Bluebell
A Novel

by

Mrs. G. C. Huddleston

Double 9
BOOKS

Bluebell
A Novel
by Mrs. G. C. Huddleston

ISBN: 978-93-63053-97-7

Published by

DOUBLE 9 BOOKS
2/13-B, Ansari Road
Daryaganj, New Delhi – 110002
info@double9books.com
www.double9books.com
Tel. 011-40042856

ABOUT THE AUTHOR

Mrs. G. C. Huddleston, a notable author of her time, penned the captivating masterpiece "Bluebell: A Novel." Set against the backdrop of a bygone era, this literary gem weaves a tapestry of intrigue, romance, and societal complexities. Through vivid prose and rich character development, Huddleston brings to life the enchanting world of Bluebell, immersing readers in a tale of love, ambition, and the pursuit of happiness. As the narrative unfolds, readers are drawn into the lives of the novel's characters, each grappling with their own desires, dilemmas, and dreams. From the spirited heroine to the enigmatic hero, Huddleston's characters leap off the page, captivating readers with their depth and authenticity. Against a backdrop of societal norms and expectations, "Bluebell" explores themes of identity, resilience, and the transformative power of love. Through its evocative storytelling and nuanced exploration of human nature, the novel invites readers to ponder timeless questions of fate, destiny, and the pursuit of fulfillment. "Bluebell: A Novel" stands as a testament to Mrs. G. C. Huddleston's literary prowess and her ability to craft a compelling narrative that resonates with readers across generations. It is a timeless tale that continues to captivate and inspire, reminding us of the enduring power of the human spirit and the timeless allure of a well-told story.

CONTENTS

CHAPTER I
SWEET SEVENTEEN

I see her now—the vision fair,
Of candour, innocence, and truth,
Stand tiptoe on the verge of air,
'Twixt childhood and unstable youth.

It was the "fall" in Canada, and the leaves were dying royally in purple, crimson and gold. On the edge of a common, skirting a well-known city of Ontario, stood a small, rough-cast cottage, behind which the sun was setting with a red promise of frost, his flaming tints repeated in the fervid hue of the Virginian creeper that clothed it.

This modest tenement was the retreat of three unprotected females, two of whom were seated in silent occupation close to a black stove, which imparted heat, but denied cheerfulness. The elder was grey and tintless as her life,—harsh wisdom wrung from sad experience ever on lips thin and tight, as though from habitually repressing every desire. The younger, a widow, was scarcely passed middle age, small of stature, but wizened beyond her years by privation and sorrow.

A smell of coal-oil, that most unbearable of odours, pervaded the interior of the cottage, revealing that the general servant below in lighting the lamp had, as usual, upset some, and was retaining the aroma by smearing it off with her apron.

Presently a quick, light step tripped over the wooden side-walk, a shadow darkened the window, and a vision of youth and freshness burst into the dingy little parlour.

A rather tall, full-formed young Hebe was Theodora Leigh, of that pure pink and white complexion that goes farther to make a beauty than even regularity of feature; her long, sleepy eyes were just the shade of the wild hyacinth; indeed, her English father always called her "Bluebell," after a flower that does not grow on Transatlantic soil.

But they were Irish-eyes, "put in with a dirty finger," and varying with every mood. Gooseberry eyes may disguise more soul, but they get no credit for it. Humour seemed to dance in that soft, blue fire; poetry dreamed in their clear depths; love—but that we have not come to yet; they were more eloquent than her tongue, for she was neither witty nor wise, only rich in the exuberant life of seventeen, and as expectant of good will and innocent of knowledge of the world as a retriever puppy.

Apparently, Miss Bluebell was not in the suavest of humours, for she flung her hat on to one crazy chair, and herself on another, with a vehemence that caused a sensible concussion.

"My dear, how brusque you are," said Mrs. Leigh, plaintively.

"So provoking," muttered Bluebell.

"What's gone wrong with the child now?" said Miss Opie, the elder proprietress of the domicile.

"Why," said Bluebell, "I met the Rollestons, and they asked: me to their picnic at the Humber on Friday; but how *can* I go? Look here!" and she pointed to a pair of boots evidently requiring patching. "Oh, mother! could you manage another pair now? Miss Scrag has sent home my new 'waist,' and I can do up my hat, but these buckets are only fit for the dusthole."

Mrs. Leigh sighed,—"A new pair, with side-springs, would cost three dollars. No, Bluebell, I can't indeed."

"I might as well be a nun, then, at once," said the girl, with tears in her voice; and a sympathetic dew rose in Mrs. Leigh's weary eyes at the disappointment she could not avert from her spoiled darling.

"Bluebell," said Miss Opie, "if you read more and scampered about less, your mind would be better fortified to bear these little reverses."

"Shut up!" muttered Bluebell, in the artless vernacular of a school-girl, half turning her shoulder with an impatient gesture.

The entrance of the tea-things created a diversion, but the discontented girl sat apart, while the hideousness of her surroundings came upon her as a new revelation. Certainly, in Canada, in a poverty-stricken abode, taste seems more completely starved than in any other country.

Bluebell, in her critical mood, noted the ugly delf tea-things, so badly arranged; the black stove, four feet into the room, with its pipe running through a hole in the wall; the ricketty horsehair chairs and wire blind for the window, "gave" on the street, where gasping geese were diving in the gutters for the nearest approach to water they could find.

Scarcely less repugnant were the many-coloured crotchet-mats and anti-macassars with which Miss Opie loved to decorate the apartment; nor was a paper frill adorning a paltry green flower-vase wanting to complete the tasteless *tout ensemble*.

The evening wore on; Mrs. Leigh proceeded with the turning of an old merino dress; Miss Opie adjusted her spectacles, and read *Good Words*. Bluebell sat down to the piano and executed a selection from Rossini's 'Messe Solennelle' with force and fervour.

"You play very well, child," said Miss Opie.

"That is fortunate," said Bluebell, "for I mean to be a governess."

"You mean you want a governess," retorted the other. "Why, what in the world do you know?"

"More than most children of ten years old. I might get a hundred dollars a year. Mamma, I could buy myself new boots then."

"You are nothing but a self-willed child yourself, unable to bear the slightest disappointment," said Miss Opie.

"Never mind," said Mrs. Leigh, coaxingly; "I'll see if I cannot get you the boots. They will give me credit at the store."

"No, no; I know you can't afford it; they were new last April. Mamma is oil to your vinegar, Aunt Jane."

"And you the green young mustard in the domestic salad—hot enough, and, like all ill weeds, growing apace."

"Then it is field mustard, and not used for salad," said Bluebell, anxious for the last word. And, escaping from the room, went to place some bones in the shed, for a casual in the shape of a starving cur, who called occasionally for food and a night's lodging.

About twenty years ago, when this melancholy Mrs. Leigh was a lovely young Canadian of rather humble origin, Theodore Leigh, a graceless subaltern in the Artillery, had just returned from leave, and, going one day to the Rink, was "regularly flumocksed," as he expressed it, by the vision of Miss Lesbia Jones skimming over the ice like a swallow on the wing. And when she proceeded to cut a figure of 8 backwards, and execute another intricate movement called "the rose," his admiration became vehement, and, seizing on a brother-officer he had observed speaking to her, demanded an introduction.

"To the 'Tee-to-tum'? Oh, certainly."

Miss Lesbia was very small, and wore the shortest of petticoats, which probably suggested the appellation.

Fatigued with her evolutions, she had sunk with a pretty little air of *abandon* on the platform, and her destiny, in a beaver coat and cap, was presented by Mr. Wingfield.

After this, a common object at the Rink was a tall young man, in all the agonies of a *début* on skates, and a bewitching little attendant sprite shooting before and around him, occasionally righting him with a fairy touch when he evinced too wild a desire to dash his brains against the wall.

At all the sleighing parties, also, Miss Lesbia's form was invariably observed in Mr. Leigh's cutter, with a violet and white "cloud" matching the robe borders and ribbons on the bells; and he and the "Tee-to-tum" spun round together in half the valses of every ball during the winter.

Perhaps, after all, the attachment might have lived and died without exceeding the "muffin" phase, had not the "beauty," Captain of the battery cut in, and made rather strong running, too, partly because he considered her "fetching," and partly, he said, "from regard to Leigh, who was making an ass of himself."

Jealousy turned philandering into earnest. Theodore went straight to the maiden aunt, with whom Miss Jones resided, and, after most vehement badgering, got her consent to a private marriage within three days. The poor spinster, though much flustered, knowing his attentions to Lesbia had been a good deal talked about, felt almost relieved to have it settled respectably, though so abruptly.

On the appointed day, having obtained a week's leave, Theodore, with his best man, the last joined subaltern, dashed up to the church-door in a cutter, just in time to receive Lesbia and her bewildered chaperone.

After the ceremony, they started off for their week's honeymoon to the Falls; and the best man, absolved from secrecy, spread the news through the regiment.

Theodore had scribbled off the intelligence in reckless desperation to his father, of whom he was the only child, and Sir Timothy Leigh, a proud and ambitious man, never forgave the irrevocable piece of folly so cavalierly announced to him.

Theodore received a letter from the family lawyer, couched in the terms of sorrowful reprehension such functionaries usually assume on similar occasions.

"It was Mr. Vellum's painful duty to inform him that Sir Timothy would decline to receive him on his return to England; that two hundred a year would be placed annually to his credit at Cox's; but the estates not being entailed, that was the utmost farthing he need ever expect from him."

Such was the gist of the communication, and Theodore, hardened by his father's severity, and unable to bear the privations of a narrow income, absented himself more and more from their wretched lodgings, and tried to drown his cares by drinking himself into a state of semi-idiocy.

There is little more to relate of this ill-starred marriage, of which Bluebell was the fruit; for soon after her birth young Leigh was killed by being upset out of a dog-cart.

Driving home with unsteady hands from mess one night, he collided with a street car, which inevitably turned over the two-wheeled vehicle. Theodore was pitched out, his head striking on the iron rails, and never breathed again.

Whatever grief Sir Timothy may have felt at his son being snatched from him, unreconciled and unforgiven, did not show itself in mercy to the widow.

Mr. Vellum was again in requisition, and proposed, on behalf of Sir Timothy, to make Mrs. Leigh a suitable allowance on condition that she remained in Canada, and delivered over the child to her grandfather, to be brought up and educated as his heiress. In case these terms were refused, she would continue to receive annually two hundred a-year; but no farther assistance would be granted.

Lesbia, in her loneliness and bereavement, was heart-broken at this unfeeling proposition, and Bluebell being too young for a choice, she consulted the voice of Nature alone, and refused to part with her child.

The maiden aunt, Miss Opie, willingly received them. She had a mere pittance, and lived in a boarding house; but, by joining their slender purses, they took the cottage in which we find them.

Thus in extreme poverty was Bluebell reared until her seventeenth year, though by personal privation Mrs. Leigh sent her to *the* school *par excellence*; attended by most of the girls in the city, whether their parents were "in" or "out" of society. Bluebell having the *prestige* of an English father, own son of a baronet, and military into the bargain, was considered in the former class, and included at an early age in the gaieties of the winter.

A new friend, who had been particularly kind to her, was Mrs. Rolleston, wife of the Colonel of a regiment quartered there, and to her Bluebell repaired to make sorrowful excuses for the projected picnic, and also to confide the scheme that possessed her mind of earning money as a musical teacher or nursery governess.

Mrs. Rolleston felt half inclined to laugh at the unformed impulsive child, who was such a pet in their household, but seemed far too babyish and unmethodical to be recommended for any situation; yet remembering her mother's straitened circumstances, and that the girl probably wanted some pocket-money, she listened sympathetically, and promised to turn it over in her mind.

Music she knew Bluebell thoroughly understood and excelled in. She had for years received instruction gratis from the organist at the Cathedral, who, originally attracted by her lovely voice singing in the choir, took her up with enthusiasm, and taught her harmony and thorough bass. Thus, instead of only practising a desultory accomplishment, she was able to compose and arrange her tuneful ideas correctly.

A dark striking-looking girl interrupted them. This was Cecil Rolleston, the eldest daughter of the house, or rather she stood in that relation to the Colonel, being the offspring of his first wife.

"Come out and play croquet, Bluebell," said she; "the children are having a game; they only let me go on condition of bringing you,"—and she led the way through the window into a charming garden, with large shady maple-trees just beginning to drop their deep-dyed, variegated leaves on the turf; the bluebirds were already gone, but the red and ashen-hued robin, nearly the size of a jay, still rustled through the boughs.

A little white dog, with a ribbon on, was holding a ball within its feathery toes, and playing with it as a cat does a mouse; a gardener was refreshing the thirsty flowers, which had outgrown their strength; and Fleda, Estelle, and Lola, twelve, eleven, and nine, were playing croquet with the zest of recent emancipation from lessons.

The governess, a dark, sallow expositor of the arts and sciences, also wielded a mallet, and Cecil and Bluebell completed the six.

The sides were pretty equally cast, and the combatants were in a most interesting crisis of the game, when Colonel Rolleston entered the garden.

He was a very handsome man, and as is often the case with the only male in a family of women, so studied and given in to by all his female *entourage*, that he would not have been pleased, whatever their occupations, if he were not immediately rallied round by a little court of flatterers.

"Estelle," said the governess, "offer your papa your mallet, and ask him to be so kind as to play with us." The child's face lengthened; she had not much hope of his refusing it, but advanced with her request.

"Must I?" said the Colonel.

"Oh, yes!" said the chorus of voices; "be my partner—be mine."

"Don't tear me to pieces among you," said he, with a deprecating gesture.

"Take Bluebell on your side, papa," cried Cecil; "she is very good, and we'll keep Miss Prosody, who is equally so."

And thus they proceeded, the Colonel radiant with every successful stroke, and blaming mallet, ball, and ground when otherwise, reiterating, "I can't make a stroke to-day."

Bluebell was very fond of the Colonel, who liked pretty faces about him, and had been kind to her; but she could not resist a slight feeling of repulsion at what she considered an abject maneuver of Miss Prosody's. His ball, by an unskilful miss, was left in her power; her duty to her side required her to crack it to the other end of the ground, but a glance at the irritable gloom of his countenance induced her to discover it to be more to her advantage to attack one rather beyond, and, judiciously missing it left her own blue one an easy stroke for him.

The shadows dispersed, and, all playfulness, the Colonel apostrophized his prize, which he succeeded in hitting. "Here is my little friend in blue; shall I hurt it? no, I will not harm it." By-play of relief and gratitude on the governess's part, as he requited her amiability by merely taking two off, leaving his interesting friend in blue unmoved.

This naturally did not enhance the interest of the children who felt it was not the game of croquet that was being played. Cecil, replying with a laughing glance to the indignant eye-telegraphy of Fleda, began to play at random; and Bluebell and Lola, not finding much antagonism from the other side, soon pulled the Colonel through his hoops and won the game. After which, Bluebell retraced her steps across the common, accompanied part of the way by Miss Rolleston, to whom she also confided her governess's projects.

Cecil was very fond of her; she had few companions, and her sisters were mere children. All the time the younger girl was talking, she was silently revolving a plan. It so happened this Cecil was in rather independent circumstances for a young lady, maternal relative having left her a legacy at twelve years old which, by the time she was twenty-one, would bring in a thousand a year.

In the mean time, she drew half that sum annually, and, of course, contributed to the domestic expenses. How much pleasanter it would be for Bluebell to live with them than with strangers. She might be *her* musical teacher; singing duets even brought out her own voice surprisingly; it would be delightful to practise together; the children had no taste for music, neither did Mrs. Rolleston care for it. Besides, she felt a generous pleasure in the prospect of assisting her friend, poor Bluebell, who often had to deny herself a mere bit of ribbon from want of a shilling to pay for it. It might require a little management at home, so she would not hint at it yet, and, with a warm caress and a gay farewell nod, they separated.

Next morning, Mrs. Leigh, still engaged in the resuscitation of the merino dress, was surprised by a visit from Mrs. Rolleston. That lady, for a wonder, considering her errand, had come alone, for it was seldom that any little domestic arrangement was entered on without the personal supervision of the Colonel.

However, there was a counter-attraction at barracks this morning, and having, so to speak, held a board on Cecil's proposition, and opposed, argued, and thoroughly talked it over, Mrs. Rolleston was empowered to suggest to Mrs. Leigh a plan for taking Bluebell into their family as musical companion to Cecil and nursery governess to Freddy, the heir apparent, aetat. four. The poor little lady did not seem much elated at the proposal. "I know my child will wish it," she said. "I can give her no variety, no indulgences, and she is of an age when occupation and society are a necessity to her. I sometimes feel," she murmured, with a sigh, "that I have stood in her light by not agreeing to her grandfather's conditions."

A look of curiosity from Mrs. Rolleston elicited an explanation, and she heard for the first time the whole history of Bluebell's antecedents.

"Why," cried she, much excited, "I remember that Sir Timothy before I married; there are so many Leighs, it never struck me he might be your father-in-law. I recollect hearing he had disinherited his son, but he has adopted a grandnephew, which, I am afraid, looks bad for Bluebell." And she listened with renewed interest to Mrs. Leigh's diffuse reminiscences, while her *protégé* appeared to her in a new and romantic light, and she pictured half-a-dozen possibilities for her future.

From a miniature of the graceless Theodore which Mrs. Leigh produced, there could be no doubt of the resemblance to his daughter in air and feature; the long sleepy eyes were identical, though the slightly insolent expression of Theodore's was, happily, wanting.

"He was the best of husbands," whimpered the widow, on whose placid mind the shortcomings of the dissipated youth seemed to have left no impression; "but he was hardly treated in this world, and so he was taken to a better."

Before Mrs. Rolleston left, it was arranged that Bluebell was to make her first essay in governessing on Freddy Rolleston, her Sundays to be spent as often as possible with her mother; and ere another week had passed, she and her effects were transferred to the Maples.

A bed was made up for her in a little room of Cecil's and the tuition of Freddy carried on in the nursery; for Mrs. Rolleston having some doubts as how the amateur and professional governess might amalgamate, avoided letting her entrench on Miss Prosody's premises.

That lady, indeed, was disposed to look upon her with suspicion and incipient dislike. She had always been treated with great consideration—quite one of the family, and cared not for "a rival near her throne." Who was Bluebell that she should be made so much of?—a little nursery governess with no attainments, and yet Cecil's inseparable companion! She was a prime favourite with the Colonel, whose "ways" she had made a judicious study of, and treated with considerable tact. He always mentioned her as "that dear invaluable creature, Miss Prosody." She could occasionally put an idea into his mind which he mistook for his own, as, for instance, when he observed to his wife,—"What a pity that girl has such a preposterous name, and that you all have the habit of calling her by it. The other evening that idiot, young Halkett must needs say, 'What a lovely pet name!' I can tell you I took him up pretty short. You really must not have her down so much, if these boys think they may talk nonsense to her."

Mrs. Rolleston was rather surprised at the irritation with which this was said; to be sure she had heard Miss Prosody, previous to young Halkett's foolish remark, lamenting that Bluebell "did not show more reserve with gentlemen guests, and that she put herself so much on an equality with Cecil." The Colonel was a domestic man, and liked cheerfulness at his fireside, of which he himself was to be the centre and inspiration; anything approaching bad spirits, silence, or headaches he always resented.

Bluebell was well enough as contributing to the liveliness of the little society—a pretty smiling young girl is seldom *de trop*; but then she must be satisfied without lovers, whose presence the Colonel considered subversive of all rational comfort.

Good-natured Mrs. Rolleston pursued the even tenor of her way, the Colonel's fidgets had a soporific effect on her nerves and created no corresponding alarms; her idol, Freddy, was satisfied with the new administration, and ceased to wage internecine warfare with his nurse; and certainly the unwonted tranquillity consequent was a decided boon to the rest of the household.

CHAPTER II
BERTIE

In the greenest growth of the Maytime
We rode where the roads were wet;
Between the dawn and the daytime
The spring was glad that we met.

Swinburne.

Two or three months passed, the bluebirds and robins had all disappeared, and the snow-birds, hardy scions of the feathered tribe capable of withstanding the rigours of a Canadian winter, were alone to be seen. The Rinks had been flooded, and skating was going on with vigour; the snow was not quite in a satisfactory state as yet; but a few sleighs jingled merrily about with their bright bits of colour, the edging of fur robes and ribbon on the sleigh bells. A general impulse of joyful anticipation ran through all the young people as winter unlocked her stores of amusement, and the keen sabre-like air, so bracing and exhilarating, stirred the life in young veins, and set their spirits dancing with exuberant vitality.

The Rollestons, who had only come out in the spring, were attracted with everything. Not a sleigh passed but there was a rush from the children to the window, and Colonel Rolleston, who was building one, received fresh suggestions about it most days from his excited family.

Every morning Cecil, under Bluebell's tuition, practised skating at the Rink, and had devised an original and becoming costume to be assumed as soon as she had attained sufficient command of her limbs not to object to a share of public attention. In the afternoon the Rink was generally crowded, and many of the Colonel's regiment evinced an eagerness to help Cecil along, and pretend to receive instruction from the skilful and blooming Bluebell; so poor Mrs. Rolleston was then invariably detailed by the Colonel for chaperone duty, and sat shivering on the platform while Cecil was being initiated in the mysteries of "Dutch rolls" and "outside edge." On one of these occasions she was roused by a well-known voice calling her by name, and turned round in joyful surprise to greet a young man just come in.

"My dear Bertie, were have you sprung from? Have you been to our house?"

"Just left it and my traps. Lascelles suddenly gave up his leave, which I applied for, and have got a week certain, and most likely all of it, for there are plenty of Captains down there; so I thought I would look you up to begin with."

"To begin with! You must stay here all the time—make it head quarters, at any rate. You have been travelling all the summer, and there's nothing to do now."

"Moose," murmured Bertie. "Ah! there's Cecil."

Cecil, skating hand-in-hand to the tune of "Paddle your own canoe," was not sufficiently disengaged to remark her mother's companion. His eyes followed her with a keen, comprehensive glance, which Mrs. Rolleston observed complacently.

"Don't you think her much improved?—much prettier?" asked she.

"Skating always suits a well-made girl. That black and scarlet get-up, too, is very becoming, but pretty—hardly."

"She is, however, very much admired," said Mrs. Rolleston, warmly, for a step-mother.

"Ah!" cried Bertie, with a slight accent of bitterness, "reasons enough for that. How well some of these girls skate! Who is that shooting-star?"

The planet in question gyrated towards them, dropped on one knee on the platform for the relief of strained ankles, and, as she addressed Mrs. Rolleston, caught a look of decided admiration on Bertie's face.

A Canadian girl is nothing if not self-possessed; she sustained the gaze with the most perfect calmness.

"Bluebell, this is my brother, Captain Du Meresq. Cecil ought to rest; will you go and tell her to come here?"

"Who is that young beauty whom you addressed in the language of flowers?" asked he.

"Nonsense, Bertie! she is Freddy's governess. You must not begin to talk absurdity to her; you will annoy Edward."

"He don't object to fair faces on his own account."

"Well, this particular one is more bother than pleasure to him. You know his horror of 'danglers'; he is afraid of aimless flirtations with Bluebell, who, being also Cecil's companion, is constantly in the drawing-room."

"Ah, my beloved niece," said Captain Du Meresq, as he gave Cecil considerable support from the ice to the platform.

"What has given us this unexpected treat?" said she, with a warmer hue than usual in her clear, pale cheek.

"My anxiety to see your new companion."

"Whose existence, I suppose, you have just heard of."

"It has been my loss," retorted he. "Fascinating young creature! The name Bluebell just describes those wild hyacinth eyes."

"Oh! Bertie," said his sister and Cecil together, "how absurd you are about girls."

"And then," persisted he, "that charming tawny hair and milk white skin."

"One might think you were describing an Alderney cow. It's a pity she is not called 'Daisy' or 'Cowslip.'"

"Girls are all alike," said Captain Du Meresq, sententiously. "Even you, my beloved Cecil, who are a woman of mind, can't stand my wild admiration of—Cowslip."

Cecil raised her eyebrows, and a scornful beam shot from the dark eyes that were her chief attraction.

"Nor could the 'dairy flower' herself, I should think. It's no use rhapsodizing before me, Bertie; I shall not tell her in any confidential communication, whatever you may think."

"Ah, well," said Captain Du Meresq, with a sigh, "let us hope the ingenious child may understand the universal language of the eyes, for I hear papa would not approve of my speaking to her."

Mrs. Rolleston was becoming fidgetty. To some women, as they advance in years, an inability of separating chaff from earnest becomes more pronounced, and the uppermost wish of her mind at present was to see a real attachment between Bertie and Cecil. Albert Du Meresq was only her half-brother; but he had become her charge in infancy under terrible circumstances, which we will briefly relate.

When Mr. Du Meresq married his mother, a wilful Irish beauty, Mrs. Rolleston was a shy, reserved girl of thirteen, and became very jealous of her father's exclusive devotion to his bride and neglect of herself.

Lady Inez looked upon her as rather a nuisance, and was coldly critical upon her appearance and manner. She was an unsparing mimic, and frequently exercised the faculty on her step-daughter, whose nervousness became awkwardness in the constant expectation of being turned into ridicule. Consequently, she cordially disliked not only Lady Inez, but the little step-brother, who was made of so much importance, till one ghastly day changed the aspect of events.

Like a fearful dream it had seemed—a strange carriage rolling to the door, from which emerged her father and another gentleman carrying a terrible burden, looking supernaturally long in a riding-habit. White scared faces flitted about; but life was extinct, and there was no frantic riding for doctors.

There had been a hunt-breakfast that morning, and she well remembered the envy she had felt at seeing Lady Inez ride gaily forth with the rest on a favourite horse.

"She has everything," thought Bella, "'Reindeer' was promised to me when he was a foal, and I have never been on his back."

But Lady Inez was lying there, with the mark of "Reindeer's" iron hoof on her temple. They had come down together at a blind fence; the horse, entangled in her habit, struck out *once*, as thorough-breds will, but it was a death-blow.

The voice of the child, crying alone and neglected in the nursery, aroused Bella from a horror stricken stupor. Her father's despair made him unapproachable, but she might comfort Bertie, forgotten by his attendants.

From this time she became almost a mother to him, for Mr. Du Meresq went abroad, and they were left alone in the deserted house for some years.

Bertie had left Eton, and just obtained a commission in the — — Hussars, when his father died, leaving him a moderate fortune, which steadily decreased as years went by. It had approached attenuation by this time, and Mrs. Rolleston felt as distracted and perplexed as a duckling's hen foster-mother, at the vagaries of the happy-go-lucky, reckless Irish blood in Bertie, which did not flow in her own veins.

She looked forward to marrying him to Cecil, as the best chance of relieving his pecuniary difficulties and reforming his unsteadiness.

Captain Du Meresq had stayed with them for six weeks some time ago, when he and Cecil became inseparable companions, and it was then that the idea had dawned upon her. She would not openly discuss it with her brother—that would have too much the appearance of a plot: but her lively satisfaction at the prospect was apparent enough, and Bertie knew her co-operation would not be wanting.

He had thought of it more than once. What chance had he not calculated to get him through his sea of difficulties; but a thousand a year alone seemed scarcely sufficient temptation to matrimony, to which he did not seriously incline. Indeed, his warm impressionable nature was not the temperament of a fortune-hunter.

He was attracted with Cecil, and got rather fond of her in the six weeks he had been trying to make her in love with him, not with any mercenary view, but because such was his usual custom with girls.

But he was afflicted with a keen eye for beauty, and Cecil was plain to most eyes, and too colourless for his taste, though she possessed a lovely figure, thorough-bred little head, and a pale, intelligent, expressive face.

Bluebell's lilies and roses and Hebe-like contour caught his eye in a moment, of which Cecil felt an instinctive conviction; but though, with a woman's keenness, underrating no point of attraction in her friend, she considered her wanting in style, which deficiency she dwelt on now with secret satisfaction. For though not in the least anxious to monopolize general admiration, that of Bertie Du Meresq was unfortunately a sensitive point with Cecil, for that six weeks had been the intensest period of her life—the dawning of "love's young dream."

She had never met him since childhood till then, when they were thrown together with the intimacy of near connexions. There was not, of course, the slightest real relationship, but Bertie jestingly called her his niece, perhaps, to establish a right of chaperonage.

He used to make her come down to breakfast *en Amazone*, and took her the most enchanting rides in that Seductive April weather. Her equestrian experience previously had been limited to steady macadamizing on the roads. Bertie took her as the crow flies, never pulled a fence, but merely gave her a lead, and Cecil, who had plenty of nerve, exulted in the new excitement. The farmers might not have thought it a very orthodox month for this amusement; but hunting was scarcely over, though the copses were filled with primroses, and violets scented the hedgerows; the birds sang as they only do when the great business of their year is commencing. And then she had such a mount, a perfect hunter of her *quasi*-uncle's. It never refused, and took its fences with such ease a child might have sat it.

Or they would ride dreamily on in woody glades, both alike susceptible to the shafts of sunlight, quivering on the leaves, the sudden gush of fragrance after a shower, and all the myriad appeals of spring to those who have that touch of poetry in their clay which is the key of fairy-land, their horses meantime snatching at the young green boughs as they sauntered lazily on; and Du Meresq, who had travelled in all sorts of strange out-of-the way places, described weirder scenes in other lands, and pictured a fuller, more vivid life than she in her routine existence had dreamed of.

Bertie was always all in all to the woman he was with, provided no other was present; and Cecil, young, and full of sympathy and intelligence, was a delightful companion. His appreciation, felt and expressed, of her quickness of comprehension was most agreeable flattery; the more so as he confided in her so fully, even consulting her about his own private affairs, for he was very hard pressed at this time, and she, who had never known the want of money, took the deepest interest in it all.

He seemed never able to bear her out of his sight. If she played, he was hanging over the piano; if he had letters to write, Cecil must do it from his dictation; and yet he would avow sometimes before her such extravagant adoration for some pretty girl, that Cecil, chilled and surprised, would feel more than ever doubtful of her own influence; and the honeyed words she had treasured up, faded away as void of significance. And then one day,—suddenly,—on her return from a croquet-party, she heard he had received a telegram, and gone, leaving a careless message of adieu.

Poor Cecil! with the instinct of the wounded animal to its lair, she rushed to her own room, locked the door, and walked about in a tearless abandonment of grief, disappointment, and surprise. How could he leave her without one word? She felt half stunned, and her brain seemed capable of only the dull reiteration that "Bertie was gone." Tears welled up to her eyes then, when the sound of the first dinner-bell drove them back. She felt she must battle alone with this strange affliction; and trying to efface from her features all evidence of the shock she had sustained, descended to dinner, looking rather more stately than usual.

It annoyed her to observe that her step-mother glanced deprecatingly at her, and was inclined to be extra affectionate. This would never do. Like most young girls, she was generally rather silent when not interested in the discussions of her elders. But now she never let conversation drop. The incidents of the croquet-party furnished a safe topic. Colonel Rolleston thought the gentle dissipation had made his daughter quite lively. Afterwards she took refuge at the piano, which was imprudent, for music only too surely touches the chord of feeling, and every piece was associated with Bertie. Cecil shut the instrument, and effected a strategical retreat to her bed-room, where, in the luxury of solitude, she might worry and torment herself to her heart's content. His absence was trial enough, but the sting lay in the way it was done, which was such a proof of indifference, that shame urged her to crush out all thoughts of him, and suffer anything rather than let him see the impression his careless affection had made on her.

And so Cecil passed through her first "baptism of fire" alone and unsuspected; but time had softened much of her resentment ere they met again.

CHAPTER III
GENTLE ANNIE

The time I've lost in wooing,
In watching and pursuing
The light that liesIn woman's eyes,
Has been my heart's undoing.

Moore.

"Bluebell," said little Lola, bursting into the nursery, where Freddy, rather a tyrant in his affections, had insisted on her singing him to sleep, "Ma says you have got to dine down to-night, and Miss Prosody, too. Won't she be in a way, for her white muslin never came home from the wash, and she had begun altering the *barège*; so I asked Felda to tell her," said Lola, diplomatically. "Do you know Bertie has come?" (His nieces never prefaced his name with the formality of uncle.) "Oh of course, you must have seen him at the Rink. Do you like him? He is sure to like you, at first, at any rate," said Lola, who apparently, like other lookers-on saw most of the game. "And don't tell, but I believe he hates Miss Prosody."

"Why?" asked Bluebell, absently.

"Well, one day he was whispering to Cecil, with their heads very near together. Miss Prosody was looking for a book in a recess behind the door, close to them; but they never saw her till she moved away, and I heard Bertie mutter something about an 'inquisitive old devil.' But don't tell, mind. There's the bell; I must go to tea," *Exit* Lola, and Bluebell flew off with some alacrity to her bed-room to prepare.

"Bluebell," cried Cecil, opening the intervening door, "can I lend you anything?" It pleased her to supply her friend's deficiencies of toilet when a sudden summons to a domestic field-day had been issued.

"Is it a party?" said the other. "I have only my eternal black-net dress."

"Just Mr. Vavasour and Captain Deveril," both in her father's regiment; they never either of them alluded to Bertie. "Here are some fixings for it," returning with a lapful of silver acorns and oak leaves, "unless you would prefer butter-cups. What a thing it is to have a complexion like yours, that everything goes with," —and Cecil looked with half envy at the girl, whose blue eyes were bluer, and hair and cheeks brighter, than usual, as she chattered away with a vivacity, of which, perhaps, the nattering glances of Captain Du Meresq may have been the secret spring.

Bluebell hadn't the slightest idea of assuming the demure demeanour of a governess in society; the Rollestons had been her great friends before, and did not treat her as if she was in any altered position; not so, however, Miss Prosody, who would have reduced her to the *status* of a nursery-maid had it been in her power.

That austere virgin was talking, or rather listening, in a sympathetic manner to Colonel Rolleston as the girls entered the room; but her eye had taken in every detail of Miss Leigh's costume, and disapprovingly remarked the silver oak leaves that festooned the black-net dress, and Maltese cross and bracelets that accompanied it, all of which she well knew belonged to Cecil.

The three young men were talking together.

"Du Meresq," said Captain Deveril, "you get more leave than any other fellow. You were in the Prairies in July, England in the spring, and now here you are at large again in January."

"You must have a rattling good chief," said Mr. Vavasour, "I don't think, Mrs. Rolleston, the Colonel is ever able to spare us quite so often."

"You see," said Bertie, "there's no demand for leave among our fellows just now; they are all in love at Montreal, and there's so much going on there. Lascelles most imprudently gave up his to drive Miss Ellery about a little longer."

"Oh, ah, I know her," said young Vavasour; "girl with grey eyes, and head always on one side when she's valsing; looks as if she was kissing her own shoulder."

"Will she land him, do you think?" said Deveril.

"Not she," said Bertie. "I have known him in as bad a scrape before; he'll get away to England soon; he always bolts when the family becomes affectionate."

A discordant gong resounding through the house was followed by the announcement of dinner.

"Come, my dear Miss Prosody," said the Colonel, complacently, leading her forth; he hadn't near done his recital of the morning's field-day, which required that delicate tact and judicious prompting to extort from him that, though not really Brigadier on the occasion, his opinion and authority had actually directed the proceedings.

Generally any amount of this affectionate incense was forthcoming from his wife and daughter; but to-night they both seemed a little *distrait* and occupied with Bertie, which, however, was a loss little felt with Miss Prosody present, whose motto seemed that of the volunteers, "Always ready," and her "soothing treatment" was certainly equal to that of either of the others.

"It's you and I, Miss Bluebell," said young Vavasour, hastily offering his arm, while Bertie who had hesitated an instant, gave his to Cecil. The momentary reluctance was not lost upon her, she become rather silent, ditto Captain Du Meresq; but their opposite neighbours were in a full flow of chatter.

"I saw you on the Rink, Miss Leigh, I wish I could skate like you. What is that thing you do with a broom??"

"The rose."

"Take a good deal of cultivating to produce. I should think? Are you going to the M'Nab's ball?"

"No; I am not asked. The others are."

"But you do go to balls sometimes?"

"Oh, yes; Mrs. Rolleston promised I should; but I can't go without an invitation, and I very seldom get one."

"I daresay not," said Jack hotly; "they don't want their daughters cut out."

"Stuff," cried Bluebell, with a sudden blush, which was not occasioned by the remark, but by the expression of Bertie Du Meresq's eyes that she had caught for about the third time since dinner began. It was very provoking; they had a sort of magnetic power, that forced her to look that way, and she fancied she detected a half-pleased smile in recognition of the involuntary suffusion.

"We are going; to 'fix up a prance' after the garrison sleigh drive on the 10th," continued young Vavasour; "will you come my sleigh, Miss Leigh?"

Bluebell's face brightened with anticipation; then she looked down, and demurred,—"I don't know that I shall be able to go."

"That's only a put off, I am sure; you came out last garrison sleigh-drive."

"Yes, because Colonel Rolleston took me in his, but I mustn't expect to go every time; and you see there's Freddy; but I *should* like it awfully, Mr. Vavasour."

"Well, I know they will make you come," said he confidently. "Promise me you won't drive with any other fellow."

"No fear of that; I don't suppose any one else will ask me."

"Wouldn't they," thought Vavasour. "I know two or three of our fellows are death on driving her."

"Cecil," said Bertie, suddenly, "I think you have grown much quieter."

"I am sure I might make the same remark, and for the purposes of conversation it requires two to talk."

"You are so stiff, or something," murmured he; "not like the jolly little girl who used to ride with me in the Farwoods. Those were pleasant days, Cecil—at least, I thought so."

"You got very suddenly tired of them, however."

"That I didn't," exclaimed he. "I was obliged to go."

"It was a yachting excursion, wasn't it?" carelessly.

"Yes, ostensibly; I had business too. Do you know Cecil very nearly wrote to you. But then, I thought you wouldn't care to hear from me, and might think it a bore answering."

Cecil was silent. "Did you miss me, my child?"

She forgot her resolves, and met his eyes with a dark, soft look.

Bertie pressed her hand under the table, and for a moment they were oblivious of anything passing around.

"Sweet or dry, sir?" said the deep voice of the liveried [unreadable], for the second time of asking.

Du Meresq darted a searching glance at the man, who looked as stolid as the Serjeant in 'Our's.' No one could have guessed he was thinking what a *piquante* anecdote it would be to relate to his inamorata, the cook, over their supper-beer. Bertie gave a laughing but relieved glance at his neighbour, whose eyes were fixed on her plate. They both began simultaneously talking louder, with an exaggerated openness, on general topics. Mrs. Rolleston joined in.

"You must stay over the sleighing-party, Bertie."

"I hate driving a hired sleigh," said he. "I wish I could get mine up; but the Grand Trunk would be sure to deliver it the day after the fair."

"But you have your musk-ox robes here; they would dress up the shabbiest sleigh. I only saw one set like them on New Year's Day, when we had at least sixty sleighs up here."

"How did you enjoy that celebration?"

"I think," said Cecil, "it is rather tiresome for ladies to have to stay in all day and receive, while the gentlemen go out calling. We had a spread, of course—luncheon, tea, coffee, everything. One man, who had a large acquaintance, came before breakfast, and they were rushing in all day. It would have been well enough if they were not in such a hurry; but they just swallowed a glass of wine, and the burden of all their remarks was, 'I have been to a dozen places already, and have about thirty or forty more to do.'"

"Could not you two young ladies make them linger over smiles and wine?" laughed Bertie. "We are not such duffers at Montreal."

"No, indeed. I saw Bluebell give a man a scalding cup of coffee, with the most engaging smile. There was a nervous glance at the clock. 'Oh, thank you, Miss Leigh, how hot it is! I shall never have time to drink it,' just as if he had a train to catch."

"They have an arrear of balls and dinners to call for; that is the only day in the year a good many ever can pay visits—the civilians, I mean."

The Colonel, who had now exhausted conversation with Miss Prosody, had leisure to observe the determined flirtation of young Vavasour with Bluebell. That unformidable young person being only seventeen, of course looked upon him as a mere boy, and her chaffing manner was not at all to the Colonel's taste, whose attention was drawn to it by an expressive glance from Miss Prosody; so he telegraphed to his wife, who soon signalled her female following from the room.

Bertie got to the door, and as Bluebell passed through last of the ladies, she again met that look of interest and admiration Du Meresq had practised so often.

Shyness hitherto had been no infirmity of this young Canadian; but Bertie somehow had mesmerized her into a state of consciousness—it was a cobwebby kind of fetter, but the first she had worn.

"Come and talk to me Bluebell," said Mrs. Rolleston, "as Cecil is so studious."

The former glanced at her friend, and involuntarily whispered—"*How* well she looks to-night!"

Cecil was sitting apart, utterly absent as it seemed, but her eyes were shining, and there was a soft brightness about her as she turned over the pages of a book. It was "The Wanderer,"—one that Bertie had brought with him.

Mrs. Rolleston agreed and interpreted it her own way. Bluebell drew a long rocking-chair by her side, and they fell into a pleasant little talk. Mrs. Rolleston always made a pet of this child; she was the best of step-mothers, but stood a little in awe of Cecil.

Du Meresq came in shortly before the rest; the elder girl did not even look up, but her face again lit. He stood *à l'Anglais*, with his back to the fire, talking to his sister, and occasionally, though without any particular *empressement*, addressing Bluebell, who thought his voice sweeter than any man's she had ever heard. It made her unconsciously modulate her own, which as yet had the untuned accents of early girlhood; but the spell was on her, and she felt, for the first time, at a loss for words. Yet when Mrs. Rolleston shortly after sent her to the piano, it was more of disappointment than a relief. Some one was following to turn the leaves—only Mr. Vavasour—odious, officious boy! Who wanted him?

"Pray, don't," cried she, pettishly. "You are sure to do it all wrong."

"Let me try," pleaded Jack. "If you just look at me I shall know when to turn."

"Well, see if you can bring that book" (indicating a very heavy one at the bottom of a pile) "without spilling the rest, or dropping it on your toes. Thank you. Now you had better go away; this is not at all the sort of music you would understand."

"Classical, I suppose. I am afraid my taste is too uncultivated."

"Come, Miss Leigh," said the Colonel, half-impatiently, "we are all expectation."

Bertie had approached Cecil, and taken up the book she was reading. It was open at "Aux Italiens," and he murmured low some of the verses:—

"I thought of the dress she wore last time,
When we stood 'neath the cypress trees together,
In that lost land, in that soft clime,
In the crimson evening weather.
Of her muslin dress, for the eve was hot,
And her warm white neck in its golden chain.
And her full soft hair, just tied in a knot,
And falling loose again."

Mrs. Rolleston thought they looked very like lovers bending over the same book, and their eyes speaking to each other, and in harmony with it went rippling on one of the wildest and most plaintive of the Lieders under Bluebell's sympathetic and brilliant fingers.

"What a magnificent touch that child has!" said Du Meresq, pausing to listen.

"She has quite a genius for music;" and, mentally, she commented, "I never heard her play better."

"She plays," said Bertie, "as if she were desperately in love."

"With Mr. Vavasour?" laughed Cecil.

"With no one, I dare say. It indicates, however, a *besoin d'aimer.*"

Cecil took up "The Wanderer" again, but she soon found they were not *en rapport*. The captain's temperament was now, ear and fancy, under the spell of the fair musician.

Bertie was soon by the piano, but Bluebell ceased almost directly after. He had brought from Montreal [unreadable] Minstrel Melodies, then just out, and asked her to try one. She excused herself on the plea that it was a man's song, so he began it himself. Who has not suffered from the male amateur, who comes forward with bashful fatuity to favour the company with a strain tame and inaudible as a nervous school girl's? Bertie was no musician, and his songs were all picked up by ear, but there was a passion and *timbre* in the tenor voice, fascinating if unskilful, and the refrain of "Gentle Annie,"

"Shall we never more behold her,
Never hear that winning voice again,

Till the spring time comes, gentle Annie,
Till the wild flowers are scattered o'er the plain?"

lingered with its mournful, tender inflection in more than one ear that night.

Afterwards the two young men from the barracks, muffled to the chin in buffalo robes, lit the inevitable cigar, and jingled merrily off to the music of the bells.

CHAPTER IV
SATURDAY AT HOME

Unhasp the lock—like elves set free,
Flit out old memories;
A strange glow gathers round my heart.
Strange moisture dims mine eyes.

Lawrance.

Cecil woke the next morning with the feeling that something pleasant had happened; and then she remembered that Bertie Du Meresq was actually in the house, and the old folly as likely as ever to begin again; but, not possessing the self-examining powers of Anthony Trolloppe's heroines, she made no attempt to argue herself out of her unreasonable happiness, and, indeed, dwelt far more than necessary on the warm, sudden hand-clasp so inopportunely witnessed by full private Bowers. She came down radiant, and looking positively handsome; but when did a too sunny dawn escape a cloud ere noon? Bertie seemed different somehow,—was not certain he could get more leave,—was even doubtful about asking for it; and Cecil's mental Mercury, which had been "set fair," went down to "change." In reality, Du Meresq not being so etherealized by love, felt out of sorts, and not up to the mark that morning, and, therefore, probably opined with Moore—

"Thus should woman's heart and looks,
At noon be cold as winter brooks,
Nor kindle till the night returning
Brings their genial hour for burning."

At any rate, he actually went to the barracks with the Colonel, "as if he couldn't get enough of that," thought Cecil, "when he is not on leave."

But after severe reflections on herself for caring a straw about it, Cecil had forgiven him, and a deceitful sunbeam peeped through in the prospect of meeting at luncheon, only to be again overcast, as the Colonel returned without the recreant Bertie.

This second reverse overthrew her afternoon arrangements, for she had reckoned on Du Meresq's escort to the Rink. This being Saturday, Bluebell always went home till the following day, and Mrs. Rolleston would not be available even for a drive, for she hated sleighing, and was looking forward to writing her English letters in the cozy drawing-room, and sociably imbibing afternoon tea with any visitors hardy enough to face the bitter northwester, happily so rare a visitant in that sufficiently inclement climate.

But Cecil preferred facing any weather to her own thoughts, and, encountering three Astrakhan-jacketed and fur-capped sisters under convoy of Miss Prosody, was carried off by them to enliven their dismal constitutional.

In the meantime, Captain Du Meresq, having lunched at the barracks, drove with Mr. Vavasour to the Rink, expecting to find both girls there: but speculating rather the most on the chance of having a more unrestrained conversation with Bluebell than he cared for under the eyes of her responsible guardians. His projects also were to prove futile, for that young person was speeding over the frozen tract on the common at the time. The snow was as dry and hard as powdered sugar, and her cloud was stiff with her frozen breath; her ears felt as though she had thrust them into a holly-bush, and the razor-like wind in that unsheltered spot must have arrested the circulation of any less healthy and youthful pedestrian. The morning had dawned prosperously for her, as Mrs. Rolleston had accorded permission to join the sleigh-party, the *summum bonum* of her hopes; and the gratification was rendered more complete by a charming present from Cecil of an ermine cap, muff lined with scarlet, and ermine neck-tie, fastened by its cunning little head and tail.

Bluebell was picturing their effect on the velveteen jacket hitherto so coldly furnished forth, and thinking that Cecil must have ordered them from Montreal with a view to this party, as they had arrived so opportunely. She remembered now that Lola had, apparently, been struggling with a secret for some days; and yet, when she, Bluebell, had been so ecstatic, Cecil had seemed more thoughtful than sympathetic and merely acknowledging her thanks by a quiet kiss, had escaped from the room.

Two expectant faces were peering over the blind at the cottage, watching the gay footsteps battling across the common. Even Aunt Jane looked forward to seeing this weekly messenger from the outer world, which, needless to say, kept well aloof from these poor and insignificant ladies.

Bluebell always brought every piece of gossip she could collect to feed Miss Opie's inquisitive mind who was in no way exempt from the sin supposed to most easily beset spinsterhood and her girlish spirits brightened the quiet cottage and left their echo behind through the dull week. She was by no means an unmixed good when she lived there. Her vivacity, having nothing to expend itself on, often turned to desperate fits of discontent and *ennui*, but now, coming home was a holiday and change.

All the inhabitants, old ladies, and new girl (for each successive one went away to better herself after a few weeks residence), assembled simultaneously at the hall door, and drew their visitor from the bitter blast into the stove lit parlour. One yet more humble welcomer was there of the vagabond tribe—petty larceny in every curve of his ungainly form, and his spirit so broken by adversity that he only ventured to wag his shabby tail in recognition of his benefactress.

This was Bluebell's casual—one of a too common race in Canada of homeless, starved animals there being no Refuge or dog tax to compel them to live under protection or not at all.

This reclaimed cur after overcoming his strong suspicion of poison, had supported himself for sometime on the food Bluebell placed for him in the shed and when emboldened by hunger and the handsome treatment he had received he ventured into the house, he was authorized to remain as watch dog and protector.

In the summer, too, horses were added to her pensioners and invited in to graze on the patch of enclosed grass at the back of the cottage, till it fell short from being burned up or eaten, for the common was haunted with gaunt, famished quadrupeds, who, in the drought of summer, were still left to look for the mockery of subsistence on the bare, parched ground.

It was a cheerful party gathered round the tea-table, quite lavishly set forth in honour of the guest. Scones and tea cakes were plenteously saturated with butter, regardless of its winter price (the old ladies would breakfast on bread and scrape the rest of the week with uncomplaining self-denial), and a heavy plum cake formed the *pièce de resistance*.

Trove, for olfactory reasons, was accommodated with his share on a rug in the passage. Bluebell was the chief talker, with her week's arrears of news. Captain du Meresq's arrival created a little buzz of interest.

"Is he handsome?" asked Mrs. Leigh, sentimentally, whose thoughts had flown back to earlier days.

Bluebell looked up with an odd, perplexed glance. "Upon my word, I don't know."

"Ah! there were more good-looking people in my day," said her mother. "There was Captain Fletcher, in your poor father's regiment, the handsomest man that was ever seen,—fresh-coloured, with golden whiskers, and long, drooping moustache. All we girls were wild about him. Is Captain Du Meresq at all like that?"

"Not in the least. I can't describe him—fine-shaped head, such strange eyes. Oh! I dare say you would think him hideous," with a conscious laugh.

Miss Opie coughed suspiciously. "It is unfortunate," said she, "when you are in such a pleasant situation, that any disturbing element should enter. I hope, Bluebell, you will be very circumspect in your demeanour towards this gentleman."

"What," said Bluebell, in demure imitation of her manner, "would you consider an appropriate attitude for me to assume towards him?"

"These fine Captains are too fond of turning young girls' heads," said Miss Opie, shaking her own; "'leading captive silly women,' as we read. If he attempt any foolish, trifling conversation, you should check it with cold civility."

Bluebell burst into an irreverent fit of laughter, and even Mrs. Leigh said,—"Oh, those are your English ideas, Aunt Jane; we are not so stiff in Canada."

Mrs. Opie having been a governess for ten years in the mother country, was looked upon as a naturalized Briton.

"I think the old country must be very dull," said Bluebell. "Miss Prosody is always pursing up her mouth and bridling if I laugh and talk with any of the officers; and one day I distinctly overheard her whisper to the Colonel,—'very forward,' and nod towards me."

"It is, however, well to profit by such remarks," returned Miss Opie; "there is doubtless some truth in them, however unpalatable."

"But," urged the girl, "Colonel Rolleston can't *bear* one to be silent or dull; he always asks if one isn't well; and I shouldn't think you could call Captain Du Meresq a flirt. Why, he has hardly spoken ten words to me yet,"—but a sudden glow came to her cheeks as she remembered how many he had looked.

"Well, well, I was only warning you. Fetch the backgammon board; your mother has won seven games and I nine since you went."

Bluebell complied, and, settling the ladies on either side of a papier-maché table, opened the piano, and began dreamily playing through the music of the night before. Trove, finding the door ajar, had pushed in, and lay near the instrument, listening in that strange way some dogs do if the tones come from the heart, and not merely the fingers.

Having got through the last evening's *répertoire,* she sat musing on the music-stool, and then crooned rather low an old song of her mother's, beginning,—

> "They tell me thou art the favoured guest
> In many a gay and brilliant throng;
> No wit like thine to wake the jest,
> No voice like thine to raise the song."

"Oh! that is too old-fashioned," said Mrs. Leigh, and Miss Opie coughed dryly. But why need Bluebell have blushed so consciously, as she dashed into Lightning galops and Tom Tiddler quadrilles, till Trove, like a dog of taste, took his offended ears and outraged nerves off to his lair in the lobby?

His fair mistress soon after sought her bower, a scantily furnished retreat, but, like most girls' rooms, taking a certain amount of individuality from its occupier. Everything in the little room was blue, and each article a present. Photographs of school friends were suspended from the wall with ribbons of her name-sake colour. It was in the earlier days of the art, when a stony stare, pursed lips, and general rigidity were considered essential to the production of the portrait.

Blue, also, were the pincushion and glass toilet implements on the dressing-table, and a rocking-chair had its cushion embroidered in bluebells—a tribute of affection from a late schoolfellow.

The bed was curtainless, and neutral except as to its blue valance, and the carpet only cocoa-nut matting, which, however, harmonized fairly with the prevailing cerulean effect.

Bluebell was writing in a book, guarded by a Bramah, some profound reflections on "First Impressions." She never lost the key nor forgot to lock this volume—a saving clause of common-sense protecting a farrago of nonsense.

"Ces beaux jours, quand j'étais si malheureux." Have you ever, reader, taken up an old journal written in early youth, and thought how those intensely black and white days have now mingled into unnoticeable grey, half-thankful that the old ghosts are laid, half-regretful for that keener susceptibility to joy and sorrow gone by? Then, as "the hand that has written it lays it aside," there is, perhaps, a pang at the reflection of how the paths now diverge of those who once walked together as—

"Time turns the old days to derision,
Our loves into corpses—or wives;
And marriage, and death, and division,
Make barren our lives."

But Bluebell knows nothing of that. She is at the scribbling age, and can actually endure to describe, as if they were new and entirely original, the dawning follies of seventeen.

In England a heroine might have wound up such sentimental exercises with gazing out on the moonlit scene; but nine degrees below zero was unfavourable for the wooing of Diana. The "cold light of stars" was no poetical figure, and Bluebell, frozen back to the prosaic, piled up the stove, and crept into bed, where her waking dreams soon merged into sleeping ones.

CHAPTER V
A WOODLAND WALK

I hope, pretty maid, you won't take it amiss,
If I tell you my reason for asking you this,
I would see you safe home (now the swain was in love),
Of such a companion if you would approve.
Your offer, kind shepherd, is civil, I own,
But I see no great danger in going alone;
Nor yet can I hinder, the road being free
For one as another, for you as for me.

It was Sunday afternoon. Bluebell was on her way to the Maples, and had not proceeded far when she observed a Robinson Crusoe-looking figure in one of those grotesque fur caps and impossible hooded blankets that the fashionable Briton in Canada so fondly affects. She was speculating idly upon whom it could be.

"Not Mr. Gordon, though the 'Fool's-cap' is like his; and Major Simeon has one of those. Oh, Captain Du Meresq!"

She bowed rather undecidedly, and then moved on abruptly.

But Bertie did not pass by.

"Are you returning?" asked he. "They can't get on without you. Freddy has dropped a cinder into his nurse's tea, and set fire to the straw in the cat's basket."

Bluebell laughed shyly.

"I have been to see mamma. Do not let me bring you out of your way, Captain Du Meresq,"—for he had turned back with her.

"Oh, I was only going for a walk," said Bertie, innocently,—a harmless amusement that, without any other object, he was simply incapable of undertaking. "Hadn't I better see you home; there's a brute of a dog down there who sprang out at me! I broke my stick across his head, and then, of course, I had to apologize, being disarmed."

"I know that fierce dog. He belongs to a cabman; but I always speak to him, and he never attacks me."

"Even a lion itself would flee from a maid in the pride of her purity," laughed Bertie. "But, Miss Leigh, must we positively go shivering across this bleak desert again?—isn't there some sheltered way through the wood?"

"There certainly is; but it is three miles round, and, I dare say, full of drifts."

"Never mind, all the better fun. Up this way?"

"Oh, but isn't it late? I think they will be expecting me before."

"There's nobody at home, if that's all," said Bertie. "They have gone to the Cathedral, and most likely will turn into tea at the Van Calmonts."

The scrambling walk was a temptation, the common hideous and cold.

"We must walk very quick, then."

"Run, if you like. Come along, there's a dear child."

Bluebell coloured furiously.

"Maybe I won't go at all now!"

"That is so like a girl," said Bertie impatiently; "standing coquetting in the cold. Now, you are offended. What did I say? Only called you a child."

"You had no business to speak so," said Bluebell, angry at his familiar manner, but rather at a loss for words. "Why can't you call me Miss Leigh, like everybody else?" and the indignant little beauty paused, with hot cheeks, and feeling desperately awkward.

Du Meresq bit his lip to hide a smile. He was half afraid she would dash off and terminate the interview.

"Dear me!" said he. "When you are a little older you will think youth a very good fault. Will you forgive me this once, Miss Leigh, and I will not call you anything else?—for the present" (*sotto voce*).

Bluebell was mollified, and rather proud of the good effects of her reproof, notwithstanding the half-inaudible rider. Du Meresq, also, was satisfied, for, without further opposition, they had struck into the wood. Unused to the Britannic hamper of a chaperone, Bluebell saw nothing singular in the proceeding. So they crunched over the snow, keeping, as far as possible, the dazzling track marked by the wheels of the sleigh-waggons, and plentifully powdered by the snow-laden trees; now up to their knees in a drift, from which Bertie had the pleasure of extricating his companion, who forgot her shyness in the difficulties of the path, and, not being given to silence, was laughing and talking away unreservedly.

"What a strange girl she is!" thought Bertie. "Who would think, to hear her chattering now, she *could* have made that prim little speech? I must not go on too fast; it reminds me of that Irish girl who said, the first time I squeezed her hand, 'Ah, Captain Du Meresq, but you are such a bould flirt!'"

Sheltered from the bleak wind the walk on the crisp track was enjoyable enough; the "strange eyes," being now on a line with and not confronting her, were less embarrassing, and the slight awe she still felt of him only gave a piquancy to the companionship.

"Are you not very glad we came this way?" Bertie was saying.

"If we had only snow-shoes," cried the breathless Bluebell, for the third time slipping into a drift, but struggling out before Du Meresq could do more than catch her hand.

"Poor little fingers! how cold they are," trying to put them in with his own into his large beaver gloves.

"Oh, I wish you would be sensible," stammered Bluebell, much confused.

"What's the use of being sensible," retorted he, "when it is so much pleasanter being otherwise? Time enough for that when anybody's by."

But Bluebell wrenched her hand away, bringing off the glove, which she threw on the snow.

"Is that a challenge, Miss Bluebell? Must take up the gauntlet? Good gracious, my dear child, you are not really annoyed? Well, we will be sensible, as you call it. Only you must begin; I don't know how."

"Evidently," said Bluebell, very tartly, drawing as far away as the exigencies of the track would admit. She could hold her own well enough with the young subalterns she had hitherto flirted with, but this man was older, and had a bewildering effect on her.

"Are you and Cecil great friends?" asked Bertie, presently, with the air of having forgotten the fracas.

"I hope so," coming out of her offended silence at this neutral topic. "I know I like her well enough."

"And do you tell each other everything, after the manner of young ladies?"

"No-o," said Bluebell, reflectively; "not like the girls at school. You see Cecil is older than I, and cleverer, I suppose, and doesn't talk much nonsense."

"Did she ever speak of me?" asked Bertie.

"Hardly ever; the others have mentioned you often."

"Cecil is a very sensible girl," with a re-assured countenance; "and as you never talk nonsense, I suppose you won't mention the trivial fact of our having taken this walk?"

"Why in the world not?" opening her large violet eyes full upon him.

"'Speech is silver, but silence is golden,' you unsophisticated child," returned he, enigmatically.

Bluebell considered. "Why, of course, I shall tell Mrs. Rolleston what made me so late."

"But not if she doesn't ask you?"

"But why not? There is *no harm* in it," said the girl, persistently.

"No, no; but if you had lived as long as I, you would know that people *always* try and interfere with anything pleasant. I should so like to take this walk with you every week, Bluebell."

Bluebell looked down; she was vaguely flattered by his caring to repeat the walk which she thought must be so unimportant to him,—it would be something to look forward to, for she *had* enjoyed it, though she could not tell why.

"But, Captain Du Meresq—" she began.

"Call me Bertie, when we are alone," said he.

They had entered on the street, Bluebell was wavering, but the last sentence, "when we are alone," struck her ear unpleasantly.

"How can I?" said she; "I do not know you well enough."

"Walk with me sometimes," whispered Bertie, "and that reason will disappear, but don't say a word about it to-day, there's a dear girl. I had better make tracks for the club; you will be at home in five minutes,"—and Du Meresq ceremoniously lifted his cap, for many eyes were about, and disappeared down another block.

Bluebell on finding herself alone, went through a disagreeable reaction. It was certainly only a few yards to her destination; but it was annoying to be left so abruptly, and an air of secrecy thrown over her actions too. Did she like him, or hate him? She could not determine; her fancy and her vanity were both touched, doubtless; then, remembering Miss Opie's exhortations, a gleam of fun twinkled in her eyes as she thought of what her horror would have been at Bertie's affectionate ease of manner.

All the same she crept into the house, feeling very underhand and uncomfortable. None of the party had returned, so reprieved for the present she went up to the nursery.

Freddy was roaring on his back, he had just thrown "Peep-of-Day" at the nurse's head, which had been unwisely offered to him as a substitute for his favourite trumpet, when its excruciating blasts become too unbearable.

"Oh, I'm sure I'm glad you have come back, miss, for I don't know how to abide that wearyin' child, as don't know what a whipping is. Here's your governess, sir, as will put you in the corner."

"Hold your tongue, you fool!" cried Freddy with supreme contempt.

The *suaviter in modo* was, indeed, the only treatment allowed in that nursery. Bluebell retreated with a highly-coloured scrap-book to the window, which she feigned complete absorption in. Freddy glanced at it out of the tail of his eye.

"Show me that, Boobell."

"I don't know, Freddy," said the girl, feeling some slight moral coercion incumbent on her. "Do you *think* you will call nurse a fool again?"

"She shouldn't bother," said the infant, confidentially, climbing into her lap, but declining to commit himself to any pledges of good behaviour. "Show me the book."

Half-an-hour after, Mrs. Rolleston looking in, saw a pretty little picture—the old nurse was nodding in a rocking-chair. Bluebell's fair young face was bending over Freddy, seated on her lap, with as arm round her neck, his cherubic visage beaming with interest as he listened to the classic tale of "Three Wishes." It was easier to her to continue the recital, while a dread of being questioned prevented her looking up.

"Bluebell is telling Freddy such a beautiful fairy story," said Mrs. Rolleston, to some one who had followed her to the nursery.

"I wish she would tell fairy stories to me," said Bertie.

CHAPTER VI
VISITORS

In aught that from me lures thine eyes
My jealousy has trial;
The lightest cloud across the skies
Has darkness for the dial.

Lord Lytton.

Bluebell had no difficulty in preserving silence about the Sunday's escapade. It never occurred to Mrs. Rolleston to enquire what time she had returned, and an evasive answer to Cecil was all that it entailed. But she was very much perplexed by the change in Captain Du Meresq's manner. The cold civility recommended by Miss Opie seemed all on his side. Nothing but good-humoured indifference was apparent in his manner. Their acquaintance did not seem to have progressed further than the first evening; indeed, it had rather retrograded; and she could almost imagine she had *dreamt* the tender speeches he had lavished on her in the Humber woods.

Cecil and he were out sleighing most afternoons, and Bluebell was thrown on nursery and school-room for companionship—insipid pabulum to the vanity of a young lady in her first glimpse of conquest, and who believed she had stricken down a quarry worthy of her bow. Having nothing to distract her, she considered the problem exhaustively from morning till night, and, if she were not in love with him before, she had got him into her head now, if not into her heart. His being so much with Cecil did not strike her as any clue to the mystery. They were relations, of course, or nearly the same thing; there was no flirting in their matter-of-fact intercourse.

Cecil found her one afternoon reading over the bed-room fire, in a somewhat desponding attitude. Miss Rolleston had just come in from a drive, her slight form shrouded in sealskins, an air of brightness and vivacity replacing her usual rather languid manner.

"You wouldn't think it was snowing from my cloak," cried she. "It is though—quite a heavy fall, if you can call anything so light heavy. We were quite white when we came in, but it shakes off without wetting."

"It won't be very good sleighing, then, to-morrow, and the wind is getting up, too."

"And what have you been doing, Bluebell?"

"I walked with the children and Miss Prosody in the Queen's Park," said the latter, rather dolefully.

"And it was very cold and stupid, I suppose?" said Cecil, kindly. "Come down to the drawing-room and try some duets."

There were two or three visitors below and Bertie, and some tea was coming in. They were looking at a picture of Cecil's just returned from being mounted as a screen. It was a group of brilliant autumn leaves—the gorgeous maple, with its capricious hues, an arrow-shaped leaf, half red, half green, like a parrot's feather, contrasting with another "spotted like the pard," and then one blood-red. The collecting of them had been an interest to the children in their daily walks, and Cecil had arranged them with artistic effect.

One of the visitors was a rather pretty girl, whom Bluebell had known formerly. She gave her, however, only a distant bow, while she answered with the greatest animation any observation of Captain Du Meresq's. This young lady was to be one of the sleighing party next day, and, as far as she could admit such a humiliating fact, was trying to convey to him, that she was as yet unappropriated for any particular sleigh.

"Who is to drive you, Miss Rolleston?" asked she, suspecting, from his backwardness in coming forward, that the object of her intentions might be engaged there.

"I am going in the last sleigh, with Major Fane. We take the luncheon and pay the turnpikes. He is Vice-President this time."

"By-the-bye, Du Meresq," said the Colonel, rather exercised to find a lady of the party without a swain, "whom have you asked?"

"Oh, everybody is engaged," said Bertie, mendaciously ignoring Miss Kendal's half-admission of being open to an offer. "I shall not join the drive at all, unless," he added, in a hesitating manner, as if it was a sudden thought, "Miss Leigh will compassionate me, and allow me to take charge of her."

Bluebell, confused by this unexpected proposition, and by feeling so many eyes turned upon her, did not immediately make any answer; then a vexatious remembrance intruded itself, and she replied, with what that individual would have thought most unnecessary concern,—

"I am very sorry—I mean—I believe I am half-engaged to Mr. Vavasour."

"I should think you were," said Mrs. Rolleston. "I don't know what he would say if you threw him over."

"Oh!" said Bertie, plaintively, "if that insinuating youth has been beforehand, of course there's no chance for me. Well, I am out of the hunt,"—and he carelessly whistled a bar of "Not for Joseph" in reply to a suggestive motion of his sister's towards Miss Kendal.

"I should think it so dull," said that young lady, tossing her head, "to be engaged so long before. *I* do not intend to decide till the day."

"What shall you keep all your admirers in suspense till the last moment?" said Bertie, with a covert sneer, for he was angry at her slighting behaviour to Bluebell. "What a scramble there will be!"

Miss Kendal was not altogether satisfied with the tone of the remark, so she commenced tying on her cloud, observing sharply, "Well, mamma, we shall be benighted if we stay any longer."

Bertie dutifully attended them to the sleigh, and won the elder lady's heart by the skill with which he tucked round her the fur robes and the parting grace of his bow.

She was about to purr out some commendation, when—"What a bear that man is!" burst with startling vehemence from Miss Kendal's coral lips.

"Oh! my dear, what can you mean? I thought he seemed so agreeable."

"I as good as told him," muttered the ruffled fair, too angry to be reticent, "that I had no one to drive me to-morrow; and I think it was real rude asking that Bluebell Leigh before my face,—a mere nursery governess—and not giving me so much as the chance of refusing him."

"But you said," urged Mrs. Kendal, who did not see beyond the proverbial nasal tip, "that you would not decide on your sleigh till the day."

"I only know," said the daughter, with dark emphasis, "I wouldn't drive with him now, if he went on his bended knees to ask me."

"Thank you, Bella," said Bertie, returning. "Nice little game you had cut out for me! What an odious girl!"

Cecil's jealous instinct detected the root of this animosity, more especially guided thereto by his attempt to secure Bluebell as a companion, which had surprised her not too agreeably.

"What is her crime," said she, sarcastically, "beyond a rather transparent design of driving with you Bertie?"

"She is hung with bangles like an Indian squaw, and has a Yankee twang in her voice."

"She pretended to scarcely remember me," said Bluebell, "though we were at school together."

"Jealous, I dare say," laughed Bertie. "Is she an admirer of Jack Vavasour's?"

"Fancy any one admiring a boy like that!" said Bluebell, who did not feel in charity with her allotted charioteer.

Bertie had advanced to take her cup, and as she said this, it seemed to Cecil he touched her hand caressingly under cover of it.

"I dare say," said she sharply, "Alice Kendal has as many admirers as other people, and, perhaps, can dispense with counting Captain Du Meresq among them."

Bluebell looked up, astonished at her manner; but Bertie perceived it with more intelligence, and the thought, "What a bore it will be if she is jealous," afterwards passed through his mind,—by which may be inferred he had had in contemplation the acquisition of "Heaven's last best gift."

CHAPTER VII
THE GARRISON SLEIGH CLUB

'T were a pity when flowers around us rise,
To make light of the rest, if the rose be not there;
And the world is so rich in resplendent eyes,
'T were a pity to limit one's love to a pair.

Moore.

"I never saw a prettier sight in my life," cried Cecil, as she stood with a motley group in the verandah of "The Maples," the rendezvous of the sleighing party. As each sleigh turned in at the gate and deposited its freight, it fell into rank which extended all round the lawn, till scarcely a space was left on the drive that encircled it, and the air rang with the bells on the nodding horses' heads.

"What the—blazes!" ejaculated Bertie, as Mr. Vavasour rounded the corner at a trot in a red-wheeled tandem, scarlet plumes on the horses, and the robes a combination of black bear-skins and scarlet trimming. The leader, a recent importation from England, better acquainted with the hunting-field than the traces, reared straight on end; but a judicious flick on her ear sent her with a bound almost into the next sleigh, and the tandem drew up at the hall door to an inch.

"Post? mail-cart? nonsense!" said Jack, shaking hands all round 'mid an avalanche of chaff. "Nice cheerful colour for a cold day; that's all."

"Quite scorching," said Major Fane. "Well, Miss Rolleston, if they leave us behind at the turnpikes, we shall never lose sight of them with Jack's flames for a beacon."

"How do you like your tandem, Bluebell?" asked Cecil, "and how far do you expect to get before Mr. Vavasour upsets you?" added she, *sotto voce*.

"I don't care if he chooses a good place," laughed Bluebell.

"Why, I thought Bertie wasn't going," said, Mrs. Rolleston, as that individual drove up in a modest cutter with a gentleman companion.

"I think he changed his mind when he heard Miss Kendal was going with papa," said Cecil.

"I believe we are all here," said Colonel Rolleston, who was to lead the procession, coming out with the great lady of the party, an eccentric dowager peeress, who having "tired her wing" with flying through the States, was now perching awhile before re-crossing the Herring-pond. Miss Kendal and a subaltern, pressed into the service, placed themselves in the back seat, well smothered in wolf-skins, and the first sleigh moved off to the admiration of the school-room party at the window, who, with the partiality of childhood, thought their papa's the most beautiful turn-out in the city.

"Mr. Vavasour's horse is up the bank," screamed Fleda. "How much better papa drives; he went off so quickly and quietly. I wouldn't be Bluebell! Mr. Vavasour can hardly get out at the gate."

"If papa had to drive one horse before another, perhaps he couldn't either," said Lola, who had been watching with great interest the erratic course of Jack's leader.

Twenty sleighs were off in a string, the crowd cheering them to the echo as they dashed through Queen's Park; but on gaining Carleton Street they were obliged carefully to keep the track, as the sides of the road were deep and treacherous.

"The Colonel is making the pace very slow," remarked Mr. Vavasour; "like to drive, Miss Leigh? they are going very smoothly."

Bluebell, whose knowledge of horses was about equal to her opportunities of instruction, unhesitatingly assented. Jack's gratification thereat was somewhat tempered, when he saw the bewilderment apparent in his flighty pair at the very original manner in which she handled her "lines."

"I suppose," said that young lady, with the composure of ignorance, "we are all right as long as this bald-face horse keeps its nose pointing at Captain Delamere's back."

"Quite so," said Jack, cheerily; "don't take the whip, you are only winding it round your own neck. I'll give Dahlia a lick in the face if she turns out of the rank."

They were winding down a hill, and took a road at the bottom at right angles to it. Colonel Rolleston, in the first sleigh, was blandly pointing out to Lady Hampshire the *coup d'oeil* of the whole procession as they described two sides of a triangle.

"Do you like my plumes?" asked Jack, relaxing his surveillance on Dahlia, as her left ear, which had been laid back in a suggestive manner, resumed its accustomed position.

"Like them," echoed Bluebell; "it's just like a hearse, bar the colour, which is frightful. I wouldn't have come if I had known I was to be driven in such a fire-engine."

"There now," rather crest-fallen. "I chose them because you said you were *fond* of scarlet, otherwise I should have preferred blue, except that I might have been taken for one of the 10th, who mount their regimental colours on everything."

"I like the 10th," said Bluebell, perversely; "they are all good-looking except the Adjutant, who got his nose sliced off by a Sikh, and the.... goodness what's that?" as a fearful shout, followed by a sudden checking of horses, brought the whole line to a stand-still.

"What's the matter?" was passed from one sleigh to another up to the front: the return message, shouted and taken up as each one interpreted it, became soon about as intelligible as it does in the game of Russian scandal, and for the next few minutes everybody was conjecturing at once.

"Here's Du Meresq," cried Jack, as Bertie came ploughing through the snow.

"Halloa, guard! what's wrong on the line?"

"Run into a goods' train," said he, keeping on his course to the Vice-President's sleigh.

"Du Meresq never tells one anything," said Jack; "I hate a mysterious fellow; somebody's capsized, I suppose, and he's gone for some brandy."

"Perhaps for a shovel," suggested Bluebell. "Colonel Rolleston may have come to a drift."

"Don't see how we are to reverse our engine," replied Jack, looking each side of the road, where the snow was piled four or five feet.

Bertie, however, had not gone for a shovel, which would have been perfectly useless, but to explain the situation and assist in turning round the sleighs. In front of Colonel Rolleston was a huge rampart of snow, extending for some distance. The wind setting dead in that direction, had drifted it across, and buried the track several feet. This road had been clear the day before, for Bertie and Cecil had driven it to ascertain, but the wind had changed and snow fallen during the night.

Major Fane's sleigh was successfully turned, after a great deal of assistance to the horses, who floundered up to their shoulders; and to this haven of refuge Du Meresq was conducting several young ladies, for each sleigh having to turn on the spot where their progress was arrested, a certain number of upsets was inevitable.

"Come, Miss Leigh," said a voice beneath her, "you mustn't stick to the ship any longer. Why, this is the worst bit of all. You can't jump; trust to me." And to Jack's indignation, Bertie lifted her from the wheel and carried her through some deep snow to a dry place. There was a certain amount of excuse for it, as he couldn't have deposited her in the drift, and turning the tandem took up its owner's whole attention, and the services of three or four volunteers; but he fancied Du Meresq had squeezed the little hand before he relinquished it, and ere the tell-tale blush had passed from Bluebell's face, Jack had turned, jumped out and replaced her in the tandem with quiet decision.

Bluebell, confused by the powerless way she had been handed about between her two admirers, could not rally directly, and sat meditating an early snubbing for Jack, but a ridiculous incident soon distracted her attention.

"Get out? No, thank you, Captain Du Meresq," cried Lilla Tremaine, a tall, handsome girl in the sleigh behind; "you'd find me a precious weight to carry, and I am very comfortable where I am. Turn away, Captain Delamere, we'll sink or swim together."

Thus urged, the individual called on made his effort; the sleigh turned, indeed, but on its side, and the adventurous Miss Tremaine, summarily ejected, sank to her waist in the deep snow, her crinoline rising as she descended, spread out under her arms, looking like an inverted umbrella. Jack and Bluebell were suffocating with the laughter they vainly tried to hide, and Bertie, who was on foot, took in the situation at once, and rushed to the rescue.

"Put your arms round my neck, Miss Tremaine," cried he, peremptorily.

The poor girl, half crying with shame and cold, did so, and Du Meresq, grasping her firmly round the waist, endeavoured to drag her forth.

"It's even betting she pulls him in," cried Jack, in a most unfeeling ecstasy, for Miss Tremaine was no pocket Venus—rather answered the Irishman's description of "an armful of joy."

"Oh, dear!" said poor Lilla, trembling with cold, as she found herself on *terra firma*, "I never can go on; the snow has made me quite wet through."

"Of course you can't," said Bertie, decidedly; "you'd catch your death of cold. Delamere, you drive on with the other Miss Tremaine," for they had both been in his sleigh, "and I'll take Miss Lilla home in my cutter, where she can get dry clothes. You must all pass their house on your way back, when we can fall in again; so that's all settled. Oh, Meredith, I forgot you. Hitch on to some other sleigh, there's a good fellow. I am on ambulance duty; somebody tell Colonel Rolleston—presently."

Then Bertie, who had his own reasons for hurrying, placed Miss Tremaine, still shivering from her snow bath, in the cutter, and drove rapidly off.

"Well, I am d——d," muttered Captain Delamere to Vavasour; "she has never seen the fellow before!"

"Hush, pray," said Jack, affectedly; "he *is* an officious young man. But be thankful for small mercies, old boy; you have got one left."

"That's the wrong one," growled Delamere.

After a brief consultation about the route, a unanimous vote for luncheon was passed, so they drove on till they came to an open space, the contrary side of the wood in which Du Meresq and Bluebell had walked on Sunday. Here all the sleighs formed up together, and Major Fane's larder was ransacked.

Curaçoa, mulled claret, hot coffee, etc., kept warm in a blanket, were passed round, with mutton pies, croquettes, cakes and other edibles; and circulation being restored, all was mirth and hilarity.

Colonel Rolleston alone remained dark and moody. He had just discovered the defection of Du Meresq and Lilla, and, having his own opinion of his brother-in-law, disapproved of it entirely. Miss Tremaine also was much too flighty for his taste, and he was very hard on Captain Delamere for not applying to him to get her decorously out of her delicate dilemma.

He made up his mind to curtail the drive, and call at Mr. Tremaine's at his earliest convenience.

Bertie, in the meantime, delighted at getting a *tête-à-tête* with a handsome girl, instead of driving in a monotonous string with Mr. Meredith, proceeded to improve the occasion with such success that his fair companion forgot her wet stockings, and even omitted to observe that they had passed the turn leading to the paternal abode.

When she did remark it, Bertie easily persuaded her that she must be quite dry now, and that, as they had missed the garrison drive, they had better take one on their own account. Miss Lilla, unrestrained by the detective eyes of her elder sister, was ripe for any frolic, and Bertie certainly did not find so many obstacles in the way of an affectionate flirtation as he had with Bluebell.

But our business is with the trans-Atlantic picnic in the snow, not with the "cutting out" expedition of this reprobate pair. Having distributed the remainder of the luncheon to the servants, a start was again effected. Lilla's adventure had left its impression one way or another on two or three of the party. Jack was delighted that Du Meresq was off on a fresh pursuit, and so not likely to be hanging about Bluebell; and that damsel was trying, by a reckless flirtation with Vavasour, to stifle the vexatious conviction that Bertie had only been making a fool of her on Sunday, and was now probably repeating the same game with Miss Tremaine. Yet at this period her vanity was more wounded than her heart; very different from poor Cecil, whose infatuation was of older date, and not the mere result of a few flattering speeches.

For a girl of her disposition to set her affections on a man like Bertie was certain misery. She had no rivals in those days when she learnt to care so intensely for the sympathetic companion who understood her so much better than any one else. He understood her; therein was the potent charm; her mind awoke and her ideas vivified from contact with his, as two happily-contrasted colours become brighter in hue in juxtaposition. No companion had ever suited her so perfectly, and yet Bertie had scarcely made direct love to her. It seemed a matter of course that they should care most for each other, and Cecil's young and ardent heart had drifted beyond recall ere she had done more than suspect another side to his character.

Now she perceived that Bertie's affection for her by no means made him insensible to the bright eyes of the fair Canadians; yet the more she cared for his philandering interludes with other girls the less she showed it, except that her manner grew colder, though, unfortunately, her heart did not.

Major Fane was disappointed with Cecil's preoccupied mood. He had taken some pains to secure her for this drive, and she hadn't a word to say to him. He certainly admired her, but, perhaps, it was more his horror of Canadian girls that had made her his choice for the day. He always said their only idea of conversation was chaff, and rudeness under cover of it; and as he had been the victim of many such "smart" speeches, he looked upon them with nervous aversion.

The quiet repose of a lady-like English girl gained by the contrast. There was rather too much tranquillity to-day, perhaps; so he exerted some tact to draw Cecil from her reserve, the cause of which he was unable to guess. He agreed with her in reviling the monotony and stupidity of sleighing picnics, having to follow one by one like a string of geese, long after one was perished with cold, though he failed to detect in her weariness that she was wishing for her father to stop at the Tremaines', and annex the truant sleigh to the rest.

Her discontent somewhat relieved by expression, she became ashamed of her unsociability, and Major Fane's next topic was not uncongenial. He was airing his cherished grudge, and pronouncing a severe philippic on the belles of the Dominion. Cecil was incapable of detraction, or envy at another's greater success; but in the face of Bertie's abduction of Lilla before her eyes, she did not feel particularly in charity with any daughter of Canada.

In the meantime Bluebell, in the strangest of spirits, refused to relinquish the reins, even in difficult places, and conducted herself generally with a mixture of recklessness and ignorance that gave Jack enough to do to look out.

He rather took advantage of this mood to make more decided love than he had hitherto done; but while he thought her wild with fun and spirits, she was really goaded on by vexation and bitterness of heart; and perhaps her most immediate wish was for solitude to drop the mask and be miserable in peace.

That was impossible, at present. Jack was tiresome. He was giving her directions how to steer up a hill, formidable from its narrow track and deep drop on either side. Dahlia, it seemed, jibbed sometimes, she must—Bluebell was paying no attention. Good Heavens! what was happening?—the leader backing and sliding! Jack's stinging whip and clutch at the reins could not arrest the catastrophe. Dahlia rears and falls over the edge, pulling sleigh and wheeler after her into a trough of snow.

Bluebell blinded and half suffocated—no wonder, for three bear-skins and two cushions were a-top of her (not to mention Jack, who had caught his leg in the reins, and was unable immediately to rise),—made vain efforts to extricate himself; the horses were struggling on their sides; and altogether, as the Americans say, it was rather "mixed."

Somehow or another, no one ever does get hurt out of a sleigh, even after an *impromptu* header of a dozen feet. Ten minutes later the party were *en route* again, Bluebell transferred, *en pénitence*, to Colonel Rolleston's sleigh, *vice* the subaltern; and by this time nearly every one was discontented and anxious to return.

CHAPTER VIII
FIXING UP A PRANCE

"'Tis over,
The valse, the quadrille, and the song,
The whispered farewell of the lover;
The heartless adieu of the throng,
The heart that was throbbing with pleasure;
The eyelid that longed for repose,
The beaux that were dreaming of treasure.
The girls that were dreaming of beaux."

Edward Firzgerald.

Before they got to the Tremaines' house, Bertie drove up with Miss Lilla, who was "quite dry now, thank you; not worth while bringing all the sleighs up to the door." More than one curious observer noticed the panting flanks of the horse, who scarcely looked as if he had been resting in a stable. To be sure, the delinquents *had* done that last mile rather fast, to nick in and meet the party before they should make inconvenient inquiries at Mr. Tremaine's,—Bertie, who was as good a mimic as his mother, enhancing the fright of his fair companion by an improvisation of the scene that would probably take place supposing they were too late to prevent it, and further convulsing her with a travesty of his brother-in-law in his most imposing attitude of stately displeasure.

Lilla nearly had a relapse when they met the rest, as Colonel Rolleston's face was the faithful reproduction of Bertie's five minutes before; but the ironical silence with which he received her speech, rather diminished their triumph at having escaped detection. The girls were all to return to "The Maples," dress there, and go to the dinner and dance at the barracks, under Mrs. Rolleston's sole chaperonage.

The scrambling toilette was got through with much noise and merriment.

"Oh, has any one seen my 'waist'?" and "Do smooth my waterfall," were enigmatical exclamations of frequent occurrence. Cecil's dormitory resembled a milliner's show-room from the variety of dresses spread on the bed.

These were not of a very extravagant description; papery pink or green silk seemed most in vogue, completed with rows of beads round the throat; but when viewed in connexion with the apple-blossom complexions, abundant hair and dancing eyes of the Canadian belles, the adventitious aids of dress might well be deemed as superfluous as painting the lily.

Half-a dozen covered sleighs, going and returning, transported the party to the barracks, where, escorted by their military hosts, they ascended the staircase, banked with evergreens, and lined by motionless soldiers to the ante-room, which, of course, looked as unattractive as the cordial but mistaken exertions of its proprietors could make it—all the *laissez-aller* comfort primly tidied away, and such a roasting fire as speedily drove every one to remote corners of the room.

The *mauvais quart d'heure* before dinner had the usual sobering effect, and young people, who later on would be valsing together on the easiest of terms, now shyly looked over photograph books, and discoursed with an edifying amount of diffidence and respect. Each one was to go in to dinner with his companion of the sleigh—an arrangement of questionable wisdom, and, as Bertie said, "It behoved one to be doubly careful whom one drove." Captain Delamere was furious, for, when he claimed Lilla, she calmly replied, "That having taken them both, she of course supposed he would ask her elder sister, and, therefore, had promised Captain Du Meresq."

Before Delamere had done anathematizing his folly in giving the saucy Lilla such a loop-hole to throw him over, the trumpet sounded, folding doors opened, and fifty people sat down to the cheery repast.

The table was bright with regimental plate, racing cups, and hot-house flowers. The band commenced playing "Selections," somewhat deafening, perhaps, but then it was too cold to put them out of doors.

Cecil and Bluebell were neither of them too much gratified at witnessing the furious flirtation going on at dinner between Captain Du Meresq and Miss Tremaine; but Cecil, who never looked at them, and therefore, of course, saw everything, fancied the admiration most on the lady's side, and even some of her *oeillades*, bravado. To be sure Bertie never did flirt seriously *en évidence*, if he could help it.

Bluebell, completely out of sorts, was acquiring a painful experience. Du Meresq's conduct seemed inexplicable and provoking as she pondered indignantly on her walk at the Humber, and mentally ejaculated with Miss Squeers, "Is this the hend?"

Jack, temporarily discouraged by her indifference to himself, which came on rather rapidly at dinner, gave his next neighbour the benefit of his conversation.

But this unsatisfactory repast to our heroines was not unnecessarily prolonged, the mess-room having to be cleared for the great business of the evening, which, let us hope will prove what it is sure to be called in next day's discussion "a very good ball."

Why this undescriptive phrase should be applied to every well-attended dance, with a supper, has always perplexed us; for, of course, every one really judges it by his or her own personal success and enjoyment, not unfrequently incompatible with that of some one else. Yet it is all summed up next morning in the summary verdict "good," or "bad." If there is a deficiency of gentlemen, space, supper, or *ton*, the latter; but given these indispensables, you may have been jilted for your bosom friend by your latest conquest, yet you must come up smiling, and endorse the public panegyric on the hated evening till the subject be superseded.

Bluebell, a few weeks ago, would have looked upon this ball as the acme of delight. She was in great request, and, indeed, attained that highest object of young lady ambition, being belle of the evening; but now her happiness did not depend on the many—dance after dance passed, and the only partner she cared for had not once engaged her.

Bertie had been sitting out half the evening with Lilla in a conservatory, and when they did emerge, was seized on by his brother-in-law with very black looks, and introduced to a somewhat unappreciated young lady.

Bertie had the happy knack of appearing equally charmed, whether presented to a beauty or the reverse; but he inscribed himself very low down on her card, remorselessly ignoring the intervening blanks, and then approached Cecil, who, in black and amber, was the most striking-looking girl in the room. Though inferior in beauty to many, her fine figure and expressive eyes could never pass unnoticed.

"Dear little Cecil, how well she is looking!" thought he, facilely forgetting his latest flame, and just becoming sensible of her "altered eye."

"My niece," said Bertie, in a theatrical tone, intended to disguise his perception of it, "shall we tread a measure? Let me lead you forth into the mazy dance."

"Excuse me, Bertie," said Cecil, languidly; "I am only going to dance the two or three round ones I am engaged for, and I know you do not care for square."

"I should think not," said he angrily, "when you are going to dance round ones with other fellows."

"You see you asked too late," said she, indifferently.

"Will you go in to supper with me then?"

"That was all arranged and written down ages ago. Let me see, I am ticketed for the Major again."

"As you have been all day. I never saw such a cut and-dried, monotonous programme for a party: all done by rule—no freedom of action."

"Really, Bertie, you and Miss Tremaine can't complain."

"That's why you are so cold to me to-night, Cecil," said Du Meresq, quietly.

"What can it signify to me?" retorted she, freezingly, vexed at having permitted the adversary, so to speak, to discover the joint in her harness. Her partner, who had been hovering near, now claimed and bore her unwillingly away, for next to being friends with Bertie was the pleasure of "riling" him by smiling icyness. It was the only weapon she permitted herself, as she would not condescend to any visible sign of jealousy or pique.

Bertie was simply *gêné* by her determination to be all or nothing; there was no satisfying such an unreasonable girl. Like the immortal Lilyvick, "he loved them all," yet her thoughtful mind and gentle companionship were becoming more to him than he was himself aware of.

Cecil, valsing round, looked at each turn for his tall figure leaning against the wall. It was an abstracted attitude, and he seemed graver than usual.

"Had she made him unhappy?"—she trusted so—would give the world to read his thoughts.

Some one said, "There is no punishment equal to a granted prayer." Du Meresq was wrapt in speculation as to whether they had really succeeded in getting a wild turkey for supper, which the Mess President was in maddening doubt about the day before.

That blissful moment was at hand, and the room thinned with a celerity born of *ennui*, I suppose, for very few people are really hungry, yet it is the invariable signal for as simultaneous a rush as of starving paupers when the door of a soup kitchen is opened. To be sure, there are the chaperones, poor things, round whom no "lovers are sighing," and, perhaps, supper *is* the liveliest time to them—old gentlemen, too, might be allowed some indulgence; but what can be said for dancing men, wasting the precious moments of their partners, while they linger congregated together among the *débris* and champagne-corks?

"What a clearance," said Bluebell, subsiding, with a fagged air, on to a sofa, as her partner bowed himself off with an eye to business.

"Forward the heavy brigade," said Bertie, motioning to his brother-in-law bearing off Lady Hampshire; "only room for thirty at a time. *We* must wait, Miss Leigh."

"I am ready to wait. But what have 'we' got to say to it?" said Bluebell, with her Canadian directness.

"Don't speak so unkindly," said Bertie, sentimentally, flinging himself on the sofa by her side. "You don't know all I have suffered this week."

"You certainly disguised it very well," said the girl, with total disbelief in her eyes.

"Do you think I felt nothing when I saw you all day with Vavasour, who every one knows is madly in love with you; and then dancing every dance—not leaving a corner in your programme for me?"

"You didn't ask me," said Bluebell, less austerely.

"No, for you never so much as looked my way. Besides, Bluebell, I told you we must be careful. If Colonel Rolleston guessed my feelings for you—he is so selfish, he forgets he has been young himself—I should be no longer welcome here."

"Then, I am sure," said Bluebell, the tears rushing to her eyes, "I wish you had never come. I have been *miserable* ever since I took that stupid walk, which you prevented my mentioning; and—and—"

"Let's be miserable again next Sunday, Bluebell," whispered Bertie.

"I shall not go home; or, if I do, I'll stop there. I'll *never* walk with you again, Captain Du Meresq."

"'Quoth the raven, "never more!"' I know what it is, you are tired to death. Sit still on the sofa and I will bring you some supper; sleighing all day and dancing all night have distorted your mental vision,"—and Bertie dashed off, passing the young lady he was engaged to on his way to the supper room, with an inward conviction that their dance must be about due. Having possessed himself of a modicum of prairie hen, he intercepted a tumbler of champagne cup just being handed across the table to Captain Delamere.

"Confound it, that's mine!" said the aggrieved individual.

"I want it for a lady," urged Bertie.

"So do I," said Delamere.

"My dear fellow," said Bertie, chaffingly, nodding towards a gorgeous American, "it is for Mrs. Commissioner Duloe. She must not be kept waiting."

"I won't allow my lady to be second to any lady in the room," cried Delamere who was elevated.

Bertie was in too great a hurry to chaff Delamere any longer, for, perceiving that his relatives were safely at supper, he resolved to make the most of the few minutes at his disposal, and, as he would have expressed it, "lay it on thick."

Bluebell was leaning languidly back on the sofa, watching the forms of the dancers, ever revolving past the open door to the strains of a heart-broken valse. (*En passant*, why are the prettiest valses all plaintive and despairing, quadrilles and lancers cheerful and jiggy, and galops reckless, not to say tipsy?)

Bertie, with his spoils, was by her side, and, having restored her nerves with champagne, proceeded to agitate them again with the warmest protestations of affection. The child with the day's experience before her, only half-believed him, but the spirit of coquetry woke up, and she resolved to try and make him care for her as much as he pretended to do.

But Bluebell was trying her 'prentice hand with a veteran in such warfare.

They were alone in the little room, in one adjoining a few people were sitting.

"I wish that girl would not watch us so," said Bluebell, indicating one apparently deep in a photograph book, under cover of which she was furtively observing them.

"Oh," said Bertie, with a groan, "she's been following me about ever since I asked her for a dance six off. I hope it is over."

"I dare say she's very angry at being left sitting out," said Bluebell. "I am sure I should be."

"Ah," said Bertie, "your experience will be all the other way—it's us poor fellows who will be thrown over, besides, she shouldn't have got introduced to me. I saw her going on the wrong leg and all out of step, and Jack Vavasour says she's a regular stick-in-the-mud to talk to."

A stream now issued from the supper room, and Mr. Vavasour, bowing himself free from a "comfortable" looking matron, hurried up.

"Our dance, Miss Leigh. I thought I should never be in time. She was twenty minutes at the chicken and lobster-salad, and then went in for sweets."

"I must go and give my girl a turn, I suppose," whispered Bertie. "She's guarding the outposts so no chance of giving her the slip. She'd go raging off to the Colonel. Just like him, letting one in for such a real bad thing."

A few sleighs were beginning to jingle up, but most of the girls assumed moccasins, clouds, and furs, and kilting their petticoats as deftly and mysteriously as only Canadians can, set out in parties, escorted by their partners, and stepped briskly over the moon lit snow to their respective dwellings.

Bertie saw his party off in their sleigh, tenderly squeezing Bluebell's hand, who fell to his share, but did not return with them. Indeed, he was walking soon in quite an opposite direction, by the side of a shrouded figure in a rose-coloured cloud, out of which laughed the mischievous eyes of the second Miss Tremaine.

CHAPTER IX
CROSS PURPOSES

Trifles, light as air,
Are to the jealous confirmation strong
As proofs of holy writ.

Shakespeare.

Bluebell had not visited her mother for three weeks. One Saturday Freddy had a sore throat and would not let her out of his sight, keeping up an incessant demand for black-currant jelly and fairy tales, and the next week a heavy fall of snow made walking impossible. She now very often shared the gaieties of the others. Mrs. Rolleston took great interest in Bluebell's career. She thought it by no means improbable that Sir Timothy should have provided for her in his will, or, indeed, that he might any day acknowledge her; and though she took her out, and let her dance to her heart's content, kept faithful watch to prevent any undesirable flirtation.

So the kind-hearted lady was a good deal disturbed at seeing Jack Vavasour, who came of an extravagant and far from wealthy family, first in the field. After the manner of love-lorn subalterns, he haunted and persecuted the fair object of his affections, who cared nothing about him, and treated him as a child does its toys, sometimes pleased with them, and at others casting them indifferently aside.

And all the time Bertie was gaining greater influence over her. But even Cecil, whose eyes were keen, was never able to detect any evidence of a secret understanding between them.

He regularly asked her for one valse only when they went to balls; indeed, he could not do less. Cecil, of course, could not hear what they talked about *then*.

There is a dreamy, intoxicating valse of Gung'l's, which he always made her keep for him when it was played. It was a small piece of selfish romance, for well he knew that charmed air would ever hereafter be haunted with associations of him. How many more "stolen sweet moments" he found in the day must be left to the reader's imagination. But stolen they were; for Du Meresq knew Cecil's disposition, and was far from wishing to break with her, though "why should he spare this little girl with the chestnut hair, and the love in her deep-blue eyes?" And Bluebell no longer shrank from being underhand. It did not strike her in that light now. She thought of nothing but Bertie, who was so different before the others, that she learnt to look forward to their brief chances of being alone as much as he did. And Du Meresq, with ingenious sophistry, expatiated on the charm of keeping their delicious secret to themselves, uncommented on by the cold and unsympathetic.

Thus Bluebell, from being a lively, ingenuous, outspoken child, altered into a dreamy maiden, living a hidden life of repressed excitement, whose whole interest was the fugitive, uncertain interviews with Bertie, and an interchanged glance, touch of the hand, or few fond words, ventured on when the others were not attending.

"Bluebell," laughed Cecil, as a cutter drove to the door, "here is your Lubin again." The girls had just returned from the Rink, and were disrobing upstairs.

"Oh, he is so tiresome," said the other. "I declare I won't come down."

"That you must; we should never get rid of him; he would sit on waiting for you. You have made such a goose of him, Bluebell, and he used to be such fun."

"I shouldn't mind him if he was fun now; but he just sits glowering at one, and stays so long. Why can't a person see when he is not wanted?"

"But you do want him sometimes," said Cecil. "You are always 'off' and 'on' with poor Jack. I believe, if he proposed, you would say 'No' one day and retract the next."

They entered the drawing-room, where was young Vavasour, as usual, making conversation to Mrs. Rolleston, who was at once bored and disproving. Cecil shook hands pleasantly enough, but Bluebell, not even looking at him, extended a lifeless hand in passing, and, picking up some work, appeared absorbed in counting stitches.

Jack turned over in his own mind every possible cause of offence. He couldn't perceive that it was he himself that was not wanted, and that she cared not a button for anything he had done or left undone.

He talked on perseveringly with the others, glancing stealthily at Bluebell tatting, till Cecil got up to make tea, when he moved to a seat nearer.

"I wasn't out of uniform till four o'clock, Miss Leigh, or I should have been at the Rink."

"So I suppose. You always go there, don't you?"

"When I expect to meet any one," trying to throw a sentimental look in his generally laughing brown eyes.

"It isn't usually empty: but, of course, you don't go for the skating. You'll never make anything of that."

"Any more than you will be of driving," retorted Jack. "Shall you ever forget that crumpler down the bank? Dahlia hasn't recovered the fright yet."

"Stupid thing; what did she jump over for? I was nearly suffocated. I am sure there must have been a cast of me on the snow."

"It wasn't altogether unpleasant," said Jack. "We were covered up very snug and warm, like babes in the wood. I shouldn't mind doing it again in the same company."

"Shouldn't you?" said Bluebell, indignantly. "Then you may omit the company." And so they went on whispering, to Mrs. Rolleston's annoyance, till the Colonel's voice was heard bringing in a visitor—a lady of unfashionable appearance, chiefly remarkable for the variety of knitted articles, described in work-books as "winter comforts," displayed on her person.

"*Ma tante!*" ejaculated Jack, incautiously; "who is this old Quiz?"

"Here is Mrs. Leigh," said Colonel Rolleston, "who says she has not seen her daughter for three weeks. Where are you Bluebell?"

Jack felt ready to sink into the earth, while his boyish face became the colour of a peony; and Bluebell, vexed and hurt, advanced to the maternal embrace.

Their mutual confusion was so evident, that the Colonel put another interpretation on it, and remarked, in a tone the reverse of congratulatory,—"You have not been long getting out of harness, Vavasour."

Jack muttered something, and tried to catch Bluebell's eye, agonies of contrition in his own.

"Well, my dear, and how well you are looking," said Mrs. Leigh. "But we have missed you at home, Aunt Jane and I. No, thank you, Mrs. Rolleston;

not at all tired. I caught the street-car at the corner, which brought me all the way for five cents. Very respectable people in it; only one soldier; he was not at all tipsy. I don't think your men ever are, Colonel. Thank you, Miss Rolleston," as Cecil brought her some tea. "I'll just unbutton my Sontag, or I shan't feel the good of it when I go out again, shall I?"

"I have been thinking," said Mrs. Rolleston, to whom it had just occurred that this would be a good break in Jack's attentions, "that it would be very nice if Bluebell went home for a few days, as you have seen so little of her."

"I'm sure I'm most grateful," said the little lady. "There, my dear, Aunt Jane was saying only yesterday how dull it was without the child. But are you sure she can be spared, Mrs. Rolleston?"

"Only to you," said the lady, kindly, but smiling a little, for certainly her *duties* were not very onerous.

Bluebell, an anxious listener, felt her heart sink at this proposal. What, go away and leave Bertie, whose daily presence had become a necessity to her! Besides, dreadful thought! his leave might be over ere she returned. In desperation she said, imploringly, "Mamma will not want me for more than a day or two," and gazed anxiously at Mrs. Rolleston, with a world of unspoken entreaty in her eyes.

The appeal was injudicious, only confirming her impression that it was a separation from Jack Bluebell dreaded, and she mentally put on another week to her banishment.

"There's no hurry," said the lady, decidedly; "a change will do you good. She shall walk over to-morrow, Mrs. Leigh; and I am very glad I thought of it."

Bluebell, thinking all was lost, tried not to show her dismay, which would have grieved her mother and done no good; but she remembered, with a sinking heart, that Du Meresq was to dine out that night, and she might get no opportunity of speaking to him alone before changing her quarters.

"I must be off home," said Mrs. Leigh. "Several little things to be done in your room, Bluebell. The stove-pipe has got choked at the elbow, and I must have the sweep in."

Her daughter longed to suggest that it might be more convenient to postpone her appearance for a day; but as Mrs. Rolleston said nothing, she could not either.

Jack, who had been all this time writhing with vexation at his *mal-à-propos* remark, here saw a chance of propitiating Bluebell and putting himself on visiting terms at her home.

"My cutter is at the door," said he, addressing Mrs. Rolleston. "If Mrs. Leigh will allow me, I shall be too happy to drive her home."

"Oh, he must be going to propose," thought the former lady, "and they won't have twopence between them;" but she could only reply,—

"Well, Mrs. Leigh, what do you say? Will you trust yourself to Mr. Vavasour?"

"I'm sure," said the little lady, flutteringly, "the gentleman is most kind; but I am so timid with horses unless they are quite old. Does your horse kick, sir?"

"Only if the rein gets under her tail."

"Ah, I should be sure to scream and snatch it—the reins, I mean, and they say that isn't safe driving. I had better walk; and yet it is getting dark, and I shall miss the car. What *shall* I do, Colonel Rolleston?"

"Drive, to be sure," said he, who wanted to get rid of them both. "Vavasour only upsets when he gives the reins to young ladies," with a glance at Bluebell.

"Well, I *should* like a ride in a sleigh, if my poor nerves will let me enjoy it," toddling to the door with Colonel Rolleston.

"I'll take the greatest care of you, Mrs. Leigh," said Jack, heartily, grateful for a re-assuring nod from Bluebell in recognition of his contrite gallantry. The mare, tired of waiting, became fidgety to be off.

"Oh, he is going to prance. Have you got good hold of his head, sir?" to the groom.

"Quite correct, 'm," grinned that official. "Quiet, 'Nancy,'" that being the stable version of "Banshee."

"Let her go," said Jack, who had just tucked Mrs. Leigh in. A couple of bounds, a smothering scream, and they disappeared in the evening gloom.

"That there old party ain't the guvener's usual form," meditated that bât-man, as he walked back, for the cutter only carried two. "He seems to set a deal of store by her, though. There's some young 'ooman at home, where she lives, I'd take my dying dick."

Cecil and her father, who had seen them off, stopped laughing together at Mrs. Leigh's peculiarities; and Bluebell, finding herself alone with Mrs. Rolleston, felt impelled to try if she could not curtail her sentence of banishment. Of course, her words were intended to conceal her thoughts — love's first lesson is always hypocrisy.

"I know I am not very much use here," she began, "but still I shouldn't like to think I was of none, and, therefore, I really don't want to stay away more than a day or two."

A sudden look of penetration came into Mrs. Rolleston's face, and, with more sarcasm in her voice than Bluebell's little speech appeared to justify, she said, —

"My dear, scrupulous child, we *can* get on without you longer than that, so you may, with a clear conscience, think of your mother, who is dull this dreadful weather."

Bluebell felt caught in a mesh and incapable of extricating herself, but she made no attempt to conceal her reluctance to going.

"How long must I stay away?" said she, dolefully.

"Just till the days get a little longer—a fortnight or three weeks, perhaps."

Bluebell made a gesture of despair (Bertie would be gone to a certainty by then), and looked the picture of misery. Mrs. Rolleston's suspicions were now convictions.

"My dear Bluebell," she began, impulsively, "I know there's some reason for your dislike to going," and she gazed fixedly at her. No denial. Bluebell hoped Mrs. Rolleston *had* some inkling of how things were with her and Bertie, and had she then persisted might easily have forced her confidence; which would have considerably enlightened and dismayed the elder lady, whose mind, being full of Jack, had never dreamed of Bertie.

Mrs. Rolleston, however, rapidly decided it would never do to encourage her to talk of the matter, and that she had better put her foot on it at once.

"I have guessed your little *penchant*, dear, for some one we won't talk about, for indeed, Bluebell, it never can come to any thing; you are both too young and too poor. It would be a most undesirable connexion."

"She doesn't think me grand enough for her brother," suggested Bluebell's wounded pride.

"And, therefore," pursued her Mentor, "absence is the best thing in these cases; and when you come back I trust you will have got rid of such hopeless fancies."

Bluebell was deeply mortified,—she lost all expectation of sympathy, and with a touch of pride, said,—"You must know best, Mrs. Rolleston, but I shall never care for any one else; and I must tell you honestly, *I* can't give it up if he doesn't."

"You will not see him at home?" said the elder lady, hastily. Such a gleam of hope irradiated Bluebell's face; she had never thought of that.

"Dear me, this is too bad!" continued the other, quite disheartened. "I shall take care you have no more opportunities of meeting here. Bluebell, do be warned. I only speak for your good."

"How self-interest deceives one," moralized the girl; "it is only because I am, as she says, 'a most undesirable connexion for her brother!'"

Cecil entered at this juncture, and Bluebell, hearing the Colonel's step also approaching, made a hasty escape from the room.

"What is the matter with her?" asked Cecil. "She brushed by me so suddenly, and looked so strange."

"Nearly knocked me over," said the Colonel, who had caught the last words.

"Don't notice it; I am afraid Bluebell has lost her heart to young Vavasour; and she is miserable at going home, because she thinks she will not see him."

"I am delighted you have put a stop to that folly," said the Colonel; "that boy dawdles over here every afternoon. I can't have Miss Bluebell's 'followers' everlastingly caterwauling in my house."

An expression of extreme astonishment came over Cecil's face.

"Bluebell doesn't care *in the least* for Jack Vavasour," said she.

"You are evidently not in her confidence. She told me 'she should never care for any one else'—her very words, the little goose."

Cecil seemed lost in perplexity. "And she doesn't want to go home?" asked she in a bewildered manner.

"Crying her eyes out at this moment I dare say."

"Then for goodness sake let her go home, and stay there till she is better," said the Colonel, irritably. "A love lorn young lady perpetually before me I cannot and will not endure."

His daughter's brow was knitted with thought. Bluebell was evidently in distress at going, but that it had any reference to Jack she totally disbelieved. A latent suspicion revived, and her face grew pained and hard. It was near dinner time, but, instead of going up to dress, she turned into a little smoking room to ponder it out. What motive could Bluebell have had to avow a perfectly fictitious love affair with Vavasour, unless it was to throw dust in Mrs. Rolleston's eyes and blind her to, perhaps, some underhand flirtation with Bertie? Cecil's affection for her friend received a severe wrench directly she admitted such a possibility, and then, as she meditated, two or three incidents, too slight to be noticed at the time, rose up to confirm it.

"Forewarned, forearmed, if that is your game, Miss Bluebell," thought she, resolving for the future to watch narrowly. At this moment Du Meresq, whistling 'Ah, che la morte,' burst into the room.

"Cecil here, all in the dark? Light a candle, there's a good girl, I want my cigar case. I'm awfully late".

"Who is the Leonore you are whistling *addio* to?" said she complying.

"I don't know, the air is running in my head."

"I thought it might be Bluebell, she is going to-morrow."

The match went out, so she could not see the expression of Bertie's face.

"How do you mean?" said he quietly.

"They think Lubin destructive to her peace of mind, so she is to go home for a fortnight. Singular idea, isn't it."

"Bosh!" said Du Meresq, emphatically. "Well, I'm off. Good-night, Cecil."

CHAPTER X
TOBOGGINING

We are in love's land to-day.
Where shall we go?
Love, shall we start or stay?
Or sail—or row?

Swinburne.

Bluebell thought that now Mrs. Rolleston had detected her secret, there was no necessity to keep it from Cecil. They were in the habit of sitting awhile, talking over their bed-room fire at night; and, though, of late, they had scarcely been so intimate, the practice had not been discontinued. So that evening she resolved to approach the subject with Cecil. No doubt she would stand her friend, and be, as ever, generous and sympathetic.

But, at the first outset, no icicle could be brighter and colder than Miss Rolleston's manner, who kept her communication at arm's-length, as it were, and refused to see any hardship in paying a filial visit for a week or two.

"My dear Bluebell, you are really too childish. One would think it was to be an eternal separation."

"It is evident you will not miss me much," said poor Bluebell, wounded, and thankful she had not committed herself further.

"I should if Bertie were not here," answered Cecil, with heartless intention. "But I really think this is the best time for you to be away, for I am out so much with him, I see nothing of you. When he is gone, Bluebell, and you have returned, we must begin to sing and read together, as we used to do." This agreeable speech effectually quenched all revelations on Bluebell's side, who, hurt and offended, took up a candle and retired to her inner apartment.

"They are all alike," she thought; "and Bertie understood the matter better than I did. Now, I suppose, they will try and prevent me ever seeing him again. Girls in novels think it necessary to give up their lovers if the family disapprove; the book always gets very dull then; but Bertie has never yet given me the chance to act the high-minded heroine." And then she fell to wondering why he had not said something really definite, he seemed near it so often. And yet he was his own master; no stern father loomed in the background—*that* Bluebell would have considered a possible obstacle,—for had she not seen such malign influence destroy more than one promising love affair among her companions. Of course there was no solution to such an inscrutable mystery, though Bluebell tossed awake half the night in the effort to find one.

Next morning they all met at breakfast as usual. No allusion was made to her approaching departure. Afterwards, she attended to Freddy's nominal lessons, packed her slender wardrobe, and then remained in her own room, for the first time unwilling to go downstairs without an invitation. And yet she grudged every hour that passed and brought the separation nearer. She heard Bertie whistling about the house, so she would most likely see him before starting—probably only at luncheon, though, which was the children's dinner. A minute before the bell rang Bluebell descended, and came full on Du Meresq in an angle of the staircase. She stopped involuntarily. He was beside her with a smothered exclamation of endearment, and an eager hand seeking hers. Had she dreamt it? The face was impassive, the hand dropped, and a careless voice was saying,—

"Are you really going home this afternoon, Miss Leigh?"

At the same instant she observed Cecil's upturned eyes in the hall below them. So she had the felicity of eating a cutlet in the presence of her love, but received no aliment for her heart hunger. Du Meresq was teazing his nieces, and did not add much to the general conversation, but the others made up for it, and, when they addressed Bluebell, did so in a particularly cheery tone, as to a nervous, fanciful girl, not to be encouraged or noticed in her blue fits. She had thought of walking home late in the afternoon, still hoping that something might bring about some last words with Du Meresq, or that he might even contrive to join her on the road; but Mrs. Rolleston, in the tone of one proposing a pleasure, said she would drive her back herself, and that the sleigh was ordered in half-an-hour.

Bluebell, goaded to mild exasperation, glanced hastily to where Bertie had been sitting, but he had left the room unperceived.

The sleigh was at the door, so also was Captain Du Meresq, smoking an after-luncheon cigar. I grieve to say my heroine displayed not a particle of self-respect as, pale and dejected, she seated herself by Mrs. Rolleston.

Indeed, the blue eyes were beginning to swim, when they were dried by a flash of indignation at the parting words of Du Meresq. He merely raised his hat, without attempting to shake hands, and said, in a jesting tone, — "*Au revoir*, Miss Bluebell. I hope you will be a comfort to your mamma."

As the jingle of the bells died away in the distance, Cecil felt a load removed from her heart. Bluebell had become an object of uncomfortable surmises, and her absence was an inexpressible relief.

She had a fair field now, and Bertie all to herself, and did not intend to spoil the present with tormenting suspicions of the past.

"Probably he *may* have flattered Bluebell at odd times, and turned her head; but Bertie, though he will talk nonsense to anybody who will listen to him, cares for something more than a pretty face. He will forget her directly she is out of sight, for there really is nothing in her."

Thus severely did Cecil reflect on the friend she had been the means of bringing into the house, and had loved all the more for the kindnesses she had been able to show her. But, then, who could have foreseen that the *protégée* would turn into a rival?

Her meditations were interrupted by the chief subject of them.

"What do you intend doing, Cecil, this afternoon?"

"It is very unsettling, people going away," said she, serenely. No occasion to let him see the satisfaction it gave her. "Shall we go and skate at the Rink, presently?"

"Oh, ain't you sick of that place? Let us order your cutter, and look in on the Armstrongs' tobogining party?"

"Enchanting!" said Cecil, brightening. "But, dear me! it will be nearly over."

"Not if you look sharp. 'Wings' will take us there in half-an-hour; it isn't five miles to the hill. Don't forget to leave your crinoline behind."

Du Meresq rang the bell, and Cecil re-appeared in a few minutes, innocent of her "*sans reflectum*," and in a clinging black velveteen suit, with a golden oriole in her cap, and a scarf of the same hue knotted about her waist.

"None so dusty," said Bertie, approvingly. "You look best in daring colours, Cecil."

Personal praise from Du Meresq, however expressed, was not unwelcome to Cecil, who was sensitively alive to her want of beauty. But she answered, carelessly,—"Just a refuge for the destitute. I can't wear pale shades, or blue or green."

"No, my bright brunette; but that Satanic mixture does not misbecome you,"—and he murmured the words in "May Janet,"—

"The first town they came to there was a blue bride chamber,
He clothed her on with silk, and belted her with amber."

"Come and help me down with the toboggin, Bertie. It is a-top of the book-shelf,"—and they dragged down a mysterious structure of maple wood, having the appearance of a plank six feet long by two wide, and turned up at one end. It had red cord reins, and Cecil's monogram, neatly painted, on the outside.

"We must show off our smart toboggin, I suppose; though where on earth we can put it in the cutter I can't think," said Du Meresq.

"I had rather hold it on my lap than not take it. Here comes 'Wings,'"—and a high-stepping American horse, bought out of a sulky, as not sufficiently justifying his name for racing purposes, dashed up to the door with the smallest and prettiest cutter in the city. The robes were white wolf-skins, bordered with black bear. The one hanging from the back exhibited a bear's head and claws on the white ground. Both robes and bells were mounted in scarlet and white; and the masks of two owls occupied the place of rosettes on "Wings'" head-stall.

"Well," said Bertie, "we are, luckily, not in Hyde Park; and I suppose a sleigh can't be too bizarre. Is this the creation of your festive fancy, Cecil?"

"Yes; I don't disown it. I sent a coloured sketch of what I wanted to Gaines, and he found fur and everything. 'Wings' was bought in an auction last month. He went cheap, because they never could teach him the correct 'racking' action. Papa advised me to have him, as he thought he would carry me in the summer, and I have no other horse."

"I'll tell you what, Cecil; we must extend our wings if we are to be in time. Canter him across the common, there's a capital track."

"Can't he go!" said she, exultingly, as on a hard, frozen surface they sped along. "We rush through the air so silently that if it were not for the bells one might fancy oneself flying."

"Yes," said Bertie; "I have known more unpleasant sensations than being driven ten miles an hour by a fair lady—a dark one, I should say."

"Given the lady. I don't think you much care whom it may chance to be, Bertie."

> "If a woman is pretty, to me it's no matter
> Be she blonde or brunette, so she let me look at her."

"Were you thinking of those lines in 'Lucille'?"

"Them's your sentiments to a T, I should say."

"And you ought to have lived in the days when the knight had 'Une seule' embroidered on his banner. I'll never believe that his loves were so limited; doubtless each appropriated the invidious distinction to herself."

"I know one knight," said Cecil, "who would give them plenty of reason to do so."

"Fancy," continued Bertie "riding in full armour to a crossroad, and challenging every one to single combat who declined to acknowledge his particular fair to be queen of love and beauty, and that no one else should hold a candle to her! Now we should think it great impertinence in a fellow to offer his opinion about her at all."

"No," laughed Cecil, "such public proclamation would never suit these inconsistent days."

"Can you not believe yourself 'Une seule,' Cecil, even in these days?" returned he, meaningly and tenderly.

"That would depend on my knight," said she, blushing, and uncertain how to take it. "I should not care to live in a Fool's Paradise."

"If it were Paradise, why analyze the wisdom of it?" said Bertie, gazing with surprised admiration at her radiant face, that kindled as with some hidden fire.

"I could do without him," answered she, "but if he were worth caring for I wouldn't share him with any one."

"I hope Fane isn't 'Un seul,' Cecil. For a young lady with such severe ideas of constancy, you were pretty thick at the sleighing-party."

There was something in this speech that annoyed Cecil, who turned it off with a short answer. It might have been that she did not like him so composedly contemplating such a possibility.

Du Meresq said no more, perhaps because they were approaching the toboggin hill, or perhaps, like Dr. Johnson, he had nothing ready.

Cecil was sorry they were so near. She felt more interested in the conversation than in the party, and gazed wistfully down a by road that would have led them in an opposite direction.

"I wish I dare turn sharp off," thought she. "But, no! we are conventional beings. This idiotic performance is the goal and object of our expedition. I am driving, and must do nothing so indecently eccentric."

So she gave "Wings" a flick with her whip, that sent him up to his bit with his knees in his mouth, and they drew rein on the edge of the snow mountain.

Miss Tremaine's bright face was just on a level with the top, drawing up her own toboggin.

"Here's this dear little Lily," said Bertie.

"Your diminutives are curiously applied," said Cecil. "That is a very substantial *petite*."

"How late you are," cried Miss Tremaine, rushing up to them. 'Wings,' who couldn't bear waiting, began to rear. "Gracious, Cecil, does he feed on yeast-powder to make him 'rise' so? How do you do, Captain Du Meresq? Come along; there's some capital jumps. Here's my little brother will hang on to the horse's head till we find some one else, if you are sure 'Wings' will not soar away with him, like an eagle with a lamb."

"I'd better billet him on that farm," said Du Meresq, driving off.

"And I must go and speak to Mrs. Armstrong," said Cecil.

CHAPTER XI
EFFECTS OF TOBOGGINING

With a slow and noiseless footstep

Takes the vacant chair beside me,
Lays her gentle hand in mine.

Longfellow.

A little further on, by a blazing fire, was seated the hostess and about a dozen other people on benches and rugs; a table spread with refreshments and hot liquids attracted as many more. The grey sky and white ground threw out the figures solidly, the only patches of colour being the bright petticoats of the ladies as they flashed down or toiled up the snow mountain.

"Have a 'cock-tail,' Miss Rolleston?" said Captain Wilmot, of the Fusiliers. "I have just made a capital one; and then may I steer you down on my toboggin?"

Cecil accepted both propositions. "But do take mine, for I have never tried it yet."

"What a beauty," said Lilla, enviously. "It doesn't look over strong, though; I shouldn't wonder if it broke in two. You'll have to mind the hole at the bottom; there have been a lot in already."

For the information of the uninitiated, I may as well describe how this hilarious amusement is conducted. Having first selected the highest hill the neighbourhood affords, well covered with slippery frozen snow, two individuals who purpose forming the freight of the toboggin pose themselves, the foremost holding the reins, which, however, are more for effect than use, sitting between the feet of the hindmost traveller, who steers with his hands.

As a finger on the snow alters the course of the toboggin, and a nervous push makes it slue round, scattering the inmates, it is needless to say the tyro in front is admonished to preserve the most absolute immobility. Then the vehicle receives a shove off the top of the hill, and shoots down the smooth precipice, and the novice, with shut eyes to escape the blinding snow that flies like hailstones about him, listens to the wind whistling behind, and with bated breath—the first time at any rate—wishes it were over.

"Captain Du Meresq," cried Lilla, "come along; I am going to take you down the big jump."

"Off Niagara, if you like."

"It *is* a tidy drop, the first shelf, so please I'd rather steer. I never trust my neck to any one but myself."

Bertie craned over. "Let me go down first, and see what it is like; it will give you an awful shake."

"Bosh! I have been down before; sit tight," said Lilla, adjusting herself.

It was a series of snow terraces, half natural, half artificial. The ridge they started from was very steep, and jutting out a little way down, yawned over a perpendicular drop to the next ledge, which sloped off again to ever recurring but lesser falls.

Receiving the necessary impetus from above, Bertie and Lilla slithered down at a terrific pace, and shot over the jutting ridge—a good twenty feet drop. As they touched the ground, the toboggin ploughed up the snow, recovered without upsetting, and tore on, jumping down the lesser falls the same way, and continuing a considerable distance along the level at the bottom before its impetus was exhausted.

Bertie, blind, breathless, and half-choked with snow, heard a voice behind, jerking in quick grasps—

"Did you e-ver feel such a de-light-ful—sensation in your life before?"

"Never," said he with a profound air of conviction, shaking off the snow like a Newfoundland dog. "I wonder if I could have steered as well!"

"If you are going to try, you may take some young woman who is tired of her life," said Lilla.

"I'll take myself down, anyhow," said Du Meresq, rather nettled; and, having dragged her toboggin up the hill, ran off to get another; but, in passing Cecil, found a moment to say—

"Don't let that young lunatic delude you down the jump. It is unfit for any girl but such a glutton as Lilla."

"I haven't the slightest wish to try," said she, laughing. "Lilla's a witch. Just look at her now."

Miss Tremaine, standing poised on her toboggin, was in the act of gliding down the hill. A light pole held in one hand served as a rudder, the other retained the cord reins.

"It is like a fairy in a pantomime let down from above," ejaculated Du Meresq. "That is uncommonly tall toboggining!"

A slight commotion was now apparent in the valley below. A brook ran through it, frozen except is one place, where was a large hole. Mr. Tremaine and Captain Delamere, slithering down together, ran into a runaway toboggin that had upset its occupant. This knocked them out of their course, and upset them into the rotten ice of the brook.

Mr. Tremaine was precipitated head foremost into the hole, with his heels in the air, and Lilla at the same moment coming to a halt in her acrobatic descent, beheld the apparition of a pair of legs, feet upwards, and a coarse pair of knickerbocker stockings dragged over the boots.

"Who has muffed in now? Gracious goodness, *I* knit those stockings; it is the Governor! Pull him out—quick, quick, Captain Delamere; he'll have a fit!"

That individual, who had just scrambled out, was standing rather dazed, ruefully stanching the cuts on his face. Between them they soon dragged out Mr. Tremaine, half suffocated, and puffing and panting like a demented steam-engine, but by the time he had recovered his breath not much the worse.

The toboggining was getting fast and furious, and several casualties occurred. The toiler up the hill, too, had need of all his alertness to dodge the numerous erratic cars tearing down in every direction.

An adventurous group were tying a dozen or more toboggins together, which they called an omnibus; and Jack Vavasour, in the character of conductor, was holding up his hand, and cadging for passengers.

"Any more for the Brook or Gore Vale? Room for two still in the 'Lightning' 'bus! No more?—then we are off. Link arms, ladies and gentlemen;" and the unwieldy apparatus was started. The couplings divided half-way down. About seven reached the bottom, the remaining five were upset, and were left there. Cecil was in the latter division, and having extricated herself from the *débris*, slowly ascended the hill.

She was rather tired now, and slightly bored; and began wondering what had become of her escort. He had not been in the coach, nor was he among the noisy, chattering party approaching her.

"Has anyone seen Captain Du Meresq?" asked she.

"Ten minutes ago he was death on the big jump," said Jack. "He took Delamere to start him; and I think Miss Tremaine went too."

A shade passed over Cecil's face. "Would you ask him, Mr. Vavasour, to get the sleigh? It is quite time we were going."

Another quarter of an hour passed, but no signs of Jack or Bertie. Cecil kept up a desultory conversation with Mrs. Anderson; but a vague impatience and restlessness came over her. She looked in the direction of the big jump, and it seemed to her a point of attraction that gathered up the stragglers, who all converged towards it. There was quite a crowd there now. Mrs. Anderson's platitudes became maddening. Then she observed Lilla coming from the same direction, and beckoning. She sprang to meet her.

"Cecil," cried Lilla, "don't be frightened." Why do people always use this agitating formula? "But the fact is poor Bertie has had an awful cropper. Good gracious, Cecil! don't look like that! Are you going to faint! He is not so very much hurt,—stunned a bit at first."

"How was it?" said the other, breathing again, and pressing forward.

"He was going down the drop. Captain Delamere was to push him off, which he did with a vengeance. He didn't mean any harm, though he don't like a bone in poor Bertie's body. However, the toboggin snapped in two from the concussion in landing. Bertie was shot out and rolled to the bottom, which would not have mattered, only he struck his head against some snag or stone hidden by the snow. We looked down, but he didn't seem to move, and we got frightened. I had had nearly enough jumping, but I took Captain Delamere on my toboggin—didn't trust him to steer, I can tell you, my dear—and bumped down quite safe. Bertie was insensible, with a queer cut on his forehead; so I extracted the solitaire out of his shirt-collar, and Captain Delamere gave him a nip out of his pocket-pistol, and then he seemed to pull himself together and sat up. A lot of people had collected round, and Mr. Vavasour asked me to come and tell you. Oh, here he is."

"Miss Rolleston," said Jack, "Du Meresq is nearly all right again. But he has twisted his ankle, and can't walk up the hill; so they are going to pull him up on a toboggin. I'll go and get your sleigh."

"Are you *sure* it is nothing worse?" said Cecil, who could scarcely abandon her first impression that his neck was broken.

"Quite. There he is, to answer for himself," as Bertie and his bearers crested the hill.

She walked to meet them. Du Meresq looked in pain, but cut short all enquiries. "Wrenched my foot that's all. You want to go, don't you, Cecil?"

"Oh, yes; as soon as possible. Lilla, Mrs. Armstrong is so far off, will you make our adieux?" *Sotto voce.* "She is a tiresome old goose; but I left her so abruptly just now."

"Miss Rolleston," whispered Jack, who had just brought up the cutter, "I think I'll send up the doctor from the barracks. Du Meresq did get a baddish cut on the head, and, if he doesn't stay in a day or two, it might turn to erysipelas in this climate."

"Pray do. Oh, Mr. Vavasour! just tell me honestly, is not that sometimes— fatal when it gets to the head?"

Cecil's eyes, dilated with terror, betrayed her to Jack, over whose honest face came an expression of sympathy and intelligence.

"Of course; but we will take care of that. That's why I am sending up the doctor, to prevent him exposing himself out of doors just yet."

Cecil did not find the drive back so agreeable as the previous one. Du Meresq, chafing at the confinement his fast swelling foot would probably entail, and provoked at coming to grief after Lilla's taunt was in remarkably bad humour.

Cecil saw the state of the case, and drove on fast, philosophically allowing him to grumble and growl without much concerning herself; but it was almost dark before they drew up at "The Maples."

In the meantime, Colonel Rolleston, having heard from Miss Prosody that his daughter and Du Meresq had gone off to a tobogining party, chose to be highly scandalized, and poured into the placid ear of his wife a torrent of disapprobation.

In vain did Mrs. Rolleston represent that they were out sleighing and skating together most days without his objecting.

"This was quite different—this was a public party—people would say they were engaged. He never had seen the good of their being so inseparable, but of course, his opinion on the subject had never been considered," etc.,— which last remark was rather uncalled for, as few heads of families have their womankind in better order than Colonel Rolleston.

A straw will show which way the wind blows. His wife listened with some uneasiness, for she had always hoped the Colonel tacitly approved the attachment between their respective relatives, which to her appeared so evident. She could only trust this was but a pettish effusion from their prolonged absence, and determined to guard against such causes of offence for the future.

But still they did not come. It was dark—it was dinner-time—it really was too bad. At last a faint tinkle of sleigh-bells was followed by a slight commotion in the hall. The servant was assisting Bertie into the smoking-room, for he elected to lie on the sofa there, and thus avoid the worry of questions and alarms.

Colonel Rolleston was too grand and angry to evince any curiosity by coming out, and Mrs. Rolleston, after receiving a hasty explanation from Cecil, sent her back to the drawing-room, and took charge of her brother, who was having his boot cut off, and in considerable pain.

There was not much resemblance in character or sympathy between the brothers-in-law; but they had hitherto avoided clashing. Now, however, the Colonel's outraged feelings of propriety wound him up to the determination of administering a solemn rebuke to Du Meresq, and he stood on that coign of advantage, the hearthrug, waiting to deliver it.

Cecil came in for the first tide of wrath, somewhat to her surprise; but, dreading her companionship with Bertie being prohibited, exerted considerable tact to smooth her father down, and especially made light of the accident, which she perceived was an aggravation of the offence.

"Not content with making my daughter conspicuous, he hadn't even the sense to keep out of scrapes himself," etc.

Mrs. Rolleston glanced interrogatively at Cecil as they met on the stairs. I don't know what answer her countenance conveyed, but they made simultaneously the same suggestion,—"Let us get Miss Prosody to dine down." They both knew that without the addition of an unoffending third the subject would be harped on all the evening.

Mrs. Rolleston was an excellent housekeeper; and the well-served repast, aided by the judicious conversation of the ladies, exercised a most soothing influence on the Colonel, who was rapidly attaining that harmless frame of mind in which, as the saying goes, "a child might play with him."

But a sudden ring at the door-bell, followed by the announcement of the surgeon of the regiment, brought on a relapse. What man does not hate being interrupted at dinner? And the doctor's report was sufficiently vague to re-kindle Cecil's fears, and create uncomfortable misgivings in the mind of her step-mother.

Du Meresq, he said, was suffering intense pain in the head, and a small bone in the ankle was broken, which he had set; but he could not be certain there was no internal injury, etc.

Mrs. Rolleston hastened away to Bertie, and did not return; and poor Cecil, not daring to show her anxiety, remained to entertain her father, or rather to listen to his irritable remarks on this unlucky expedition for the rest of the evening.

Never was there a more fractious patient than Du Meresq as he lay listlessly on the sofa, while the bone reunited. He had speculated on many a stolen walk with Bluebell in that unfrequented wood, where they would be far less liable to interruption than at "The Maples." He thought of his cavalier parting with her,—a bracing tonic,—necessitated by the self-betrayal of her dejected air, but which he expected to have explained away in a most agreeable manner before now. It would never do to write from this house. What a shame it was sending her away—for a mistake, too, for they had got the saddle on the wrong horse. "Still," he thought, "it is a bore when girls take things *au grand serieux*. Lilla Tremaine is quite different, as jolly as possible, but never expects impossibilities. Now Cecil and Bluebell are never satisfied without one's swearing one cares for nobody else. At least, Cecil isn't, though I don't think I ever quite said that to her yet. It doesn't matter telling Bluebell so, and she looks so pleased, and believes every word of it. I would marry that child if I could afford it." And then visions of debt, ever pressing, harassed his mind. "Well, it could not last much longer; there would be something left out of the fire when he sold out, and he could try Australia, or the Gold Coast, or—he didn't care what."

But such subjects were not exhilarating, lying alone in the smoking-room, and at last he rang a hand-bell, and told the servant to ask Miss Rolleston to come and sit with him.

Cecil complied at once, but brought with her a colour-box and sketch-book. Drawing was her great occupation, and she was now filling in from memory a sketch of the toboggining party.

"You never come near me, Cecil, unless I send for you!" said Du Meresq, complainingly.

"Poor Bertie! are you very much bored?" said she, without looking up from her painting.

"Horribly; and my thoughts and occupations are none of the pleasantest."

"Those horrid duns again," glancing at some blue looking envelopes lying near. "But you haven't opened one of them."

"Never do, nor answer them either. They keep up a pretty close correspondence considering it is one-sided."

"Bertie," said Cecil, drawing on diligently, "Can't something be done? You never seem to look into your affairs. Perhaps they wouldn't be so bad if you did. I shall be of age in August, and," colouring slightly, "I will lend you as much as you want. You can give me an I.O.U. for the amount," continued she, rather proud of her knowledge of business.

"You dear, romantic girl" (Cecil was chilled in a moment), "how could I take your money? I shouldn't have a chance of repaying it. No, I shall last as long as I can, and then try the Colonies. It is only my rascally self, after all, to think of. Thank goodness, I don't draw any delicate, fragile life after me into privation and discomfort."

Cecil bent more closely over her drawing.

"What are you doing?" said Bertie, impatiently. "I can't see your face. Come and sit by me, Cecil. I like a 'gentle hand in mine.'"

Cecil moved as if in a dream, and sat in a low chair near his couch.

"You have always been so kind and true to me," stroking her hair caressingly.

A slight movement of the handle of the door made them involuntarily separate, and Mrs. Rolleston entered.

"Cecil, your father is looking for you. He wants you to drive with him, and call on the Learmonths."

"What an infernal bore!" said Du Meresq, energetically; "and I must lie in this confounded room, with nothing to do the whole afternoon. Can't you get out of it, Cecil?"

"No, no!" said Mrs. Rolleston, hastily meeting her daughter's eye. There was unspoken sympathy between them. Her half eager look of inquiry passed into intelligent acquiescence, and, with a regretful glance at Bertie, she left the room.

The next day and the one after the Colonel required his daughter's companionship; the third day, they all went out in the afternoon, as Du Meresq seemed better, and said he had letters to write. No sooner, however, was the house quiet and deserted, than he rang the bell, and sent for a sleigh, hobbling out with the assistance of a stick and the servant's arm. For the information of that lingering and curious functionary, he ordered the driver to go to the Club, which address, however, was altered after proceeding a short distance.

CHAPTER XII
THE LAKE SHORE ROAD

But all that I care for,
And all that I know,
Is that, without wherefore,
I worship thee so.

Lord Lytton.

"I suppose, Bluebell, you keep all your fine spirits for company?" said Miss Opie, tauntingly; and, indeed, she had some reason to be aggrieved. Few things are more trying than living with a person in the persistent enjoyment of the blues; and the old, saddened by failing health and the memory of heavy sorrows, are apt to look upon gloom in youth as entrenching on their own prescriptive rights.

Bluebell was always now taking long, aimless walks, bringing home neither news nor gossip, and then sitting silent, absorbed in her own thoughts, or else feverishly expectant; while each evening she sank into deeper despondency after the day's disappointment.

"Spirits can't be made to order," answered she, shortly. "I have got nothing to talk about."

"I am afraid you are ill, my dear," said Mrs. Leigh; "outgrowing your strength, perhaps. You are such a great girl, Bluebell—so different to me; and you scarcely touched the baked mutton at dinner, which was a little frozen and red yesterday, but so nice to-day."

Bluebell shivered. She was not at a very critical age, but the culinary triumphs of the "general servant" made her practice a good deal of enforced abstinence since she had been accustomed to properly prepared cookery at "The Maples."

"People who do nothing all day can't expect to be hungry," said Miss Opie, sententiously. "If a man will not work neither may he eat."

"Then it is all right," retorted Bluebell, "as it seems I do neither."

"Not work!" cried Mrs. Leigh. "Why she has earned already more than I ever did in my life, and brought me ten dollars to get a dress with, only I shan't, for I shall keep it for her. I must say, Aunt Jane, you are always blaming the child; and, if her mother is satisfied, I think you may be."

Aunt Jane was silenced, but she wondered what Bluebell could do that her shortsighted mother would not be satisfied with. Meantime the object of the discussion had escaped from the room. She had no wish to spend the afternoon in the dim parlour, stuffy with stove heat and the lingering aroma of baked mutton; and a fancy had occurred to her to wander through the wood she had last traversed with the sole occupant of her ill-regulated mind.

Trove, now a well-to-do and unabashed dog, rolled and kicked on his back in puppy-like ecstacy as he watched her dress, and officiously brought her her muff, which, however, he objected to resigning. Trove was Bluebell's confidant and the repository of her woes, and perhaps as safe a one as young ladies generally choose.

Not a sign of the Rollestons had she seen since her arrival at the cottage ten days ago. Bluebell thought she could not have been more cut off from them if she had crossed the Atlantic instead of the Common. Going to the Rink would have too much the appearance of seeking Du Meresq, so she rigorously avoided that; but even in King Street, where Cecil's cutter flashed most days, she never caught sight of "Wings'" owl-decorated head.

There was a great deal of her father's disposition in Bluebell, and she chafed at the monotony of days so grey and eventless, and longed for she knew not what; so that it was life, movement, *pain* even, to exhaust those new springs of thought and feeling that the awakening touch of a first love had called forth, and would not now be laid.

Bluebell, like most Canadians, had had plenty of early admiration from hobbledehoys, who made honest, though ungainly, love to her; but her heart would as soon have been touched by an amorous Orson as by these youthful tyros in the art. Du Meresq had that deceptive countenance apparently created for the shipwreck of female hearts. Sometimes men called him an ugly fellow, but no woman ever thought so. There was expression enough in those luminous eyes to have set up three beauty men. They could look both demoniacal and seraphic,—tender often, but scarcely ever true; add to this a magnificent *physique*, a soft manner, a winning voice, and, what gave him an almost superstitious interest to women, that *fey* look attributed to the Stewarts. He had read and studied hard by fits and starts, for whatever possessed his mind he always pursued with ardour, and to Cecil was fond of inveighing against his useless, unsatisfying life. In spite of her infatuation, though, she judged him more truly than most people, and perceived that his fitful remorse was chiefly occasioned by pressure of money matters, and seldom lasted over pecuniary relief.

In the most secret flights of her imagination, she pictured herself in some new country with Bertie. An adventurous, reckless nature such as his, she thought, turned every gift to evil in the commonplace life where his idiosyncrasy had no play; but detached from his idle mess-room habits, and launched into a new career, when to live at all involved exertion of mind and body, would metamorphosize her hero into all she could wish.

Such was the ideal, in her conventual bringing up, of the rich and well placed Cecil; while Bluebell, to whom luxury was unknown, longed for wealth to take her into a sphere where taste was not starved by economy, nor all her horizon bounded by weekly bills. But in both cases their air castles were to be occupied with Du Meresq.

The girl and the dog sped along on their desolate walk—it was too cold to linger. Bluebell carefully followed the route she had taken with Bertie, that memory might be added by association.

"Ah, Trove," said she to the dog, who bounced up against her, "I am as much a waif and stray as you are—disowned by my grandfather, who might have made us rich, and taken up by people one day and forgotten the next; but you have drifted into harbour now, my dog, and who knows—"

A smothered growl interrupted this monologue, and then a sharp bark. Bluebell looked round to see what was exciting him; she heard a distant tinkle of bells, and listened keenly; laughing voices were apparently approaching. From an impulse that she could not have explained, Bluebell darted into an empty woodshed, dragging Trove in after her, and holding him firmly by the muzzle to stifle his growling. Through an aperture in the boards she could observe, unseen herself.

The sounds grew louder, and a score of sleighs defiled past her hiding-place. Bluebell scanned each carefully. There were the usual members of the Sleigh Club. She recognized the Tremaines, and several others of her little world. Jack in his tandem; but, faithful Lubin! no "cloud-capped" Muffin sat by his side; his companion was of the sterner sex, or, as he would have described him, "a dog." But where were the Rollestons? No representative of "The Maples" was present, not even Du Meresq. They had flashed past within a minute; but, like a fresh breeze over still water, the little incident had awakened and roused up Bluebell from her lethargy.

Her thoughts became more lively as she speculated why Bertie and Cecil were absent from the sleighing party. It was some consolation, at any rate, not to see him enjoying himself quite as much without her. The sun was setting redly as she neared the cottage, and a young moon gaining brightness. Bluebell, remembering a childish superstition, paused to wish. The passage was dark as she entered, and her mother's tones, talking with great volubility, struck her ear. "Mamma has her company voice on," thought she, which, being interpreted, meant an increase of nervousness and consequent garrulity.

She opened the door, and her heart gave a sudden leap as she became aware of, rather than saw in the dusk, the tall, broad-shouldered form of Du Meresq. Bluebell came stiffly forward, and offered a cold hand, utterly belying her heart, to Bertie, who bent over it as if sorely tempted, in spite of Mrs. Leigh's presence, to carry it to his lips. But she withdrew it abruptly, and sat down, seized with more overpowering shyness than she had ever experienced.

Miss Opie's keen, attentive eyes were taking in the situation.

"Captain Du Meresq has been kind enough to call," said Mrs. Leigh, "to say there is no immediate hurry for your return, my dear."

Bluebell raised disappointed, questioning eyes; but something in his face conveyed to her that the message was coined as an excuse for his appearance.

"I hope Cecil is well?" said she, trying to speak unconcernedly; "but I saw she was not out with the Club to-day."

"I think she is tired of it. Where did you fall in with them?" asked he.

"In the Humber," very consciously.

"Were you there?" asked Bertie, with a tender inflection in his voice, that Bluebell knew well. But she would not look up, and Miss Opie did, so he proceeded carelessly, — "I suppose they were coming from the Lake Shore Road, up the serpentine drive in the wood?"

"Oh! that is such a pretty walk in summer!" said Mrs. Leigh.

"I dare say," said Bertie, looking straight down his nose. "I went round that way once, and even in winter found it the pleasantest walk I ever took in my life."

"Ah, then," said Mrs. Leigh, knowingly, "I dare say some pretty young lady was with you."

"No such happiness," said Bertie, with an imperceptible glance at Bluebell. "The fact is, Mrs. Leigh, women detest me! I suppose it is my deep respect, making me so fearful of offending, that bores them; but I fear I am a social failure."

"In my day," said Miss Opie, ironically, "young ladies *expected* to be treated with respect."

"And that could not have been so long ago; yet now they are beyond a bashful man's comprehension," said Bertie, with an air of simplicity, slightly scanning Miss Opie's wakeful face. He had got on so well with the mamma, who was this old maid, who appeared so objectionably on the alert?

"Well, I am sure," said Mrs. Leigh, "some girls here *are* that pert and forward, I can't bear it myself; and yet the gentlemen all encourage it, and think it real smart. Lilla Tremaine, you know, Aunt Jane."

"Ah!" said Bertie, shaking his head, "a very unsteady young person."

While Du Meresq was making conversation, Bluebell sat incapable of contributing to it. She would not have believed that his presence should afford her so little pleasure; but he seemed incongruous here, and was apparently amusing himself with the simplicity of her relatives. A clatter of tea-things filled her mind with dismay. The ideas of the "help" on the subject of cleanliness were in a very rudimentary stage, and that the cloth would be in anything but its first freshness, was a moral certainty. Impossible, however, to avert the catastrophe, and the general servant, actuated by a determination to get another look at Miss Bluebell's "young man," undauntedly bore in the tray.

"Dear me, is it not rather early?" said Mrs. Leigh. "Oh, Captain Du Meresq,"—seeing him rise,—"you must stay and have a cup with us."

"Another day, if you will allow me," said Bertie, trying to disguise his extreme lameness. "I hope, having found my way here, I may be permitted to call again in this sociable manner, and have a little agreeable conversation, so preferable to gaiety, which I abhor."

"If you will take us as you find us," said the little lady, graciously, "we shall look upon it as a great favour, I am sure. Dear me, Captain Du Meresq, have you hit your foot? You seem quite lame."

"I am, rather. I had an accident. Is there not some shorter way back than the road I came?"

"Oh, yes, by Barker's Row. You know the Link House?"

"No—a," said Bertie, looking expressively at Bluebell, as a hint that she might offer to point out the road.

"Oh, surely you *must*; keep straight on King Street, and then you come to—"

"Wolfe Street?" suggested Du Meresq.

"Gracious, no! that would be quite out of your way! Go to—I'll tell you what, Bluebell shall show you where you turn off—it isn't ten minutes from here."

Bertie murmured a profusion of thanks, and, distrustful of Miss Opie, protested against being so troublesome. But Bluebell, scarce able to believe in such luck, sprang up with a sudden illumination of countenance, and the next minute the lovers were alone under the light of the moon.

"Bluebell," said Du Meresq, "I have got a sleigh here. I thought I *might* get you out of it if I pretended I was walking, and didn't know the way; but the fact is, my child, I can hardly limp a hundred yards. Come a little drive with me."

"Oh! I dare not. It is so late, and they expect me back again directly."

"Then you are going to run away the first moment we have been alone for so long!"

"Whose fault is that," said she, reproachfully.

"Not mine. I have been laid up ten days with a broken ankle. But I suppose you have been seeing Jack Vavasour every day, and forgotten all about me?"

"Bertie," said Bluebell, hesitatingly, "did they say anything to you about—"

"About Jack? Yes, they said he was spoons on you. And also, Miss Bluebell, that you were awfully in love with him."

"No, no, nonsense," said she, blushing. "I meant about yourself."

"They know nothing of that?" said he, inquiringly.

"They do, though. I don't know what you will say, Bertie, but I told Mrs. Rolleston."

"What can you mean, Bluebell? Bella told me that you cared for nobody but Jack Vavasour; and I was deuced angry, I can tell you; at first, though I thought it uncommon 'cute of you saying so."

Bluebell, utterly confounded by this extraordinary assertion, had no time to reply, for she found herself close to a covered sleigh, and the man had got down and opened the door. She drew back.

"Jump in," said Bertie, impatiently.

Bluebell shook her head.

"What do you propose?" said he, in an angry whisper. "We can't sit out in the snow, and I can't walk another yard."

She hesitated, and he gently impelled her into the vehicle, following himself, to the anguish of his injured foot, that he had struck in his haste.

"Where to, sir?" said the man, whom Bertie, in his momentary pain, had forgotten.

"Go to the Don Bridge."

"Can't, sir. I am ordered at the College by six o'clock."

"Drive to the devil, then. I mean, drive about as long as you can. I like driving."

"Hush, Bertie! how can you? What will he think?"

"How much 'old rye' he will get out of the job. Come, Bluebell; the hour is ours, don't spoil it fidgetting about trivialities. I have scarcely dared to look at you yet, my beautiful pet," trying to steal an arm round her waist. But she drew herself away, irresponsive and rigid, being uneasy and frightened at the escapade she had been led into.

"You haven't a spark of moral courage, Bluebell," said Bertie, impatiently. "You are as prim and unlike yourself as possible, just because you are wondering what that man on the box will think. Or, perhaps, you are afraid of that thin, sour old duenna at home."

"She will be inquisitive enough," said Bluebell, resignedly. "And, Bertie, I wanted to tell you, but, perhaps, you know, that they will never have me again at the 'Maples' while you are there,—Mrs. Rolleston so utterly disapproves of it."

"What *is* this hallucination that you have got hold of?" said Du Meresq. "What did you tell, or fancy you told, Bella?"

"We got on the subject. Your name wasn't actually mentioned; but she quite understood, and said something," said Bluebell, reddening as she felt the awkwardness of her words, "very strong against it."

Bertie looked relieved. He began to understand the mistake, which he considered a fortunate one.

"And did you promise to give me up?"

She turned her large, innocent eyes upon him. "How could I, when I care more for you than anything in the world?"

"My poor little Bluebell!" said Du Meresq, crushing her in his arms. But the sleigh stopped; the man was getting down.

"My time is up, sir."

"Well, drive to where you took us up," said Bertie. "Bluebell, tell me quick, where shall I see you again?"

"I can't risk driving," said she, hurriedly. "When will you be able to walk?"

"Can't I see you alone at home sometimes? When are your people likely to be out?"

"They don't go out for days together, except on Sunday, to church; and Aunt Jane would suspect something directly if I didn't go with them."

"Let her, meddling old idiot! I shall come then, Bluebell."

"No, no, Bertie; pray don't! Could you walk in a week?"

"What an eternity! Well, meet me in the Avenue in the Queen's Park, at three o'clock on Wednesday. Here's this brute getting down again. Only just time to kiss those dear blue eyes. *Addio* Leonore. How the deuce am I to get home, I wonder?"

"Bertie, you'll never be able to walk."

"Never mind me. Run back, my dearest, and throw dust in the eyes of that misguided old female, who presumes to open them on what doesn't concern her."

CHAPTER XIII
NORTHERN LIGHTS

Do you remember
Those evenings in the bleak December,
Curtained warm from the snowy weather,
When you and I played chess together,
Checkmated by each other's eyes?

The Wanderer.

Bluebell sped home, and, to evade remarks, hung up her hat in the passage, as the least embarrassing way of reporting herself, then remained, perdu, in her own room, transfigured into fairy-land by her happy thoughts. Bertie was acquitted of intentional neglect. It was only the malignity of Fate that had divided them; and there was the positive anticipation of meeting again in six days. To be sure, it involved entering on a course of deceit. Aunt Jane would, probably, be shocked, as she was at everything; mamma would not think much of it; and as for Mrs. Rolleston, she need not consider her wishes, after telling Bertie such a bare-faced fib about Jack Vavasour, evidently in the hope of making mischief between them. She was very much astonished at such unscrupulous conduct in her friend, but what other conclusion could she come to?

To be sure, common-sense whispered that looks and language such as Du Meresq had permitted himself, ought to be followed by an offer of marriage; but with common-sense Bluebell had little to do at this period, and first love cares not to concern itself with the prosaic. The mystery and romance of interviews with her love, "undreamt-of by the world in its primness," appeared far more enchanting than any authorized attachment provided with a regulation gooseberry picker.

So she came down with a slightly defiant air; but meeting with nothing worse than a gravely knowing glance from Miss Opie, sat down to the piano to escape questioning.

Mrs. Leigh's thoughts were complacently occupied with the visitor. She only wanted further confirmation to place him in the light of a future son-in-law. Adversity had not given her the wisdom of the serpent, and she never dreamed of possible danger in the attentions of this unknown young man to her beautiful, but portionless, child.

However, her mind became unsettled again by the appearance of another suitor, in dog-skin gloves of a brilliant tan, and his usual air of cheerful confidence. No guile was there in Jack Vavasour, whose prostrate adoration of her daughter was so undisguised, that she mentally deposed Bertie (whose devotion was more problematical) in his favour. Still she thought, "I should never think of influencing dear Bluebell one way or the other, and we shall see which proposes first."

Jack's visit, as usual, was a lengthy one. His fair enslaver had recovered her spirits, and no longer metaphorically turned her face to the wall. She was glad of distraction, and not ungratified by his allegiance, though without the slightest idea of returning it.

Like the boys and the frogs, she did not consider that what was sport to the one was hard on the other, and probably would not have cared if it had struck her; for, whatever poets may say, there is no more thoroughly heartless age than sweet seventeen. When he sat on till the arrival of the unappetizing meal they called a meat-tea, Bluebell did not wince at her mother inviting him to join it, simply because his opinion was a matter of indifference to her, though she carelessly recommended him not to be late for mess.

Jack, however, with magnanimous disregard of that usually important period of his day, stayed his healthy young appetite with the cold joint from dinner; and he and Bluebell amused themselves frying eggs and roasting chestnuts, which further assuaged its keen demands.

Many times during the evening did Mrs. Leigh leave the room, on the principle that young people like to be alone together. But all her tactics failed to uproot Miss Opie, who clung to her book and her seat by the fire, partly from the contrary conviction that young persons should *never* be alone together, and partly because, save in the kitchen, there was no other fire in the house.

"What shall we do?" cried Bluebell, with the faintest of yawns, tired of consuming their culinary labours. "You don't care for music, I know. There's an old chess-board somewhere; and I can't think of anything but cat's-cradle, if you don't like that."

"I can play," said Jack, stoutly, who had not attempted it since his childhood, but only wanted an excuse to remain on. So they sat down at the spidery table, saying little; Jack quite well entertained with his hand frequently coming in contact with Bluebell's on the board. He would have liked to crush up that little member in his own, and meditated the bold *coup* more than once, but was always discouraged by that far away, unconscious look in her eyes.

In this squalid parlour, where she was the only soft-hued thing in the room, he thought her more beautiful than ever. Perhaps she was, for the love-light burned steadily in her Irish eyes, and he could not tell it was not for him.

Never were more lenient or careless adversaries. Twice Jack's queen was in Bluebell's grasp uncaptured, and he could at any time have checkmated her, had he been as attentive to the variations of the game as to those of her countenance. Suddenly Bluebell swept her hand over the board, crying,—"I never saw such men, they don't fight. We have been playing half-an-hour, and have hardly taken any prisoners."

"It is a slow game," said Jack, equably; "let us try cat's-cradle. Or, perhaps," he continued, meeting with no response, "I ought to be saying good-night."

Bluebell was secretly tired of him, and could not conceive on what principle her mother began pressing him to stay.

"There's the nicest bit of toasted cheese coming up for supper," said she. "I know all officers like a Welsh rabbit. My poor late husband did, though he used to say, in his funny way, he only ate it because there was nothing else fit to touch."

"I fear I must go; but I hope you'll ask me to tea again, Mrs. Leigh, it is so jolly getting away from mess sometimes," said the young diplomatist.

"That I will," said she, highly flattered, "and I shall be very much offended if you don't come. I am only sorry you can't sit a little longer now."

Jack was not quite sure he couldn't, but Bluebell, pretending not to see his hesitation, held out her hand and said "good-night," so he had nothing for it but to go. In two minutes, though, his head re-appeared. "Come and look at the Northern Lights, Miss Leigh; regular tip-top fireworks. Here's a shawl; make haste." But when she come out, only a few weak-coloured pink clouds were floating about.

"Is that all?" ejaculated Bluebell.

"Not quite," said Jack; "it was a western light I was trying to invoke, or, rather, the light of my eyes. When may I come and see you, Bluebell?"

"I came out to look at meteors," said she, laughing at his unwonted flowers of speech; "and I don't know who gave you leave to call me by my Christian name."

"It isn't your Christian," urged Jack.

"It will be my *nom de guerre*, then, if you say it again."

"Change it if you like," quoth he, "if you will let me change your surname too."

A startled stare of blue eyes, a smothered laugh, and Bluebell had darted into the house, clapping the door after her.

"Confound it," thought Jack, "just my luck. In another moment I should have kissed her—I *think* I should; but, hang it, when a girl looks you straight in the face and talks to you as if you were her grandmother, it puts one off. Well, I have kissed lots of girls without proposing and now it's *vice versa*, for it was as good as an offer, and all I got by it was her nipping in just when I thought I had her to myself."

CHAPTER XIV
THE TRYST

Twas full of love—to rhyme with dove,
And all that tender sort of thing,
Of sweet and meet—and heart and dart,
But not a word about a ring!

Hood.

Time flew much lighter with our heroine as she counted the days to the next rendezvous with Du Meresq; anticipation is ever sweeter than reality. The cottage was no longer dull, nor existence empty, even the unrenewed and diminishing snow, dusky as a goose in a manufacturing town, was the symptoms of approaching spring and verdure. Who need think of the torrents of rain which must precede it? The little episode with Jack outside the door afforded her secret entertainment, and although she did not look upon it as a *bona-fide* proposal, that did not bias her intention of relating the anecdote for Bertie's delectation. It might be just as well to let him see if he couldn't speak out, others could, and if he were jealous, why so much the better.

Clouds were chasing each other in the sky, and the increased mildness of the atmosphere inspired Bluebell with the dread that rain was approaching, for a rendezvous under dripping umbrellas, if feasible, was not the most desirable *pose* for a romantic interview.

However, the morning rose clear and sunny, the snow was thawing, and in many places the runners of the sleighs grated on bare ground.

Bluebell was exultant. The elements evidently didn't mean to oppose her, but she was somewhat disconcerted at dinner by Miss Opie's remarks on her Sunday dress, which, being of a becoming hue, she had rashly donned.

"Are you going visiting, Bluebell, that you are so smart?"

"Oh, dear no; only for a walk."

"How foolish to draggle that mazarin blue poplinette in sloppy snow! Once let it get any snow stains on, and it will look quite shabby on bright spring days."

"It's no use having things, if one doesn't wear them," returned the girl, evasively. But when she came down ten minutes later equipped for her walk, she encountered Miss Opie again in full marching order.

"My, dear, as you are dressed so nicely, I dare say you are going 'on King,' and so am I; so we can walk together."

Consternation in Bluebell's face—it was only a quarter to three.

"I am going quite in the opposite direction," cried she, hurriedly, and, without waiting to see the effect of her words, abruptly fled.

"Just Canadian independence," muttered Miss Opie; "It makes all the girls such thoroughly bad style."

Bluebell began to feel very nervous; two or three young friends that she met on the way, she passed with a quick nod and averted face, dreading their joining her. Her eye swept the broad walk of the Avenue in an instant; no familiar figure arrested her vision, and the seats placed at regular intervals on each side were also vacant of interest.

So she was first—the Cathedral clock had struck three some minutes before, she was perplexed to know what to do with herself, and began walking slowly to the other end. Of all possible *contretemps*, the non-appearance of Du Meresq had never suggested itself; but after a couple of turns the unwelcome misgiving strengthened, and there would be only one at the tryst that day.

In a tumult of disappointment and indignation, conjecture after conjecture chased each other; while ever and anon her fancy was mocked by some one turning in at the gates bearing a general resemblance to Du Meresq, only to be dispelled by a nearer and more accurate view.

A simple explanation suddenly dawned; Bertie might have written to warn her of an unavoidable absence. The possibility of such a letter, which, had she had received it in the morning, would have been the bitterest disappointment, now seemed a resurrection from despair to hope, and with relaxed features and brightening eyes, Bluebell walked rapidly through the gates to the Post-office.

Letters were so rare and unlooked for at the cottage, that the postman never included it in his rounds; and the contents of the pigeon-hole appropriated to them at the office was seldom inquired for, except on mail-days, when there might be an off-chance of an English letter for Miss Opie. Even Bluebell, who for the first fortnight after her banishment from "The Maples" had been a regular applicant, had not been near it since Bertie's visit to the cottage.

"Two letters for Miss Theodora Leigh." One she scarcely looked at; the other instinct told her must be Bertie's handwriting; it had been lying two days at the Post-office.

> "My dearest Bluebell," ran this note, "I can't come to the Avenue on Wednesday, being now entirely confined to the sofa with my ankle, which has gone to the bad. I am only staying on now with sick leave, and the Chief very sulky at that. When shall I again see those beloved, angel-like, soft blue eyes? Don't write to me here, for, as you may remember, the orderly fetches the letters, and my august brother-in-law sometimes deals them round.

> "Your ever devotedly attached, "A. Du M."

Poor Bluebell, as she read these few and rather cavalier lines, felt for the moment as if she had never suffered till now; his hinted at departure, and apparent resignation to absence from her, was a severe shock, and, in the first hot feeling of grief, the scales fell from her eyes, and she began to see Bertie as he was, but she could not yet endure the light of reason, so resumed her voluntary blindness, and re-read the letter, and though very little of it could satisfy her expectations, she dwelt more on the few words that did. After a while, she remembered the other letter, and found, with awakening interest, it was from Mrs. Rolleston. This was written in a pleasant chit-chat style, giving an account of their every-day life since she left, and not at all avoiding Bertie's name, the tedious effect of his toboggining accident being one of the chief incidents mentioned. It wound up with saying that they expected her back as soon as she liked.

Bluebell felt rather mystified at the tone of this epistle; but was much comforted by the thought that the ban was removed, and she might go to "The Maples" and judge for herself. This was dated prior to the other letter, but Bertie appeared to have been ignorant of it.

The following day, our heroine, in a hired sleigh, was jingling back to "The Maples," and curiosity and interest all centred on one question—"Is he there still?"

As she passed through the hall, her eye glanced searchingly round on the chance of seeing some familiar property of Bertie's. There was only a pair of his moccasins; but they might so easily have been left behind as useless, now the snow was evaporating.

Mrs. Rolleston and Cecil received her very cordially, but, knowing their sentiments, that was rather an unfavourable omen, and Freddy and Lola, who had come down to see her, kept up such an incessant chatter, that there seemed no chance of obtaining the information she dreaded.

At last, in a momentary pause, she faltered out a leading remark in such a low voice that no one attended to it. A minute later, she tried again,—"I hope Captain Du Meresq is better."

"How red you have got, 'Boobell!'" said Freddy. "Look, mamma!"

"What did you say, my dear—Bertie? Oh, yes, he is very lame still; but he was obliged to go yesterday."

The sudden colour left Bluebell's cheek, and she sat for some minutes in a relaxed, drooping attitude, oblivious of all around, till becoming sensible of Cecil's gaze rivetted on her. It was a cold satirical expression, at the same time inquiring. Bluebell was very unhappy; but this roused her, and, raising her head, she looked her enemy steadily in the eyes, with a bitter smile.

She never, strange to say, suspected Cecil of being a rival, merely supposing she was carrying on the family politics; and wounded by her officiously hostile demeanour, as she considered it, resolved no trace of her sufferings should ever be witnessed by this cold friend.

And thus it happened that the topic was jealously avoided by each; though, with mutual occupation and amusements, they became friendly again, now the disturber of their amicability was removed.

Bertie and Cecil had been inseparable the last week. His premature exertion in calling at the cottage had thrown him back; and really ill, and, in enforced inaction, he could not bear her out of his sight.

So day after day Cecil passed in the smoking-room, only hurrying out for a short drive or constitutional; and half-repaid by the gloomy complaint, "How long yon have been!" when she re-entered.

Du Meresq's correspondence, too, as we have before hinted, was not calming. A half-indignant letter from a friend whose temporary accommodation had not been repaid, a bill at three months wanting renewing, a tailor threatening the extremest rigours of the law, and similar literature, familiar to a distressed man, was punctually brought by the Post-office orderly for his delectation.

"You seem interested, Cecil," said he, as, with the uncerimoniousness of a trusted *confidante*, she glanced through the variations of the same text. "Do you young ladies ever get up behind each other, and back each other's bills?"

"You haven't opened some, Bertie; and they are not all bills."

"You can, if it amuses you," hobbling across the room. "Why, Cecil, my foot is almost sound again. We'll drive somewhere this afternoon, anyhow."

"See what the doctor says. Look here, Bertie, here's a letter marked private, so I didn't go on."

"Where did you find that? I never saw it." As he read, his brow grew dark, and he pondered several minutes; while Cecil, devoured with curiosity, and half-apprehensive of evil, remained silent.

"Will you get me a railway-guide, Cecil? There's one in the dining-room."

She complied, most unwillingly.

"Are you really going, Bertie?"

"I must, to-night."

"Why?" she more looked than asked.

He glanced through the letter again, and tossed it to her. "You see I have no secrets from you, Cecil, though I should not care for any one else in the house to be acquainted with its contents."

It was a confidential letter from his Colonel, saying, if absolutely necessary, he would give him more sick leave; but advising him, if possible, to return at once and settle some of his most urgent liabilities, which, having repeatedly come to his ears, he could no longer avoid taking notice of, unless he took steps to get the more serious ones shortly arranged.

"What *will* you do, Bertie?"

"I don't know that anything but jumping into the Lachine Rapids would solve the difficulty," returned he, lightly; "and even that must be deferred till the river is open."

"How much is it?" impatiently.

"I dare say six hundred might soothe the chief's sense of propriety, and give one a little breathing-time. But I can't get that, so the smash must come a little sooner than it otherwise would."

"You tell me that, and tie my hands by refusing to let me help you. Bertie, if you could just hold on till August, when I might draw any cheques I pleased—"

"You dearest little angel!" interrupted Du Meresq, warmly; "what have I done that you should be so kind to me? But all women are alike—generous and true-hearted when a fellow is down in the world; and—"

"Then you promise? You will count on the money?" said Cecil, not much flattered at being supposed only to act up to the inevitable instincts of her sex.

"Good heavens, Cecil! no; I am not such an unprincipled brute as to rob you of a penny. Under no possible circumstances could I touch—"

"Under *no possible* circumstances?" leapt out before she could restrain her speech. Had the meaning escaped him, the eloquent blood which rushed over neck and brow must have betrayed it completely.

Bertie, who had been speaking without motive, was taken by surprise as the sense of her impulsive words flashed on his brain.

"My darling Cecil!"

Cecil, the colour of a carnation, and expiring with embarrassment, raised her eyes, and encountered his fixed on her with a fond, sad, but *not* responsive expression. If shame could kill, she had received her *coup de grâce* that moment. He had understood, and yet said nothing.

The most rapturous gratitude on his part would hardly have reconciled her to herself; not to be met half-way was ignominious rejection.

It had all been the work of one moment, and relief came in the next with the entrance of Colonel Rolleston. Cecil, feeling as if delivered from a spell, got out of the room, and entrenched herself in her own, where her thoughts became almost unendurable.

In horror at what she had done, her first wish was never to see Bertie again. Every particle of pleasure in his society must now be over since that one mad, unguarded sentence.

"I might have known," thought she, bitterly, "that that false, caressing manner of his never meant anything. I have seen it with a dozen girls—even Bluebell,"—here she winced; "and yet in the face of all probability I must needs believe myself more to him than any one, because it suits him to make me the receptacle of his worries. Well, he is disinterested, at any rate, since all my money has no more attractions for him than myself."

A stormy hour did poor Cecil pass with her wounded pride, when she was interrupted by Lola, the Mercury of the establishment, who came to tell her that "dinner would be an hour earlier, because Bertie was going away."

Cecil received the intelligence very shortly, and nipped in the bud her evident intention of lingering by declaring herself "busy," which that astute young person, seeing no signs of employment, interpreted as "cross."

"I must face it," thought she, as the last peal of the gong jarred on her nerves. She descended just in time to see Colonel and Mrs. Rolleston disappear into the dining-room. Du Meresq, who had waited, eagerly placed her hand under his arm, and drew her back a moment.

"Cecil, where have you been hiding all this afternoon?"

I suppose he had the key to the answer, for the changing hues of her complexion, in which pride struggled with confusion, was the only one he got.

"You utter little goose!" said Bertie, emphatically, crushing the hand under his arm as they entered the dining-room. Curious to relate, Cecil scarcely felt so ashamed as she had an hour ago. Not a chance would she give him, though, of speaking a syllable in private; and very soon after dinner he departed, taking leave of Cecil before all the rest, with no more distinguishing mark of affection than a long hand-clasp, which seemed as if it would never unlock.

"Only his odious flirting manner!" said Cecil to herself; but she did not think so, and felt a good deal less self-contempt than she had before.

Next day, when Mrs. Rolleston announced Bluebell's expected return, Cecil felt quite in charity with her, and resolved to make things pleasanter than they had been, though this relenting mood was nearly dissipated by her unconscious rival presuming to look miserable at the tidings of Du Meresq's departure.

CHAPTER XV
AN ENIGMATICAL LETTER

'Tis Spring, bright Spring, and bluebirds sing.

I was monarch supreme in my cloudland.
I was master of fate in that proud land;
I would not endure
That a grief without cure,
A love that could end,
Or a false hearted friend,
Should dwell for an instant in cloudland.

Mackay.

Nothing but rain, pouring rain, for the next few days, washing the walls of snow down the unmetaled streets, a very slough of despond to all beasts of burden. Once more the sight of green grass relieved the eye, weary of the one monotonous hue it had rested on for weeks, and still it rained as if determined not to stop till it had fulfilled its mission, and dissolved every sooty patch that in chilly spots still obstinately lingered.

At last the clouds parted, the sun came out, and Cecil, regardless of mud, and impatient of long confinement, started off for a gallop on "Wings."

On her way she met the Post-office orderly with letters, who stopped and gave her one. It isn't such a very easy thing to read your correspondence on horseback, with the wind catching the sheets, and the sun shining through the paper, mixing the writing on the other side with the one you are reading. Still less feasible is it in a crowded street; so, though Cecil at once recognised the handwriting of Du Meresq, it had to be consigned to the saddle-pocket till the traffic was threaded, and she had entered on a quiet corduroy road by the lake. Then she opened it with a flattering feeling of expectation, and was half-disappointed at its calm commencement.

Bertie, with his usual dependence on her sympathy, began by telling her that he had been able to make a temporary arrangement, which had squared things for the present. "But," he continued, "the evil day must be no longer deferred. I will try and find out every shilling I owe. It will be more than I expect, I dare say, yet my commission ought to cover it, and, altogether, I shall probably save enough out of the fire to be a small capitalist in Australia. Much as I hate it, I must cut the service, for if my debts were paid to-morrow I should have just as many in two years. Dearest Cecil, I know you do not exactly hate me; I wish I were more worthy of the affection of such a dear, true-hearted girl. Will you trust me, Cecil, and believe in me a little longer, even if I say no more at present? I don't think your father likes me; I wish now he did. Let me see your dear handwriting soon. I believe you have more head than any girl I know, and more heart, too; and no one can appreciate your sense and affection more than yours, ever devotedly,

"A. Du MERESQ."

Cecil rode thoughtfully on, as she turned the letter over in her mind, trying to penetrate Bertie's meaning.

"Why does he not speak out more plainly?" thought she. "He will never be any richer unless he marries me, so it is useless waiting for that. I will not, any how, be in too great a hurry to understand him this time. If his debts are paid, and he leaves the army soon, he must say more—or nothing." And at that chance Cecil turned rather pale, and giving Wings his head, who had been fretting some time, started off at a good refreshing galop. They were on the race course now, and, excited by the turf, he gave her quite enough to do to hold him.

"What fun station-life must be," thought she. "Always riding in a wild, strange country,—birds, animals, plants, scenery, and ideas, all different and unhackneyed. Canada is well enough, but it mimics England too much, and is fifty years behind it." Before she got home, she had composed a clear-headed and sympathetic, but not at all lover-like, letter to Bertie, who was disappointed at the tone of it; and—"as the nymph flies, the swain pursues"—he wrote a much more affectionate one back, and then Cecil suffered her thoughts to take a more decided shape, and they dwelt especially on a "lodge in some vast wilderness" of her colonial paradise,— picturesque, but not luxurious—an exquisite climate, and Bertie combining the life of a happy hunter and enterprising colonist, returning to sup on a kangaroo steak, and to wake up to another day of movement and adventure.

Cecil passed a great deal of her time in this ideal log-house, sometimes garrisoning and defending it, during Bertie's absence, against a war party of savages, for danger was by no means excluded from her scheme of felicity, except perhaps one, like St. Senaun's isle, her—

"Sacred sod,
Should ne'er by Woman's feet be trod."

In such dreams and the companionship of Bluebell, who gave no further offence, now that she had learnt self-command and the necessity of keeping her feelings to herself, the spring advanced apace, and the first bluebird, alighting on the garden rails, was descried with a shriek of ecstacy by Lola.

The children, who unlike their elders, had had no gaieties, or sleighing and skating parties, to wile away the rigours of the snow king's reign, were emancipated from dulness by the approach of summer. Their lessons could be carried on in the garden; and, one day, Lola, who had shut her eyes while repeating to herself an irregular verb, saw, on opening them, a jewelled humming-bird balancing itself in the air on a level with her hat, and apparently inspecting that head-dress with wonder and curiosity, after which it flashed off and dived into a flower.

The garden was alive with fairy wonders; wild canaries came to it— pure saffron, except their black-flecked wings,—the soldier-bird, so bold and scarlet,—robins were a drug in the market, and only tolerated for their tameness and vocal powers. But none could weary of the bluebirds, whose azure took so vivid a hue in flight, from the sun shining through their wings.

Then there were excursions to the Humber woods in search of wild flowers, all new, rare, and delicate,—too much so to bear the pressure of eager hands, for they seldom survived the transit home. Often Cecil, Bluebell, Miss Prosody, and the children drove there in a waggonette, with a luncheon-basket, and spent the whole day in the golden woods, or rowing on the Humber river. Cecil's craze at this time was to paddle her own canoe; and occasionally Lilla Tremaine, who had become pretty intimate with her, joined the aquatic party.

The Colonel had rather demurred at first, thinking there was a *soupçon* of fastness and independence in it. Visions of possible anglers and unchaperoned river flirtations disturbed his mind; but eventually he satisfied himself, by requiring Miss Prosody to be always of the party, who followed with the children and a boatman in a flat-bottomed tub.

On one of these occasions they had been pulling about the beautiful bends of the river. Cecil, paddling her canoe, with a trolling-line out at the end of it, and Bluebell rowing a boat, while Lilla fished with a very especial spoon-bait of her own devising. Despite, however, the seductions of the gaudy red cloth and tassel of long hair from a deer's tail, not a fish impaled itself on the circle of formidable hooks prepared for its reception, and the mid-day sun began to dart fiercely on them.

"All nature speaks of luncheon and repose," cried Lilla, beginning to wind up her line, after the frequent weed had repeatedly mocked her hopes with its dull, dead pull. "Let us moor the fleet under this overhanging fir-tree, Cecil; it makes quite a bower."

"It feels like thunder, the fish don't bite, and the mosquitoes do," assented Cecil. "We must signal for the Infantry, though, who are also the Commissariat."

Bluebell tied a silk handkerchief to her oar, and waved it wildly.

"I wonder if that old nuisance enjoys herself," speculated Miss Tremaine, as Miss Prosody's prim visage appeared in the stern of the other boat. "So like you English, always carrying your propriety about in the shape of a foil."

"Don't abuse our treasure," said Cecil, demurely. "Ask papa what he thinks of Miss Prosody."

"I should get a more impartial opinion from Estelle and Fleda, who are always being kept in and bullied."

"Well, I really think the other children are enough for to-day," said Cecil. "What a fuss Freddy made to get after Bluebell into that tituppy little boat of yours."

"Yes, and you would all have been beseeching him not to till now, if I had not taken him by the scruff of the neck and dropped him into the other!"

"Well, dear," said Cecil, languidly; "we don't all possess your strength of mind and biceps. What have you got there, Lola?" as the boatman deftly shot the other boat under the overhanging branches.

"Water-lily leaves for plates! See now stiff and shining they are, and washed up so clean."

"Then, I suppose we must not use these wooden ones, my fanciful fairy?"

"Don't be so foolish, Lola!" snapped in Miss Prosody. "You'll spoil your frock; throw them away!"

"We can put them over the platters," said Cecil. "Hand out the edibles, Bluebell. What have you got?"

"Here's a pie, a cake, a tart, croquettes; no knives, about a pound of salt, and some butter in the last stage of dissolution."

"No knives!" cried Miss Prosody. "There must be!" plunging desperately into the basket.

"That is more untidy than a lily-leaf plate," remarked Lilla.

"No, positively not," said the governess. "How very remiss of Bowers, particularly as I observe he has provided forks!"

The children looked disappointed. They had been reckoning on the phenomenon of Miss Prosody, subjugated by hunger, eating pie with her fingers.

"Here be a knife!" said the boatman, wiping on his trousers the blade of his clasp-knife.

"Let as put a polish on," said Lilla, laughing at Cecil's face; and, jumping on to the bank, thrust it several times into the earth. The children, tired of their cramped position in the boat, wished to dine on shore; but it was thickly wooded, and there was no clear space; so Freddy was wedged into a fork of the tree, and Lola swung on another bough, where they chattered like two pies, handing down a basket on a string when they required fresh supplies.

Cecil lay on the bear-skin in her canoe, with her hat over her face, declaring it too hot to eat, but consuming, under protest, a croquette occasionally tossed in for her sustenance. Miss Prosody, quite genial and urbane after luncheon, was deep in consultation with the boatman as to the locality of certain ferns she proposed spudding up for her pet rockery at "The Maples," where her lighter hours were diurnally spent in washing and tending her spoils.

"I suppose this is all very sylvan and jolly," said Lilla, handing the remnants of the refection to the boatman; "yet somehow, candidly, it's slow."

"Possibly," said Cecil, "it is the absence of the other sex that makes you find it so?"

"Perhaps," said Lilla, frankly, with furtive enjoyment of Miss Prosody's stiffening face. "Well, ladies, I should like my little smoke; can I offer anybody one? You will find them very mild,"—and she drew forth a neat case of Latakia cigarettes, selected one, and, striking a match on the heel of her boot, lit it.

"Of course, if you choose to be so unlady-like, we cannot prevent you," said the governess, icily.

"Dear me!" said Lilla, innocently, "I never dreamt of your objecting; for I have heard you tell Colonel Rolleston, when he has been smoking, how fond you were of it in the open air."

"Colonel Rolleston would most decidedly disapprove of *your* doing it."

"He does, I believe, of most of my actions; but he is very kind to me all the same. Look at this wretch of a mosquito actually stinging through my glove. I'll just touch him up with the red ash of my cigar."

Miss Prosody knew of old that Lilla was incorrigible, and, having no hope of support from Cecil in any attempt to snub her, resolved to discountenance the proceeding by going away, and summoned the children from their tree, who were quite ready for a fresh start. The girls declared it was too hot to move. Lilla continued to puff away lazily, the zest rather gone now there was nobody to be shocked at it. Bluebell, mingling her voice with the birds, was singing the "Danube River," while Cecil, with shut eyes, lay in her canoe, and gave herself up to the dreamy music, till, aroused by its sudden cessation, she looked up, and saw a boat half checked in its speed, and Major Fane and Jack Vavasour doffing their billy-cock hats.

Cecil's return bow was freezing, and Major Fane, who had rested irresolutely a moment on his oars, shot the boat on with vigorous pulls. She felt half penitent as she saw his discomfited face, but her coldness arose from having become alive to a possible danger.

Colonel Rolleston had lately very frequently asked him to dinner, even when there was no one else, and he always fell to her share to entertain. Now Major Fane was a very good match in every way,—quite what parents and guardians would approve; so, thought Cecil,—"I can't have any mistakes about that, or it will only settle papa against Bertie."

"Did you summon those two from this vasty deep, Lilla?" cried she. "But, I forgot; I don't think either of them sail under your flag."

"My colours are too rakish and privateerish for Major Fane; and as for Jack, I am afraid he has the bad taste to prefer Bluebells to Lilies."

"If you think him worth your acceptance," said Bluebell "I will make you a present of him."

"He may be yours to keep, my dear, but not to give away. At present I am not 'on for matrimony,' and, to flirt with, I don't know any one better fun than Bertie Du Meresq."

The other girls were both too conscious to reply to this audacious remark, and after awhile they resumed fishing, Lilla's gaudy bait still unsuccessful, though Cecil had landed one or two pike. Bluebell grew tired of rowing steadily to keep her companion's line extended, and persuaded her to wind it up; then Lilla took the sculls, and they fell into conversation.

"Were you at that tobogganing party where Captain Du Meresq hurt his ankle?" asked Bluebell, diligently examining the corolla of a water-lily.

"Why?" was the counter inquiry.

"Because I never heard how it happened."

"How was that?" said Lilla, launching into narrative. At the close of it she said,—"Cecil pulled him through that time. I shouldn't have thought nursing much in her line; but she was very hard hit, you know, and I rather wondered Bertie didn't propose before he left so suddenly. Very likely he did though."

Bluebell's eyes opened in horror at this unpalatable suggestion. "What *are* you dreaming of, Lilla?" gasped she. "Cecil! why she looks upon him as an uncle or something."

"Oh, Bluebell, you blind little bat, it would be as well if you looked upon him 'as an uncle or something.'"

But the other sat aghast and speechless. Lily glanced at her sympathetically.

"Well, perhaps he mayn't care for Cecil. He has been talking nonsense to you, too, I see, as he has to us all three, for that matter. I feel so angry about it, I have a great mind to tell you all he said to *me*."

"I don't want to hear," said her companion, coldly; "nor do I at all agree with you about Cecil"

"All right," returned the other. "Only remember he can't afford to marry, whatever he may have pretended to you—not but what that subject is about the last it ever occurs to him to enter upon."

Bluebell at first utterly refused to receive this intolerable suggestion into her mind. Lilla must be inventing—in love with him herself, and trying to make mischief. Nothing should induce her to believe it. How irritating she was, too, with that knowing, quizzing expression in her face!

So when Cecil, tired of solitude, proposed coming into their boat, Bluebell eagerly took possession of the canoe, and went off on an independent paddle, ostensibly to look for Miss Prosody.

CHAPTER XVI
DETECTED

His passion is not, he declares, the mere fever
Of a rapturous moment. It knows no control;
It will burn in his breast thro' existence for ever,
Immutably fixed in the deeps of the soul.

The Wanderer.

"Why did you shoot on so quick, Major?" said Vavasour, in an injured tone, after the dumb scene before referred to. "We might as well have stayed and discoursed those young women."

Fane growled something about not choosing to intrude.

"I don't suppose they would have minded. That spicy little party, Lily Tremaine, was smoking. I wonder who finds her in cigars?"

"I hate Canadian girls!" said Fane. "And when they pretend to be fast they are more unbearable still."

"Oh, come," said Jack, warmly, for was not Bluebell of that maligned nationality? "they must have used you badly, Major. They are far more unaffected and natural than English girls, who always ride to orders; and as for beauty —"

"You have only got to look at Bluebell Leigh. Well, slope back to them, Jack. You shan't have the boat, because I should never get it again. But if you like to plough through that long grass to their bivouac, I daresay the mosquitoes will receive you warmly if the young ladies don't."

In the meantime, Bluebell, tempted by a shady creek, abandoned her canoe, and, flinging herself down on a bed of wild flowers, remained a prey to the consideration of this new view of Lilla's, which would account, in the most unwelcome manner, for the inconsistency of Du Meresq's conduct with his professions.

Cecil a rival! Much as she wished to disbelieve it, corroborative evidence, unheeded at the time, now recurred with such startling distinctness that she marvelled at her own previous blindness. Still, Bluebell was not cured. That he cared most for herself she continued to believe, though Cecil's fortune might have tempted him away. Plan after plan for obtaining an explanation was discarded as unfeasible; and, at last, Bluebell, in despair, hid her face in her hands, and burst into the unrestrained grief of the young.

She was disturbed by a slight rustling in the bushes, and, looking up, beheld Jack Vavasour in an attitude of confusion and consternation, apparently meditating flight.

"I beg your pardon, Miss Leigh; I was going away before you saw me. I'll go at once. My darling Bluebell, what *is* the matter?"

"I don't know," said she, relieved to see it was "only Jack." "I am very hot and—miserable."

Vavasour sat down, and tried in his honest and unsophisticated way to console her. "Was there any one he could pitch into for her? He would do anything she wished, etc., if she would only say what was vexing her."

Bluebell could hardly help laughing, but was so unaccustomed of late to sympathy, that she felt half tempted to take him into council, and confide her misplaced attachment and perplexities.

It was rather heartless, knowing his sentiments; but callousness to the pangs of a lightly won and unvalued heart is not uncommon in Love's annals.

However, he was too precipitate for her.

"Bluebell," he began, blushing rather, and looking, as she thought, almost handsome in his eagerness, "do you remember what I said to you the other night when we were looking at the Northern Lights?"

"I remember some absurd chaff."

"It wasn't," said Jack, with emphasis suited to the solemnity of the declaration. "I meant every word of it; and now I say, like the Beast in the fairy tale—'Beauty, will you marry me?'"

"And she always said,—'No, Beast,'" said Bluebell, laughing; "and then he went away, 'very sorrowful.'"

"Yes, but that's the difference. I shan't go away, or let you, till you say 'Yes.'"

"I couldn't, really," said she, treating it as a joke. "So we shall be starved to death, and covered up by birds, like the babes in the wood."

"No; we will live happy ever afterwards," passing an arm round her waist with an air of proprietorship. "Shall I tell Colonel Rolleston to-night?"

"Oh, this is too serious," cried Bluebell, energetically freeing herself. "If you really want an answer to such stuff, most decidedly 'No.'"

Jack, in furious mortification, for he saw she was now thoroughly in earnest, poured forth reproaches, accusing her of coquetry and purposely deceiving him, caring not if his words were just or unjust; and Bluebell's conscience was not altogether guiltless. Perhaps her own disappointment made her better understand his; for she waited patiently till the torrent of words had a little subsided, and then, laying her hand persuasively on his arm, said with gentle archness,—

"Don't be angry, Jack. What should we live on? *I* haven't a penny, *you* can't always pay your mess bill, and I am afraid an officer's wife couldn't go on the strength of the regiment, and take in washing."

"I didn't think you were so mercenary," said he, looking into her liquid eyes, that were fast quenching the angry light in his.

"I suppose I must be," said Bluebell, *naively*; "for I hate poverty so. You know my father married—just as you want to do—a pretty girl without a dollar to her name."

"You are pretty, my darling, and you know it," said Jack, bitterly.

"I don't know why people care for me if I am not, for I'm afraid there isn't much in me; and at the age of seventeen one may at least lay claim to *la beauté du diable*. Well, as I was going to say, my father married just as imprudently, and got disinherited for his pains."

"No fear of that with me," said Jack. "I am number seven, and they have all good constitutions. Destiny has decreed that I must live by my wits, without even providing me with any."

"So you see," continued she, "as we have neither money nor brains, it is no use thinking of it!"

"You are wise in your generation," said Jack, darkly. "You are pretty enough to get a rich husband any day; but whoever it is, for Heaven's sake, don't let it be Du Meresq!"

Bluebell's fair brow contracted, and her dark lashes swept her cheek, as she said, in a low, pained voice,—"No fear of that."

"I trust not," said Jack, severely, and quite unconvinced. "You are but a child, Bluebell; and, though you won't take me, I shall watch over you, and see that you do not throw yourself away; though if any good fellow wants you, I suppose I must grin and bear it."

"Thanks, my stern guardian. I hope you won't die of old age in the mean time. And now, do go, dear Jack. I must paddle after the others."

"Say good-bye first. May I, Bluebell? Only this once,"—and, without waiting for consent, he imprinted a kiss, grave as an officiating priest's to a new made bride. Touched by his love and resignation she voluntarily returned it, and, turning away, encountered the two mischievous eyes of Miss Tremaine in the stern of her boat, which had glided up unobserved.

I suppose there is no dereliction from the Eleventh Commandment, in which people would more joyfully welcome an earthquake than being taken at a similar disadvantage. No explanation or extenuating circumstances can be attempted in that deep confusion.

Lilla raised her eyes to heaven with a most edifying expression of pious horror, and shook her head disapprovingly.

"Jack," muttered Bluebell, in a tone of concentrated anguish, "I shall die of it!"

Vavasour suppressed an expletive more forcible than parliamentary, and strode down to pull the boat in.

"Oh, here you are," cried Cecil, innocent of the foregoing pantomime, for she was rowing, and had her back to them. "Mr. Vavasour, where do you spring from?" She noted, as she spoke, his strange expression and Bluebell's heightened colour with quickening curiosity and pleasure.

"I left Fane further down the river," said he; "and Miss Leigh and I sat listening to the—bull-frogs." Here Jack cast a look half-imploring, half-furious, at Lilla, who had assumed a most Quakerish expression, and hummed the air, "A frog he would a wooing go."

"Well, get in Bluebell," said Cecil, smiling; "we are going home now. Come and see us soon, Mr. Vavasour."

Jack liked Cecil very much; but he only bowed gloomily, and placing Bluebell in her canoe, disappeared, as might be inferred, to Fane; though afterwards that gentleman bitterly complained that he had, on returning home,—after waiting, to his great inconvenience, an hour or more, anathematizing Jack,—found that he had walked back to barracks totally oblivious of his companion.

Bluebell's return drive was far from a peaceful one. Lilla, it is true, abstained from remarks before the children; but there was no escaping her provokingly wicked glances, which argued ill for her future discretion.

Cecil, on the contrary, was unusually suave and considerate to Bluebell, and had rather the air of shielding her from Lilla; which would have been less incomprehensible had she known that in the interval of disembarking and entering the waggonette, Cecil had been made a participator in that malicious damsel's discovery.

At bed-time, Miss Rolleston, contrary to her wont, entered Bluebell's room, hair-brush in hand, as if disposed for a cozy confab. But that employment, so provocative of feminine disclosures, appeared futile this night, and the raven and chestnut coils were brushed to the sheen of a bird's wing ere Cecil had discovered what she had come for.

At last, under cover of lighting her candle, she said, with a disarming smile,—"You are very reserved, Bluebell. May I guess what Lubin said to you in the Humber, to-day?"

"I dare say you can," said the other, simply. "He will forget all about it soon, I trust."

"Do you mean you gave him no hope?" a suspicion of Lilla's veracity mingling with her disappointment.

"Certainly not," with great energy.

"But why?" asked Cecil, with asperity.

Bluebell turned her melancholy eyes full upon her, and the two rivals gazed steadily at each other. Then Cecil's head was impatiently flung back, her level eyebrows went down, and, without further remark, she rose and left the room.

CHAPTER XVII
DID YOU PROPOSE THEN?

A lover came riding by a while;
A wealthy lover was he, whose smile
Some maids would value greatly.

More Bad Ballads.

The summer had not been a very gay one. The heat was so intense as to throw languour on the garden and croquet-parties, which replaced the winter balls and sleigh drives. Thunder was in the air, and growled and muttered around; but the joyfully-hailed clouds floated away without affording a drop of rain; or if one black flying monster poured itself like a water-spout on the parched city, laying the flowers with its violence, the thirsty earth licked it up, scarce leaving a trace. Summer lightning quaked in long sheets over the horizon; the geese were lying dead on the common from drought; and the restless night was haunted by the tramp of straying horses on the wooden side-walks.

"Round trips" were advertised in all the papers, and brackish bathing-places on the St. Lawrence were already crowded. The Saguenay and Marguerite rivers had carried off their fishing votaries, the black fly worked its wicked will at Tadousac, where the "property" whale of the — — hotel had already been seen spouting, according to the waiter, as he attended at the matitudinal *table-d'hôte*. At any rate, seals might be seen with the naked eye, and shot, too, by a wary seal-slayer in a boat. Two such trophies were already in the hotel, affording unlimited excitement to the visitors, who, indeed, were somewhat in need of extraneous amusement, for the only resource the place could boast was pulling a boat against the strong tide of the two rivers meeting, with the alternative of a garment-rending scramble in the woods, a prey to the nipping fly, and coming sometimes in undesired proximity to a wild cat.

Twice a week the Quebec boats, with Saguenay trippers, chiefly Americans, halted at the hotel for an hour or two, and turned in their freight, who invariably commenced dancing to the more amiable than tuneful strains of an amateur performer in the public drawing-room.

This pleasure was partaken of quite as "sadly" as if they were our own unfrisky compatriots; but it passed the time, and the males still further diversified it by "smiling" at the bar.

The Rollestons, vacillating between Tadousac, the Falls, a trip in the "Algoma," and a journey to Boston, their large party being an objection to each and all, were finally attracted by an advertisement of a fishing-lodge to be let or sold on Rice Lake.

This would be a *pied à terre* for disposing of the impedimenta of the family—governess and children—during the hot months, leaving the others at liberty for flying excursions. The price was so ridiculous that Colonel Rolleston bought it outright, jestingly saying to Lola that it should be her marriage portion.

There had been a croquet party at "The Maples," but nearly every one was gone except two or three who were remaining for dinner. Among these, with a movement of vexation, Cecil observed Major Fane, her father's persistent encouragement of whom began to cause her serious uneasiness. Why, this was the second time within four days he had been asked to dine! "Can he possibly have spoken to papa first?" thought she. "It is just the sort of matter-of-fact thing he would do." Revolving it over, she walked slowly towards her step-mother, who was revelling in a packet of English letters just received, and began reading out portions to Cecil, who listened absently at first, till a passage in one of them, from circumstances, arrested her attention.

It was from a cousin of Mrs. Rolleston's, and chiefly related to her only daughter, who was heiress to a considerable property. This child had always been backward and excitable, and apparently incapable of the fatigue of study. The letter went on to say that Evelyn was developing a passion for music, even attempting to compose, and that the writer desired to find a good musician to reside with them, who should be also young and cheerful, and likely to tempt her on in other branches of education as well.

"Mrs. Leighton is exactly describing Bluebell," said Cecil, quietly.

"Oh! and she would suit them so perfectly. I *wonder* if it would do! Bluebell will be crazy with delight, she has such a wish to see England; but I doubt if her mother would part with her to such a distance."

Cecil despised herself for saying,—"If you were to put it very strongly to Mrs. Leigh, and show her the advantages to her daughter,—for they are rich as Croesus, and would pay anything for a fancy,—surely she would not stand in her way."

Mrs. Rolleston was meditating, and answered, rather inconsequently,—"I feel greatly interested in Bluebell. I think she is very conscientious and right-minded. Mr. Vavasour never comes here now; and I am sure she has never encouraged him since I gave her a hint on the subject."

Cecil remembered the scene in the Humber, and Bluebell's suggestively-conscious face that evening, so did not rate so highly the heroism of her friend. But the stragglers now drew round them, and they went in to prepare for dinner.

Cecil had also kept Lilla Tremaine, for latterly she had shrunk from a *tête-à-tête* with Bluebell, who, sensible of their estrangement, yet sadly acquiesced in it, as her new-born suspicions had been strengthened by seeing Cecil receive a letter in Bertie's handwriting.

Lilla, who could not forget the *tableau vivant* she had witnessed, was continually persecuting her hapless victim with inuendoes and allusions, whose anger and powerlessness to exculpate herself gave an additional zest to the amusement. Therefore, finding this young lady was to remain the evening, Bluebell took refuge in the school-room tea, and did not appear at dinner.

Conversation fell on the new purchase, and their approaching departure for Rice Lake; and, observing this did not appear to have a very exhilarating effect on the Major, Colonel Rolleston continued,—"When will you come down and see us, Fane? We shall get very tired of our recluse life, and want some one to bring us the news."

The Major's face brightened, but, stealing a glance at Cecil's, which only expressed consternation, it was speedily overcast, and he returned an evasive answer. Looking gloomily for the relief he expected to discern in her countenance, he received a swift glance of gratitude, which uncomplimentary graciousness completed his discomfiture.

Soon after dinner some garrison duty summoned away Colonel Rolleston, and the others returned to the garden, where daylight struggled with the newly-risen moon. A soft breeze came up from the lake, reviving after the glaring day. Cecil was *distraite* and silent, so Lilla's vivacious tongue attracted around her the gentlemen of the group, and, without any effort of his, Major Fane found himself somewhat apart with Miss Rolleston.

Though heart-whole when we first introduced him, he was now really in love with Cecil,—that is to say, he approved of and wished to marry her.

As an eligible, many determined efforts had been made for his capture, and the absence of any desire on her part to attract him gave first the feeling of security which soon led to a stronger one. If not pretty, she was graceful, especially so just now, he thought, in that unconscious, reflective attitude.

Fane became nervous: it wasn't often he got the chance of being alone with her, and she might immediately rejoin the others; but just then Cecil, coming out of her reverie, looked up, and said,—"Don't you want to smoke? Not here, but come over to the summer-house where the children do their lessons."

This proposal from the reserved Cecil, who had lately been so conspicuously repellent? He thought the change too good so be believed, and, without another asking, accompanied her to the arbour; but she insisted on the ostensible motive of their going there being carried out.

"Do you think, Cecil," said he, darting on his opportunity, "I want anything else when I am alone with you?"

Fane had, as he thought, broken the ice; but the next instant he was uncertain if she had heard or understood. A moonbeam showed him her face,—it was very pale with a look of determination on it, and her eyes were bright and steady.

"Yes," said she, after a pause, "I am glad we are alone. Major Fane, I have known you such a long time, I want to ask a favour of you, and tell you a secret."

The most confident lover might have found something ominous in these words. Fane felt as if he had made a false step; but he answered, stiffly, perhaps,—"You must have known me to very little purpose, Miss Rolleston, if you are not assured how gladly I would help or be of use to you in any way."

"Don't think me mad," cried the girl, impulsively; "but could you stay away—I mean, not come here quite so often."

Fane was too much astonished to speak, and Cecil plunged desperately on. "You have been so kind to me," she faltered, "I am afraid of its misleading papa, and his thinking that you have wishes and intentions—"

"That I might wish to marry you, Cecil? Is that the misconception you are afraid of?"

"Pray don't imagine *I* think so, but *he*, might; and, oh! Major Fane, I care most deeply for some one whom I know would not be acceptable to papa. You, on the contrary, would be everything he could wish—don't you see? the disappointment would make the other all the more objectionable to him."

"I do see my unenviable position," said Fane, shortly, for it was bad enough to be thrown over himself without being expected to be interested in a rival. "What do you wish me to do, Miss Rolleston?"

"To forget, if you can, every word I have said," cried Cecil, in an *accès* of embarrassment now that she had done it, and the excitement was over. "What *must* you think of me!"

Fane was silent for some time, for he was struggling with mortification. Fortunately for Cecil, he was a gentleman, or he might have revenged himself by assuring her she had totally mistaken his intentions.

"I can't under-value the sacrifice you ask of me," said he, presently. "I do not blame you, for you have never pretended to spare me any affection from the lover you are so true to. I hope he is worthy of it."

A pang seized her, as the doubt whether she was not throwing away true gold for counterfeit obtruded itself. "We are good enough for each other," said she, simply, "but, at present, his prospects are so discouraging, that we are not even engaged." A curious expression passed over Fane's face. "But I have money enough for both," pursued Cecil, "and if papa is not dazzled and attracted by more brilliant—by you, in short, he must see there is sufficient, and, if I remain firm, eventually consent."

Her extreme eagerness infected Fane too, and relieved the awkwardness of her strange appeal.

"Still afraid of me!" said he, sadly. "My poor child! I fear there is trouble before you. Will it satisfy you if I get six months' leave, and go to England? By that time, perhaps, your complications may have arranged themselves."

Cecil's dark eyes beamed on him with the most speaking gratitude. "You *are* a true friend," cried she, warmly, "but how selfish and exacting of me to banish you!"

"Oh, as to that," said he, with a short laugh, "I shall not dislike it. I should have got away long ago if I had known what I do now."

Nothing a woman detests so much as friendship from the man she cares for, and yet she always offers it to the suitor she rejects.

"I never thought you would care really," said she softly "I hope I have not lost my friend by putting too much confidence in him."

"I ought to thank you for your honesty," said he, with a reaction to bitterness, and they rose and returned to the others, met by many a significant look and shrug. Fane observed it, and determined to go. He was in no humour to be watched and commented on as a suitor of Cecil's. His dog-cart hadn't come, but he lit a cigar, and walked to meet it. "So that's settled," thought he. "And now the sooner I get out of this horrid country the better. I wish I hadn't refused a share of that moor; I should have been just in time for it. Well, she is a nice girl—far too good for that scamp, Du Meresq. I might have suspected what was going on there. Poor child! what a life he will lead her if it comes off, but most likely it won't. It *must* be Du Meresq; for, though I was evidently meant by the Colonel, I remember that Madame never seemed especially pleased to see me."

How unfeeling women are! Cecil forgot her remorse at Fane's disappointment in exultation at having so successfully removed a serious obstacle from her path, and her eye sparkled with wicked amusement as she noticed the marked coldness of Mrs. Rolleston's manner, due to her supposed flirtation with the Major.

The Colonel, too, who returned shortly afterwards, glanced round and inquired for Fane.

"Gone, I think," said Cecil, innocently; and he also threw upon her a look of gloom and reproach. No engaged young lady could be gayer than Cecil the rest of the evening. She became the life of the party, would keep everybody as late as possible: and certainly more than one shared the opinion of Mrs. Rolleston, whom her daughter mischievously tried to confirm in it, that the arbour had been the scene of a proposal and acceptance.

As the elder lady was slowly undressing that night, Cecil, still with the same provoking brightness on her face, peeped in.

"Are you sleepy, mamma?"

There was something in her manner that brought Mrs. Rolleston's annoyance to the culminating point. She thought the faithless damsel had come to announce her engagement, and demand sympathy and congratulations. So, with a view to arrest any aggressive gush, she said, with some asperity,—"I am glad you have come, for I wanted to tell you, Cecil, how bad it looked your walking off in that way with Major Fane."

"I suppose it was rather strong," said the girl coolly; "but I like him so much. I had no idea he was so nice."

Mrs. Rolleston took refuge in the ill-assumed dignity of rising anger.

"I suppose, mamma, he is very well off? Papa often wonders that he goes soldiering on."

"Really, Cecil, whatever your speculations may be, it was not a delicate act, sitting apart with him for half-an-hour in a dark arbour."

"I thought he might propose,"—Mrs. Rolleston's face expressed, "Are you mad?"—"or give me a chance somehow of saying what I wanted to. And what's more," she continued, "I am not certain whether he meant to, or not. To be sure, I didn't give him much time."

"Did *you*, propose, then? Cecil, if you don't wish me to disbelieve my own senses, tell me at once what you were about in the summer-house."

"Refusing eight thousand a year," was the short reply.

A puzzled, not unpleased expression, was dawning. "I thought you said he did not propose?"

"Well, no; honestly, he didn't. We had a little conversation, and the upshot was, he has promised to go to England for six months."

Mrs. Rolleston was not a proud woman, and the relief was so great, that she folded Cecil in a silent embrace.

"Perhaps, mamma," continued the girl, demurely, "you won't think it necessary to mention this to papa. It wouldn't be fair to betray Major Fane!"

Mrs. Rolleston was only too convinced, and replied, "that she should consider it Cecil's secret, and say nothing about it." Whereupon the damsel ran merrily off, humming the air, "I told them they needn't come wooing to me." But, arrived in her own room, her evanescent high spirits vanished, and a bitter and clear-sighted mood succeeded. "Bertie," she thought, "your evil influence is over us all. Mamma, till now the truest of step-mothers, is only thinking of ensuring you my fortune. I disoblige papa, send away a true love, hate Bluebell for her too attractive soft eyes, am harassed by doubts even of you—is it worth it? I might yet recall Lucian Fane; he is very calm, and would not expect too much. What folly! No, if I am to be miserable, it must be my own way, with the only man who interests me heart and soul. I suppose, if we marry, I may reckon on one year of happiness, though hardly any one who knew Bertie would expect him to be constant even for that time. But by then I should have got immense influence, for, though I am not clever and attractive like him, I have far more will, and, in the long run, it is character more than talent that shapes our life. If Bluebell would only go to England!"

Then she detached from the wall and began to pack up a little possession that always travelled with her. It was only an old print of a cavalier, and no one but Cecil had observed that a twin soul to Bertie's looked out of its dreaming eyes.

CHAPTER XVIII
LYNDON'S LANDING

All the fairy crowds
Of islands that together lie
As quietly as spots of sky
Among the evening clouds.

Unknown.

Bluebell had begun to feel herself in a false position. Freddy's lessons were, of course, a farce; and Cecil now seemed never to care to practise with her. Miss Prosody, with every hour of the day marked out for herself and pupils, made sarcastic reflections on her want of occupation; but, unhappy though she was, she could not make up her mind to leave the Rollestons, and thus dissever the chief link with Bertie. Besides, she had heard (a piece of information derived from Fleda) that he was shortly expected to join them at Rice Lake. Therefore, when Mrs. Rolleston unfolded the project of sending her to England to cultivate the musical predilections of Evelyn Leighton, Bluebell showed such repugnance to the scheme, that Mrs. Rolleston did not press it further; and, though surprised, being personally indifferent, soon dismissed it from her thoughts, with an inward comment that girls never knew their own minds a month together.

Cecil, however, marvelled at her mother's want of penetration and could not refrain from increased coolness to Bluebell.

White horses were curling the broad waters of Ontario, as the huge river-steamer "St. Michael" was getting up the steam for its run to Quebec; and, from the crowd on the wharf waiting to embark, it might be surmised that even the sofas in the saloon would be at a premium for sleeping berths. The Rollestons were surrounded with acquaintances, either going themselves or seeing others off, till the bell rang, when there was a rush to the tug, and the big paddle-wheels got in motion. The children ran up and down the long, narrow saloon on to the decks at each end, while Miss Prosody was vainly trying to wrest the key of a sleeping-berth from the purser, who, the supply not being equal to the demand, was having rather a hot time of it.

"Two double cabins," cried Colonel Rolleston, presently; "the rest must have berths in the ladies' cabin, and trouble enough to secure that. However, here are the keys. How shall we divide?"

"Shall Estelle and Lola sleep in the wide lower berth of one cabin, and I in the upper?" said Cecil.

"And we must take Freddy, I suppose?" said Mrs. Rolleston; "and Miss Prosody, Bluebell, and Fleda, go to the ladies' cabin."

"Oh, Cecil!" cried Lola, as they unlocked their domicile off the saloon, "what a little—little bed! If you turn, you'll tumble into ours; and how will you get up? Won't I catch your foot!"

"No bath!" exclaimed Estelle; "only two small basins! And what a looking-glass! it makes one squint!"

"It is better than the ladies' cabin," said Fleda, dolefully, "with the stewardess sitting there, and two or three sick-looking people, and the berths all open like the shelves of a bookcase."

"It is only for one night," said Cecil. "We land at Cobourg to-morrow afternoon. Look! the waiters are laying the long tables for luncheon, or dinner I suppose it is. Come out on the deck till it is ready. Oh, dear! there is not a patch of shade left for us. How they over-crowd these boats!"

"There's a gentleman holding his umbrella over Bluebell," said Lola.

Cecil's eyes opened in some amazement. She would have thought it rather impertinent in a stranger offering such familiar accommodation, but Bluebell availed herself of it with the frankest *nonchalance*, and, in the conversation that ensued, lost her place in the first rush of diners, who, at the ringing of the bell, instantly occupied every vacant chair.

"They seem to be having a very good time," observed Fleda, who had picked up some Americanisms.

Somewhat aghast at his daughter's precocity, the Colonel stepped out on the deck, and, with grave dignity, offered Bluebell his arm to conduct her to his seat, which, quite unconscious of his disapprobation, she accepted with civil indifference.

And the young subaltern lit a cigar to console himself for the withdrawal of the clear blue eyes that looked so deep under the shadow of the umbrella, and tried to find as much piquancy in the "funny book" he had recently purchased at the St. Michael's book-stall, while the good ship went ploughing on, past wooden villages, brown houses picked out with white, and perhaps here and there a little orange-frocked child giving a characteristic dash of colour.

Then, as the sun sank lower, the most gorgeous hues came into the sky. But, while every one was on deck gazing on its almost tropical vividness, a film stole between, a shivering dampness pervaded the air, and soon a dense fog drove the chagrined passengers back into the saloon.

The captain went to his bridge, and the tea-bell rang soon after. People were beginning to talk sociably to their neighbours, and a mild hilarity reigned, when a violent concussion, followed by a sudden cessation of the paddles, caused a general rush from the table.

Bluebell, in the act of receiving the second supply of coffee, was aroused from her immediate bewilderment by a scalding *douche* down her neck—the waiter, a young German with heart disease painted on his livid lips and pasty complexion, having held the coffee-pot suspended topsy-turvy for an instant, and then fallen in a fit on the floor.

All the men had crowded on deck, and it soon became known that they had run into a log raft, which, though no lives were lost had been nearly swamped, and much injured by the collision. The "St. Michael," too, had received a bulge, which rendered a little tinkering at the first port desirable.

The first alarm of the passengers being lulled, and the panic having subsided into the excitement of a danger passed, public interest became concentrated on the young waiter, who still lay in a death like swoon, till, eventually resuscitated by means of one of the numerous little brandy-flasks that popped out from sympathetic female bags, he was borne off by his napkin flapping fraternity to their crystal cave of tumblers.

Little sleep did Cecil get on her narrow perch that night, for her sisters, in their dreams, were ever in a sinking ship, or struggling in the foam-driven rapids. Even her heart beat quicker when the paddle-wheels suddenly ceased, and ominous voices, indistinctly heard, appeared in agonized consultation. A familiar sound of knocking and hammering, however, suggested that they must have put into port for the repairs determined on; and, grasping her scanty complement of bed-clothes that were slipping to the floor, Cecil conveyed the re-assuring intelligence to her sisters, and they composed themselves to sleep at last.

Another day's progress down the beautiful river,—narrow enough at intervals to see both shores, the Stars and Stripes in American villages, as well as the Union Jack in those of the "Dominion," as it is now called,—and then they entered among the thousand islands of the great St. Lawrence.

Everybody was on deck watching their changing shapes, some apparently all rock, and others a bower of greenery, and admiring the skilful steering of the large vessel among them. Soon after noon the first rapid was shot, a bubbling, seething whirlpool, with clouds of white foam beaten up by the jagged teeth of the sunken rocks.

Winding in and out among the islands till late in the afternoon, they reached their port, and repaired to the hotel, to pursue the rest of their journey by land.

A ricketty waggon—not an English hay-cart, but a spidery trap, with high wheels, so called—and a dilapidated buggy were placed at their disposal. Two children and the old nurse remained to follow in the coach, and the advance guard started, after an anxious consultation as to whether the wheel of the buggy could be trusted to revolve the twelve miles without dislocation.

The corduroy roads were in their usual inefficient state,—whole planks had disappeared in places, and were loose in others,—so locomotion became a series of jolts and bumps. The drivers wished to save two miles by crossing a river, and spoke confidently of a bridge, which, on arriving at, proved to be only some pieces of timber cast wholesale into it, some of them negligently nailed together.

Mrs. Rolleston, who was not of an adventurous nature, though much advanced in that direction since her residence in Canada, wished to return, and go round; but four miles lost was too serious a consideration; so she shut her eyes, clutched her husband, and prayed audibly, as the driver, with a screech of encouragement to his cattle, after a few struggles and flounders, landed the waggon on the opposite side.

But Miss Prosody declared that the wheel of the buggy would certainly be torn off in the attempt, and, losing her usual prudery in terror, whipped off her stockings, and proceeded to wade, to the exposure of a very attenuated pair of calves.

Freddy and Lola hung upon Cecil, powerless with laughter, comparing her to the thin-legged aquatic birds in the Zoo; but the Colonel, with rather a suspicious guffaw, rushed to her aid, relieving her from her hose, and, as she afterwards recollected in deep confusion, a pair of knitted garters.

The buggy bumped over somehow, and they got *en route* again, the road winding through woods golden in the setting sun. Occasionally a raccoon, playing about the trunks of trees, beguiled the loneliness of the way; or a strange bird, with harsh note, but gay plumage, flashed across their track. Colonel Rolleston, however, was not so much entranced as his children at discovering that the road stopped at the hotel on the lake, not coming within half-a-mile of his new property, and that they must embark and cross over in boats to Lyndon's Landing, as it was called, after the former occupants.

The evening was calm, and the sunset dyed their sail redly as it floated the barque lazily across the slumbering lake to their port at the bottom of a sloping lawn. The path, winding up hill, led them to a sylvan-looking lodge, where, instead of a bell, hung a hunting-horn.

Cecil executed a sonorous blast, but dropped it hastily, it being answered almost simultaneously by an ancient menial left in charge. Their own servants were coming on by coach, and they were much comforted by perceiving that this provident person had prepared a substantial repast, combining supper and tea, in a small, snug room.

The young people rushed about on a tour of inspection, and found plenty to satisfy their curiosity. The hall, to begin with was filled with trophies of the chase—antlers of moose, stuffed aquatic birds, Indian spears, and strange carving. A long, low, narrow room opened on it, in which were chairs of the weirdest description, fashioned out of boughs of the forest nailed together almost in their natural shapes. The late owner was a man of eccentric and various accomplishments, and his handiwork appeared in every detail of the house.

Pictures from his brush were on the walls; of the lake in every mood—stormy and slumbering, golden sunsets, and tempest-torn clouds, a canoe stealing through the rice, a flight of wild ducks overhead, and one swirling down to the gun of its occupant; again, the lake frozen over, and a sleighing party careering upon it.

There was a screen of his carving, and two or three couches, the latter more comfortable than the rest of the furniture, being covered with moose and seal skins. Other skins were stretched on the floor. The table-legs, like the chairs, were made of fantastic branches of wood, having rather the effect of antlers when visible under the embroidered cloths, probably the production of the squaws in the Indian village. Mr. Lyndon was the architect of the villa itself, and his whimsical fancy came out in every detail. Long, rambling passages squandered space, while queer-shaped rooms appeared up and down steps, and in unexpected places and corners, as if squeezed in by an afterthought, yet the humblest commanded a pretty view. Many of the ceilings were decorated with Cupids, Mermaids, and Dryads carelessly painted in, apparently the resource of wet afternoons.

Colonel Rolleston's voice summoned them from these attractive rooms to supper, and certainly the *menu* was varied enough to suit all tastes.

Prairie-hens and snipe were flanked with Indian corn, salsify, maple sugar, and cocoa-nut cakes; tea at one end, and a disipated-looking bottle of "old rye" at the other. But hasty justice was done to this repast by Lola and Freddy, who were dying to go down to the landing, and witness the disembarkation of their sisters, and introduce them to their discoveries; so soon as the boat was descried, they flew down with Colonel Rolleston, waving a flag hastily caught up in the hall.

Mrs. Rolleston and Cecil went to arrange the distribution of bed-rooms, the latter choosing for herself a queer little triangular nook in a gable. Perhaps she perceived that a room of less modest proportions would inevitably have to be shared with Bluebell. It might have been a watchtower from the extent of its view, which swept the lake up to the Indian village.

The children below were full of the stories the boatman had told them. That black island there was called "Long Island," and the other, with scarcely any trees, "Spate" or "Spirit Island," because it was the burying-ground of the Indians. Another was "Sheepback," from its shape, and full of poisoned ivy, which, if accidentally touched, infected the blood, and caused swelling like erysipelas.

The younger ones, with Cecil and Bluebell, were too restless to stay in the lamp-lit room they had supped in, but wandered about, finally settling in the long drawing-room, where they could watch from the windows the moon silvering the lake, and the antlered furniture throwing strange shadows on the floor.

Then Bluebell sang the "Lorelei," and Cecil invented legends for the lake, till, their rooms being at last prepared, the old nurse swooped down on her charges, and bore them away from the domain of Undines to that of Nod.

Colonel Rolleston had soon exhausted the resources of his new purchase, and duck-shooting having not yet begun, he went down to Quebec, taking Cecil with him, for an excursion up the Saguenay. She was rather unwilling to go, for, though the elders got tired of a place without roads, she was perfectly content to be all day long in her canoe, fishing, sketching, reading, or picnicing with the children on the island. But perhaps her strongest reason for not wishing to absent herself was the continual expectation of Du Meresq's appearance.

They had had no tidings of him since they had settled at the lake; but nearly all Bertie's advents were sudden and without warning. From her nook in the gable she commanded the hotel landing, and few boats left it without being reconnoitred through Cecil's binocular.

But then the Colonel wanted a companion, and was convinced it would be delightful for Cecil; so she prepared to go with well-assumed expressions of pleasure, devoutly hoping that no such *contretemps* as Bertie wasting any days of his leave by coming in her absence might befall.

To be sure, as she was in correspondence with him, nothing, apparently, was easier than to mention her intended trip, which, of course, would prevent his choosing that time to come to the lake; but it happened that Cecil had written last, and since a certain fatal speech, which even now maddened her to remember, she had been very particularly careful to let him make all the running. Still, not wishing to be left in the dark should he arrive during her absence, she said, carelessly, — "I hope, mamma, you will write now and then, and let us know how you are getting on in this dear little place."

"Really," returned Mrs. Rolleston, smiling, no *arrière pensée* having struck her, — "I more depend on hearing from you. Bluebell can write her fishing experiences, and how often they have tea on the islands; but all I expect to do is to travel over a good deal of my point-lace flounce before you return."

While Cecil went away to put on her travelling dress, as sometimes happens, the true bearing of the speech flashed on her; and when her step-daughter returned, arrayed *en voyageuse*, Mrs. Rolleston considerately remarked, — "How dull I shall be without you! I think I'll write to Bertie;" and the quick, grateful glance of intelligence in Cecil's eyes encouraged her to say much more in that letter than she would otherwise have done.

CHAPTER XIX
CALF LOVE

I gat my death frae twa sweet een,
Twa lovely een o' bonnie blue;
'Twas not her golden ringlets bright,
Her lips like roses wet wi' dew—
Her graceful bosom lily white—
It was her een sae bonnie blue.

Scotch Song.

The arrival of the Rolleston family created a good deal of interest in the limited society of the lake, and not entirely of a friendly nature. Needless to say, the adolescent members of it were all more or less engaged to each other, which, being rather the result of propinquity than uncontrollable preference, the maidens noticed with angry surprise the admiration excited in the bosoms of their swains by the apparition of Bluebell on their hitherto uninvaded waters. Alec Gough and Bernard Lumley, both morally placarded "engaged," having, as a matter of course, plighted their troth to two neighbouring fledglings, were wild for an introduction; and no sooner did Bluebell's canoe leave Lyndon's Landing, than two corresponding ones were sure to shoot out, apparently actuated by the same persuasion that there was no more likely place for a fish than the snag round which she was trolling, and ready to gaff a maskinonge, or help to land an obdurate bass, if occasion offered.

Any such incident might have commenced an acquaintance, were it not that Miss Prosody, with a boatful of children, was never far off, and had a scaring and terrifying effect.

Bluebell rather despised very young men. Still, she was not insensible to admiration, and was quite aware of these two young aborigines following in her wake as surely as a gull in that of a vessel.

One day Alec Gough was able to render her some slight assistance, her line being obstinately entangled in the snag; but Miss Prosody sternly brought up the boatman to complete the service, and bowed off the interloper with such extreme severity, that Bluebell could not resist bestowing a coquettish and dangerously grateful glance, which set his heart bumping, and instantaneously obliterated the image of his sandy-haired little love.

It was too bad of Alec, for he had been engaged a year, and had already cleared (he was a lumberer) space enough in the backwoods to start a farm, and he was now on a short visit to his betrothed to report progress and pursue his suit. So he had no business to get his heart entangled with the line, and his legitimate affections disengaged with the string he was clearing, under Circe's azure eyes; and why need he, in that tactless manner, talk of her at tea as "The Lady of the Lake"? which, if such a senseless *sobriquet* was worth having at all, Miss Janet Cameron considered she had an indisputable right to, for could she not row, swim, dive, and paddle with the best?

Then again, after tea, he actually stole out in his canoe, muttering something about "looking for ducks," to which Bernard Lumley gallantly remarked that he "needn't leave home to find them." He certainly *did* take a gun, but was also provided with a little flageolet, the companion of his lonely life in the woods; and waiting till nightfall, by the light of a waning moon, this absurd and reprehensible young lumberer paddled himself off to Lyndon's Landing.

There he carefully reconnoitred the house, wondering which could be Bluebell's casement. The insensible building afforded no hint, so he pulled out his "howling stick," as Bernard called it, and timorously breathed forth a lay of love, which certainly must have been first cousin to the one that encompassed the extinction of the cow.

The inmates were apparently asleep, and Alec, getting bolder, played every suggestive air he could think of. I don't know whether he expected Bluebell would open the window and enter into conversation; but, in point of fact, the lattice under which he was serenading was Mrs. Rolleston's, who not particularly expecting any lovers, was sleeping the sleep of the just far too soundly to be disturbed by it.

There being no policeman to direct him to "move on," Alec continued his dismal repertory till he was tired, and then paddled off, not wholly discouraged, as he hoped that Bluebell, though she would make no sign, might have been secretly listening to, even watching him, and conscious of the admiration he sought to convey.

The Lake families called within the next few days. Bluebell did not appear when the Camerons, mother and daughter, came; and, as Mrs. Rolleston happened to say *her* daughter was away, they were quite mystified as to whom the dangerous stranger could be. Then Coey and Crickey Palmer came with their mother's cards; and as at that time Bluebell was present, reading to Mrs. Rolleston, they naturally took her for one of the daughters, and made acquaintance after the manner of girls; and, I have no doubt, had Bluebell committed a murder and absconded next day, either of these young ladies could have given a more complete and accurate description of her person than detectives are generally furnished with. Notwithstanding the reluctant admiration that the inspection resulted in, Coey (Bernard's affianced) heroically hoped, as she rose to take leave, that Miss Rolleston would spend the afternoon and stay to tea the following day.

Mrs. Rolleston glanced at Bluebell, who was rather dimpling at the prospect of a change, and carelessly replied that "her daughter was at Tadousac, but that her young friend Miss Leigh would be very happy."

I suppose she was, for she certainly was rather solicitous about her toilette for the occasion—only an innocent brown-holland dress; but two hours were spent in knotting up some wicked blue bows for throat and hair, and re-trimming her gipsy hat with the same shade. It is, of course, an undoubted fact that women dress for their own satisfaction only, and in accordance with their instincts of "the true and the beautiful;" so it would be mere hypercritical carping to suspect coquetry of lurking in the deft folds of that unpretending blue ribbon, or that, in the face of her *grande passion* for Du Meresq, she could for a moment occupy herself with the foolish admiration of Alec and Bernard.

Well, Bluebell is our heroine, and we must make the best of her,—to some people admiration never does come amiss; and if a demure *oeillade* can play the mischief with the too inflammable of the rougher sex, I don't know who is to be held accountable except the father of lies.

"Palmer's Landing" was a less original building than Lyndon's but on a more accessible side of the lake. The establishment and furniture were of the rough-and-ready order. When a too independent help, finding her mistress didn't suit, gave herself an hour's warning, and went up North, Coey or Crickey would resignedly cook the family meals till an opportunity arrived to get another, and as, in addition to those occasional calls upon them, they were their own dressmakers, they had less time to get discontented with the monotony of the lake than might otherwise have been the case.

Bluebell was taken round by the two girls to visit their garden and poultry-yard. The latter was a source of profit, as they supplied the house, and drove hard bargains with their mother for the chickens and eggs. She also was shown their own room, and the rose-wreathed, green tarlatane, which Miss Crickey explained with conscious pride she was to wear at a city assembly next week. "I am to stay with my uncle—he has a large dry-good-store at — —, but he lives on Brock." She was also warned off trespassing by the full account of Coey's engagement, and by that time Bernard had arrived to escort the girls for a ramble in the woods.

Crickey, on the principle of doing as she would be done by, marched Bluebell on in front, so that the others might linger behind, and make love upon the usual pattern. It was customary at the lake for to tuck their *fiancées* under their arm, and cast incessant sheep's eyes at them, much conversation was not *de rigueur*.

Bernard, however, was somewhat discontented: he thought there were innumerable opportunities for that kind of thing; so his eyes wandered from the face of his love to Bluebell's round waist and waving hair. Instead of incessantly squeezing her arm, he barely held it, and finally dropped it to remove a briar from the skirt of his distractor.

Bluebell smiled with her big blue eyes, perhaps more gratefully than the service demanded, which encouraged the youth to commence conversation. The few platitudes he attempted might have been the most sparkling wit from the animation with which they were received. Surprised to find himself so agreeable, he lingered by her side. Crickey, expecting him every minute to fall back, remained by Bluebell, so poor Coey trudged behind, and began to experience what jealousy was.

After a while, the others tried to bring her into the conversation by appeals to her opinion, but Coey was not to be so easily propitiated, and returned austere answers.

Then Bernard, thinking he might as well be hung for a sheep as a lamb, became all the more engrossed with his captivator, and it was in at one of strong discontent that he exclaimed, as they were returning, — "Why, there's Alec and Janet Cameron coming down to the house!"

Their unexpected arrival was rather a relief to the Palmer girls, Bluebell only saw more mischief before her, but Bernard's impatience at the sight of Alec whose motive for coming he easily guessed, was quite undisguised.

The latter accounted for himself by saying "that Janet wished to make Miss Rolleston's acquaintance, and, therefore, he had accompanied her."

"Oh, I am not Miss Rolleston," said Bluebell, "I am the governess."

"I have had the advantage of seeing the governess," said Alec, demurely, "and she is old enough to be your mother."

"But I am the musical one and Freddy is my pupil entirely."

"Are you really?" said he, brightening "Then you *like* music?"

"I am sure that is not a necessary consequence," said Bluebell, rather mystified by the meaning tone of his voice, but Alec, believing she had heard his nocturnal serenade and assuming a secret understanding on the strength of it, lingered by her side talking in an undertone—really about nothing in particular, for, like most spoony boys, he trusted more to his eyes than his tongue. Still it had all the effect of a flirtation, and when the girls went upstairs to prepare for tea, Bluebell found herself quite out of court without the support of the other sex. Coey was already turned into a very belligerent little ring-dove, and Janet watched her askance, for she had never before known Alec so keen about partaking of tea at Palmer's Landing. Crickey, whose feelings were not so powerfully engaged, supplied her with toilette requisites, and such conversation as hospitality demanded.

Bluebell was rather flattered by the apprehension she excited, and, with mischievous ostentation, produced from her pocket a weapon of war in the shape of a blue ribbon, and began weaving it into her chestnut fuzz, too naturally wavy and long to require frizettes. Coey, who was rather pretty in the white kitten style, had sparse pale hair, never properly combed over her "water fall," as she called it, which obtruded itself like a crow's nest. This attractive peculiarity was more apparent than ever to-day, the frizette having been caught by a bough in the woods.

Bluebell observed that her decorative preparations were restricted to a dab of violet-powder on her nose, and a slight application of lip-salve. "I can't let her go down such a figure," thought she, "though she is dreadfully angry with me," and, seizing a comb, began silently to effect a reformation in Coey's *chevelure*.

"Oh, thank you," said the other distantly. "Isn't it right? Never mind. Dressing is such a waste of time."

"Hugger-muggering with Bernard is not, I suppose?" thought Bluebell, resolutely continuing her task.

But it was Janet's turn to be angry, when, at tea that evening, utterly oblivious of the vacant chair next herself, her faithless swain manoeuvred into one next Bluebell.

"Are you fond of music by moonlight?" he took the first opportunity of whispering.

"I like it anywhere," replied she, innocently. "I can't say I ever heard it by moonlight."

Much discomfited, Alec gazed incredulously, and then burst out laughing.

Bluebell naturally inquired what she had said to amuse him; but he evaded the question, as Janet was evidently listening. Later on, when the former was at the piano, and he pretending to turn over, he whispered, —"I wonder under whose window I was making such a lovely noise the other night?"

"How should I know? And why did you do it?"

"I wanted to give you a welcome to the Lake; but perhaps I serenaded that vinegar-faced governess instead."

Bluebell was playing rather a pathetic sonata; but the time got decidedly erratic, as she stared bewildered at Alec, and then went off into a fit of laughing. "How could you be such a goose? If Colonel Rolleston had been at home, he would have fired his ten-shooter at you."

"Tell me which is your window," he whispered, "and I'll give you plenty of music by moonlight. I hope it is the one with the balcony."

"Why?"

"Because," said Alec, audaciously, "you would look so beautiful stepping out on it, like Julia in 'Guy Mannering.' And we could talk, you know."

"Very well," said Bluebell, who opined it was about time to shut him up. "Suppose we refer it to Miss Cameron. I understand your heart and accomplishments are all made over to her. Perhaps she would assist at the balcony scene!"

Alec bit his lip, and looked rather ashamed. Such a rebuff would not have embarrassed Bertie, nor awakened in him a slumbering conscience, as it did in this young lumberer, who was ridiculous enough to be in earnest in his infidelity.

But Bluebell, knowing she had no quarter to expect from the girls if she returned to them now, was far from wishing to bring him to a sense of his duty before the evening was over, so smiled as engagingly as ever, and continued to accept his attentions, till Janet, fizzing in high dudgeon, announced her intention of going home, which, of course, involved the escort of her recreant young man.

"Wait here a quarter of an hour," whispered Alec to Bluebell, "and I will run back and row you home."

"Gracious, no!" said she, with rather the sensation of a child who has been sent out to spend the afternoon and has misbehaved. "Here is Mrs. Rolleston's servant come for me. Go back with Miss Janet and make it up, for I am never going to speak to you again,"—and she turned away to make her adieux to Mrs. Palmer, a motherly-looking old lady, who had been nodding half asleep on the sofa all the time.

"Such a charming musical evening—such a treat!" said she, brisking up, and quite unaware of what had been passing round her the last two hours.

"Miss Leigh was quite untireable," sneered Janet. "One could not have *asked* her to exert herself so much."

"Must you really go?" interposed Crickey, fearing now the music was over the harmony might cease also.

Bluebell pleaded a promise to return early.

"I am sorry to be the means of taking away any attraction that might have induced you to stay," put in Janet, determined to give her "one" before she went.

"Thank you," said Bluebell, sweetly, declining to understand; "but I could scarcely expect you to stay to amuse me."

"That, I feel sure, would be quite out of my power!" said the other, bent on provocation; and Crickey nervously dragged Bluebell away to get her hat.

Alec lingered till she was fairly off, fearing that Bernard would try and escort her home. He, however, was thoroughly sulky at the way Gough had monopolized her the whole evening, and was quite as ready as Coey to pronounce her an arrant flirt; which so mollified the latter, that when, a few days later, she and her sister were asked to return Bluebell's visit at Lyndon's Landing, she accepted without the slightest hesitation, in a perfectly charitable frame of mind.

Alec and Janet, of course, quarrelled going home; but it being not the first time by a good many, it blew over without a rupture, the gentleman, for the future, cautiously avoiding Bluebell's name, though he tried all he knew to meet her alone, in which respect Fortune did not favour him; and there being no more efficient chaperons than children, with their sharp observation and fatal habit of repetition, they might meet every day on the blue water without his obtaining more than a saucy glance or a few commonplace words, which he would try and put as much meaning into as he could.

CHAPTER XX
THE PRINCE PHILANDER

A division of souls may take place without a word being exchanged. One reminded of those mists that rise into a cool stratum of air soon to redescend in flakes of snow....

Human Sadness.

The day that the Misses Palmer were to spend at Lyndon's Landing turned to rain in the afternoon. The children had a half-holiday, and so the weather was a double misfortune; and after "What shall we do?" had been asked in every minor key of querulous despondency, they eventually grouped themselves, some sitting, some lying on buffalo robes scattered on the floor, and demanded stories from the elder girls. From the darkness of the sky, twilight had come earlier, and Freddy had closed the curtains, to give greater mystery to the fairy lore they were invoking.

Previous to this they had had a grand dressing up and a fancy ball. Crickey retained the turban and Indian table-cloth which had been her "make-up" as an "Eastern Princess." Freddy was a wild beast; and Lola, by dint of a long pair of military boots, seal-skin gloves, and "pretending very much," was "Puss in Boots." The old nurse's cap and spectacles were, with a peaked hat, the salient points of a "Mother Hubbard." But they were tired of it now, and no sound was heard except the sullen moan of the storm on the lake, and the voice of Bluebell, half-inventing and half-relating from memory.

"And so the Princess remained in the strong tower of the Giant Jealousy; for though the doors were all open, and you would suppose she had nothing to do but walk out and be free, yet if she did get a little way some invisible power always drew her back again, after which the Giant seemed more tormenting than ever. For no one could really release her but the Prince Philander, whom she loved, and he only by remaining true to her alone (which, perhaps, was not always the case, and that was how she had strayed into Castle Jealousy), and coming himself and overthrowing the Giant, who would then be instantly dissolved into smoke, and—"

But the ultimate fate of the bewitched Princess was never known, the story being arrested by a shout from the children as they caught sight of a tall, dark figure, half-concealed by a carved screen, and even in the dusk Bluebell discerned the expression of amused attention and half-satirical smile on his lips.

"I saw him first!" cried Lola, jumping up exultingly. "He has been standing there ever so long, but he made me a sign not to tell."

"I wanted to hear Miss Leigh's story," interposed Bertie; "but it is only the plain Princesses *that* Giant gets hold of, and then the fairy Princes are too busy with the beauties ever to come and rescue them!"

Bluebell was almost unnerved by the surprise of his unlooked-for appearance. A real Prince Philander had come at her invocation; whether he was to overthrow the Giant, or strengthen his hands, remained to be proved.

She had a dim impression of presenting him to the Misses Palmer with a mortified recollection of her own absurd "make-up," and then sat down, quite faint from the uncontrollable beating of her heart.

Perhaps it was to relieve her he was so amiably making conversation with Coey and Crickey; and exceedingly well they were getting on, she began to think, recovering rather rapidly when not the object of any particular attention.

"And you have been shut up here all day without any exercise?" she heard him say. "That's very bad. Suppose we play hide-and-seek and run about all over the house;" and, clamorously supported by the children, the motion was carried, and the game commenced.

Bluebell, who was under the influence of strong feeling, thought it most sickening folly, and wished that Mrs. Rolleston would come in and stop it; but she was charitably reading to a sick fisherman close by, and, perhaps, weather bound. Miss Prosody was taking a peaceful afternoon snooze; and if she did hear the scampering about the house, they were not unaccustomed sounds on a wet day.

It had struck Bluebell that the game might have been a *ruse* of Du Meresq's to get a word with her in private; but Estelle came up in fits of laughing, to tell her that Bertie and Crickey were hid together in the cupboard. This was too much, and she walked coldly downstairs and out of the game.

Coey went in search of her sister, who bounded down directly after with a very red face; and soon Mrs. Rolleston came in, full of exclamations and inquiries.

Du Meresq said,—"He and Lascelles had got a week's leave, and had come to the hotel for some duck-shooting."

"And Cecil won't be back till Thursday," said Mrs. Rolleston, regretfully.

The significance of this remark was not lost upon Bluebell, who stole a furtive glance at Bertie's face.

"I thought I had got to an enchanted hall," said he. "I daren't wind the horn lest I should fall under the spell. The portal yielded to my touch, and I entered the first room, where conceive my surprise to see, fantastically dressed, and reclining in Eastern fashion on skins and cushions, a galaxy of beauty. They were silent, too, except one, who, in a hushed, mysterious, voice, was improvising an allegory."

"In short," said Mrs. Rolleston, in a matter-of-fact tone, "the children were dressed up and telling stories." She began to wonder where Miss Prosody could be. It was no use Bertie prejudicing his chance with Cecil by getting up an idle flirtation with these Lake young ladies, who were already blushing so ridiculously at him; and would have been further confirmed in this conviction had she guessed that ten minutes ago he had tried to kiss one of them in a cupboard.

She offered him a bed, but willingly accepted his excuse that Lascelles was all alone, and he had promised to go back, but would bring him to dinner next night. And then he went away through the rain, and Bluebell was left with her thoughts.

Well she had never pictured such a meeting as that! And how disagreeable it had all been. Of course she did not mind his not having paid her much attention before the children, who repeated everything, but to go on in that silly romping away with Crickey was ineffably disgusting. She did not at all recognise it as a poetical justice on her for tampering with other people's lovers a few days before, but mentally denounced that young person as bold and unlady like to the last degree.

The evening continued so stormy, that Mrs. Rolleston kept the girls all night, and Bluebell, much against her will, had to entertain them, which was the more irksome as they were both expiring with curiosity about Bertie, and could talk of nothing but his extraordinary behaviour. Crickey hadn't even the sense to keep his impertinence in the cupboard to herself, and Bluebell, who had only suspected before, was provoked into the most trenchant expressions of condemnation.

"How could I help it?" asked Crickey, indignantly. "How should I know he would be so impudent?"

"Why need you have got into the cupboard with him?" said Bluebell. "It is just what you might have expected, in fact, it was inviting it."

"It wasn't," said Crickey, almost crying, for she had previously been inclined to take it as a tribute to her charms. "Freddy and Estelle had hid there before, and Captain Du Meresq said it was the best place in the house."

"For that, no doubt," began the other. But Coey came to her sister's assistance with a Biblical allusion to the mote and the beam, and Bluebell saw that if personalities were to be avoided, they had better go downstairs at once. So the party of ladies passed a quiet sleepy evening, — Mrs. Rolleston mentally resolving not to encourage those girls about the house while Du Meresq was at the lake, and wishing she could expedite Cecil's return. How much more danger there was from Bluebell she never suspected, Bertie had been so very cautious.

As they went up to bed, Crickey, who had become rather sobered by the dull evening, entreated Bluebell not to mention the cupboard scene in hide-and-seek, which was impatiently promised. To think that she should be asked to keep any girl's secret about Bertie! "And now," thought the poor bewildered child, "it will be almost more difficult than ever to see him alone, and I must ask him if there *is* anything between him and Cecil." For that seed of bitterness sown by Lilla had borne "Dead Sea fruit"; and, much as she struggled against the hateful idea, it really seemed the only clue to Bertie's inconsistencies.

The next day Mrs. Rolleston had some letters, and reading one attentively, she threw it over to Bluebell. "You didn't seem to care for this some weeks ago, but you see you can think twice of it. I *did* write rather enthusiastically about your music, which, really, is too good to be wasted on my children, and the result is Mrs. Leighton is quite wild to have you."

A singular expression flitted over the girl's face as she mechanically took the letter—it was only to gain time, she wasn't reading it; and the large salary and kind promises of a happy home took no effect on her mind.

She was thinking of Du Meresq. Suppose he was only trifling with her, and all those warm protestations of affection were really to end in nothing! She might even have to see him married to Cecil! The thought was unendurable, yet it was possible; and, if so, how could she remain with the Rollestons? And it would be almost as bad as returning to the cottage, once "so rich with thoughts of him." Chance had thrown Du Meresq again in her path, and she was determined to find out the truth. Chance also offered her this retreat, which would put the ocean between them if he failed her, and then no distance could be too great for her wishes.

"Can you give me till the mail after next to decide?" said she, as she arrived at this point of decision.

"Oh, of course," said Mrs. Rolleston, smiling at the almost tragic tone of resolution in which it was uttered. "You will have to consult your mother, and she might not wish you to go to England. Why child, how pale you are!"

Bluebell forced a wintry smile and escaped, for a lump was rising in her throat, and she could not but remember that she must expect no sympathy or support from Mrs. Rolleston, who had once said, "It would be a most unsuitable connection." She passed the day in reviewing the situation. This was the first time she had ever been called on to think seriously and painfully, and act for herself without a friendly word to support her. Perhaps Du Meresq's behaviour the day before had not a little braced her to the energetic course she had determined on. It was, indeed, no easy task to extort from a man who professed so much the simple question in black and white which could alone give value to his addresses. With no witnesses present, she had little doubt that he would be as ardent a lover as ever; but that would no longer satisfy her. She had arranged her plan, and relied on two feelers to settle the matter one way or the other.

The first was to repeat to Bertic what Lilla had said about himself and Cecil, and then judge of the effect of her words. If unsatisfactory, she might tell him she was going to take a situation in England, "and if he makes no effort to stop *that*, it will, indeed, be over, and I will go," was the necessary conclusion.

Du Meresq and his friend, Captain Lascelles, came to dinner. Were either to die, exchange, or marry, the other would doubtless feel much inconvenienced, not to say injured. In England, their hunters, rooms at Newmarket, stall at the Opera, or whatever would bear division, were all joint-stock affairs; and either would, with perfect cordiality, have lent the other money, which a long unpaid tradesman would have found exceedingly hard to extract from him.

Both were unquiet spirits in the regiment, abhorring the monotony of drill and stables, and insatiable for leave. Yet on field-days, even their most pipe clay of colonels admitted that there was no smarter turned out troop than Lascelles', and no better squadron leader than Du Meresq.

The party was so small at dinner that conversation became pretty general. Captain Lascelles at first tried to be *au mieux* with the only young lady present; but he didn't make much way, and began to think her rather stupid, and to wish that those lively girls his friend Bertie had told him of would swim or paddle themselves across. To Bluebell the evening was little short of purgatory. Never had she known Du Meresq so altered. Scarcely a sentence had passed between them, and his manner was conventional and guarded. Formerly he had been equally cautious in public, yet they were always *en rapport*, and some slight glance was certain to be exchanged in assurance of it.

This night she knew from internal consciousness that they were not, and that a palpable change had taken place. Her heroic resolutions of the morning passed away in inconsistent and impotent longing for one word or gesture to break down this impenetrable wall that seemed to have arisen between them, and to recall the old happy love-making days. Mrs. Rolleston asked her to sing. A bird robbed of its nest could not have felt more disinclined, yet she would try, though her voice sounded strange to herself, and was harsh and wiry.

Du Meresq wondered what had jarred those silvery tones, and stolen the melody from the voice he had once thought almost seraphic. Music, and especially Bluebell's, had ever a potent charm for him. She had abandoned the song at the end of the verse, and glided without stopping, into an instrumental piece. There was a subdued hum of voices, but Bertie's was not among them, and Bluebell knew he was listening as of old. She had arranged some variations to their favourite valse, and some impulse made her select that. Keeping the subject cautiously back, and only allowing suggestions of it to steal into the modulations, it seemed like fugitive snatches of an air borne on a gust of wind, and overcome by nearer sounds,—the breeze in the trees, the tinkle of sheep-bells, the brawling of a brook.

Bertie listened curiously, thought he had caught the air, lost it, and doubted, till he recognised, in the mocking melody that continually eluded him, the valse he had so often danced with Bluebell. He shot one glance of intelligence at her as she finished, but Lascelles, who could not bear the piece, was so loud in admiration, and found so much to say about it, that Du Meresq could not have got in a word had he wished it.

Bluebell turned impatiently away, and snatching up some work, went to a secluded part of the room, under cover of requiring a shaded lamp there. "If there is any truth in magnetic attraction," thought she, "Captain Lascelles shall not come near me, and Bertie shall." She excluded every other thought from her mind, and *willed* steadily. Du Meresq became restless, rose from his chair, and stood aimlessly looking at something on a table. Bluebell continued her mesmeric efforts, every fibre quivering. He was coasting in her direction; in another instant he would be close, and have sat down on the sofa by her. Then she looked up, and their eyes met and mingled. It might have been for half-an-hour to her overwrought sensations; the past was forgotten,—she was gazing in a trance. What impelled Mrs. Rolleston at that moment to say,—"I heard from Cecil this afternoon, Bertie, and if they catch the boat at — —, they will be here to-morrow evening?"

The passionate eyes drowning themselves in the love light of Bluebell's became thoughtful and colder. The spell was broken. Du Meresq turned away, and began talking to his sister about the expected travellers.

The reaction was painful as the killing of a nerve, and the cause of it so cruel, that she made no attempt to endure it. A swift glance round showed her she was unobserved, and springing to the door, she fled from the room, to weep out her blue eyes in senseless, hopeless repining.

No one noticed her exit but Lascelles, who, going through his social *devoirs* with mechanical propriety, had his powers of observation quite disengaged.

"I can't make the girl out," he soliloquized. "She is aggravatingly pretty, plays very uncanny, unpleasant music, and looks at me with about as much interest as if I had called to tune the piano or regulate the clocks. I wonder if she is expected to go to bed at ten! I fancy there is a very stringent code of rules for a companion. She was sitting in such a nice inviting corner, to. Du Meresq seemed sloping off for a spoon; but when he doubled back, and I was just ready to bear down, she shot out of the room, like Cinderella when she had 'exceeded her pass.'"

The two friends looked in next morning. They were going in a yacht as far as the Indian village, and Bertie said if the Colonel and Cecil would be likely to have arrived, he would come in on his way back. There was some discussion about trains and connecting boats, and a guide-book was fruitlessly hunted for.

"Oh, I recollect," said Mrs. Rolleston, suddenly; "I put it in the table-drawer in the next room,—right-hand drawer, Bertie," as he went to fetch it. He found a little more than he sought, for there, alone, with every appearance of being caught, was Bluebell. Du Meresq would, perhaps, have avoided the *contretemps*, had he been prepared for it. As it was he advanced towards her, and, clasping her in his arms, kissed the cheek from which every ray of colour had vanished, and said, tenderly,—"What has turned my Bluebell into a Lily?"

"I have heard something. I want to ask you a question," came out almost mechanically.

Du Meresq had not expected so serious an answer to a *banalite*, and his countenance altered.

"Why are you so grave, Bluebell? You take life too seriously, my child. A young beauty like you need never be unhappy—only make other people so."

But his theories were no longer taken as gospel.

"Oh, I am quite happy," said she, with an involuntary ironical infusion in her voice, "but I don't often see you alone, Bertie, and there are one or two things I want to ask you."

"We'll soon square that", said Du Meresq carelessly, "What do you think of Lascelles?"

"Think of him?" repeated Bluebell, with passion "What should I think of him? I don't care if he dies to morrow!"

"What, a good looking fellow like that?" said Du Meresq, jestingly, "and he admires you awfully." What a flash of those violet eyes—regular blue lightning! But a sudden gush of tears extinguished it, and, breaking from him, Bluebell rushed out of the room.

A look of extreme annoyance came over his face and he whistled thoughtfully. Lascelles shouting his name, burst into the room.

"Where is that book? 'His only books were women's looks, and folly all they taught him.' Oh Bertie I fear me you are a sly dog."

"What the devil do you mean?" said Du Meresq with much irritation.

"What do you? Keeping me here all day, while you are spooning the pretty companion. She bolted out of this so quick,—nearly ran into my arms, and seemed taking on shocking. Oh, you strangely ammoral young man!"

"By Jove!" said Du Meresq, "it is lucky it was only you. Well, let us be off now, and shut up, there's a good fellow."

CHAPTER XXI
A PERILOUS SAIL

Our birth is but a sleep and a forgetting,
The Soul that rises with us, our life's Star
Hath had elsewhere its setting,
And cometh from afar.

Wordsworth.

By this the storm grew loud apace,
The water wraith was shrieking,
And in the scowl of heaven each face
Grew dark as they were speaking.

Campbell.

There was a bright moon that evening, and Colonel Rolleston and his daughter were crossing the lake. A yacht passed them, sailing rapidly before the wind. Some one on board took his hat off.

"Who was that?" asked Cecil.

"It was very like Lascelles," said the Colonel. "I wonder what he is doing up here."

Cecil's colour rose. The name of Lascelles suggested Bertie. She knew they usually hunted in couples, and her busy mind was alive with conjecture. She wondered if the same idea had occurred to her father. She thought he looked a shade grimmer; but he smoked his cigar in silence, and a few more pulls from the sinewy arm of the boatman shot them into Lyndon's Landing. And then it all seemed to Cecil as if the same scene had been enacted in a previous state of existence. Where before had she seen his dark figure thrown out just so by the moonlight? Certainly not in a dream. Could one's life be repeated? She almost felt, by an exertion of *memory*, she might tell what was coining next.

A deep, calm satisfaction stole over her as Bertie helped her from the boat, and his eyes sought hers under the stars. She heeded not that Colonel

Rolleston's greeting was apparently cool and formal, nothing signified—life had suddenly become intense again. What could ruffle the golden content of the present? Happiness is a great beautifier, and as she sprang to shore, her graceful figure so undulating and spirited, and her soul beaming warm in her radiant eyes, he wondered that he could ever have thought Bluebell more beautiful. She often recurred to him hereafter just as she stood that night, shrouded in a crimson Colleen Bawn, under cover of which her hand remained so long in his.

Du Meresq did not stay very late. Both he and Cecil were quiet and dreamy. To be in the same room again was quite happiness enough for the present. Mrs. Rolleston also was entirely satisfied, diverted her husband's attention with creature comforts, and made no effort to detain Bertie. Given a love affair, and a certain interest in it, the most unscheming nature becomes Macchiavellian in tact and policy.

And Du Meresq unmoored a canoe and paddled himself off, unwitting of a young, desolate face pressed against an upper casement. From thence she had watched him waiting for Cecil at the landing, and, with eyes sharpened by anxiety, had detected their happiness in meeting. She could not go down to receive confirmation of what required none. Better receive the *coup de grâce* from his own lips than to undergo gradual vivisection while looking helplessly on.

Bluebell was young and credulous, her heart had been flattered away by this man, who had had so many before and did not want it now, and yet, poor child, could she have looked beyond, she might have seen cause for thankfulness that the thing most hotly desired was withheld for this early love had not root enough for the wear and tear of life. It was a hob day romance, born of the senses, the bewildering fascination of a graceful presence and winning voice, and well for her if her guardian angel stood with even a flaming sword in the way.

The two girls did not meet till the morning, when Cecil, preoccupied as she was, could not but notice the blanched weariness of Bluebell's face which, owing a great deal of its beauty to colouring, appeared by contrast almost plain.

"You should have come up the Saguenay with us. I am sure Rice Lake cannot agree with you," said she, launching into a glowing and graphic description of their adventures. In reality, Cecil had detested the whole expedition, having been in a continual fever to return; but, now that her mind was at ease, memory brought out the notable points in a surprising way, and she quite talked herself into believing that she had enjoyed it immensely, and had witnessed everything with the utmost relish and curiosity.

They were sitting in the garden over-looking the lake, and a tiny sail shot out from the hotel landing and stood towards them. A light stole over the face of the brunette, but the features of the blonde became rigid as they marked its progress. Neither alluded to the circumstance—Cecil continued her narrative, and Bluebell made the requisite replies; but when the boat had made Lyndon's Landing, and Du Meresq and Lascelles jumped out, Cecil found she was receiving them alone.

The latter was come on a farewell call. The two friends meant to sail to a railway station five miles up the lake, where Lascelles would take the car, and Du Meresq bring the canoe back. After a short visit, Mrs. Rolleston and Cecil strolled down to see them off.

"I have never tried the canoe with a sail up," remarked the latter. "With this wind it must be absolutely flying."

"Not quite so dry," said Lascelles, laughing. "Du Meresq is such a duffer; he ships a lot of water."

"Cecil," said Bertie, giving a pre-conceived idea the air of an *impromptu*, "come up to Coonwood with us; it's lovely scenery all the way, and I should have a companion back."

"What do you say, mamma; may I go?" dropping her eyes and speaking in an indifferent voice, to disguise her delight in the anticipation.

"May I go?" mimicked Lascelles to himself. "Bertie is always sacrificing me to some girl or other. She will swamp the boat,—it's within an inch of the water already with my portmanteau,—and very likely make me miss my train, or get wet through pulling her out." This in soliloquy, but he looked courteous and smiling.

Mrs. Rolleston hesitated; in her heart she acquiesced; but what would the Colonel say? The younger ones took silence for consent, and Cecil was reclining on a bear-skin at the bottom of the canoe, Lascelles kneeling in a cramped attitude, with the steering paddle, in the bow, and Bertie in charge of the sail, before words of prohibition could come from her.

"Dear me! I don't half like it," said she, nervously. "How stormy it looks in the west. How long will it take you?"

"We shall have the wind back," said Bertie. "About two hours and a half—three at the outside. I'll bring her home in good time for dinner,"—and Cecil kissed her hand in laughing defiance while he spread the sail to the wind, and, catching the light breeze after a flap or two, they glided gaily on their course.

"Don't move about, Cecil," said Du Meresq; "we are rather low down in the water."

No one knew better than Cecil, who had quite appreciated the small spice of risk in weighting the frail bark with an additional person; but then it was worth it to sail back alone with Bertie.

"You are getting dreadfully wet, I am afraid, Miss Rolleston," said Lascelles. "Ease the sail a bit, Bertie."

"You shouldn't keep her head to the waves," argued the other, "as if it were a boat. Keep her broadside to them, and we shan't ship half so many."

There was a fresh breeze when they left the landing, but, after getting three miles or so on their way, the wind rose almost into a squall; white horses raced on the lake, and, in spite of every effort of the two young men, about one wave in ten flung a curl of spray over Cecil. Bertie threw off his coat, and made her thrust her arms into it as well as she could, and Lascelles followed suit by spreading his over her knees. The sky became stormier, and the wind howled ominously. They had started full of spirits, and gay talk and chaff had been bandied among them. No one could quite tell when it dropped, for it had been kept up with an effort after the threatening appearance of things had sobered them.

Cecil was drenched to the skin, but they ceased to express solicitude on that account, for a more pressing apprehension filled each mind, that the canoe so weighted could not live through it much longer.

The girl was stiffening in the rigidity of her reclining attitude. The least movement would have capsized them, and each wave larger than the rest she expected to swamp the canoe. Suddenly she remembered Du Meresq having once said he could not swim, and then, for the first time, her heart sunk, and a sickening horror came over her.

Lascelles, she supposed, in the event of their being upset, would endeavour to save her. But Bertie! He would drown before her eyes, for the water was deep, and the shore for some time had been only a nearly perpendicular rock. Probably Lascelles so laden might be unable to land even her. Looking upon Du Meresq as doomed, that contingency did not disturb her. Drowning, she had heard, was a pleasant death. It didn't look so though, with that cruel steel water lapping thirstily for its prey. After the one supreme moment when she sunk with her love, would they rise again in the land where there is neither marrying nor giving in marriage, with the Platonic serenity of spirits, all earthly passion etherealized away?

She looked up; Lascelles was baling out the water with his hat. "Du Meresq, you had better haul down the sail and take the paddle," said he significantly.

"Our only chance is to make Coonwood," returned the other; "there's no landing nearer. We should never get there paddling. I must keep up the sail and run for it."

He glanced at Cecil as he spoke, who met his eyes with a calm, strange smile.

A muttered consultation between Du Meresq and Lascelles alone broke the silence for some time. The latter continued to bale, rejecting Cecil's offer of assistance, only entreating her to continue perfectly still. The canoe was almost level with the water. "It must come very soon now," she thought, and, shutting her eyes, tried to realize the great change approaching.

Her favourite day-dream of sailing away to a new strange country with Bertie recurred to her. What if this was to be the fulfilment of it, and they were to explore for ever an unknown land beyond the skies! But would it be so? No sooner should the frail bark sink from under them than she would feel Lascelles clutch her in a desperate grip, and be dragged through the water, and placed alive, though half-suffocated, on the shore. But Du Meresq would be sucked down in the blue lake, and travel to that bourn alone.

Cecil shuddered, and formed a rapid resolve. "Who was Lascelles that he should separate them? Let him save himself if he thought it worth while. Whatever was Bertie's fate should be hers also."

Thus determined, Cecil waited for the end. She had only to elude Lascelle's grasp at the critical moment, and her fate was as certain as Du Meresq's. She gave a regretful thought to her father; but he had other children, and Cecil had no strong family ties.

As she waited in a state of half exaltation, a quiet little thought crept in,—how was it, after all this time, the boat still lived? Why they could not be far from Coonwood! Lascelles was still baling, but Bertie, from improved dexterity in the management of the sail, evaded the waves more successfully.

Cecil continued to watch, and the tension of her mind yielded to a flutter of hope as she saw the water no longer gained on them.

"We should be pretty near now," observed Lascelles.

"Yes, here we are!" rose in almost a shout of triumph from both, as, on rounding the point, the wished-for harbour appeared in view. With one last effort the envious waves dashed over, drenching them through and through as they landed.

"A drop more or less doesn't much matter now," cried Cecil, gaily, wringing her dripping garments. And they all shook hands in their elation of spirits, with short expressions of relief, and congratulations at their escape, which all confessed to have been in doubt of at one time.

"You are a regular heroine, Miss Rolleston," said Lascelles, heartily. "If you had jumped up, or gone into hysterics, as some girls would, we should have gone under pretty soon. As it was, I thought I had my work cut out, for do you know that Du Meresq can't swim?"

"Yes, I know," grudgingly, for she could not bear Bertie to be at a disadvantage. "But I am sure it is quite miraculous how he managed the sail through that squall."

"Only if we had swamped, Lascelles must have saved you," whispered he, regretfully; "and I would never have forgiven him!"

Cecil did not make any verbal answer, but, as usual, her face was not so reticent. Lascelles felt himself rather *de trop* as he concluded,—"Well, if they are on for a spoon already, I may as well be looking after my car."

"There's your Bullgine," cried Du Meresq, with some alacrity. "I daresay it has been there an hour: no fear of losing a train in this leisurely country!"

"Well, adieu, Miss Rolleston; I trust you will not suffer from your soaking. You will have an hour or two to wait, I am afraid, before the gale goes down, and Du Meresq will hardly fulfil his promise of getting you home in good time for dinner."

"We are only too lucky to require another dinner; but I suppose we shall be in an awful scrape," answered Cecil, speaking quickly and nervously, for somehow she began to half dread being alone with Bertie. "Good-bye, Captain Lascelles. Here's your coat, which you were so good as to spare me;

I am afraid it is not a valuable acquisition in its present spongy state;" and "Good-bye, old man," from the two friends as Lascelles ran off; shooting a momentary humorous glance of intelligence at Du Meresq.

The former, as he settled himself in the locomotive, thought rather seriously of the "situation" he had left his friend in. He rather wondered at Bertie, who appeared dangerously in earnest this time. To be sure, she was a nice enough girl, and very "coiny," he believed; but though convinced that such a marriage would be a piece of good fortune for his friend, remembering the convenience of their mutual partnership, he sincerely hoped he would "behave badly," and get out of the scrape somehow.

CHAPTER XXII
AT LAST

The breeze was dead,
The leaf lay without whispering in the tree;
We were together.
How, where, what matter? Somewhere in a dream,
Drifting, slow drifting down a wizard stream.

The Wanderer.

"It is just as well," said Du Meresq, laughing, "we have not got to take him back again. The experiment of three in that birchen bark is too expensive to repeat; and we could not throw him over as a Jonah, since he is the only one of us who can swim."

"I ought never to have come! And, now we can think of wordly things again, only fancy what a rage papa will be in about it all. It is a curious fact, Bertie, the very last time we were out together, an accident made us late—at the tobogganing party, you know."

They had entered the station, which appeared perfectly deserted. The last official had gone up with Lascelles' train. A fire, however, was still burning, and the coal-box only half empty.

Du Meresq threw the coals on the waning embers, which responded with a cheerful fizz to the needed aliment, and then began unlacing Cecil's wet boots as she sat before the fire.

These two had often been alone together without the slightest embarrassment, but now, perhaps from the reaction, and being a little unstrung, she felt a most distressing sensation of it, besides which the anticlimax of his occupation after her overwrought anticipations of their mutual fate, gave her an hysterical inclination to a peal of laughter.

He did not speak, and silence was too oppressive to be endured, so she cast about desperately for a topic of conversation. The *entourage* was not particularly suggestive,—four white-washed walls and the chair she was sitting on comprised the furniture. Clearly she could not take in ideas with her eyes, which, indeed, were fixed with a magnetic persistence on the mathematically straight parting of Bertie's back hair, which would scarcely furnish subject for remark.

"There go a ruined pair of Balmorals," said he, placing them in the fender. "Your stockings are wet through, too; why don't you take them off?"

"I prefer them wet," said Cecil, rather scandalized.

"Shall I go and walk about outside while you dry them?" asked he, with a smile.

"Yes, do. Walk away altogether if you like."

"But you might drown yourself going home alone, and haunt my remaining days.

> 'They made her a grave too cold and damp
> For a soul so warm and true,
> And all night long, by a fire-fly lamp,
> She paddles her white canoe,'" —

quoted Bertie, jestingly.

Cecil disliked his manner, and felt irritated; but there she was, imprisoned, bootless, in her chair, while those appendages smoked damply in the fender.

"Dear me," she said, impatiently, "will that wind never drop! When shall we be able to start, I wonder?"

"Don't you think we are more comfortable here?" said he, lazily. "Remember what a row there'll be when we get home."

"Yes, you always get me into scrapes. Why did you bother me into this idiotic expedition?"

"Didn't you ask me to take you?" provokingly. "I am sure I understood you wished to come."

Cecil coloured angrily, and then burst out laughing.

"I can't afford to quarrel with you in this disgusting desolation, it would be like the two men in the lighthouse; but remember, sir, it goes down to your account when I am restored to my friends."

"The captive should not use threats. I am not intimidated. What should now forbid that I whirl you away on the next car to *Ne Yock*, and marry you right off? and then you would have to obey me ever afterwards."

"Bertie, you forget yourself," with great dignity and rising colour.

"I can't help my unselfish nature. I never do think of myself. Seriously, Cecil, would it not be a good plan?"

"I hardly understand how you would effect it in broad daylight against my will."

"Nothing more easy. I shouldn't put you into the train till it was just going, and I am sure you would have too much self-respect to make a disturbance. If you did, I would point to my forehead, and shake my head expressively. Then, probably, the guard would assist me. After we were married, I should shut you up for a time to reconcile you to the situation, and by degrees, if you pleased me, I would allow you more liberty."

"Suppose I ran away and never returned."

"Oh, you would always be watched, I should, perhaps, let you get a little distance to encourage you, and then bring you back again."

Cecil would not vouchsafe a retort. She thought Bertie's behaviour in the very worst taste, and had never known him so little agreeable. But there they were incarcerated, and the wind still howled. "How was it they were so little in tune," she wondered, "wasting time with this tactless badinage?" Bertie, too, whose greatest charm was his lightning perception of all her thoughts and feelings, could he possibly think—and here a hot glow mounted to her cheeks, which were not cooled by feeling her hand suddenly captured by Du Meresq, as he whispered in her ear,—

"As we always get into scrapes together, don't you think, Cecil, for the future we had better only be responsible to each other?"

"I think," said she, flaming up at last, and her bright eyes flashing indignantly upon him, "that your conduct is idiotic and ungentlemanly: What right have you to make me the subject of your silly jokes?"

"I have made you look at me at last," cried he, "though I am almost 'blasted with excess of light.' Dearest Cecil, you must know what I have come to Rice Lake for, and that you can make me the happiest or most miserable fellow breathing."

Bertie's eyes were glowing with earnestness, and his whole manner was as eager as it had before been inert. Cecil was dumb from contending emotions, love, pride, and doubt, all at war; yet a small voice in her heart kept repeating "At last!"

"You must have known my wishes ever since we parted at Montreal," pleaded Bertie. ("I was by no means so certain," thought Cecil.) "I could not speak then; your father will, perhaps, think I oughtn't to now. Yet, at least I can say honestly, will you marry me, my dearest little Cecil?"

At the asseveration, "I can say honestly," a sudden illumination came over her face, as if every cloud had been instantaneously swept away.

Persons conversant with such subjects maintain that the plain words, "I will," are generally first used by the bride in church, when she promises to worship M. or N. with her body. No doubt, Bertie was answered somehow; but as there are no reporters in Paradise, so happiness requires no chronicler, and we drop the curtain while Cecil becomes engaged to her ideal and only love—a fate sufficiently uncommon in this world of contradictions.

The wind was lulled to a whisper, and a golden sunset was reddening the lake, ere our lovers remembered, with a start, that they had to get home.

"Now comes the rude awakening," cried Du Meresq. "Dinner spoiled, and a very stern expression of paternal opinion to you, my poor Cecil. Very grumpy to me. By Jove, I won't tell him to-night! Here's your half-baked boots. We shall never get them on. Shall I carry you to the boat, and roll your feet in the bear-skin?"

"I feel as if a hundred years had passed since we were last in the canoe," said Cecil, evading this obliging proposal. "But how the lake has calmed itself down; it seems sleeping, and the shore and the islands cast long shadows on it."

"'Tis one of those ambrosial eves
A day of storm so often leaves,"

began Bertie, with his incurable propensity for quoting. "What made you so shy at the station, Cecil? I was obliged to put you in a rage to get you natural again."

"After the pleasing picture you draw of our domestic felicity, I can't think how I ever accepted you."

"I was just going to begin when I was unlacing your boots, but the idea struck me that to propose holding a lady's foot instead of her hand, would be too ludicrous a variation from all precedent. What a sensitive girl you are, Cecil! I am sure you knew what was coming, for I felt you drawing into a shell of consciousness, that would have made me nervous too, if I had not been impertinent instead"

Cecil was not far from a relapse, for dreamily happy as she was, she had already begun to torment herself. She had accepted Du Meresq so readily,— good Heavens! she might almost say thankfully,—and, disguise it as he might, he must know it. Could a thing be really valued that was so easy of attainment? When Cecil was shy she was usually dumb, it never revealed itself by hasty, foolish speech, or an artificial laugh. Her countenance, however, was not so silent; and Bertie, as he watched her changing hues and varying expression, thought how much more he admired that mobile, sensitive face, than the pink and white of a soul-less beauty.

"Where is your hand, Cecil?" stretching out a long arm to feel for it. "I am sure a dragon of propriety might trust a loving pair in this wabbly little craft, which an attempt at osculation would upset."

There was just breeze enough to fill the little sail, which bore them swiftly and gently along. A pale star came out in the sky. Though dusk, it was far from dark, night in a Canadian summer being of very abbreviated duration. The lovers had relapsed into dreamy reverie, but, as they began to approach more familiar objects, stern reality resumed its sway. Cecil was the first to give evidence of it, by saying, in rather a subdued voice,—

"Don't you think, Bertie, as you must go away to-morrow, you had better get it over to night?"

"Heaven forbid!" cried he, rousing up, "let us have this evening in peace. You see, my dearest little Cecil, he will hate it anyhow, and to-night will be awfully put out at my bringing you home so late; so this would be the very worst opportunity to choose. To-morrow, after dinner, I'll try what I can do with him. I am a shocking bad match for you, Cecil, and that's the fact. But when I went back to Montreal, thinking of nothing but you, I considered and pondered over every possibility of putting my prospects in a fair light to your father. To the amazement of my creditors, I asked for their accounts. Then I made a little arrangement with Green, the senior lieutenant. He is the son of a money-lender, and very sick of being a subaltern; so he paid the over-regulation down on account for my troop, and will shell out the rest, with an extra thousand, directly my papers are in. The over-regulation money, with a little stretching, covered my debts. To be sure, Green had to part pretty freely, but his pater will get it out of some one else. Now, my idea is to realize what remains of my slender fortune, and try my luck in Australia. You see, my darling, you are all right, for all your money will be settled on yourself; so that if I smash up there, the worst that can happen will be your having to maintain me till I can 'strike ile,' or bring out a patent horse-medicine, or become riding-master to young ladies."

"I put my veto on the last," laughed Cecil. "But really, Bertie, I can hardly believe such good news as your being actually cleared up at last; indeed, I almost feel a sentimental attachment to your debts, for it was about them you first got confidential that Spring you stayed with us in England."

"That visit did my business for life," said Bertie, with a wooer's usual disregard of veracity. "But you are far more beautiful now, Cecil, than you were then."

Not even Du Meresq could persuade Cecil that she had any claims to boast of on that score; indeed, she had once overheard him say that he hardly ever admired dark women, so she passed it by with a half smile of incredulity, as she observed, —

"I really begin to have some faint hope of papa consenting. Your being out of debt will weigh tremendously with him."

"And I am sure you will like Australia," cried he, enthusiastically. "It is the most charming climate, and the life delightful. I will send you up a lot of books on the subject."

Cecil was ashamed to confess how many she had read already. "You *must* go by that boat to-morrow night, I suppose?" said she, meditatively.

"Yes; no help for it. But as I shall send my papers in at once, most probably I can get leave till I am gazetted out."

"Oh! I wish that *mauvais quart-d'heure* with papa were over," sighed Cecil. "All to-morrow in suspense!" "Cecil," said Du Meresq, in his most persuasive tones, "it is better to be prepared for the worst. I know you are true as steel, and far firmer than most girls. Promise that you *will* marry me, —with his consent, if possible; if not, without."

They had landed just before, and were walking up to the house. What presentiment checked the unqualified pledge he would have imposed on her?

"I promise," she cried, "to marry no one else while you are alive."

CHAPTER XXIII
LOLA'S BIRTHDAY

She is not fair to outward view,
As many maidens be;
Her loveliness I never knew
Until she smiled on me.
Oh! then I saw her eye was bright,
A well of love—a spring of light

Hartley Coleridge.

Mrs. Rolleston had passed a terrible day of anxiety. The sudden rising of the wind so soon after their departure first aroused her alarm, which, as the utmost limit of the time they were to be away passed, became augmented tenfold. The absence of the Colonel, who had gone inland, at first a relief, now increased her desperation, for there was no one to make an effort for their preservation or to ascertain their fate. She and Bluebell, who suffered scarcely less, could only rush to the boatmen for either consolation or assistance. They got little of the former, for with the usual propensity of the lower classes to make the worst of everything, they expressed a decided opinion that the canoe so overladen could not have weathered the squall.

"But they might have put in somewhere," cried Bluebell, seeing Mrs. Rolleston speechless with consternation.

"How far would they be got, ma'am?"

"They must have been gone nearly an hour before the wind began to howl."

"Then they'd be nigh the black rocks, and no place to land closer than Coonwood, unless they turned back and got on to Sheep Island."

"Oh! go and see!" cried Mrs. Rolleston, beside herself with terror, palling out her purse in answer to the mute unwillingness on the man's face.

"It won't be no manner of use; but if it will be a satisfaction to you, ma'am," looking expressively at the purse, "and my mate will come with me, I'll go out for them. They ought to come down 'ansome," he muttered, "if I finds the bodies."

The two ladies waited to see him off, fretting inwardly at the delay of repairing a plank in the boat and fetching his mate. It was a good substantial old tub, very different from the fairy canoe freighted with those precious human lives. Then they returned to their weary watch in Cecil's bird's-nest of a room, which commanded the most extensive view of the lake. Bluebell's young eyes were the first to discern the tiny white bunting, and hope battled with suspense till they could be sure it was the sail they sought. With the field glass they made out two forms.

"Cecil is safe!" cried Mrs. Rolleston, recognising her large, shady hat. "But still," she thought, "Bertie might be drowned, and Captain Lascelles bringing her home. Oh, Bluebell! can you recognise him?" for the girl had the glasses. They were very strong ones, and her vision keen. A spasm passed over her face.

"Captain Du Meresq is quite safe," said she, bitterly. She had looked at the moment when Bertie stretched out his arm for Cecil's hand, and was carrying it to his lips.

Mrs. Rolleston's raptures were too oppressive just then. Bluebell felt thankful to hear a slight disturbance, which betokened that the Colonel had returned. His wife, quite unnerved by the transition from despair to joy, could conceal nothing, and, rushing down, poured into his ear all the dread and relief of the past hours. The Colonel hearing it thus abruptly, and unsoftened by previous anxiety, only felt intense anger at Cecil's having gone alone with these two men; and the danger and exposure to the storm that she had undergone aggravated the offence considerably. He felt too strongly to say much to his wife, who, indeed, had suffered quite enough already; and the sting of it all—his growing fear of Du Meresq's influence over Cecil—he was not disposed to confide to her.

"I have been too careless," he reflected, "and I cannot trust Bella, who will never see a fault in her brother. However, he will be gone to-morrow, and I will take care they never meet again till Cecil is married."

Mrs. Rolleston, in the restless activity of a lightened heart, had hurried away to order large fires to be lit in their rooms, and hot cordials and everything imagination could suggest placed ready. Indeed she racked her brains to remember what restoratives were usually applied to drowned persons. Holding them up by the heels or *not* doing so (whichever it was), and hot blankets, were the only prescriptions she could recollect; and then the culprits themselves came in, looking particularly fresh and pleased with themselves.

Cecil she proposed instantly to consign to a warm bed, but the girl laughed her to scorn, and would not hear of being shelved in that manner; and, finally, they all came down to dinner, talkative from a delightful sense of reaction. This superfluous effervescence, however, was soon flattened by the unsympathetic gloom of the head of the family. It was very unlike his usual manner, and not a good augury, thought two of the party, who ascribed it to the right cause.

Cecil, however, was determined to resist the damping influence as long as she could. She rattled off lively French airs at the piano, and challenged her father to chess; but he only drily remarked "that after having passed the day in wet clothes, she had better take some ordinary precautions and go to bed." Indeed, her slightly feverish manner perhaps warranted the advice.

"Good night, then, Bertie, and mind you are here early to-morrow for Lola's picnic."

It was the child's birthday, and she had written roundhand invitations to all of them, to spend the day on Long Island and lunch there.

"Tell Lola," said Bertie, smiling, "I would not miss it for the world. She will think me very shabby, but I can't get her a present at Rice Lake."

He went away himself a few minutes after, half hoping to obtain from Cecil a second and more affectionate farewell, but could see nothing of her. Just as he stepped out, though, a casement shot open, and her bright face appeared for an instant as she threw down a rose, round the stalk of which was a slip of paper with the word "*Courage?*" scratched upon it. She put a finger on her lips warningly, then kissed her hand, and vanished.

Bertie picked up the rose. It was one she had plucked as they entered the garden, and worn in her dress that evening.

As he got into one of the various canoes at the landing, another one passed, paddled by a good-looking youth, who half stopped, and gazed intently at Du Meresq, then catching sight of the flower in his button-hole, an expression of baffled rage came over his boyish face, and he shot away.

It was Alec Gough prowling around with his flageolet, intent upon addressing some minstrelsy to Bluebell, and much disconcerted by the sight of Du Meresq coming from that house with a trophy in the shape of a faded rose.

About two hours after, Cecil, too feverish from the exciting events of the day to sleep, became sensible of some strains of music, apparently from the lake. She sat up to listen. Could it possibly be Bertie? No; he was too good a musician for that barrel-organ style; some wandering person from the hotel it must be. The air was familiar to her, though she could not immediately recall the name. At last she recollected it was one of Moore's melodies, and a verse of it, really intended by Alec for an indignant expostulation to Bluebell, came into her head. —

> "Fare thee well, thou lovely one,
> Lovely still, but dear no more;
> Once the soul of truth is gone,
> Love's sweet life is o'er."

One is more prone to fancies and superstitions in the night-time, and something in the sentiment saddened her. The unknown musician did not weaken the effect by playing another air; and Cecil towards morning fell into an unrefreshing slumber, in which her dreams seemed to parody the day's adventures.

Sometimes she was struggling in the water; and then the scene changed—she was being married in a small church, or rather it more resembled the white-washed room at the station. Bertie was presenting her with a rose instead of a ring, while she was trying to conceal 'neath the folds of her bridal dress her feet encased in shapeless Balmorals. Then Colonel Rolleston suddenly appeared and forbade the ceremony to proceed, while the bridegroom seemed to have changed into Fane, and Bertie, as best-man, slowly chanted—

> "Fare thee well, thou lovely one.
> Lovely still, but dear no more."

"Cecil," cried a gay voice, "are you singing in your sleep? Get up. It's my birthday," said Lola, energetically shaking her shoulder.

"Oh, Lola, is it you? I am so glad you woke me! Many happy returns, my child. Have you had any presents?"

"Oh, yes, pretty good ones. I put my stocking out last night, and it was stuffed. A white mouse from Fred in it, too. It ran away and up the bell-rope, and we have been catching it ever since; but," hanging her head, "there was nothing from you, Cecil."

"Well, Lola," remorsefully, "it is never too late to mend. Would you like a locket? Fetch my dressing-case and you shall choose one."

Cecil was too happy herself that morning not to be amiable to others, and Lola was her favourite; so she would not hurry her, and waited patiently the child's indecision and chatter as she turned over the trinkets.

"Actually Miss Prosody gave me a dictionary; horrid of her, wasn't it? Perhaps she'll ask me to say a column a morning. I think I'll leave it by accident on one of the islands."

"I'll buy it of you," said Cecil, smiling. "I don't think I learned columns enough when I was a child."

"Likely you'd do it now, though, as you are not obliged! Well, Cecil, I think I'll take this dear little blue one with a pearl cross on. It is such a hot day! What dress are you going to wear? It must be a pretty one, because it is my birthday."

Cecil smiled contentedly. It was the birthday of something besides Lola—the dawn of a new life to herself. "Here, miss will this do?" asked she, holding up a fresh grey muslin for her sister's inspection.

"Middling," discontentedly, "Bluebell looks well in those cool, simple dresses; but you are never really pretty, Cecil, except in a grand velvet dress, and then you are splendid."

"Fine feathers make fine birds," replied the other, rather hurt. It was not a morning on which she could bear to be told that her attractions must depend on her toilette; but, half-an-hour afterwards, as she knotted some carnation ribbon on the grey dress and in her dusky hair, a shy smile came over her face, for she saw she was beautiful with the light of love. A warm tinge coloured the usually pale cheek, the lips had taken a deeper red, and were parted with a rare *fin* smile—the velvet eyes were softer and of liquid brightness.

So thought Bertie, as his expressive glance but too well revealed when they met at breakfast. He made no attempt to conceal his devotion; his eyes scarcely left her face, and his voice took a different tone in addressing her. Fortunately for Bluebell's peace of mind, she was not present. Mrs. Rolleston noticed it, and rejoiced; the Colonel was equally perceptive, and made an inward resolve.

CHAPTER XXIV
LITTLE PITCHERS

If aught in nature be unnatural,
It is the slaying, by a spring-tide frost,
Of Spring's own children; cheated blossoms all
Betrayed i' the birth, and born for burial,Of budding
promise; scarce beloved ere lost.

Fables In Song.

The whole party were gathered on the lawn after breakfast, preparing for the start, and continually running backwards and forwards for something forgotten. Du Meresq and Cecil were talking apart: the Colonel was to be told that evening after dinner; and Bertie had to get to Cobourg, and catch the night steamer there.

"If we are late back, there will be hardly any time," said the girl.

"Long enough to explain my magnificent prospects, or rather projects. Oh, Cecil, you will be firm, anyhow!"

Her answer was prevented by a clinging sister rushing up. She hummed the words of a favourite air. "Loyal je serai durant ma vie."

Bertie picked a rose and gave it to her. "It exactly matches your ribbons," said he.

It reminded Cecil of her dream, when he gave her a rose instead of a ring, and turned into Fane, and a superstitious chill came over her. At this moment Colonel Rolleston stepped out.

"It is time you people were off. I am only coming with you as far as the hotel to get a trap. I find I must go to Cobourg for letters. I wish, Cecil you would drive with me."

What? give up all those hours with Bertie! His last day, too, and the first of their happiness!

In utter consternation, Cecil cast a most imploring glance at her father; but he, appearing not to see it, continued nonchalantly,—

"It is a long, dull drive, and I shall really be glad of your company."

Du Meresq ground his heel into the gravel with vexation, and Mrs. Rolleston attempted a feeble remonstrance. "The children will be disappointed if Cecil goes away," —which sentiment they eagerly chorussed.

"Well, you must spare her to-day," said their father, "for I want her too. It will be much better for Cecil to take a quiet drive after her exposure yesterday, than to grill on those islands all day."

It was quite evident opposition would be useless. In sullen resignation she entered a boat with the Colonel, and, taking the rudder lines, steered a course away from Long Island, which the picnic party were now making for. She had seen Bertie standing angry and irresolute, and, apparently, not going; and then he must have changed his mind, for as they were just pulling off, he stepped into the vacant place of a boat containing Mrs. Rolleston, Freddy and Bluebell. Not for a moment was she deceived as to the Colonel's motive in causing her to forego her day's amusement. It was not her society that he wanted—it was to separate her from Du Meresq; and who could tell that he might not intend to bring her back too late to see him before he went?

This she determined to resist to the utmost. She did not feel as if she could endure the suspense, if Du Meresq lost this opportunity of speaking, however doubtful might be the result.

Revolving the difficulties in her path only made Cecil more resolute. She would never give Bertie up, neither would she wait to grow prematurely old with the sickness of hope deferred.

If her father refused consent, would a long secret engagement, promising to remain faithful to each other, be their only resource? Cecil smiled at the idea. She did not forget she was an heiress and of age. Love is for the young, and she was far too proud to meditate bestowing herself upon Bertie when years should have quenched hope and spirit, and stealthily abstracted every charm of youth. And as to him? Well, his antecedents had certainly given no promise of the long suffering fidelity of a Jacob.

Colonel Rolleston was pretty well aware of what was passing in his daughter's mind, for his eyes were now fully opened; but he did not choose to show it.

They arrived at Cobourg, where he found his letters; and then the horses were put up to bait, and they went to the hotel for luncheon.

Cecil expressed a hope that they would be able to return when the horses were rested.

"Certainly," said her father; "we will drive back to dinner."

And, much relieved, she brightened up considerably.

Now the Colonel would rather have detained her long enough there to ensure passing Du Meresq on the road; but the *ennui* of spending so many hours in so uninteresting a place, and the absence of any excuse for waiting, favoured Cecil's wishes.

Still the time seemed interminable to her in that dusty inn parlour, with its obsolete Annuals, cracked pianoforte, and ugly prints on the walls. Surely no horses ever required so long a rest, and when her father suggested ordering her some tea, it seemed almost like *malice prepense* to occasion a further delay.

However, they were off at last, and as they rattled along in their shaky conveyance, she became painfully conscious of its discomfort. Every jolt was anguish, and her head and all her limbs were aching. Was it the ducking yesterday, or only this dreadful springless buggy?

They reached the landing before any of the party had returned, and Cecil sought her gable and threw herself on the bed, trusting to rest to remove some of her unpleasant sensations.

As she closed her eyes, she fell into a not unhappy reverie. True, there were opposition and difficulties to contend with, but Bertie was her own, and she would never doubt him more. How disinterested and straightforward he had been in freeing himself from debt before he spoke at all? Even her father must acknowledge that; also that he had sufficient money for the career he had chosen, and only valued her fortune as a security and comfort to herself.

The unutterable luxury of being able to think of him unrestrained only dated from yesterday; for before there was always the humiliating dread that her idolatry was only returned in the same measure in which it was distributed among his somewhat numerous loves. But now distrust had all melted away, and she cared not for the many who had hooked, and lost, since she had landed him.

Aroused by the splash of oars on the lake, Cecil tried to spring from the bed, but her limbs were stiff and heavy, and she dragged herself languidly to the window. They were all on the landing but Du Meresq, and the quick pulsation stilled again.

"I suppose he went first to the hotel," thought she, and began arranging her hair, disordered by the pillow. She heard Lola running upstairs, and called her as she passed.

"I am coming, Cecil. I have got a message for you from Bertie, which is, that he has only gone up to the hotel, and will be here in ten minutes."

Cecil kissed the welcome Mercury, and drew her into the room shutting the door.

"Well, dear, and did you have a pleasant day? What did you do?"

"Oh, yes," said Lola, whose eyes were glittering with excitement, and who had altogether rather a strange manner. "That is to say, pretty well. We didn't do much."

"How was that?"

"Why, Bertie and Bluebell were so stupid. They went away by themselves for ever so long."

Cecil felt as if a hand had suddenly clutched her heart and frozen the blood in her veins. Could that pale face, with wildly gleaming eyes, be the same so sweet and tranquil, that was carelessly smiling at the child an instant before?

"And do you know, Cecil," pursued Lola, warming with her subject, and speaking with intense excitement, "Bertie kissed Bluebell. I saw him do it."

A pause, and the child, apparently gratified by the interest she had awakened, continued,—

"I think Bluebell was crying, and he trying to console her; at any rate, I heard him say he 'loved her very much.'"

One has noticed some years warm weather set in delusively early, and blossoms of fruit and flowers nursed in its smiles peep prematurely forth; and then a biting frost and northeast wind will spring up, the sun all the while treacherously shining, and in one hour destroy the bud and promise for ever. No less swift was the scathing power wielded by that innocent executioner. Every word, fraught with conviction and crushing evidence, sank deep down into her heart. She sat so still that Lola got frightened, and entreated her to say what was the matter; but Cecil appeared unconscious of her presence, and, scared and bewildered, the child shrank away.

Then the girl rose up, and with rapid, uneven steps paced the room. After a while, first bolting the door, she unlocked a sandal-wood box, where, tied with a ribbon and carefully dated, was a packet of Bertie's letters. One by one she patiently read them through, noting and comparing passages, then tying them up, wrote the day of the month and the hour on a slip of paper, and finally enclosed all in an outer cover, which she sealed with her signet-ring, and directed to Du Meresq. This done, the restless walk was resumed. Her head was burning, and throbbed almost too wildly to think. One line seemed ceaselessly to ring in it, that had mingled with her dreams last night, and recurred with hateful appropriateness, —

"Once the soul of truth is gone, love's sweet life is o'er."

Contempt of herself for having been so duped added bitterness to these thoughts. How long and easily had Bertie and Bluebell hoodwinked her to be on the terms they were, and doubtless had often laughed over her simplicity and short-sightedness! But Lola had described her in tears, not smiles; and then Bertie appeared baser than ever. He loved Bluebell, yet would sacrifice her for Cecil's fortune; for the unhappy girl no longer believed in his disinterested professions of the day before. No! she was dark and unlovely, and her rival beautiful, in his favourite style! And Du Meresq was black and treacherous, as a smothered instinct had sometimes warned her.

Mrs. Rolleston came to the door and begged her to come down. Lola's account had startled her. Cecil entreated to be left alone; "she had a splitting headache, and wished to be quiet;" and on her step-mother effecting an entrance, the sight of her face left no doubt of the validity of the excuse.

"Bertie will be so disappointed if he does not see you to-night," cried she regretfully. A bitter smile, and the reiteration, "I cannot come down."

"Your hand is burning, child. You are in a fever. What *is* the matter?"

Cecil coldly withdrew it, in the same somnambulistic manner, and said she would lie down; and Mrs. Rolleston went out, hurt by her want of confidence, and much bewildered by many events of that day.

Lola next invaded her, sent by Bertie to entreat for admission. "He only just wants to come in for a minute, and see how you are."

"I can't see *any one*, my head is too bad; tell Bertie so. I am going to lock the door, and go to bed."

But she only threw herself on it. The light waned and darkened, and the moon arose. Then Cecil stole cautiously to the window and watched. Presently Du Meresq came out alone, and she knew he was on his way to the boat. He would look up, she was sure, and she entrenched herself behind the curtain. By the light of the moon she saw his gaze rivet itself on her window, as though it would pierce the gloom. His face was strangely pale, and even sad, and her rebellious heart throbbed wildly as she felt how perilously dear he still was to her. He turned away. Whatever he wore or did, there was a picturesque grace about him, thought Cecil; and as his boat became smaller and smaller in the distance, she wished, in the bitterness of her heart, they had both sunk in the squall of yesterday, e'er she had discovered how falsely he had lied to her.

Lola again disturbed her. "Papa says he is coming up in ten minutes to see you. Bertie told me to tell you he was very sorry you would not speak to him, or say good-bye."

Lola had dined late, it being her birthday, and wore Cecil's locket on a ribbon, but she looked scared and depressed. "It was so dull downstairs," she said. "Mamma had gone away after dinner, and talked a long time to Bluebell. Bertie had not come out of the dining room till it was time to go, and she had had no one to speak to but Miss Prosody—not a bit like a birthday."

"Lola," said Cecil, much too preoccupied to attend to her complaints, "has the letter bag gone down to the boat yet?"

"I saw it still open in the passage."

"Then run down quick with this big letter—you understand? Don't stop to speak to any one, but put it in the bag and come back and tell me when it is done."

The child looked at the address "Why, Cecil," said she, curiously, "this is for Bertie! What a pity I couldn't have given it to him before he went! What a lot of postage stamps it takes!"

"Never mind, dear, run away with it," anxiously.

Lola was but just in time before the Colonel came out, locked the bag, and went upstairs to his daughter.

Pre-occupied as he was, he was startled at her changed appearance. A shawl was thrown around her, and she appeared shivering, while a fever spot burned on either cheek. The Colonel was alarmed and irritated. "It is all that folly yesterday. Have your fire lit, and go to bed, but I must say a word or two first."

No assistance from Cecil, he took a turn or two about the room, surprised at her apathy. It was very difficult to begin, he wished to be kind, but was determined to be firm. How indifferent she seemed. Perhaps she would not care so very much.

"Cecil," he began, "you will guess what I wish to speak about. I don't know whether I was more surprised or annoyed at Du Meresq's preposterous proposal for you to-night."

"What did he say, papa?"

"Why," perplexed at her unusual manner, which exhibited no surprise and little curiosity, "all he had to say was, that he wished to abandon his profession, and take you on a wild goose chase to the Antipodes. That in itself would have been quite sufficient, but there are other reasons, I have not a good opinion of Du Meresq, and I had almost rather see you in your grave than married to him." Cecil made no sign, and the Colonel continued, — "It may seem hard now, but you will live to thank me. I wish you, Cecil, since he will not be satisfied with less, to write a few lines and tell him all must be at an end between you."

She rose mechanically, brought her writing-desk, and took out pen and paper.

"What shall I say?" she asked, tranquilly.

The Colonel, who was prepared for determined opposition from his strong willed daughter, knew not whether to be most relieved or confounded by this apathetic submission. "I will leave the composition to you," said he, gently.

"Thank you," said Cecil "I should prefer writing it from your dictation."

"Say, then," returned her father, not ill pleased to get it expressed strongly "that you find I am so irrevocably opposed to your marriage with him, that you have no alternative but to give up all thoughts of it for the future, and that he must understand this decision to be final."

Deliberately, and with the same stony indifference, she wrote it word for word, handed it to her father to read then sealed the letter with her own signet-ring, and returned it to him.

"It will be Fane yet," thought the bewildered Colonel, with a secret glow of hope. "I was mistaken, her heart is not in this business—if she has one," was the irrepressible doubt, for though Bertie's ardent suit had left him inflexible, his daughter's insensibility almost disgusted him.

Muttering to himself, "That job's over," with a lightened heart he sought his wife, and directed her to go to Cecil, whom he thought far from well. But an interview with Bertie's sister just then was too distasteful to the unhappy girl, and she only answered Mrs. Rolleston's request, that she would open the door, by entreaties to be left in peace and allowed to sleep.

It would have been better had she admitted her not only into her room, but her confidence for the kind lady knew what even Cecil might have acknowledged to be extenuating circumstances, but she now felt completely alienated and distanced by the forbidding reserve of her step daughter, of whom she was not altogether devoid of awe.

The next day an express was on its way to Peterboro' for a doctor. Cecil was down with rheumatic fever, and delirious.

CHAPTER XXV
CHANGES

I remember the way we parted.
The day and the way we met;
You hoped we were both broken hearted;
I knew we should both forget.

A hand like a white wood-blossom
You lifted, and waved and passed
With head hung down to the bosom,
And pale, as it seemed at last.

Swinburne.

Du Meresq in indignant dismay at the abduction of Cecil on the day of the picnic stood awhile silent and bitter, deaf to the impatience of the children, who wanted to be off. While thus irresolute, he chanced to glance at Bluebell, whose countenance betrayed an agony of suspense. The entreating look in her eyes she was probably unconscious of, for the child had not yet learned to command her face. Bertie yielded to it by a sort of magnetism, and flung himself into the boat where she and Mrs. Rolleston were already seated, but remained silent and thoughtful as they floated monotonously along. His sister was equally occupied with uneasy reflections, and Bluebell seemed as spell-bound as the rest. For one soul deeply moved and agitated often affects by electricity another in a receptive condition. Does not the atmosphere in a tempestuous mood thrill and disturb our nervous system?

She was next to Bertie, and noted that, though concealed by rugs and waterproofs, his hand did not seek hers as of yore.

They were joined on Long Island by the rest of the party, and all kept pretty much together at first. There was luncheon to be unpacked, the fire to be made and some fish to be grilled in a frying-pan. Du Meresq partially shook off his gloom, and assisted the children in their preparations; and, from the noise that ensued, a stranger would not have suspected the mental disquietude of three of the number.

After luncheon, Bluebell wandered away in search of wild flowers, the children hunted for cray-fish, Miss Prosody spudded up ferns, and Mrs. Rolleston drew from her pocket her favourite point-lace.

Du Meresq, hungering for that exclusively masculine solace, tenderly brought forth the pipe of his affections, nestling next his heart. There was too much air on the beach, and he sauntered away in search of a more sheltered situation in which to woo his divinity.

Some "spirit in his feet" must have led him "who knows how," for ere long he found himself seated on a log beside Bluebell. I cannot tell what spell that syren had used to attract his footsteps so unerringly, for, little accustomed as he was to resist female influence, in thought at least Du Meresq was loyal enough to Cecil.

He made no attempt to kiss her, as he would have done before in a similar situation, but talked a while in that half-fond, half-bantering manner that had misled the inexperienced child. The sun poured its level rays upon them, and a little brown snake, with a litter of young, crawled from beneath the log. This occasioned a hasty change of quarters, and they found another seat o'ershadowed by a tangle of blackberries. It was very secluded and still, and here, with her whole soul, in her eyes, Bluebell abruptly asked Bertie her dreaded question.

Rather taken back, he answered evasively. But the ice once broken, she was not to be turned from her purpose, and repeated, as if it were a stereotyped form of words she had been practising, "I only wish to ask one single thing, are you engaged to Cecil?"

Du Meresq was no coxcomb. He was distressed at the repressed agitation in Bluebell's voice, her hueless face, and the hopeless look in eyes he remembered so beaming, and for the moment heartily wished he had never seen her.

"How young she looks, with her lap full of flowers. Like an unhappy child," thought he remorsefully. "I must tell her the truth; she'll soon get over it."

Very gently he took her hand, and said, gravely,—"I asked Cecil yesterday to marry me, and she said yes."

Bluebell staggered to her feet, with perhaps a sudden impulse of flight, but so unsteadily that Du Meresq involuntarily threw a supporting arm round her. At that moment Lola, in search of blackberries, and herself concealed by the bush she was rifling, peeped through the brambles, and remained a petrified and curious observer.

Bluebell, struggling for composure, tried to speak, but the effort only precipitated an irrepressible flood of tears, and Du Meresq, grieved and self-reproachful, in his attempts to console her, used the fatal words that Lola afterwards repeated to Cecil. The child escaped without her presence being detected.

Bluebell's emotion had passed over like a storm that clears the atmosphere. It left her calm and cold, and only anxious to be away from Du Meresq.

There is a bracing power in knowing the worst. He had gained her affections without the most distant intention of matrimony, and resentment and shame restored her to composure.

She turned her large child-like eyes on him with mute reproach.

"You should have told me before," were her first articulate words. "No wonder Cecil hated me when you were pretending to care for me behind her back."

Bertie murmured,—"There was no pretence in the matter."

"Then why do you marry Cecil?" asked Bluebell, with the most uncompromising directness. "Is it because she is rich?"

"Confound it," thought Du Meresq; "I trust she won't suggest that to Cecil."

"Can't I love you both?" cried he, somewhat irritated; and just then Miss Prosody and her brood appeared in sight.

"I return you my share," exclaimed Bluebell, breaking abruptly from him, and, running down the path, joined the governess and children.

Du Meresq had rather a bad quarter of an hour over the pipe which this sentimental episode had extinguished; but he could not regret, in the face of his new engagement, the *finale* of a past and now inopportune love-affair.

Bluebell did not come down to dinner that day nor see Du Meresq again; but afterwards, Mrs. Rolleston, who was in nobody's confidence, and had the uneasy conviction that something was going desperately wrong, came into her room.

Bluebell's state of repression could endure no longer. She began by entreating Mrs. Rolleston to accept Mrs. Leighton's situation, and let her go to England at once; and after that it did not take much pressing to induce her to make full confession of all that had passed.

It must be remembered that Bluebell was under the impression that her friend had always known of the flirtation between herself and Bertie; but now for the first time the horror-stricken Mrs. Rolleston had her eyes opened to what had been passing before them.

Everything burst on her at once. Recollection and perception awoke together. To keep it from Cecil seemed the most urgent necessity, and the removal of Bluebell the thing most to be wished for.

Bluebell was disposed to keep back nothing, and answered every question with frank recklessness. She told of their first walk in the wood, their frequent interviews at "The Maples," and Bertie's visit to the cottage, laughing at the idea of having ever seriously cared for Jack Vavasour.

Mrs. Rolleston remembered that Cecil had not shared her delusion on that subject, and anxiously inquired if she had ever acknowledged to her her *penchant* for Bertie.

Bluebell answered in the negative, giving as a reason that, though unable to guess the cause, her manner had always repelled any approach to confidence on that subject.

Mrs. Rolleston remembered Cecil's strange behaviour that afternoon, but she had not even seen Bluebell since the picnic. It remained unaccountable.

She reflected with vexation on the fatality that had made her refuse the child's confidence so many months before; but yet she hoped no harm was done, since Bluebell averred that Bertie and Cecil were engaged.

The letter to Mrs. Leighton was written that night ready for the morning mail; another was also despatched to Mrs. Leigh at Bluebell's request, who was anxious that Mrs. Rolleston should break the rather summary measures to her—not that the latter anticipated much difficulty there. All Canadians have a great idea of a visit to England, which they tenaciously speak of as "home," and "the old country." And she would probably be glad that Bluebell should see her father's birthplace.

At the child's express wish, it was also arranged for her to go home at once, as companionship with Cecil could now be agreeable to neither of them.

Mrs. Rolleston had only seen Du Meresq for a moment before he went away, yet his manner, no less than her step-daughter's, clearly indicated that something was wrong. Even Colonel Rolleston had taken up an attitude of impenetrable reserve, and his wife was completely at fault. Next day, however, the shock and terror of Cecil's illness fell upon them, turning her mind to a more immediate subject of anxiety.

Bluebell could not do less than offer to remain, and share the vigils in the sick room; but even in delirium Cecil became palpably worse when her rival approached, so, in a few days, with much sadness, she bade farewell to those who had made the world of her "most memorial year."

While Cecil was hovering on the borderland of mental darkness, a note came for her from Bertie, written on receipt of the packet that Lola had posted and was as follows:—

> "What can I imagine, Cecil, from this parcel of my letters returned without a word beyond the date and hour? You must have packed them up at the very time I, as we had agreed, was asking for you from your father. I shall not speak of the almost insulting way in which he received my proposals, for that we had anticipated; but you had promised in any event to be true to me. You could not have changed in a summer day, I know your nature, my dearest little Cecil, and you would not have deserted me in this crisis unless your vulnerable side, jealousy, had been awakened. Indeed you have no cause for it. I cannot come back to the Lake, for your father would not receive me, but shall make no plans till I hear from you.
>
> "Yours, as ever, devotedly,
>
> "B."

It was three weeks before Cecil could read this letter, and the following day Du Meresq got hers, written at her father's dictation.

It was not a soothing one for an ardent lover to receive, and Bertie was at first furious, and considered himself very ill used. With it all, though, he never believed that Cecil had really changed. He thought very probably his unfortunate flirtation with Bluebell had come out; returning his letters looked like an *accès* of jealousy, and the one she had written was probably prompted by the same cause.

Any way, though, he was at a dead lock. Her father, of course, would not allow her to see him, and while she was in this mood writing was useless. His papers were in, and tired of inaction at Montreal, he obtained leave to go to England. He lingered time enough to have received an answer to his letter, and, none coming, he took the first steamer homeward-bound.

Du Meresq had not acquainted his sister of his engagement to Cecil; for being aware of the Colonel's inimical disposition, he did not wish to draw her into any difficulty about it. She did not even know that he had written to Cecil since he left, as the letter had fallen into her husband's hands, who, though not intending to withhold it altogether, considered it a document that might very well wait her convalescence.

Mrs. Rolleston wished to apprise Bertie of Cecil's dangerous illness, but she had allowed one mail to pass, and they only recurred once a week, so that Du Meresq was embarking at Quebec the day her letter arrived at Montreal.

Cecil made a slow recovery. The rheumatic fever, caused by sitting so many hours in wet clothes, and aggravated by the shock she had since received, hung about her many weeks, and as soon as she could be moved they took her back to Toronto. Then her father most unwillingly gave her Du Meresq's letter. He was too honourable to destroy it; but, looking upon him as the frustrator of his plans for Cecil, and the indirect cause of her illness, viewed with impatience any chance of a renewal of intercourse.

Cecil read it repeatedly; but though her heart longed to believe, her mind remained unconvinced. She shrank from all mention of the subject with her step-mother, knowing how one-sided a partisan she would be, but could not deny herself the self-torture of questioning Lola again. The child relentlessly stuck to her text, painting the scene with a vividness that did credit to her descriptive powers; and being one of those vivacious and ubiquitous children never to be sufficiently guarded against, was able to mention one or two other occasions on which she had "popped on them."

And all that time Bertie had apparently been devoted to herself! This was decisive. Lola could have no interest in deceiving her. She must not answer his letter or be his dupe again.

Bluebell's approaching departure to England still further corroborated Lola's story. At that picnic on Long Island, Bertie had evidently acknowledged his engagement to herself, which she now fully believed to be a mercenary one, as, doubtless, he had also assured her rival. But perpetual lonely walks and rides were unfavourable to oblivion, and had Du Meresq been but on the spot, I think even then the mists between these two lovers would soon have been drawn aside.

Mrs. Rolleston wondered that she had not heard from Bertie, but imagined he was somewhere on leave. Cecil would not speak on the subject, but she mentioned it sometimes to Bluebell with surprise, who was much perplexed to guess what could have divided them. Her own conscience was easy; she had told Cecil nothing—indeed, they had never met since the latter's illness. Bluebell was now with her mother, preparing for her journey to England, and had persistently avoided going to "The Maples."

A very cordial acceptance had come from Mrs. Leighton, who said Evelyn was all impatience for her musical friend. Mrs. Rolleston, who was now a frequent visitor at the cottage, laughed a little at the letter, which was very gushing, and told Bluebell they were an emotional pair. Evelyn was strangely brought up,—every fancy, however extravagant, gratified, partly on account of her delicate health, and partly from the sentimental sympathy of her mother. One whim was, she would never learn from ugly people, and the supply of beautiful governesses being limited, her education was proportionably so also.

Mrs. Leighton sent minute directions. She would pay Miss Leigh's passage-money, giving her rather less salary the first year. Of course she was to come under protection of the captain, to whom the *rôle* of heavy father to unchaperoned girls is usually relegated; and on arriving at Liverpool the railway journey to Leighton Court would be only a few hours.

Mrs. Rolleston gave her a pretty travelling dress, and otherwise replenished her slender wardrobe. She also contributed a little good advice as to abstention from flirting, explaining that in her unprotected situation she could not be too sceptical of the honest intentions of would-be wooers.

Bluebell indignantly repudiated the possibility of thinking of such a thing for the present, if, indeed, ever, and professed the most ascetic sentiments.

It was rather hard on Mrs. Leigh, this far-away separation from her only child—indeed, she could not understand why she was not engaged to one or other of the whilom visitors at the cottage, but comforted herself with the reflection that there were doubtless many rich husbands in England. Bluebell, like her father, seemed of a roving disposition, and she must let her fledgling try her wings.

Mrs. Leigh was romantically inclined, and thought a heroine setting out on her adventures should be provided with some talisman, and, in this case, proof of her origin. So she disinterred from the old hair-trunk, where it was usually entombed, the miniature of Theodore Leigh. How young he looked! more like Bluebell's brother. "You must never lose it," said she to her daughter; "for if your grandfather left his money to you after all, I dare say the lawyers would try and prove you were some one else; so it is as well to have your father's portrait to show, and your eyebrows are brown and arched just like his."

Though at a loss to comprehend why lawyers should display such unprovoked enmity, Bluebell gladly received the miniature. Her unknown father represented to her another and more brilliant life; and when most discontented at the penury of the cottage, she was fond of picturing to herself her paternal relations, whom she imagined very grand people, and in a very different position to that in which she had been brought up. In these last days, Bluebell thought a good deal of Cecil with some return of her old affection. She remembered how generous and dear a friend she had been till Bertie came between, and thought how ungrateful she must consider her to have clandestinely stolen away the only treasure she would have been unwilling to share with her. Still, even were they to meet, nothing she could say would do any good, for Bluebell knew of old how difficult it was to speak to Cecil on any subject she was determined to avoid, and it was not likely she would be particularly approachable on this one.

So, upon the whole, it would be a relief to get away, and break new ground, leaving painful associations behind; and the bustle of preparation for the voyage was not without interest.

Miss Opie presented her with a brown-holland bag, divided off for brushes, slippers, etc., which she enjoined her to hang up in the cabin. "Habits of neatness are always of great importance in a confined space; and I have put in a paper of peppermint lozenges in case of sea-sickness," she added.

It was the last evening at home, and every bit of furniture in the once despised house seemed instinct with a meaning no other place could have for her.

There was the old piano, on which she used to dream away so many hours; and that arm-chair seemed still haunted by the vision of her handsome, faithless lover, as she had seen him in the gloaming.

How long they had lived there! The little china dog on the shelf was the same she used to play with on the floor before she could walk. Dull and trite, and only too well known as these objects might be, a sentimental interest seemed now to hallow them. Youth is selfish, and takes all affection as its due; but even the slight brush with the world Bluebell had already sustained, gave her the consciousness that, tired as she might be of her limited life at home, never need she expect to meet elsewhere such unselfish tenderness as a mother's.

CHAPTER XXVI
CROSSING THE HERRING POND

A few short hours, the sun will rise
To give the morrow birth;
And I shall hail the main and skies,
But not my mother earth.

Childe Harold.

The morning rose clear and brilliant. The partings were over, and Bluebell, on the deck of the river steamer, was gazing her last on the long flat shore, with its high elevators, and waving adieu to the diminishing forms of Mrs. Leigh and Miss Opie, who had seen her on board,—the latter with many injunctions to ascertain that two old-fashioned hirsute trunks containing her wardrobe were really put into the steamer at Quebec. Bluebell had treated herself to a smart little portmanteau for the cabin, being rather ashamed of her antediluvian luggage. She had ten sovereigns in her purse, that had been scraped together among them as a provision for any emergency. The Rolleston children had sent her a travelling-bag; but not even a message came from Cecil, which saddened Bluebell, but did not make her resentful, for she could not but suspect that the former's engagement to Bertie had come to an end, and that, in some way or other, she herself had been the cause of it.

A touch of frost during the last fortnight had worked a transformation on the foliage. The thousand islands were changed from green bowers to the semblance of shrubberies of rhododendron, so brilliant were the crimson and red of their leaves. They were associated in her mind with Cecil, whose artistic eye revelled in the autumn tints, and was perpetually painting and grouping them during the last fall.

It was rather lonely and monotonous in the river steamer. There was no one on board that she knew, and, as each hour increased the distance from all familiar places, a feeling of friendlessness stole over her.

Arrived at Quebec, every one seemed to push before and jostle her away; but patiently following in the stream, she found herself, with a sensation of relief on board the huge Leviathan steamer that was to be her home across the broad Atlantic.

Some misgivings respecting luggage obtruded themselves. A porter had put her portmanteau and bag on board, but the two trunks she had never seen. No one seemed to attend to her till one man gruffly replied, — "That if they were properly addressed, they would be put into the hold all right." And Bluebell took comfort in the remembrance of the labels plentifully nailed on by Aunt Jane, that she had then thought looked so nervously ridiculous.

She sat for some time alone in the saloon, waiting till the rush for state rooms should have a little subsided before making a timid request for her own.

Several people were now returning, apparently with disburdened minds, for anxious wrinkles were smoothed out into complacent curiosity. Bluebell made an incoherent attack on the stewardess, who swept by, without attending, and after being passed on from one official to the other, she found herself half-proprietess of a dark confined den, with two berths, two wash-hand-stands, and a sofa. Her partner in these luxuries had apparently taken possession and gone, for rather a queer shawl lay on one berth, and a singularly tasteless hat hung on a peg.

These significant articles deprived the little dungeon of all charms of privacy, and, feeling as if it belonged so much more to the other lodger, and she herself were somewhat of an intruder, Bluebell left her small effects in the portmanteau, which she stowed away in the most unobstrusive manner, not even venturing to hang up the brown-holland contrivance of Aunt Jane.

Then she found her way on deck, where most of the passengers were congregated, and, sitting down on a centre bench, in rather inconvenient proximity to a skylight, was sufficiently amused in speculating on her fellow travellers.

"My comrade can't be among them," she thought, "for she has left her hat below."

Most noticeable were a young officer and his bride, as Bluebell immediately decided the latter to be, partly from her helpless *exigeante* demeanour, and partly from the extreme newness of her fashionable get up.

The minuteness and height of her heels were more conducive to the Grecian bend than preserving a balance on a sloping deck, and her fanciful aquatic costume of pale-blue serge more adapted to a nautical scene in private theatricals than for contact with the drenching spray of the rough Atlantic.

But ere the anchor weighed she shone pre-eminent, and had the gratification of making a dozen other women feel shabby and dissatisfied.

In contrast to these was a sickly-looking, middle-class person, with two children tastefully arrayed in purple frocks, red stockings, and magenta comforters. They were clinging to a coarse-looking girl, also with a preference for cheerfulness of hue, who carried a felt donkey, and seemed to be the nursery-maid.

The head of this household, apparently, was not going to accompany them, and, indeed, appeared in rather a more elevated condition than could be wished. He addressed Bluebell, and inquired if her cabin was near his wife's, and, on professing ignorance, said he trusted it might prove so, as "he naturally felt great anxiety at her travelling so lone and unprotected like,"—a slight unsteadiness of gait showing how irreparable was the loss of her legitimate defender. The people around stared and smiled, but he continued to gaze, in a mournful and approving way, at Bluebell, while his wife sat in a state of repressed endurance, calculating how many more minutes he would have for exposing himself before the tug separated friends from passengers.

After a playful feint to throw one of his children overboard, he became calmer, and relapsed into a maudlin monologue till the bell rang, when he was hustled off, much to Bluebell's relief as well as his wife's, whose set mouth relaxed as if a care had rolled away.

Two or three officers on leave were pacing up and down, and with them another young man, but, whether he were civil or military, Bluebell could not decide. He was not exactly like either; there was a slight oddness about his dress, which, though well cut, was carelessly put on, and rather incongruous in different parts. The neck-tie was a little awry, and not the right colour for the coat; still he seemed gentlemanly—rather distinguished-looking than not.

These were all the portraits she took in till the bell rang for luncheon, and there was a general desertion of the deck. Being, by this time, very hungry, Bluebell followed in the string, but felt dubious where to seat herself, as she found people had already appropriated their places by pinning their cards on the table-cloth.

The captain, who had just come in, observing her, asked if she were Miss Leigh, and then took her to a seat next but one to himself.

"You must look upon me *in loco parentis*," said he, good-naturedly, with a strong Scotch accent.

Being the first friendly word she had heard, Bluebell thanked him with a heartiness of gratitude that caused her neighbour on the left to glance at her with furtive interest. It was the young man with the deranged neck-tie. On her right was a haughty dame, who evidently considered herself a person of position. Next the captain, on the opposite side, was an elderly widow lady, with weak eyes and rather methodistical appearance; and on her left a fussy, brisk-looking little woman, of about thirty-five. Then came the bride and bridegroom, a doctor, an aunt and niece, and the rest were out of range of our heroine.

Days at sea are very long, and this first one seemed nearly interminable to Bluebell. She walked on deck till she was tired, and read a book till she shivered, and then retreated to her cabin, to find the fussy little lady of five-and-thirty extended on the sofa. "Ah!" cried she, "I have been wondering all day who my fellow-lodger was to be; let me introduce myself, as we are to have such close companionship. I am Mrs. Oliphant, of the 44th; you are Miss Leigh, I heard the captain say. I am lying down, you see, for I have such a dread of sea-sickness, and it is such a good thing for it."

They were not out of the river and it was like glass. Bluebell, feeling particularly well, laughed inwardly, as she inquired if Mrs. Oliphant was a bad sailor.

"Middling; very much like the rest. You see I have been settling everything conveniently—while I can."

She spoke as if she had just made her last will and testament, and certainly everything was very commodiously arranged—for Mrs. Oliphant. Not a peg or a corner was left for any properties of Bluebell's, who perceived she would have to keep all her effects in the portmanteau, and drag it out for everything she wanted.

"But I always try and cheer up other people," said the little lady, complacently. "I have a bad bout, and then I go and visit others, and keep up their spirits—going round the wards I call it. When I came out, Mrs. Kite, of our regiment, and Mrs. Dove, of the 100th 'Scatterers,' would have laid themselves down and died if it hadn't been for me; but I roused them—Mrs. Kite, at least—for poor Mrs. Dove gave way so, she wasn't out of her berth for a week, and could keep down nothing but a peppermint, and the stewardess never came near her."

"But surely everybody won't be ill!" said Bluebell, somewhat appalled by these statistics, and, with the close air of the cabin, feeling her head swim a little. "I believe it is better not to think about it."

"Certainly; let us change the subject. Will you hand me my eau-de-Cologne? And so you have never been to England before."

"Never," responded Bluebell, not inveigled into giving any further information by Mrs. Oliphant's look of curiosity.

"Perhaps you are going out now to be married?" (archly.)

"No," said the girl, composedly; "if that were the case I should hope my intended husband would come and fetch me."

"Well," said the lady, finding she was to extract nothing, "I suppose we must be getting ready for dinner. In the P. and O. it used to be full evening costume, but one soon has to give that up on the Atlantic; so you see I just change my body for a white Garibaldi, and put a coloured net on. I have four nets, mauve, magenta, green, and blue; these make a nice change."

But in spite of her extreme satisfaction in her own arrangements, she felt secretly disgusted at the freshness of Bluebell's appearance in an uncrushable soft *barége* trimmed with blue. It was also rather a blow to observe those thick shining coils of chestnut hair were not supplemented from the stores of any Translantic *coiffeur*.

When they came to dinner, a little more motion was perceivable as they were entering the Gulf, and the table was mapped out with ominous-looking frames of wood for the confinement of plates and glasses. The bride came down gorgeously attired in a Parisian garb of mauve silk, cut square, but looking slightly white and less secure of admiration than she had in the morning.

"That is not a very serviceable dress for a sea voyage," whispered Bluebell's neighbour, seriously. A few remarks had already passed between them, and she had discovered him to have large, demure, brown eyes, that never appeared to notice anything except for the gleams of secret amusement that occasionally danced in them. "It quite sets my teeth on edge seeing those stewards tilting the soup close to and trampling on it."

"She must be a bride, I suppose," returned Bluebell, "and has so many new dresses, she doesn't care about spoiling one or two."

"Heavens! what a view of matrimony! And these are the reckless opinions of young ladies of the present day! Why, Miss Leigh, the greater part of my great-grandmother's *trousseau* still exists in an old trunk; and my cousin Kate went to a fancy ball in her tabinet paduasoy, which was as good as new."

"How tired they must have got of their things! I should like to have a new dress every day of my life, and a maid to take away the old ones," cried Bluebell recklessly.

"How much does a dress cost—making, trimming, and all."

"Oh, some would be simple and inexpensive, of course—say, on an average, £6 all round."

"That would be more than £1,800 a year, without counting Sundays. You'll have to marry in the city, Miss Leigh."

"I shall have to make £30 a year supply my wardrobe—and earn it," returned she, lightly.

This admission did not lower her in the estimation of the chivalrous young sailor, for such he was, though it cooled the already slight interest taken in her by the portly lady on the other side.

Mrs. Oliphant, who had made acquaintance with everybody, was gabbling away with her accustomed volubility.

"Oh, my dear Mrs. Rideout, have you tasted this *vol-au-vent*? You really *should*. I have got the bill of fare" (with girlish elation). "There's fricandeau of veal, calf's-head collops, tripe à—" here she stopped short, confused at the shocking word.

Bluebell and the young lieutenant had arrived at sufficient intimacy to exchange a merry glance.

In the mean time, the bride was enacting the pretty spoiled child, and resisting the solicitations of her husband—a spoony-looking infantry captain—that she would endeavour to eat something. "Every one says it is so much better," reiterated he.

"But I am not hungry," said the baby, with most interesting *naiveté*.

"Try a *rawst* potato, ma'am," said the captain, in his broad accent. "There's many a one will eat a *rawst* potato who can't care for anything else."

The bride made a little *moue*, and shook her head, then admitted that she fancied a piece of raspberry tart, though the captain protested that if she would eat anything so injudicious, a gentle nip of whisky would be advisable to correct it.

Captain Butler, the happy bridegroom, was evidently still in the adoring stage, so he listened complacently to his wife's silly badinage with the skipper, whom she informed, apparently for the information of the company, that she was just nineteen, but winced a little at her further admission that they had only been married a week.

A slight but monotonous roll and general chilliness, seemed to portend they were getting into a more open sea, and, as the motion increased, the saloon began to thin a little. The bride's prattle deepened into moanings and complaints; she was laid on the sofa, covered with shawls, and supplied with sal-volatile and smelling-bottles by her devoted spouse, who began to look deadly pale himself.

Mr. Dutton, Bluebell's neighbour, had gone for a smoke with the skipper. Mrs. Oliphant was also an absentee; she had tottered from the saloon the instant the wind freshened, with a contortion of countenance that betokened her dallyings with the *vol-au-vent* would be severely visited. Mrs. Rideout, the lady of position, went off on the arm of her maid, who had not yet succumbed.

Bluebell, determined to resist the whirling in her head, took out some work on which she tried to fix her attention. The elderly widow was looking over a missionary book with woodcuts, and they occasionally exchanged sentences.

The discomposing rocking of the vessel continued, and the moan of the winds mingled with the incessant complaints of Mrs. Butler on a distant sofa, who was as communicative respecting her anguish as her age.

Tea and the return of some of the gentlemen a little relieved the monotony. Bluebell was languidly experimenting on a piece of dry toast, when the loud crying of a child attracted her attention, and, the steward leaving the door open, a little girl of four plunged in. She recognised her as one of the children with the tipsy father. The mother had dined in the ladies' cabin, and retired to her berth to lie down, and this lost lamb was searching for her.

"Come here, my dear," said Mrs. Jackson, the widow lady. "Don't cry, what's the matter?"

But "I want mamma," was the only reply, without any cessation of shrieks.

"Oh, hush! look at these pretty pictures; here's Moses in the bull-rushes."

A momentary glance, and then the cries redoubled.

"Phoebus, what lungs!" ejaculated Mr. Dutton. "Come here, child," authoritatively, holding up a lump of sugar.

A slight lull, and a hesitating zig-zag movement in his direction. He made a grab as she came within reach, placed her on his knee, and pushed a bit of sugar into the month opened for a roar.

"I am quite ashamed of you, making such a noise. Don't choke, there's more sugar in the basin. Wipe your eyes, and see if you can possibly look pretty."

Bewildered, but distracted by the sugar, the tears ceased.

"What is your name? Mary, I suppose."

"No, no," indignantly, "H'Emma."

"H'Emma! You little cad, what is the H for? Say Emma. You can't? Then no more sugar."

"Emma," repeated the astonished child.

"That's right; here is another lump. Miss Leigh, may I ask you to reach me a very pretty book of coloured animals I saw behind you? Now, Emma, there is a tabby cat, just like you have at home."

"No, mamma drove it away;" and, the grief returning, "Oh! where's mamma?"

"She isn't coming while you make that noise, and I fear she must be a wicked woman to drive a poor cat away,—she will never have any luck. Now, what's that?"

"A 'orse," triumphantly.

"Where *were* you riz! Say horse. That's right; don't forget. A pig, a sow, a goose," and so on, half through the book. "Now I'll shut it, and you can go to bed."

"No, no; see the rest," said the now excited child.

"Which would you rather have, mamma or pictures?"

"Pictures. Show them quick."

"Very well; then mamma may go to blazes. We don't want her bothering here till we have done. What did you say was the name of that animal?"

"A 'orse."

"What did I tell you? You will never be a lady if you leave out your h's."

At this moment the mamma appeared. "Oh," said Mrs. Jackson, "your little girl was crying so for you, till that gentleman succeeded in amusing her."

"I 'ope, sir, she 'asn't been very troublesome? The baby, 'e 'as been so fretful with 'is teeth, or I should 'ave come for H'Emma sooner."

"The gentleman said H'Emma was vulgar."

"Don't you tell stories, miss. The gentleman wouldn't 'ave you called hout of your name."

Bluebell laughed at Mr. Dutton's slightly confused appearance, and asked if he thought his corrections would survive the force of example.

"I might have known whom she had learnt it from."

Then, after a moment's hesitation, he asked Bluebell if she could play chess; and, on her replying in the affirmative, he produced a pocket-board.

"I always take it to sea with me," said he, "and make out problems."

Bluebell was beaten, and he tried to teach her a more scientific game. And the evening passed away pleasantly to those two at any rate.

On retiring to her cabin, she perceived a strong smell of brandy, and found Mrs. Oliphant ensconced in the lower berth. Evidently the time for "cheering other people" had not arrived, for her complaints were incessant. The ship was rolling considerable, and Bluebell found some difficulty in undressing, and more in clambering into her berth. She had not been there many minutes when she was startled by the apparition of a man walking straight into the cabin, who explained his errand by unceremoniously putting out their lamp.

Then she fell into a dreamless slumber, but was not long allowed a refreshment denied to her companion, who, in all her wakeful moments, insisted on keeping up a querulous conversation, till Bluebell, in despair, feigned sleep, and would no longer reply.

CHAPTER XXVII
HARRY DUTTON

But hapless one! I cannot ride—there's something in a
horse That I could always honour, but never could indorse.
To speak still more commercially, in riding I am quite
Averse to running long, and apt to be paid off at sight. In
legal phrase, for every class to understand me still, I never
was in stirrups yet a tenant but at will; Or, if you please, in
artist's terms, I never went a-straddle On any horse without
"a want of keeping" in the saddle.

Hood.

The next morning was rougher than ever. The stewardess brought Mrs.
Oliphant's breakfast; but Bluebell, eager for more congenial companionship,
dressed, and went down to the saloon, where she received a cheery welcome
from the captain, who said he had hardly hoped to have his breakfast-table
graced by the presence of any ladies on so wild a morning.

The widow was also stout-hearted, and, evidently considering it right to
take the only young lady under her chaperonage, advised her after breakfast
to remain below and work with her. Bluebell was of a grateful disposition,
and acquiesced, but secretly thought it rather dismal, so, when Mr. Dutton
came down and begged her to go on deck, as they were passing through
some magnificent icebergs, she willingly pocketed her tatting and went up.
The young lieutenant got a couple of rugs and arranged her comfortably.
Certainly the roll of the ship was much more bearable on deck.

Mr. Dutton remained to amuse her, and, both being young, they
speedily became confidentially communicative. She learnt from him that
he had just been promoted out of his ship, and was going home till he got
another. "At least," he amended, "it is more my home than any other. I am
going to stay with my uncle, who would like me to give up the service, and
remain with him altogether."

"Is he so very fond of you?"

"Why, yes, in a sort of way. You see he has got no one else. He never wished me to go to sea, but when I was at school a brother of one of the fellows came, who had just passed as naval cadet, and he had such a lot of tuck, and tin, and presents, that we were all wild to go too. My governor had some interest, and I never ceased tormenting him, till at last he got me appointed to the 'Sorceress.' After I had been a month at sea I had had quite enough of it; but we were on a five years' cruise, and by the end of that time I liked the life as well as any other."

"Then why should your uncle want you to give up your profession?"

"Because," blushing slightly, "he always says I shall be his heir, and he wishes me to take an interest in the estate, and learn to be a country gentleman. But after I have been on shore a month or so the monotony of it is awful, and I feel as if I must do something desperate if I stop quiet longer."

"I thought English country gentlemen found plenty of excitement in hunting and shooting."

"Not all the year round," with a smile; "and, besides, I can't ride! Now, Miss Leigh, if you were an English girl, you would never speak to me again! I don't fear the obstacle, and would ride anything anybody likes to trust me with; but I know, and the *horse* knows, he could get rid of me at any minute. I hunt sometimes, and go straight if the quad. I am on is fond of jumping; but I cut a voluntary as often as not, and then some fool is sure to come up and say,—'You had no business to have parted at that fence, Dutton; the horse took it well enough!' Then I have no 'hands,' I am told. Certainly, whenever I take up the rudder-lines to put his head for any particular course the brute takes it as a personal affront, and begins to fret, go sideways, and bore and all but tell me what a duffer he thinks me. There's my cousin Kate, who will spoon with me by the hour in a greenhouse, and dance as often as I like to ask her, but at the cover-side she is so ashamed of me she shuns me like the plague; and then, of course, next ball it is, 'Dear Harry, *do* introduce me to Major Rattletrap,' or some such soldier officer, 'I like the look of him *so* much.'—'I just offered to,' says I, 'but he didn't seem to rise; said his card was full. Seems sweet on that girl in pink, with black eyes.' That's a school friend of Kate's, whom she is mortal jealous of."

"As if she believed a word of it!"

"Oh, didn't she, though! She bit her lip, and looked shut up. I have great moral influence over Kate that way."

"There's a grand iceberg!" cried Bluebell, after an amused pause, in which she had been trying to picture Cousin Kate: "What a strange shape; it must be hundreds of feet high. How cold it makes the air, though."

"And you are shivering; I'll run and fetch another rug. It is warmer by the funnel, only there are a lot of fellows smoking there."

"But, Mr. Dutton," said she, hesitatingly, "why don't you join them? You have given me all your warm things, and must be cold yourself."

"I'll go if you tell me to," said the lieutenant, looking full into Bluebell's eyes. She was silent, and the long eye-lashes came into play while she considered. She had promised Mrs. Rolleston not to flirt, but there had been no question of that hitherto. Why should she throw away a little pleasant companionship when she was so lonely? "I only spoke on your account." But she had flirting eyes, which said, only too plainly, "Go, if you can."

"I don't think any one could feel cold near you," he whispered,—and then they both blushed. A minute after he ran off for the rug, and Bluebell was left—to repent. "Oh, dear!" thought she, with very hot cheeks, "we must *not* begin this sort of thing already, or there will be an end to all comfort—and as if I could ever forget!"

She received the rug with matter-of-course indifference, and looked up at him with the serenity of a nun; the young lieutenant was quick to perceive the change. He thought it wiser to follow suit, and they were at ease again, though each remembered the other's blush.

"I came upon a very touching tableau in the saloon," said he; "the bride was reluctantly pecking at some chicken, and that ass, Butler, feeding her with a fork."

"Ah! those are your nationalities," laughed Bluebell; "we don't do such silly things in Canada."

"No, you are very stiff and stand-offish there, I know; that is why you don't require chaperones."

"What are the duties of a chaperone in England, beyond sitting up against a wall all night, like an old barn-door hen?"

"But they mustn't roost," said Mr. Dutton; "they have to guard their charges from the insidious approaches of ineligible youths, and assist them to entwine in their meshes the sons of Mammon."

"But it must be rather difficult at a ball to distinguish who are eligible as you call them."

"Oh, an astute and practised chaperone knows pretty well who everybody is. They have books of reference, too,—the 'Peerage' and 'Landed Gentry.' I believe now, though, a good deal of matrimonial business is done in the city."

"And men have no objection to heiresses either," said Bluebell, darkly, as a memory came over her. "There's the dinner bell." He collected her rugs, and helped her down to the saloon, where they were betting how many knots the steamer had made that day, and raffling for the successful number. Mrs. Oliphant was present, almost as brisk as usual, for the wind had moderated, and the steamer laboured far less. After dinner some of the ladies joined in a game of shovel-board on deck. The bride, now quite bright again, insisted upon being instructed by Mr. Dutton, and became, with a view to his fascination, more helpless and infantine than ever, for she was one of those women who cannot bear any one to be an object of attention but themselves.

However, as she was not successful in detaching him entirely from Bluebell, she conceived a dislike to her, in which Mrs. Oliphant cordially participated, and they afterwards whiled away many an hour in the dear delight of detraction. Bluebell was pronounced an unprincipled adventuress, determined to use every art to entrap this unsophisticated young man, and each act and look on her part was treasured up by the two censors for private analysis and discussion.

Mrs. Butler, it is true, had less provocation to be spiteful than the elder lady; for being young and silly, she *was* a certain object of attraction to some of the officers; but the very indifference of Mr. Dutton gave a value to his admiration, and made her more eager to obtain it than that of the rest. Besides, the vacuity of mind and employment at sea, a brisk flirtation is sure to attract lookers-on, and become a fruitful incentive to malice and envy. Bluebell could not account for the unfriendly interest she excited, as her Canadian education had taught her to regard fraternizing *pro tem.* with any sympathetic masculinity a very unimportant matter, and about as much a precursor to matrimony as if her companion were of the same sex; and she had been far too hard hit to bear any down-right love-making from another man so soon after. Mr. Dutton was, perhaps, as inflammable as most sailors, but he could not make Bluebell out. She evidently liked his society, and became pleasant and animated when they were together, which they were pretty constantly; yet if ever he ventured on anything tender she had a way of putting it by in the most unembarrassed manner possible, which piqued while it perplexed him.

On one occasion, when she had let some warmer speech than usual glance off, he chose to take it as a snub, and, pretending to be offended, betook himself to masculine society and smoking. Bluebell was alone all day, a prey to the ill-natured watchfulness of her two enemies, whose quickened observation and exultant faces proved they had noticed the cessation of his attentions. Once or twice he passed her without a word or look, regardless of the innocent surprise in her eyes. "Perhaps he is trying to gain 'moral influence over me,' as well as his cousin Kate," thought she, with a little laugh. At dinner he dropped into a seat next Mrs. Butler instead of his usual one by herself, and, from the bride's incessant giggle, was apparently devoting himself to her entertainment. Bluebell had no one to speak to except the kind old captain, with whom she was rather a favourite, and who chatted away willingly enough, till she ceased to hear that disagreeable and affected laughter.

"Miss Leigh," said a penitent voice in her ear, "will you come on deck? There's a little land bird in the rigging."

"No, no," said the captain. "I won't have this young lady disturbed; it is very cold on deck, and she is better here."

"I thought you would like to see it," said the lieutenant, gloomily. "It is very tired—blown off shore, I should think."

"Indeed, I'd like to give it some crumbs," said she, hesitatingly. "Will you take it some, Mr. Dutton?"

"Certainly not," seeing his advantage, "unless you come too—in fact, I thought of shooting it. It would be pretty in your hat—or Mrs. Butler's."

"That would be, indeed, a feather in your cap," said Mrs. Oliphant with an unpleasant sneer.

"Quite right, my dear," said the captain, as Mr. Dutton walked away, "not to do everything a young man asks you;" and he assured Bluebell, who was still solicitous about the bird, that it would not venture down for crumbs.

Our heroine was vexed at Mr. Dutton's disagreeable manner, and began moralizing on the inevitable way in which she succeeded in estranging her female companions, and offending those of the other sex.

The old captain was just going off to his bridge, when by some afterthought, he stepped back, and asked Miss Leigh if she would like to sit awhile in his cabin. "You'll find no one there but the cat and the parrot," he said; and, on her gratefully assenting, led the way to a small oasis of comfort.

The cat, a great brindled Tom, arched his back a yard high, and made a sort of back jump up to his Master's hand, where he rubbed his head with a sociable miaw. Bluebell soon had him on her lap in a cozy arm-chair.

"I think Master Dutton will be rather puzzled where to find you," observed the old skipper, with a twinkle, as he was leaving the cabin.

"Dear me," said Bluebell, with a conscious blush, "I hope you don't think—that there's anything—of that sort—"

"I think you have been letting that young man keep you all to himself up in a corner quite long enough," retorted he, "and you may as well show him you can do without him;" with which he left her to her meditations.

"How disagreeable good advice is!" thought the girl. "Dear old thing! But it is so dull at sea—one must do something. I do wish though Mr. Dutton wouldn't try to spoon—he was awfully nice before he thought of it."

Of course these two drew together again next day, and, though Bluebell still evaded with Madonna eyes all approach to love-making, the lieutenant accepted the situation, and contented himself with flirting *sous le nom d'amitié*.

CHAPTER XXVIII
ROUGH WEATHER

I would be a mermaid fair,
I would sing to myself the whole of the day;
With a comb of pearl I would comb my hair,
And still as I comb'd, I would sing and say,
"Who is it loves me? who loves not me?"

Tennyson.

One day there was a gale. It came up suddenly, and some ladies sitting on a bench were swept off by a roll and sudden lurch. The deck was soon cleared of the feminine element, with the exception of Bluebell, who enjoyed an immunity from *malheur de mer*, and knew she would not be much better off in her cabin, where Mrs. Oliphant had gradually ousted her from everything but sleeping accommodation.

A huge roller had hurled itself over the steerage, and broken a man's arm; but the part of the vessel she was on kept pretty dry. Stormy petrels were hovering in flocks; the ship, plunging head foremost into deep troughs, seemed as if it must break its back or be swallowed up, but always borne on the crest of a wave only to repeat the header next minute.

Bluebell was lying (for no other position could be preserved) on some rigs by the wheel, and holding on by a rope to prevent sliding about. She felt excited by the grandeur of the situation, and, in the pauses of the wind, sang low some wild German Volkslied.

"Are you a Lorelei?" asked Mr. Dutton, who was never far off. "What do you intend to do with the steamer?"

"I don't mean any harm to the ship, but I shan't lull the winds yet. How delightful and magnificent it is!"

"If you really don't mean to engulf us, and won't comb your golden hair, pray go on singing. I'll risk it."

Bluebell nodded, and gave full play to her magnificent voice in the wildest Lieder she could remember. The man at the wheel, if he had ever heard of a Lorelei, might have been excused for mistaking her for one. A lady to sit and sing in such a gale was not an every-day experience. Her bright hair was only covered by the hood of a deep-blue cloak, from which her large eyes seemed to have caught a reflection, so dark were the pupils dilated with enthusiasm.

"You might be a corsair's bride," said Mr. Dutton, admiringly, "you are so indifferent to discomfort and danger. I can't fancy you shut up in a poky school-room, taking regular walks, and teaching Dr. Watts to tiresome children."

"I have only one pupil of a musical and romantic turn. You are altogether wrong in thinking me indifferent to luxury; I am quite longing to be in a comfortable house again."

"Your penance will be over in a day or two. Why do you stay out to be drenched with spray and perished with cold?" very discontentedly.

"How can I be either with all these wraps? and, when you are not sulky, your society *is* preferable to Mrs. Oliphant's!"

"Yes; that is about my place in your—what shall I call it? Regard is a nice, proper word,—just more acceptable than the plainest and most spiteful woman on board."

"Rather more than that," said Bluebell, gently. "It would have been far worse without you; but after this voyage we are not likely to meet again, though I shall never think of it without remembering my friend."

"What a nice word!" savagely. "Why don't you add,—

'Others may woo me—thou art my friend?'

Do you know that song, Miss Leigh?"

"Yes," laughing.

"'Lonely and sadly his young life did end;
Pause by my tombstone, and pity thy friend.'

It's enough to draw tears from one's eyes."

"Well!" said the lieutenant, "I never met a Canadian girl before, but I see now they are the coldest, most insensible—oh! of course, you only laugh. How do you know we shall never meet again? Suppose I call on you in your new—situation."

"Governesses are not allowed 'followers.' I mean, male visitors would be considered as such."

"Couldn't I get a tutorship in the same family?"

"There are no boys. Gracious! what a wave. Surely it is getting rougher, Mr. Dutton?"

"Well, yes. I think I must take you down. The next roller may wash over you. Lean all your weight on me, or you'll be blown off your feet."

In a most incoherent manner she reached the gangway, and, clinging to the banisters, reeled into her cabin, where was Mrs. Oliphant in hysterics. The stewardess was in attendance, and she was insisting on her immediately fetching the captain, as, without his assurance that there was no danger, she declined to be calm.

"As if the captain could leave his bridge!" said Bluebell, laughing. "And I am sure the ship would go down if he did."

Another shriek from Mrs. Oliphant, who, with a desperate effort, seized on a life-belt, and called to the stewardess to assist in its adjustment.

"Oh, dear!" cried Bluebell. "And what is to become of me? However, you are quite welcome to it. I had sooner be drowned at once than bob about on a wave, with sharks nibbling at my toes for an hour or two previously."

"Perhaps, ma'am, now this young lady be come, who seems to have a good heart," said the stewardess, "you will let me go to Mrs. Preston and Mrs. Butler, who have been wanting me ever so long."

"No; I will not be deserted. Mrs. Butler has her husband and Mrs. Preston has her maid."

"Oh, she is worse than all! She sent down for Mrs. Preston to come up and speak to her, as she was dying as fast as she could, and the poor lady couldn't as much as lift her own 'ead."

"And you are not so very bad," said Bluebell, encouragingly. "Think of Mrs. Dove, of the 100th 'Scatterers,' and don't give way."

So, partly by laughing and partly by gentle determination, she brought her round, and favoured the escape of the stewardess.

It was not a very agreeable task soothing this selfish and cowardly woman; and she was by no means assured that there was no cause for anxiety. Her thoughts reverted to Bertie. Suppose they were all drowned. In theory she hoped Cecil would be happy with him. Still there was a *soupçon* of gratification in imagining him mourning in secret anguish and remorse over her untimely end. She remembered his favourite poem in the "Wanderer" that Cecil used to read, and the lines,—

"I thought were she only living still,
How I could forgive her and love her."

Only in this instance forgiveness was more due from her.

Mr. Dutton here knocked at the door, to offer to help them up stairs to dinner; but Mrs. Oliphant had dropped asleep, exhausted by her emotions, so they went up alone. Only a few gentlemen were in the saloon, and the widow lady, whom everybody had begun to like, she was so unselfish and contented.

Dinner was consumed in a picnic fashion. Bluebell's modicum of sherry had to be tossed off at once in a tumbler, for the glasses were dancing a hornpipe on the table, plates required a restraining hand, and their contents to be conveyed to the mouth with as much accuracy of aim as was attainable.

She thought compassionately of the careworn mother of H'Emma, who probably would have been quite neglected during the gale, and determined to take her something, and get Mr. Dutton to carry it and steady her own footsteps. Nothing could exceed the discomfort in which they found them. The nursery-maid was imbecile from terror and prostrate with sickness, and the harassed mother doing the best she could.

To begin with, H'Emma had received a whipping, which, however undeserved, was probably the most judicious course, by inspiring fortitude, and cutting off all hopes of undue indulgence.

The poor woman was very grateful for the visit. "No one had been near them," she said; "and the girl was so frightened, and H'Emma had screamed so, she was at her wits' end."

"I am surprised at you, Emma!" said Mr. Dutton. "When, you are grown up you may be as frightened as you please; but if you don't practise self-command as a child, you'll be very properly whipped."

At this allusion to her misfortunes another howl seemed impending, only that her attention was arrested by an orange tossed carelessly in the air.

"Whoever catches it may have it. Don't look at mamma; she has abdicated for the present, and we are here to put the kingdom to rights. Don't you think, Emma," in a whisper, "it would be a very good thing if that squalling, bald-headed young fraternity of yours were slapped?"

"Mammy says it is his teeth."

"No reason he should set ours on edge. I'd compose him if I had the chance! Well, Miss Leigh, if I can't fetch anything else for this lady, I'll go on deck, and return presently to report progress and help you back again."

The storm raged for many hours more, and struck terror into the hearts of the women and children. Mr. Dutton and some of the other gentlemen were up all night, as well as the captain and officers; but the morning rose calm and delicious over a sleeping sea, and cheerfulness and high spirits reigned in the ship. They were within a day of land, too—a more welcome prospect than ever, after the perils and dangers of the night. The dinner-table had scarcely an absentee, and was far more lively than it had ever been yet.

"One can sleep comfortably to-night, being so near land," cried the thoughtless Mrs. Butler.

"There have been more shipwrecks off the coast of Ireland than any other," said Mr. Dutton, sardonically. He was the only one who did not display unmixed delight at reaching England; and, when other people are exuberantly rejoicing at the very thing that is annoying ourselves, to moderate their transports a little is a satisfaction.

"Oh, how can you be so shocking! But I don't believe you. Once we are in sight of land, if there were any danger, what would prevent us getting into boats and rowing to it?"

And then Mr. Dutton plunged into a ghastly tale of a steamer that had struck on the Irish coast at night, and the passengers had to take to the boats in their bed-clothes. One poor mother, with a baby tied on her back with a shawl, and another child in her arms, found the shawl empty, the infant having slipped out into the sea; and how they remained beating about for hours before they could land, nearly perished with cold from insufficient clothing.

Everybody seemed provided with similar anecdotes, and yarn succeeded yarn till late in the evening, when a message from the captain that Ireland was in sight brought them all on deck. The moon was shining softly over the beautiful mountains and valleys of ——. A more exquisite little picture could hardly have been presented to the eye wearied of perpetual gazing on the pathless ocean. Exclamations of delight were heard on all sides, while some prosaically remarked it was almost as fine as scenes in "Peep o' Day" or "The Colleen Bawn." To Bluebell it was fairy-land. To begin with, she had never seen a mountain, and the picturesque in Canada is on too large a scale for the little details that give beauty to scenery. Her conception of the Emerald Isle, founded on Lover's ballads and Lever's romances, was completely realized.

"How haunting!" said she, in a hushed whisper. "What a pity to go any further, and be disenchanted, perhaps!"

"I wish," said Mr. Dutton, "you would think you might go further and fare worse in another case,"—which ambiguous speech, it must be supposed, was not intended to be taken literally; for, though youthful susceptibility and propinquity had given birth to a hasty passion, and he was savage enough at the prospect of parting, to a young man dependent on an uncle and residing chiefly at sea a penniless wife might have its embarrassments.

Bluebell had glided down the companion again. The mails were landed, the pilot came on board, and next morning they were steaming into the Mersey. Many of the passengers had got letters, and were talking of their plans and fussing about luggage.

"How refreshing it is to see some one without that business look!" cried Mr. Dutton to Bluebell, who was leisurely reading in the saloon. "But have you no goods or chattels, Miss Leigh? And ought not you to have a letter with sailing orders?"

"I have two boxes somewhere in the hold. No, I didn't expect a letter, I was to telegraph at Liverpool, and come right off. This is the address:—

"Mrs. Leighton, "Leighton Court, "Calmshire."

"Why, that is my line!" said the sailor, mendaciously. "I can travel with you as far as Calmshire."

"Can you really? How very strange! But I suppose England *is* a small place," said Bluebell, *naively*.

"Oh, extremely insignificant! I shall be able to see you safely to your journey's end. So that's all settled. Now I will go and look if your luggage is coming up, for I suppose we shall land in an hour or two."

Bluebell's curiosity was excited by the *Times* newspaper, which a gentleman had just laid down. It was only the advertisement sheet, for some one else had immediately snapped up the rest, and she glanced vaguely down the first columns, puzzling over such enigmatical insertions as "Our tree, our bridge, our walk," "What shall we do with the Tusk?" and that

"John is entreated to write and send remittances to his afflicted Teapot,"—
when her eye lit upon the following name among the deaths:—

> "On the 22nd inst., at Leighton Court, of scarlet fever,
> Evelyn Cora, only child of Mrs. and the late Henry
> Leighton, Esq., aged eleven years."

Bluebell sat petrified,—the ground cut beneath her feet,—she could
only be shocked for the poor child whom she had never known. But what
was to become of herself in a strange land, with no place to go to? Besides
Leighton Court there was not a place in all England, except an inn, that she
would have a right to enter; and in a few minutes more the shelter of the
ship would be withdrawn,—even now she could see the smoke of the tug
coming to disembark them. Perfectly appalled and unnerved, she pushed
the paragraph towards Mr. Dutton, who had just entered, and gazed
helplessly at him with large frightened eyes.

He took in the situation at a glance, and the thought that had struck
him before of the strangeness of sending this beautiful girl, like a bale of
goods, to an unknown country, where she had no connections, returned
with confirmed force. How friendless she was! But slenderly supplied with
money, of course. A daring possibility had darted into his mind. It was an
irresistible temptation,—and sailors are proverbially reckless. Matrimony
hitherto had never entered into his views. It would entail leaving the navy
and living with his uncle, who, though kind, was arbitrary enough, and
would have very decided opinions upon whom his choice should fall.
Connection, money, he knew would be a *sine qua non*. More than one well-
born and tochered *débutante* had successively been indicated to him as a
bride that would in all respects suit Lord Bromley's views; and Bluebell, as
far as he knew, fulfilled none of these conditions. All the same the struggle
in his mind was in combatting the difficulties that opposed his resolution
to marry her.

Bluebell, of course, could not guess his thoughts, and she only felt very
desponding that he seemed unable to suggest anything.

"Oh, Mr. Dutton," she cried, "do go and tell the captain, and ask him
what I had better do! He is sure to think of something,—for a day or two,
at any rate."

The young man looked up with a strange smile, but there were other
persons present. "Certainly," he said, with rather a constrained manner. "I

will go and tell him,"—and Bluebell, mistaking his reserve for coolness, felt disappointed.

The captain was very busy, and not too well pleased at being interrupted, but when he had mastered the intelligence he gave it his whole attention directly.

"Eh, the puir lassie!" he ejaculated, "wha's to become of her!"

"There's only one thing that I can do," said the lieutenant, briefly.

"You!" said the skipper, whose remark had been an exclamation, not an interrogation. "What the mischief could you do? I am doubting what the guidwife will say, but I am thinking I must *jeest* take her home."

"Oh, how good of you, sir!" said the young man, seizing his hand, unobservant of the dry cynical look in his eyes. "But I trust it will not be for long, as I must tell you, in confidence, if she will only consent, I intend—I hope to marry Miss Leigh immediately."

"You be d—d! I will have no such goings on. If the lassie comes to me, she will act conformable; and, if you think you are in a position to maintain a wife, you may consult your *feymily*; I'll have no such responsibility."

"You are, of course omnipotent in your own ship," said the young sailor, angrily, "but you need not forget you are speaking to a gentleman."

"As far as I can see they are no honester than other people. I only belong to the respectable class myself, and I'll no have it."

"What a fool I was to tell you! But surely," half laughing, "matrimony is an honourable institution."

"I kenna—I kenna. I'll give the bairn shelter till she hears from her kin, but I'll have no marrying or such like, to be called to account for mayhap afterwards."

But Mr. Dutton, only made more eager by opposition, sprang away to the saloon, where Bluebell was sitting.

"Yes, I have a message for you," said he, in answer to her inquiring look. "Will you come on deck? Here are your cloak and hood."

He led her away, with rather a pale face, to the most secluded part of it.

"What did the captain say?" she asked.

"The captain is a canny, suspicious, pigheaded old Scottish-man!"

"Of course, of course," very despondingly, "no one can do anything for me. I must go to a lodging, and advertise for another situation."

"They will want a recommendation from your last place."

"Well, I can get it from Canada."

"And that will take a month. Bluebell, listen to me; for there's no time to beat about the bush. I love you, my sweet child; but that you know already. Will you marry me? Don't start. I know it is sudden, but it will be all easy. Directly we land we can drive to a register office; they will ask no questions, but marry us right off, and we can have it done over again in a church, if you like."

Bluebell began to wonder how many more sensational minutes this hour was to contain.

"Mr. Dutton," she gasped, in a horrified tone, "what *are* you saying? You must know it is impossible."

"Summon all your moral courage, Bluebell. You were not afraid in the storm. Why do you shrink from acting a little out of the common?"

This speech was so like what Bertie would have said, that it nearly brought the tears to her eyes.

"Pray say no more," said she, shrinking away from him. "How could I ever *dream* of such a thing!"

"*Can't* you care for me, Bluebell—ever so little?" pleaded Harry Dutton.

"But that would be so *very* much!"

Her strange wooer grew more eager, for the moments were passing, and Bluebell was at her wit's end, when the skipper came rolling up to them. The delight and relief with which his proposal of taking her home was received was far from pleasing to Mr. Dutton, and Bluebell, in her lightened heart, felt some self-reproach at the sight of his gloomy countenance.

The captain was hurrying her away, but she lingered a moment, and, with one of those speaking glances he had learnt to look for and love, put out her hand to the young sailor.

"Stay with me," he whispered; "it is not yet too late." She shook her head, "I believe you hate me!" he muttered, savagely.

"No," said Bluebell, impulsively saying more than she felt. "I like you only too well—but not enough for that."

"Any more last words?" said the skipper, who had stood aside good-humouredly, master of the situation.

"I have nothing further to say," said the young man, stiffly, making way for her to pass.

A minute more, and she was rowing to shore in the captain's boat, who then put her into a cab to drive to his home.

Now, the good skipper, such an autocrat on board his vessel, was by no means so under his own roof-tree, and sundry misgivings obtruded themselves as to the welcome he might receive from the wife of his bosom when a comely young lady was to be included in it.

"She'll no jest like it at first," he muttered, half aloud; and as the moment approached and apprehension intensified, he repeated the remark still louder.

This moderate expectation was amply justified by the event. The good lady received the explanatory introduction with a snort, and a countenance expressive of contempt and disbelief, while she ironically "feared there would be nothing in the house good enough for her."

Bluebell endeavoured to excuse her unlucky presence, the best argument she could think of being that she would advertise for another situation immediately. Only for the fear of offending the captain, she would have added that she was prepared to pay for her board, which, by putting it on a business footing, would doubtless have commended itself to the dominant passion of her hostess's mind, and dispersed the misgivings she at present entertained of this "fine madam."

The general stiffness was relieved by the boisterous greetings of the captain's boys, who had just rushed in from school; but it was a terrible evening to Bluebell, feeling *de trop*, and unable to calculate how soon she should be released.

"Ye'll jeest put her in Phemie's room," the skipper had said. (Phemie was a daughter lately married.) "How will I do that," was the responding retort, "when the carpet is up, and the iron bedstead was broke by Rab a week syne?"

"Well, then, Rab will jeest let her have his bed," said the captain, equably brewing himself some whiskey-and-water,—and so on through the evening, during which Mrs. Davidson by no means softened the trouble and inconvenience Bluebell's presence occasioned, whose spirits fell to their lowest depth.

Was it to be wondered at that Harry Dutton recurred pretty constantly to her mind? She could think calmly now of the proposal that had so startled her before. It was, at any rate, a sincere, straightforward offer of marriage, and so far he contrasted favourably with Bertie, whom she had determined to forget. But, then, she had dismissed him—he had gone away to his uncle's, and they would probably never meet again; and as when a thing is out of reach it becomes immediately enhanced in value, she began to regret her lost lover, and to think that there, perhaps, might have been a short cut out of her difficulties. We are aware that this unlucky admission must depose her at once from the rank of a heroine, as it is well known a heroine never for an instant suffers interest to enter into the sacred claims of love.

CHAPTER XXIX
BLUEBELL'S DEBUT IN THE OLD COUNTRY

Says "Be content my lovely May,
For" thou shalt be my bride.
With her yellow hair, that glittered fair,
She dried the trickling tear,
And sighed the name of Branxholm's heir,
The youth that she loved dear.

Scott.

Next morning Bluebell rose early, and wrote out an advertisement, in which she described herself, more truthfully, than diplomatically, as a young person of eighteen, proficient in music, but not skilled enough in other branches of education for advanced pupils.

The captain promised to write to Mrs. Leighton, reporting her arrival, and explaining that "Miss Leigh would not think of intruding on her in her bereavement, but only requested permission to be allowed to apply to her as a reference when she heard of another situation." He added, "That in the meantime Miss Leigh was remaining in his family."

Armed with the advertisement, Bluebell pensively walked off to get it inserted in the *Liverpool Mercury*. The captain lived in a suburb of the town, and had given her clear directions how to find the office. It was a disagreeable walk, and she was obliged to concentrate all her attention on not losing the way, so her thoughts could not well stray to Harry Dutton; but ere she had proceeded many streets—she met him! He was looking very haggard, but eagerness and triumph lighted up his large brown eyes as he perceived her. Bluebell was in a state of half terror, half delight, and whole bewilderment.

"How is it you are still in Liverpool?" she gasped.

"I have been walking about all day in hopes of meeting you!" cried he, disregarding her question.

Bluebell felt as if she had recovered an old friend. She told him of her rough reception by Mrs. Davidson, and how annoyed she was at being forced to remain there an unwelcome guest.

The answer to this was obvious, but the lieutenant would say nothing now to scare her.

"Why we have got to the river," she said, after some unheeded period of eager conversation, "and my advertisement! It must be miles from the office!"

"Much too far to go back," said the sailor "Give it me, I will insert it for you."

"Thank you," said the heedless Bluebell. "That will be so much pleasanter, and we need not thread those horrid streets again!"

There was nothing more to do but to go home, and yet she didn't directly. There would be only Mrs. Davidson in, who was so ungracious and disagreeable, and she lingered half an hour or so, talking to Harry Dutton, who would, perhaps, be gone by to-morrow, but he wasn't, nor the next day, nor the next. They never made any assignations, yet day after day Bluebell met him, and for a brief space they were together.

Harry Dutton was only twenty-two, he had been at sea all his life, and had never been seriously in love before. But now he had completely lost his head, and all considerations were swept away by this overmastering passion, which his knowledge that Bluebell did not fully return only seemed to augment. His uncle was a selfish, exacting old man, but he had been kind enough to this boy who, with the usual ingratitude of human nature, forgot everything to gratify the fancy of the moment.

Dutton had never been thrown in contact with so pretty a creature, and, notwithstanding the apparent aberration of mind displayed in thus jeopardizing his prospects, laid his plans coolly and cleverly enough. Bluebell still talked of her impending governess life, and he kept his own council, though firmly resolved never to lose sight of her again.

She was beginning to wonder that her advertisements had elicited no replies, and Mrs. Davidson had been especially unpleasant about it, when one day the wished-for letter arrived.

"Mrs. Giles Johnson, having seen 'B.L.'s' advertisement in the *Liverpool Mercury*, is requiring such a person to instruct and to take entire charge of the wardrobes of five little girls, one of whom, being nervous, she would be required to sleep with. Mrs. G. J. trusts she is obliging, and would have no objection, when the lady's-maid has a press of work, to assist her with it, or make herself generally useful in any other way. 'B.L.'s' attainments being apparently limited, and Mrs. Giles Johnson having an abhorrence of music, she can only offer a salary of eighteen pounds a year."

Bluebell alternated between tears and laughter on the perusal of this letter.

"Why, at the Rollestons'," she cried, "I had thirty pounds a year, only Freddy to teach, and did what I liked! But they were friends," — and a home-sick feeling came over her.

"If ye just turn up your nose at every situation, ye'll never be placed," said Mrs. Davidson.

"Oh, perhaps I shall get another letter to-morrow. I would go back to Canada if I had money enough."

Bluebell put on her hat. Whichever way she went she was quite certain of meeting Mr. Dutton, to whom she wished to display this wonderful document. It was all very well to laugh, but it certainly was most discouraging and vexatious. Yet Mr. Dutton, when she saw him, gravely affirmed it to be "quite as good an offer as he had expected, and was only surprised at her getting any answers at all," — which well indeed he might be, considering that the advertisement never appeared in any paper, and that the liberal proposals of Mrs. Giles Johnson were an emanation from his own brain.

He proceeded to relate the most uncomfortable anecdotes of governess life in England, making it appear that they were treated like white slaves, and expected to know everything.

Bluebell, though only half believing it, began seriously to question whether her small attainments were saleable at all. Her friend the captain would go to sea again shortly, and having prevailed on Mrs. Davidson to receive a small contribution towards her board, the ten pounds were dwindling away.

Then, when she was reduced to the depths of perplexity and depression, Harry Dutton cautiously pleaded his cause, and, as a strong will bent on one object will always sway an irresolute mind, Bluebell listened, and for once tried to realize what it would be. She had been frightened at Dutton's precipitancy in the first instance; but now he had become in a manner necessary to her, and she certainly liked him, — immensely. Still, of course, after her experience of the *grande passion*, this mere *entente cordiale* could not be mistaken for the real article. But there was another question: had she not, by meeting him so often, given him a right so to speak, with fair expectation of success? She had heedlessly walked into the snare with her eyes open, and felt no resisting power to break through the mesh of circumstances that environed her.

Bluebell wavered and hesitated. Harry followed up his advantage. Ere a few stars twinkled out, "single spies" on their colloquy, the struggle was over, and the bold wooer had extorted from his *fiancée* a promise to marry him the following morning but one at a register office in Liverpool.

The very next day they would probably not meet, as he had everything to arrange, and also to prepare a lodging for her, for they had determined to leave Liverpool immediately afterwards.

One thing only Bluebell retained her firmness sufficiently to stipulate for, which was, that the kind old captain should be told of it. Mr. Dutton agreed, on condition that she did not breathe a syllable till after their marriage, when he promised to write himself and acquaint the skipper.

Bluebell could scarcely trust herself to think as she walked slowly home. She felt quite reckless, and as though she were fated to do this act, that seemed so desperate. What would all her friends in Canada say? Somehow she did not look forward to telling the news to Mrs. Rolleston. She supposed Cecil would be pleased, and it might clear up matters between her and Bertie. Ah! if it were only him she was going to be married to! Why does one always like the wicked ones best? She wished to imagine him desperate, remorseful, beside himself with jealousy. But she knew that would not be so. At the utmost he would, perhaps, toss off a brandy-and-soda, give a tremendous sigh, and ejaculate, "Ah! poor, dear little Bluebell!" and then reflect that he would rather like to meet her again, when there would be no question of marrying—the only thing he was unprepared to do for her.

From which tolerably accurate surmise our reader will perceive that our heroine has rather come on in penetration since we first presented her fresh and verdant in these pages.

Then she thought of her mother, and how disappointed she would be at not being present at the marriage. She had written to her on landing, but this letter had been posted in Ireland. Since then she had acquainted her with the facts of Evelyn's death, and of her own exertions to obtain another situation, lodging in the mean time with Mrs. Davidson.

On her re-appearance Bluebell was received somewhat coldly by the old captain, who asked her where she could find to walk so long every day. It was very disagreeable having to answer evasively, and he did not appear satisfied—on the contrary, eyed her askance all the evening.

The reason was, he had accidentally observed Mr. Dutton coming out of an hotel, and was unable to conjecture what kept him in Liverpool, unless he were lingering there on Bluebell's account. Connecting this with her frequent absence from home, he began to think it time to be relieved from the responsibility of this dangerous young guest. He did not reveal his suspicions to his wife, but the following day kept something of a watch over her, and proposed himself to accompany her out.

Somewhat surprised by the placid gratitude of her reply, his suspicions were still further allayed by seeing no sign of the lieutenant, for whom he kept a sharp look-out. He told the girl—narrowly watching her all the time—that there were many snares in Liverpool, and that unless he could see her safely placed in a *feymily* before the next trip of the "Hyperion," he must arrange with the owners for the passage-money, and take her back to her friends, trusting to them to, repay him.

"How generous you are, dear Captain Davidson!" was all she said. But he noticed she turned deadly pale, and two bright drops stood in her eyes.

The idea was so tempting for a moment, with the irrevocable step of the morrow hanging over her like a troubled dream. What if she could return to the old, happy, careless days, and leave this smoky, foggy England, where care and anxiety rose up at every step! But there is no going back in life. What should she do in Canada? Her connection with the Rollestons was played out, and for every one's happiness it was better severed. There was scarcely any demand for governesses in the Dominion, as the children commonly went to school; so she would encumber her mother with the expenses of the voyage, with no prospect of contributing anything to her very slender fund.

All this passed rapidly through Bluebell's mind; but it soon settled into an acceptance of what appeared the inevitable, while the good captain talked on, hoping to induce her to place some confidence in him, if she did know of her admirer's presence in Liverpool.

The girl fathomed the old man's drift, and most heartily wished she had not promised to conceal it from him. It would be an unspeakable relief if this fatherly captain could only countenance and witness her marriage, to say nothing of being spared the treachery of deceiving him after all his kindness. But, there!—she had promised Harry, and must abide by her word.

Only, that evening at bed-time, observing Mrs. Davidson buried head and shoulders in a cupboard she was straightening, Bluebell suddenly threw her arms round the old skipper's neck, gave him a silent hug, and glided from the room, and in the solitude of her own wrote, as fast as pen could scribble, an impulsive, affectionate letter of adieu, confessing what she was to do on the morrow, which her husband (she did not mention his name) would then write and announce to him.

"Eh! is the lassie daft?" had half murmured the not ill-pleased captain; then, perceiving that the salute had been bestowed without the detection of his partner, a large slow smile expanded itself all over his broad face.

"Wha are ye girning for like an auld Cheshire cat?" inquired the unsuspicious lady.

"Nonsense, my dear; nonsense!" complacently stirring his grog and looking rather foolish. His Scotch head had disapproved of what his good heart, of no nationality, had decided with regard to Bluebell. I am not sure now, though, that he did not think the money might be worse risked than in taking this personable lassie another trip across the Atlantic.

CHAPTER XXX
NO CARDS

Love will make oar cottage pleasant,
And I love thee more than life.

Tennyson.

A dense November fog ushered in the dawn of the following day. Bluebell had been awake for hours. Some men were mending the streets, and, as she listened to the monotonous blows of their pickaxes and hammers, a lugubrious fancy crossed her that just such sounds would a criminal hear when workmen were erecting the gallows that was to close his mortal career. By ten o'clock a new page of her life would be turned over, if, nervous and unstrung as she was, she were able to carry out the first part of the drama. Suppose the captain should object to her walking abroad, or offer again to accompany her! And even if she effected a start, might he not, his suspicions awakened, quickly follow! The eight o'clock breakfast bell rang, and Bluebell came down with a white, scared face and dark rims to her eyes. The captain appeared unobservant. To tell the truth, the stolen kiss, which he probably considered "naughty, but nice," had made him somewhat conscious. So he looked demure and rather sly; but the girl had forgotten the circumstance.

The old Dutch clock ticked louder than ever, and, as usual, recorded the quarters with an internal convulsion. At half-past nine the boys would go to school, and, in the commotion of their departure, Bluebell resolved to pass from the threshold and go forth to her fate. She got her hat, — unnoticed and unquestioned was in the street, and groping her way through the fog with swift, unsteady steps. In two turnings from the door Dutton met her, a relieved, triumphant smile lighting his features as he placed her in a cab. The man, previously instructed, drove rapidly off to the register office. Bluebell, now the die was cast, felt almost fainting; but Harry's strong arm was round her, and in less than a quarter of an hour these two youthful lunatics were as securely and irrevocably married as though the ceremony had been performed by an archbishop in full canonicals. The gold circlet was on her finger, with a pearl one to guard it—of no great value, for Harry was aware there would be sundry demands on his ready money. Bluebell, of course, could have no luggage, and he had put himself in the hands of a patronizing lady in an outfitting establishment, and procured her a small stock of necessaries. He had received his pay, and not long since a liberal cheque from Lord Bromley; so the "sinews of war" were not wanting for the present. They drove straight from the register office to the station, and were in the train and far on their journey before Bluebell had the least idea where they were going to; indeed, if she had known, she would scarcely have been wiser, all places in England being equally strange to her.

Dutton, rapturously in love, now that his schemes were successful, was in a state of exulting happiness almost overwhelming to Bluebell, secretly oppressed with a sense of the irrevocable. She even caught herself, when they stopped at stations, wishing that some one would get in. Very different was the first-class carriage from the long cars, containing sixty or seventy persons, that she had previously travelled in. But yet there were four vacant seats, which in spite of the rush for places, continued unoccupied. Now and then their door was hastily clutched by some passenger, but a guard seemed invariably to turn up and bear the individual away to another carriage. About three o'clock they stopped at a very small station, where only one or two persons got out.

"Here we are, Bluebell," cried Harry, grasping rugs, sticks, and umbrellas, and throwing them to the porter.

She sprang up and looked around with intense interest. They were nearing her first *pied-à-terre* as a married woman. But the journey was not yet ended, and they transferred themselves to a fly, in which an old grey horse waited sleepily.

"Lucky I thought of ordering it," said Harry; "it is the only one here, of course."

"Harry!" cried Bluebell, rubbing her eyes, as if only just thoroughly awake, "have you got a house? Where in the world are we going to?"

"I couldn't think why you didn't ask that before, you little fatalist, taking it all in such a predestined way. I hope you don't think it a case of the Lord of Burleigh over again? It is only a cottage, Bluebell; but I think it is comfortable, and one mercy is no one will be able to find us here!"

The extreme advantage of this isolation scarcely seemed so apparent to her; and as the above sentence was the only connected or rational one Harry gave utterance to, conversation, properly so called, was *nil* during the drive. After skirting a hanging wood, and passing some water meadows, where red Herefordshire cows with white faces grazed under the low wintry sky, they drove through a primitive village, and, turning down a bye-road, drew up at a queer gabled cottage. It was very picturesque and odd-looking, and Harry, during his last leave home, had spent a night there on a visit to an artist friend, who was making sketches in the neighbourhood.

Its proprietor, a carpenter, sometimes lived in it, and sometimes was able to let it to gentlemen coming down to fish in the river. On receiving Dutton's telegram, he and his wife, who had given up all hopes of letting it for the winter, gladly laid down their best carpets, brought out their summer chintzes, and arranged everything in apple-pie order, for the cottage was taken for a month certain.

Harry had not forgotten to order a piano to be hired from the nearest town. After their long journey it all looked very home-like and attractive. They ran about the house like two children, examining everything. The sitting-room was the prettiest, with its two bay-windows at right-angles, low roof and rafters. The artist had gone abroad, and had left some of his pictures on the wall in charge of the carpenter—a bewitched Greuze, copied in the Louvre; the inevitable study of a bird's-nest and primroses; a girl standing at a wash-tub by an open window, on the sill of which outside leaned an Irish peasant, with his handsome, blarneying face. Then there were sketches taken in the neighbourhood. "I remember this one half finished on his easel," said Harry. It was a glade of a forest; in the foreground a huge oak, knee-deep in bracken, and tall blue hyacinths. "Look Bluebell, here is your name-sake flower."

"Oh, that is it! Well, I never saw one before; we have none in Canada."

"I wish it were June now," said Harry; "summer weather is what this place wants;" and he glanced out of the bay-window looking on a lawn, with a spreading cedar encircled by a seat. Some pinched chrysanthemums— those flowers that always look born in adverse circumstances—and one or two hardy roses still lingered. The clematis made a bold show on the porch, though the north wind had begun to detach its clinging embrace from the masonry, and make wild work in its tangled masses.

"It must be lovely in summer," said Bluebell, shivering, and feeling a slightly depressing influence creeping over her. They wandered out by the banks of the river to a ruined abbey, which always attracted tourists during the season. It was especially sketchable, and "bits" of it were carried away in many an artist's portfolio. But it was desolate now, and flocks of jackdaws came screaming out of holes in the walls.

I am painting from Bluebell's point of view, who could not shake off the weird feeling that possessed her, to which, perhaps, fatigue, mental and physical, not a little contributed. Yet when they came in no depression could withstand the cheery look of the lamp-lit room, with its snowy cloth laid for dinner, blazing fire, and closely-drawn curtains; and they both were unmistakably hungry, for the breakfast they had been too nervous to eat had been their only previous meal.

The carpenter waited. Bluebell felt desperately conscious. His manner was so benign and protecting, and he coughed so ostentatiously before entering the room, she was perfectly sure he had guessed that they had run away that morning. He imparted shreds of local information to Harry while changing the plates, who answered good-humouredly, but would have preferred to hear that the whole neighbourhood was wintering in Jericho. A sociable Skye terrier, who strolled in with the first dish, was rather a resource to the new-made bride, who found it easier to bend over Archie, sitting up for bones, than to sustain with imperturbability the curious if furtive observation of the carpenter.

A day or two after this evening, Harry, coming in from a smoke, saw Bluebell, with a pleased, intent face, writing, as fast as the pen could scratch, over some foreign paper.

"Oh, Harry," cried she without looking up, "we must not forget to walk into the town this afternoon. It is mail-day, I have no stamps."

Dutton's face became suddenly overcast. He jerked the end of his cigar into the fire, and threw down his hat.

"Whom are you writing to?" he asked.

"To my mother, and everybody," said Bluebell, gleefully. "I am telling them all about it."

"The devil! My dear child, stop a little."

"Why?" looking up surprised. "Oh, do you want to put something in? It would be nicer. I'll leave half a sheet."

Harry looked the picture of vexation and perplexity. He had never realized Bluebell's relations, and here it seemed she was in regular correspondence with her mother and other friends.

"My dear girl, for goodness' sake stop! My uncle does not know it yet, and you mustn't say a word to any one."

Bluebell seemed rather bewildered. "Why don't you tell your uncle, then? And surely my mother would be equally interested!"

Dutton sat down for a long explanation, "I shouldn't so much have cared about offending him before, but now I have you, Bluebell, it would be ruin. I have nothing but my profession and what he allows me; and he disinherited his only son for a marriage that displeased him."

She gave a half start here. "What is your uncle's name."

"Lord Bromley."

"Oh, of course; you told me so before. Well, go on."

"I shall run down to 'The Towers' presently, sound the old man, and break it to him, if possible. If I could only take you, my darling, it ought to do the business! By Jove, I have a great mind to try!"

"But," said Bluebell, reverting to her own immediate anxiety, "I must tell them at home what has become of me. Fancy, Harry, what a state they would be in, not hearing! Let me, at any rate, say I am married, but cannot tell my name for a few weeks."

"Well, mind you don't say more," very gloomily. "I dare say there will be no end of a row, and they will be sending people to try and trace us. Impossible for a month, though," he reflected.

"And, Harry, did you write to Captain Davidson?"

He shook his head.

"Oh, do, pray, or let me!"

"Now, my dear Bluebell, haven't we just agreed the fewer people who know it the better? You say you left a letter telling him you were to be married, and it is no further business of his. Besides, he is a suspicious old nuisance, and would very likely come boring down here; and then I should be sure to quarrel with him. Come along, put on your hat, and let us go out."

"I must re-write my letter," said she. It was much shorter than the other one, and a sober look had dawned on her fair face when it was finished.

More than once she resumed the subject, but never got any satisfaction from Dutton. "What did she want more? Could anything be jollier than the life they were leading, with no one to bother them? Every one was alone in the honeymoon; and, once their marriage was confessed, it would be the beginning of ceaseless annoyance, disagreeable advice from relations, shindies without end."

Harry was still in the seventh heaven—more ardent in love with his wife than ever; and this sweet little quiet home, with "the mystery and romance of it," he was unwilling to tear himself from. To Bluebell it bore a different aspect. Marriage had deprived her of all her friends, and raised a barrier between the present and the past. There had been no time to grow to Harry, and he demanded so much. She was never alone, never free from this all-pervading passionate love that she felt quite powerless to equal. Sometimes Bluebell marvelled he did not perceive this, though nothing she dreaded more, for, since the discovery of how much he had risked for her, she was always blaming herself for not feeling the exclusive devotion that could alone recompense him.

To be suddenly deprived of all occupation, and sent to some unfamiliar place to be absolutely happy for a month, is an ordeal custom imposes on most newly-wedded pairs; but a runaway match has severer conditions still, since no letters of affectionate interest can be expected from friends, and the bride has not even a trousseau to fall back upon.

One morning after they had been married three weeks, a batch of letters was forwarded to Dutton by his agent, to whom he had only lately given his address. One was from Lord Bromley, and had lain there some time. On coming in from a walk that same afternoon, they found cards on the table.

"Just impertinent curiosity," growled Harry.

"Why?" cried Bluebell. "For my part, I think it is rather fun to have a visitor. Dear me, though, *I* have no cards;"—and she coloured deeply as she remembered that her marriage was still unacknowledged, even on pasteboard.

"Bluebell," cried Harry, impulsively, "I'll go to-morrow and make it all right with my uncle at once."

"Oh, I *wish* you would," with deep energy.

"And you don't mind being left?" he asked tenderly.

"Oh, anything to have the secret at an end!"

"Bluebell, for goodness' sake don't expect too much! What if my uncle disinherited me? It is not at all unlikely."

"Ah, Harry," said Bluebell, softly, "that comes of marrying me. Why did you not think of it first? I should be no worse off," continued she, musingly; "I could give music lessons. It's hard on you, of course; but, Harry, do, pray, whatever are the consequences, tell him."

"But you don't realize the consequences. I should be obliged to go to sea, leave you alone, and have scarcely any money to send you. But if he took it pleasantly, he could make it worth my while to leave the navy, which he has always wished me to do, or let us have sufficient coin for you to come to any port I am stationed at. As long as it was only myself, I didn't care so much; yet Bromley Towers *is* worth saving, if possible." A pause. "But I can't think what you will do while I am away."

"Shall I cultivate our visitors, Mr. and Mrs. Stevens?"

"Not for the world; we must let them slide quietly, and then people will begin to understand we don't wish to be called on."

"I daresay you are right; this house must be an *oubliette* till your awful uncle is confessed to." Bluebell spoke with some asperity; the concealment had become so unbearable. What would the Rollestons think if her mother imparted to them her improbable story of being married to a man who could not acknowledge her? And that dear old captain would most likely imagine the worst without her being able to undeceive him. But Harry was deep in *Bradshaw*, and unobservant.

"I shall sleep in London, I think, and go down next morning. Let me see, I shan't be able to get away till after the new year. Lord Bromley has the usual family gathering on for Christmas."

"Won't the time of your return somewhat depend on the way your communication is received?" asked Bluebell, demurely.

"Well, rather," laughing. "It won't do to bring it in head and shoulders. I must stay a little while first and watch my opportunity."

Bluebell walked with him to the station next day. It was freezing hard—a bright, bracing morning; and when he had taken his place, and the train had whistled off, she was shocked to find how her spirits rose. Of course, she told herself it was because there would soon be no occasion for concealment; but there was a sensation of present relief not quite to be accounted for by that.

Young people care quite as much as their elders for occasional solitude— more, perhaps, for they have generally brighter thoughts to fill it. Bluebell, from the reasons before mentioned, in her anxious compliance with his every whim, had become quite a slave to Harry, and a little breathing-time was far from unwelcome. After all, she had a good deal exaggerated his sacrifice, which was made entirely to please himself!

Leaving the road, Bluebell struck a path across some fields leading to the river, and amused herself throwing sticks for Archie to fetch off its half-frozen surface—a diversion which soon palled on the Skye, who was not fond of water; so Bluebell wandered on, soliloquizing, as usual. Suppose this uncle, who loomed in her imagination like some dread Genie in his disposition over their fate should receive the intelligence by cutting off the supplies and hurling maledictions at Harry's head, what on earth would they do? She had always been very fond of acting,—indeed, had been quite an authority in drawing-room theatricals and charades at "The Maples," and with her magnificent powerful voice, what a pity she could not go on the stage! She had read in novels of girls offering themselves to a manager and realizing fabulous sums, and eighteen pounds a year seemed to be her net value in the governess market. Then Harry might go to sea for a year or two,—they were both so young,—and by that time things might look brighter, or the Genie relent.

She and Archie had a good time that bright winter day, and tired themselves out completely. He could pass from the immediate enjoyment of a meal to a snooze on the rug before the fire; but after Bluebell had had some tea, there remained many hours at her disposal before bed-time. She would have liked to have written a long letter to her mother; but if it must be worded so guardedly, where was the good? So she flew to her unfailing friend, the piano, and interpreted Schumann and Beethoven to a late hour, while the carpenter and his wife, listening in the kitchen, "wished that the lady would play something with a bit of tune in it, and not be always practising them exercises."

CHAPTER XXXI
BROMLEY TOWERS

Had yon ever a cousin, Tom'
And did that cousin happen to sing'
Sisters we have by the dozen,
But a cousin's a different thing

Hon. Mrs. Norton.

Harry had stayed the night in London, and rather wished, for the present, it might be inferred that he had been there all the time. It was some distance from Bromley Towers, and quite dusk as he drove through the park. Snow was on the ground, and still falling slowly, the two roaring fires in the hall, as the doors were thrown open, flung a red light on the holly berries and gigantic bunch of mistletoe suspended from the chandelier, and flickered on dark oil paintings let into the panels. The footmen were unfamiliar, but the old butler beamed on the young heir he had known from a boy.

Harry shook him heartily by the hand, and asked a dozen questions in a breath. There was a sprinkling of visitors already in the house, so, shirking the reception rooms, he made straight for a private passage, where in a certain study, he knew he should find his uncle.

Lord Bromley seldom had his large house empty and there were ample means of entertainment for guests, but, like a good general, he had a secure retreat from the perils of boredom in a sacred suite of rooms, to which no one but his nephew had access. To Harry himself this particular study was invested with a certain amount of solemnity, he had been summoned there on so many notable occasions, —once to be sentenced to a thrashing from a malevolent tutor who had reported him, afterwards, before going to school, to receive good advice, not unsweetened by a tip. Cheques had been dealt out there, and his uncle's views for his future guidance inculcated on him. Dutton entered now with somewhat of the feelings of a truant schoolboy, for had he not been on shore a month without coming near the place or even writing?

He murmured something about London and business, which the old peer received with the merest elevation of the eyebrows, and was evidently not going to be unpleasant about it. He knew his nephew was just off a voyage and in possession of a handsome cheque, and was not ill pleased that he should have had his fling, and have done with it before coming down.

Besides, if some plans of his succeeded, he would soon have to *range* himself.

Finding it was all right, and Lord Bromley disposed to be sociable, Harry made himself as entertaining as possible, and was communicative enough about everything but the proceedings of the last few weeks.

"I think you know most of the people in the house," said his uncle, as Dutton was retiring to dress, "except, perhaps, one or two men. Lady Calvert has brought her daughter here. She was not out, you know, when you last went to sea."

"I remember her, though; projecting teeth and —"

"She will probably drop into all that Durnford property now Lionel is dead."

When he came down to dinner, Lord Bromley introduced him very particularly to the few strangers present, who all thought how fond his uncle seemed of him, and that he would surely be the heir.

Dutton, like most careless dressing men, looked best in the regulation simplicity of evening clothes, in which the despotism of fashion curbs all vagaries of fancy. More than one feminine critic smiled involuntary approval of the handsome young sailor, whose easy, slightly unconventional manner, though singular, was not unattractive.

He had been told off to take Lady Geraldine Vane in to dinner, and went to renew acquaintance with her at once. She was dressed in a cloud of blue tulle, and wore a heavy white wreath on her hair, which was very light. Complexion she had none. She was pale without being fair. Her features were irregular, lips thin, with projecting teeth, and eyebrows scarcely apparent at all. Yet these defects were partly redeemed by one sole attraction, a pair of large, light eyes, with a great deal of heart in them. They could glisten with affection and brighten with interest, and were the faithful mirrors of a modest, sensitive, and naturally amiable disposition. But Harry thought her, dress and all, the most colourless object, and longed to offer even a damask rose to break the cold, sickly effect.

There was another young lady present, of a very different type to Lady Geraldine,—not exactly pretty, but evidently aiming at being *chic*. Her dress was of the latest fashion, and in a slightly audacious style, likewise the arrangement of her hair. She had a pretty, neat figure, and a way of seeing everything through half-shut eyes. This was Harry's cousin Kate.

Perhaps it would be too much to say he was very fond of this young damsel; but, at any rate, he was delighted to find her there. "She is such a jolly girl in a house!" he said to himself.

Kate, then a finished coquette of ten, used to try her hand at flirting with the big schoolboy; and when she had him in a state of helpless adoration, and all his pocket-money was gone in presents to her, would turn him off in favour of his particular friend, who was spending the holidays at Bromley Towers. The two boys blacked each other's eyes in consequence; but the capricious fair only remarked that "they had made such frights of themselves, the sooner they went back to school the better."

As they grew up the intimacy continued. Kate would make use of him as an escort, and allow him to kiss her as a cousin. She also confided to him her love affairs, which at first made him very angry, but afterwards he sometimes suspected their veracity.

Harry could not help watching her at dinner. He saw the amused face of her neighbour, Colonel Dashwood, and sometimes caught her lively repartees.

Lady Geraldine was rather tame, and not even pretty; it was up hill work talking to her, and he was just in the humour for a chaffing match with cousin Kate. After dinner it was just the same: she was surrounded by men, and Lady Geraldine, the only other girl, sat apart, with rather a plaintive, neglected look.

"Why can't she talk to some of those old women?" thought Harry. But he felt bound to try and amuse her, and, after a little desultory conversation, ingeniously evaded the necessity of boring himself further by asking her to sing. She complied very amiably, and, as he stationed himself near to turn over, saw it was one of Bluebell's songs. Lady Geraldine had been well taught, and sang accurately; but, oh! the contrast of the thin, piping voice and expressionless delivery to the rich tones and almost dramatic fervour with which Bluebell poured forth her "native wood-notes wild"! Then Kate came to the front, followed by a devoted cavalier, who took her gloves and fan, and was forthwith despatched in search of a very particular manuscript book somewhere in the half.

En attendant she rattled off a sparkling French *chansonnette* with such *élan* that every man in the room, musical or otherwise, was soon round the piano. Her voice was harsh and wiry; but there was an oddity and originality in her style, while she pronounced the words with a vehement clearness, that drove their meaning home to the dullest ear. Mr. Hornby returned with the manuscript book, fastened by a patent lock, and ornamented with an elaborate monogram.

"I never keep any songs that other people have, so I am obliged to guard my *spécialités* under lock and key,"—and she held out her arm to Colonel Dashwood to unclasp a bracelet, the medallion of which opened on touching a spring, and disclosed a gold key.

Colonel Dashwood retained the wrist while pretending to examine this miracle, and Kate shot one of her dangerous glances out of half-closed eyes.

A personal assault upon Dashwood would have been consonant to Harry's feelings at the moment. He was not yet quite proof against twinges of jealousy about cousin Kate, who was now turning over the leaves of her book with an unconscious air.

"This song Mr. Forsyth brought me from Mexico. Such crabbed copying, only an expert could read it; so I merely scribbled down the words, and made him sing the air till I had caught it. That Charley Dacre got from a boatman at Venice; and this little Troubadour thing" (sentimentally) "was composed by a friend of mine, who has promised never to let any one possess it but myself."

"I hope you bought up the whole edition," put in Harry.

"And here—even you, you dear, unmusical boy, are represented. Do you remember it, Harry?" (playing a few bars.) "The air you were always whistling, and said the sailors sang at watch."

"Yes, that was it," said he, with brightening eyes. "How could you recollect?"

"Well, when you went to sea I got somewhat plaintive and dull; used to hum it about the house, and set down the notes."

"But these are not the right words."

"Oh, no," said Kate, casting down her eyes with modest candour; "they are my own."

Now Harry at the same moment felt almost certain he had seen the lines somewhere before; and, being rather apt to stick to a point, turned it over in his mind, while his cousin poured forth a flood of song like a skylark soaring. Ere she desisted, Dutton had left the room, and discovered the words in an old Annual on a top shelf in the library.

CHAPTER XXXII
THE SPRING WOODS

But, Tom, you'll soon find, for I happen to know,
That such walks often lead into straying;
And the voices of cousins are sometimes so low,
Heaven only knows what you'll be saying.
And long ere the walk is half over those strings
Of your heart are all put into play
By the voice of those fair demi-sisterly things,
In not quite the most brotherly way.

Hon. Mrs. Norton.

More snow fell that night, and Lord Bromley's gardeners were sweeping the walks from an early hour next morning. Robins lingered about with bright eyes, soliciting crumbs, and shaking off showers of snow as they flew from yew-hedge to holly-bush. Breakfast was over at "The Towers," except for a few late individuals; and Harry Dutton, in a pair of long boots, and, I am afraid, a pipe in his mouth, was taking a quarter-deck walk in front of the ball-room windows. He was thinking pretty hard, and the subject was evidently not pleasing, as it was with a sensation of relief he observed a deft figure crossing the ball-room, in a fur-trimmed cloth costume, remarkably well kilted up over a resolute-looking pair of small boots. She signed to him to open the windows and let her out. Harry made a feint of emptying his pipe, but received gracious permission to "puff away."

"That killing get-up can't be for me," thought he. "I'll give her the tip she wants."

"A certain good-looking Colonel of Hussars has gone to play a match at billiards till luncheon."

"Why that blunt and abrupt observation, *à propos* to nothing?"

"You must excuse my sea manners. I should have used more circumlocution, but they don't put much polish on us on board."

"No, they don't, and you boast of it, hence that phrase. You never hear a soldier apologizing for his 'army manners'!"

"Speaks well for their modesty! Well, Kate, where are you bound for? You are not rigged up in that way merely to coast about here."

"I meant to walk round the spring woods."

"And as Dashwood has sloped perhaps I may sail in consort. The walks won't be swept, of course, and that dainty scarlet petticoat will look like an old hunting-coat."

But a gardener asserting that the men had been at work since daylight, the cousins departed on their ramble.

A gravel walk a mile round encircled the inner ring of a wood left wild, except where rides were cut, showing vistas into the park beyond. Here and there it was cleared into a rosary, with a summer-house, a Dutch garden with a fountain, a glade with a fish-pond, etc. The trees were magnificent, and many a foreign specimen was represented, while the shimmering tints of grey-green, from their great variety, were of shades innumerable. Sometimes the bordering turf became wider, and flowering shrubs grew each side of the walk,—an intoxicating spot in spring, when the wild flowers carpeted the woods, and the bird *artistes*, returning from starring in other lands, recommenced their "popular concerts."

Even now, in winter dress, its attractions were but changed. The lichen-covered kings of the forest revealed their bold limbs undisguised by foliage, the feathery birch showed its delicate tracery against the clear winter sky, and Dutton sighed as he gazed on that fair demesne, and thought how hard it would be to give it up.

Kate's thoughts had apparently wandered in the same direction, for she said abruptly,—"What a happy fellow you are, Harry, to be heir to all this!" But she was thinking more of the first-rate style in which it was kept up, and the magnificent, comfortable house, than of its picturesque features.

"There's many a slip," said Harry, moodily, between the whiffs of his pipe. "We all know Uncle Bromley, Kate."

"Do you know," said she, mysteriously, "I hear he actually keeps his eyes, so to speak, on that grand-daughter in Canada. The agent who pays the annuity reports to him."

"The deuce!—you make me quite hot, Kate. Are you inventing just out of chaff?"

"No, honour bright. Mamma was talking about it; and seems he heard rather an unpleasant rumour the other day."

"Come, that's better. What has the young woman been a-doing of?"

"Run away, or something. I overheard mamma telling old Lady Calvert; but they nodded and winked and interjected I couldn't clearly make it out. I was writing a letter at the davenport, and in the glass opposite observed them. I don't generally burden my mind much with the conversation of my elders, but something in the alertness of their attitudes and flutter of their caps made me contemplatively bite my pen and—attend. A breach of confidence on the maternal side, I should surmise, for she declined satisfying my laudable curiosity when I pumped her afterwards, and seemed alarmed at my having heard anything."

"I had no idea," exclaimed Harry, "that he took the slightest interest in that girl; and, hang it all, Kate, she *is* the rightful heir. Perhaps he looks on her as a second string in case I don't carry out all his arbitrary wishes."

"Yes, I shouldn't recommend your running counter to him gratuitously. To tell you the truth, I thought you rather a lunatic keeping away so long after coming on shore,"—and Kate gazed searchingly into Harry's face, who blushed, and then frowned under the scrutiny.

"Ah!" murmured the fair inquisitor, "then there *was* something—a woman in the case, of course: there always is."

"I tell you what," cried Dutton, recovering himself, "if you begin supposing improbabilities about me, I'll turn detective on you and Dashwood."

"Sea manners again! and when I was so kind—putting you on your guard. But, never mind, Harry, though I *think* what I please, I shan't peach *if you don't.*"

"Let us seal the treaty," passing one arm round her waist. "Give me a kiss, Kate—you haven't yet."

"Anything in reason, which sealing treaties in a vista opposite Uncle Bromley's study windows is *not.*"

A few paces rectified that objection; but Dutton relapsed into a brown study, and Kate fell to thinking of Colonel Dashwood; and so they wandered on till the girl spoke again.

"What port have you left your heart in, Harry?"

"My dear, I have none. I left it in your charge when I went to sea, and have never asked for it back again."

"I expect I shall have to return it now, as I think my uncle has some views as to its disposal, and may inquire for it."

"He always has chimeras of that sort. I say, Kate, how perilously plain Geraldine has grown up."

"You discern the finger of Fate there. She has, indeed. I wonder she is not ashamed of herself."

"Speak not thus harshly of a misfortune."

"It's just as much a fault. Do you think *I'd* submit to be plain? Never. Give me only one good feature, I'd pose up to it, and make it beautify the rest. Large goggle eyes like hers might be thrown up with a heavenly expression—so—(but I am afraid mine are rather earthly). A bad figure even could be rectified. She need not indulge much in the poetry of motion. *I* am not pretty, but I dare say you never found it out. No, you haven't, so you needn't assume that look of regretful dissent; and I repeat, that any girl so spiritless as to give in to being ugly *deserves* to be left out in the cold."

"That, my dear, you can never be. You carry brimstone enough to set every one in flames about you. But to return to our—sheep. Don't say, Kate, I am expected to range alongside such a figure-head as that!"

"She will have a very valuable consignment of—timber, however, when she comes into Forest Hill."

"Which adjoins 'The Towers!' The Avuncular will be death on it! What an unfortunate idea to take up!"

"Can't you do it?" asked the girl, looking askance.

"I don't want to offend his Lordship. I'd ride for a *fall*. Any chance of a refusal, Kate?"

"That wouldn't satisfy him. He thinks a man ought never to be beat; and that

'It isn't so much the gallant who woos
As the gallant's way of wooing.'

But I do hope, Harry, you won't have to marry Geraldine. Fancy *her* mistress of 'The Towers!'—no go!—no fun! and she would collect the stupidest people in the county."

"What a brilliant little chatelaine some one else would make!" quoth wicked Harry.

A glance—one of Kate's own—which few men could stand and feel perfectly cool. With all her flirtations,—and at present she was most in love with Colonel Dashwood,—she never forgot that if bereaved of their uncle by an opportune fit of the gout, few better matches could fall in her way than cousin Harry; so that a little quiet love-making with him was a useful investment in view of such a contingency; though, of course, she could not wait, if this dear uncle, as, indeed, was sadly probable, lived on indefinitely with Harry's future still unassured.

Dutton blushed a little under Kate's gaze, which affixed a serious meaning to his insincere words; but his eyes returned the challenge in hers, though the girl saw in an instant that the expression was not spontaneous, and Harry felt equally sure that the passion latent in his cousin's was more for "The Towers" than himself; and then he laughed inwardly as he thought how different it would be if she knew he was married.

Several days passed, and the object of Harry's visit was still unfulfilled. Indeed, a good opportunity for the disclosure seemed more remote than ever. Kate monopolized all the men in the house, and, being at home, Dutton, in common decency, could not suffer Lady Geraldine to be neglected. There were only those two girls staying at "The Towers." Others sometimes came to dinner with their parents, and an *impromptu* dance was often got up. Geraldine had begun to listen for Harry's step, seat herself near a vacant chair, and thrill with delight when he took it. No man dislikes such unconscious flattery, and Dutton, ill at ease in mind, felt himself soothed by her kindness.

On these occasions, Lord Bromley appeared bland and agreeable, Lady Calvert voluble and unobserving, and there was a sense of *bien-être* over every one, Kate, perhaps, excepted.

Dutton had received one letter from his wife. He had had a five mile-walk to get it from the post town he had bidden her address to, and opened it with a strange mixture of curiosity and yearning. It was a very bright letter, made no complaints of loneliness, and was rather divertingly written, considering the limited topics at her command; and yet Harry crunched it up in his hand with a sensation of half anger and whole disappointment. It was their first separation,—they had not been married seven weeks,—and there was scarcely an expression of affection in it!

He felt like a schoolboy who has coveted and caught some pretty wild animal for a pet, yet cannot succeed in making it fond of him.

He laughed rather bitterly as he retraced his steps. It was scarcely worth the cold, companionless walk, or the pains he had taken to evade the rest.

Why should he risk offending his uncle to please her? If that, indeed, were all, he did not know that he should. But new considerations came in. We were on the eve of drifting into the Crimean War; the papers were getting more and more threatening; and, in the event of hostilities being declared, he had applied for a ship on active service.

Could he, then, when he might never return, leave Bluebell with their marriage unacknowledged? "Though," thought he, in his moody reverie, "if *that* were all right, I don't believe she would care a pin if *I* were knocked over by a round shot."

Some curiosity and a good deal of chaff greeted Dutton on his return; but Kate did not fail to remark how little he entered into, and how quickly turned it off. That cousin Harry had some mystery of his own, the astute damsel was pretty well convinced, though to the rest he appeared light-hearted and hilarious, and enjoying to the full his enviable position.

"What a lucky young fellow that is?" had been remarked at different times by nearly every guest in the house. And the days slipped by, Harry very much "made of" by Lady Calvert, while Lady Geraldine's preference was of an unobtrusive and reticent nature—impalpable, yet grateful to the senses as the fragrance of an invisible, leaf-hidden violet.

And Bluebell, all alone in her retreat, and each day passing without tidings, began to think she had over-estimated Harry's once troublesome adoration, and almost to doubt if he would ever return.

In truth, he was ashamed to write. The longer the confession was deferred, the harder it became; and he had now assigned himself a date. On receiving sailing orders to the Baltic, he would tell all, and make it, perhaps, a last request to his uncle to acknowledge his wife. In the mean time why plague himself about it? Things must take their course.

They were sitting one day in a pretty breakfast-room. Kate rather angry with her Colonel, who lingered on, always apparently at boiling point, yet never so far bubbling over as to commit himself in words. Harry, too, was looking actually interested in Geraldine, whose large, honest eyes were beaming with a sort of tender happiness. Lord Bromley was not in the room. Clearly he must be detached.

"Doesn't this dear old room remind you of childish days?" cried the artless damsel. "It used always to be summer or Christmas then; and we had tea here in such beautiful china, so different from the horrid school-room crockery."

"And sometimes we were so long over it, they couldn't clear away before the company passed through to dinner, and we got under the table to watch them," said Harry.

"And we used to put out the little sofas and jump over them, King Charles's beauties looking down on us from the wall so grand and gracious. And there was always mignonette and nemophila in window-boxes, so sweet in the evening air? And the honey? Oh, Harry, do you remember the honey?"

Her reminiscences succeeded in breaking up the *tête-à-tête*, and, lo! the wicked little dominant spirit who pulled the wires had indirectly influenced every one in the room. Harry, mesmerized by eye artillery, had dropped into confidential converse with Kate; Geraldine was suffering a *serrement de coeur* at being so lightly left; and the Colonel, his occupation gone, was reduced to twisting those tried friends in perplexity—his pendulous whiskers and moustache.

"How silly a hairy man looks drinking tea," Kate had whispered; "like a thirsty rat dipping its whiskers and tail in!"

A rather pleased expression pervaded Harry's countenance, which was as smooth as a billiard-ball. His cousin soon had him beautifully in hand, and then extorted a promise to do the thing he hated most, *i.e.*, to escort her out hunting the following Friday. She hadn't the smallest intention of remaining with him after they found. Then she would ride with her Colonel, who acquitted himself more creditably in a hunting-field; but, as she was not allowed to start with him alone, it was necessary to impress Harry into her service.

"That's all settled," cried she, rising. "Remember, honour bright! And now go and talk to dear Geraldine, who looks as if she were going to cry." For Kate had heard Lord Bromley's step in the passage. He came in with Mr. Hobart, who had just returned from London. "Have you heard the news?" said the latter; "war is declared; the army, Guards and all, are ordered to the East, and the fleet is to go to the Baltic."

How these few words went straight to their mark, contrasting with the frivolities that had amused them all day! It had come at last. Chances of distinction, redemption from stagnation, the much-coveted active service. They were all brave men in that house—soldiers or sailors, most of them; but the "bitter sweet first shock" and rush of new ideas kept them, at first, rather pale and silent.

After dinner though, when the wine had circulated and the first strangeness worn off, chaff and jest flew lightly about, for a general excitement pervaded the whole party.

"Shall you order those new clothes now Dashwood, you had so many patterns for this morning?"

"No! they would be out of fashion, perhaps, when we return. I was just going to order a new tunic, too! That sinful extravagance may be cut off."

Harry, who, perhaps, had most cause for anxious thoughts, was foremost in the fun. If his spirits were forced, that was his own affair; and, to avoid Kate's over-keen eyes, he (the last thing he ought to have done) devoted himself the whole evening to the more restful society of Geraldine.

Pre-occupied as he was, he began to be sensible of a change in her manner—she seemed struggling with some indefinable agitation; her voice shook, and sounded strange when she spoke.

And when he laughingly hoped "he should be covered with medals next time they met," uncoquettish Lady Geraldine looked a moment in his face with a glance he could not misunderstand, while a large, unavoidable tear fell on her hand. To capture and press it tenderly was but obeying a remorseful impulse. Geraldine immediately became composed, and her sensitive face brightened. The embarrassment that had left her seemed to have passed into Harry, who felt the greatest relief when a flutter of skirts and general rising betokened that the ladies were about to retire.

But the little incident had forced resolution on Dutton's vacillating mind. "That settles it," he soliloquised. "She is far too nice to be deceived. I know Kate won't let me off to-morrow, but I will have it out with my uncle directly I come back, and go to London by the 8.30."

CHAPTER XXXIII
LORD BROMLEY INTERVIEWS DUTTON

Ere long a challenge and a cheer
Came floating down the wind;
'Twas Mermaid's note, and the huntsman's voice
We knew it was a find.
The dull air woke us from a trance
As sixty hounds joined chorus,
And away we went, with a stout dog fox
Not a furlong's length before us.

Lawrence.

Nearly every one was going by a late train the following day, intending to hunt in the morning; for it was a favourite meet in some of the best country of — —shire. Kate was the only fair equestrian, and Harry was to escort her.

There was one old hunter in the stables who loyally carried the young man without taking advantage of his maladroitness. Kate always insisted, when he accompanied her, on his being committed—I may say to the *care* of this faithful equine, who knew its business far better than its rider, and, if it did not lead him to glory, at least avoided disgrace.

Whatever she might have felt about the approaching departure of Colonel Dashwood certainly did not appear, for Kate was in glorious spirits,—her pretty figure, always well on horseback, set off still more by the elastic action of her beautiful dark chestnut.

Where is the thorough-bred without "opinions?"—and when of that excitable colour, you may generally reckon on a handful! "Childe Harold" was vexed at galloping on a different strip of turf to his companions, and delivered himself of seven buck-jumps successively. Kate, quite at her ease, was repressing his efforts to get his head down, with the same smile on her face that some absurdity of Harry's had provoked; but just as she began to tire a bit, and fancy her hat was loosening, "Childe Harold," who might then, perhaps, have had one conquering buck, as suddenly gave it up, in the fatuous way a horse will, when he is nearest success, if he only knew it.

"Two or three of those would have settled me," said Harry, good-humouredly coming to her side. "What an ass a fellow looks who can't ride!"

"Well, I will say for you you don't funk," said Kate consolingly; "and I suppose all sailors ride like monkeys.—There are the hounds going on; we are only just in time."

Coquettish Kate was soon surrounded. If she rode fair and didn't cross men at their fences, still less did she want assistance at any practicable leap. "Childe Harold," too, was indifferent to a lead; so, beholden to none, she rode her own line, and, with her merry smile and gay tongue, with the whole field, from the gallant master to the hard-riding farmer, there were few greater favourites than Harry's cousin Kate.

The universal theme at the cover-side was, of course, the declaration of war; but even that absorbing subject sunk to silence as the first low whimper, taken up more confidently by hound after hound, proclaimed that poor Reynard was being bustled through the underwood.

A relieved smile played over the features of the owner of the cover, and "Always a fox in Beechwood" came approvingly from the master's lips as he crashed out of the spinny. Kate's gauntleted hand was held up warningly, for the "Childe" was apt to let out one hind leg in excitement. Then there was a screech from an urchin in a tree, and they were away with a straight running fox pointing to Redbank Bushes, eight miles off as the crow flies.

Not much of the run was Harry Dutton destined to see that day; his presumed mission was to stick on and follow Kate, who thought no more about him once they were away. He had flopped over the first fence without a mistake; but coming on a bit of road the old horse faltered, a few yards more he was dead lame. Harry jumped off, and found a shoe gone. Dashwood had a spare one he remembered, and there was a blacksmith, not half a mile distant. He looked round—no sign of him of course; he was sailing away with a good start, fields ahead, in that contented ecstasy that stops not for friend or foe. There was nothing for it but to plod on to the forge, trusting to nick in later in the day. As the shoe had to be made, delay was inevitable. Dutton lit a cigar to while away the term of durance, and was disconsolately looking out at the door of the smithy, when he observed one of the Bromley grooms trotting smartly down the road.

He hailed the man, who touched his hat with alacrity. "I was riding to find you, sir; his Lordship has sent your letters."

The train was late, and the post had not arrived before they had been obliged to start that morning. He tore open a large blue official envelope, "On Her Majesty's Service," and read his appointment to H.M.S. "Druid," one of the Baltic fleet.

Harry stood intent a minute, with compressed lips, then signed to the groom to give him his horse.

"I have got letters for Colonel Dashwood and Mr. Hobart, too, sir."

"Well, 'Figaro' will be shod in five minutes. But you won't catch them this side of the Bushes; they were going straight for them half an hour ago."

And he galloped away with his loose sailor seat in the direction of "The Towers." The hour had come. That letter was the self-imposed signal for the acknowledgment of his marriage, and, perhaps, extinction of all hope of inheritance. One watchful figure at the library window perceived his red coat winding through the trees on his way to the stables. Lady Geraldine had caught sight of the blue envelope, and, with the prescience of love, had divined the whole. She had not wandered far from the window that morning, being too restless and miserable for anything else. Now, as she perceived him, her heart stood still. He must be going that very day.

"Well, she would see him once more, at any rate. Adieux must be spoken, and, after last night, surely something more, something to dwell on when they were apart." The carriage was rolling up to the door for the daily drive. Lady Calvert and Kate's mother came down well muffled up. "Geraldine, my dear, are you not ready! Oh, you had much better come, or you will be left alone in the house."

Geraldine, hitherto all transparent candour, shook her head dissentingly. "Oh, no, thank you; much too cold. I am going for a walk presently."

She forbore to inflame the maternal curiosity by mentioning Dutton's return, and the elder ladies drove off on a shopping expedition to the market town.

Harry, in the meanwhile, had entered the dining-room, and, eliciting from a footman that his uncle was in, poured out something from a decanter on the side table, and, without waiting to refresh himself further, went down the passage leading to Lord Bromley's sanctum.

"'The lion in his den, the Douglas in his hall,'" muttered he to himself. "I shall be a man or a mouse when I come out."

We need not go through the whole interview of the uncle and nephew. The latter's appointment was, of course, the first subject of discussion; and never had Harry known Lord Bromley show more cordiality and warmth of manner. He himself was becoming confused and tongue-tied with the importance of the confession at hand.

"I think of going to London this afternoon," said Dutton, still fencing. "There's a few things to arrange, as I am to join on Monday."

Lord Bromley coughed, poked the fire, and then observed,—"That brings me to a subject that I wish to explain to you. I have brought you up in the expectation of succeeding me at 'The Towers,' and, naturally, I expect you to make a suitable marriage,—as well you may with such prospects before you. I have noticed with great pleasure that your inclinations seem to have forestalled my wishes. The young lady, too, does not appear averse. But before you go, if you would like to explain yourself to her—in short, bring it to an engagement, you would have my most cordial approbation— in fact, I think it's the best thing you could do."

Harry grew a shade paler as the opportunity he wanted appeared.

"I am very sorry, sir," said he, shortly, "but I can never marry Lady Geraldine."

"Why, the devil not?"

"Because," faltered he, "I have a prior attachment. Indeed, am bound—"

"Prior attachment! d—d stuff!" cried the angry peer. "Whom have you seen, I should like to know, except some garrison hack at the ports you have stopped at! By — —, it is not Kate, I hope?"

Dutton shook his head. He would have been amused at any other moment.

"No, much worse, no doubt. Listen, Harry. It is bad enough your having made a fool of that very nice girl; but, if ever you wish to be master of this house, the sooner you get rid of all disgraceful entanglements, the better."

Dutton's good angel battled hard with the tempter, but the latter held him silent.

Lord Bromley spoke again, but his voice, though stern, was broken.

"I disinherited my only son for a marriage that displeased me, by which you have benefited. He died unreconciled to me. You may judge what quarter *you* would get in a similar offence!"

The old peer's face had turned to granite. A variety of expressions shifted across Harry's while his uncle continued,—"Yes, you had better go to town, as you have raised expectations here you seem to have no intention of fulfilling—*at present*," and he rose from his chair and held out his hand to his nephew. "Good-bye, Harry. You have something else to think of now; and when you return I hope you will have more sense."

It was not manly—it was not heroic—but with the wisdom of the children of this world, Dutton passed from his uncle's presence with his secret still unrevealed.

The watcher at the library window saw another carriage drive round. This time it was a double dog-cart, and two or three leather portmanteaus were being disposed on it at a side door.

Already! Geraldine grew nervous. He might come in at any moment, or perhaps would not know any of the ladies had remained at home.

"Still, he could *ask*," whispered her heart. She had not long to remain in suspense. Harry came out, jumped into the dog-cart, and gathered up the reins; then he looked up and saw Geraldine's stricken face. He blushed hotly as he took off his hat, and shot one sorrowful glance from his eyes ere he drove off, at headlong speed, to the station.

CHAPTER XXXIV
HARRY GOES TO THE BALTIC

Is this my lord of Leicester's love,
That he so oft have swore to me?
To leave me in this lonely grove?
Immured in shameful privity?

Unknown.

Bluebell, a lonely little recluse at the cottage, seemed to have passed a lifetime there, so long were the uneventful days. She was not exactly unhappy, being too young and healthy to be a prey to low spirits. Still, her life could hardly be called satisfactory. In the first days of their marriage she would exclaim in her heart. "Oh, to be sometimes alone;" then, with the suddenness of a transformation-scence, her wish had been but too abundantly accomplished.

It was weeks since she had heard from Dutton, whose first letter had never been repeated, and she begun to believe that the headlong passion that had led him to force her, almost against her will, into marriage with him was as short-lived as it had been quickly kindled.

She remembered Bertie Du Meresq, who had appeared quite as desperate at first, and then had quietly transferred his affections to Cecil. Like the Psalmist, she could have "said in her heart, all men are liars."

Harry near—adoring—*exigeant*, could be an evil; but Harry away, engaged every thought; and if thinking of a person is the first step to love, he ought to have been satisfied with the way Bluebell was employing herself.

One evening she was sitting in her bed-room with the window open. There was a light breath of spring in the air though the nights were frosty. It was near midnight, and starlight, which has ever attractions for the young; later on, a warm fireside and creature comforts are more congenial. Archie, the dog, with his nose on his paws, bore her company; presently he gave a low growl, and pricked his ears—a moment after, Bluebell fancied she could hear the sound of wheels on the frosty ground. It became clearer and clearer; presently she could distinguish the red lights of a fly, and then she knew that Harry was come.

That his mission had been unsuccessful, she read at once in avoidance of her questioning eyes, yet, strange to say, it seemed of secondary importance. Dutton himself, for the first time, was of all-absorbing interest to Bluebell. His presence seemed to break the lethargic spell that had bound her, while no small detail of appearance and dress escaped her, even that his hair was parted differently. Dutton, who had dreaded the first meeting, was relieved by Bluebell's manner, and saw at once they were more *en rapport*. He was only too willing to procrastinate bad tidings, so it was not till the next day that she realized the whole fatal truth. Harry was going to the war with their marriage still unacknowledged.

He related, truthfully enough, his conversation with Lord Bromley. Even then, in her deep interest as to its result, Bluebell vaguely noticed the curious coincidence of his uncle also having disinherited a son, but, having a more dominant idea in her mind, that was left in a vacant corner, to crop up at some future time.

Dutton was vexed that she could not see he had no other alternative but silence.

"It would have been simply giving away 'The Towers' to have blurted it all out then."

To Bluebell's unsophisticated mind, honesty seemed more importunate than expediency.

"Then, if you do get 'The Towers' now, it will be on false pretences."

Harry reddened. He had all along been goaded by a vague sense of dishonour. "It's useless crying over spilt milk," exclaimed he, impatiently. "Now would have been the very worst time—just as he wants me to marry some one else. But when I come back—"

"Then he may be dead."

"By Jove! I think he has quite as good a chance of surviving me—not a shade of odds either way. Look here, Bluebell, I will write a letter containing a full confession, enclose our marriage certificate, and seal it with this ring he gave me. If anything happens, send it to him, and I believe he will take care of you, but not while I am alive."

"Send it to him at once, Harry."

"You used not to be so indifferent to poverty, Bluebell. You told me, in the steamer, that you had a longing for luxury and riches."

"Luxury and riches," echoed Bluebell, "seem as improbable as ever. I should like to be able to look my friends in the face."

But it was all in vain. Dutton, though remorseful, was obdurate; there was much to arrange, and he had only twenty-four hours to remain. Lord Bromley had omitted the accustomed parting cheque, which Harry had reckoned on, and money was scarce with the two young people.

"Will you go back to Canada, Bluebell, till the war is over, and I will send you all the money I can?"

"What, as Miss Leigh?"

And he could say no more. The same difficulty prevented her writing to the Rollestons, or any one else. Long and anxiously they talked over their dilemma; Dutton had only money enough to pay his bill at the cottage, and Bluebell was resolute to earn something for herself.

She answered an advertisement in the *Times* he had brought with him, naming, as reference, the mother of Evelyn Leighton. To her she also wrote, begging that any applicant might have the recommendation she had received of her from Mrs. Rolleston.

Dutton had gone, but expected to be able to return for a day or two before the fleet sailed, and Bluebell was left alone with her thoughts—too full of horrors for solitude to be endurable. Each night she dreamed of Harry, dying, and mangled by shot or shell, only to renew the vision in her waking hours; and, as she pictured such a termination to their brief married life, a vague tenderness took the place of her former apathy. The very weakness he had shown in concealing their marriage made him more a reality to her by giving her an insight into his nature—not an endearing trait, perhaps; yet sometimes the failing that one tries to counteract in the very effort it arouses awakens an interest.

Bluebell felt thankful that her hours at the cottage were numbered, for lately she had begun to fancy people looked askance at her, and the carpenter's wife had developed an inquisitiveness akin to impertinence.

Mrs. Leighton sent a very kind answer, assuring her of the recommendation as she had received it from Mrs. Rolleston. It was addressed to "Miss Leigh," and a crimson flush rose to her temples at the unpleasant smile with which the postmistress handed it across the counter. Harry, when he wrote, having posted it himself, ventured to address his letter to "Mrs. Dutton"; the only other she had received was from her mother, directed, as requested, to B. D. This letter had been rather distressing—filled with vague fears, inspired, she was sure, by Miss Opie, and conjuring her, with promises of inviolable secrecy, to reveal her name.

The lady whose advertisement she had answered, apparently attracted by her musical professions, replied immediately, and, the reference to Mrs. Leighton being satisfactory, she was shortly engaged at a fair salary.

Then Bluebell, writing the account to Canada, could not refrain from slipping in a private scrap to her mother, on which, in the strictest confidence, she acknowledged her wedded name. This circumstance, however, she did not mention to Harry when he returned on two days' leave, knowing he would be sceptical as to Mrs. Leigh's power of secrecy.

Of course he was relieved that she had an asylum provided, and equally, of course, raged inwardly at his wife's having to support herself in her maiden name. He was the more remorseful as Bluebell made no further allusion to it, and seemed more occupied with making the most of his last days.

But he only called himself a confounded rascal, and trusted things would come right in the end.

Bluebell was to remain one more night at the cottage after her husband left. Her wardrobe, though slender, was new, as it consisted of what Harry had bought at Liverpool. None of it was marked, as she remembered with satisfaction; so there was nothing to betray her but her wedding-ring. She removed and suspended it round her neck on a piece of ribbon. The miniature of Theodore Leigh, which had not been forgotten the day she eloped, was also carefully secreted in a trunk.

The bill was paid, the fly at the door. One tender parting only remained; this was with Archie, who had sprung into it after her, for he and Bluebell had become inseparable. They could scarcely drag him away, and she buried her face a minute in his rough coat with almost equal regret.

"Would you like to keep him, ma'am?" said the carpenter's wife.

"I cannot now, but when Mr. Dutton comes back, and we are settled, will you let me have him?"

"Ah, well," said the woman, half disappointed, for she did not care for Archie, "ye'll have forgotten all about it by then."

CHAPTER XXXV
A DISCOVERY

There woman's voice flows forth in song,
Or childhood's tale is told;
Or lips move tunefully along
Some glorious page of old.

Hemans.

Bluebell was settled in her new abode, about fifteen miles from London: and certainly few governesses have the luck to drop into a more sunshiny home. Only two little girls, pleasantly disposed; no banishment to the school-room. They all mingled sociably together after lessons were over,—walked, drove in an Irish car, or played croquet and gardened as the spring advanced.

Mr. Markham was a barrister in London, and came down to dinner most days—not always, though; and his wife, still a young woman, was glad enough to find a companion in Bluebell. Beauty, too, unless it excites jealousy, is agreeable to look at, and she soon became interested in the young Canadian. But after a while she was puzzled by her. There was a far-off, touching look in her eyes that had come there since marriage, and she was reserved about herself, though the stiffness of first acquaintance had long ago given way to affectionate intimacy. For a girl apparently so frank to be at the same time so guarded suggested something to be concealed. Mrs. Markham, being a woman, could not refrain from speculating about it. She had elicited many lively descriptions of Bluebell's life in Canada, and the children were never weary of sleighing and toboggining stories. But these were general subjects; her narratives were never personal ones.

"By-the-bye," observed Mrs. Markham, one day, "how strange it was that poor child, Evelyn Leighton, dying just as you were going there! Her mother told me of it when she enclosed Mrs. Rolleston's letter. But you arrived in October, I think. Where were you those few months?"

"I was staying with a friend," replied Bluebell; but her hand shook and she became crimson.

Mrs. Markham did not fail to note this, and suspected that during that friendly visit some love passages might have arisen. "She seems very sensitive about it," thought the kind lady. "I will get her to tell me some day. It is such a shame ignoring that sort of thing with governesses, just as if it were a crime! And if there is really anything, he might come and see her here sometimes."

But Bluebell remained nervous and out of spirits the rest of that day.

One morning they were sitting together in the pleasant drawing-room; the children had a holiday, and were playing with their dogs out of doors; Mrs. Markham was colouring a design for her flower-beds, and lamenting the non-arrival of some seeds the postman was to have brought. "The year is getting on," murmured the aggrieved lady; "they really ought to be sown, and it is such a lovely day for gardening."

"Let me go to Barton and fetch them," cried Bluebell, who was always ready for a walk. "I shall be there and back before luncheon."

"Would you really?" said Mrs. Markham. "But it looks so hot! Are you sure you don't mind?" And declaring it was the thing of all others she should enjoy, Bluebell set off.

It was one of those glorious, sultry days that sometimes occur early in the year, when summer seems actually to have arrived for the season—a delusion invariably dispelled by the biting blasts of the blackthorn winter. Lovely as it appeared it was a very oppressive day for a long walk; the white, glaring road seemed endless, and she half repented her offer.

Bluebell was scarcely so strong as she had been, and, having to hurry a good deal to be back in time for luncheon, was quite pale and exhausted on re-entering the drawing-room, prize in hand.

The second post was on the table, and the girl stopped short in the midst of a message from the seedsman, for a deep black-edged envelope, addressed to herself, caught her eye. Mrs. Markham observed her with furtive anxiety. It is terrible to watch the opening of a letter evidently containing sad tidings, yet she was hardly prepared to see Bluebell, after perusing it drop prone on the ground as though she were shot, her forehead striking against the table in the fall. Ringing the bell, Mrs. Markham flew to her assistance, and, unfastening the collar of her dress, something was disclosed to view which gave that lady a second sensational shock, more thrilling than the first. Hurriedly she closed the dress again, despatching for water a sympathetic servant who had just entered, then swiftly, dexterously, possessed herself of a ribbon encircling the girl's throat, on which hung a wedding-ring.

Bluebell recovered only to fall from one fainting fit into another. Her strength had been exhausted by the walk, and she had none to bear up against the shock that awaited her. The letter was from Miss Opie, announcing Mrs. Leigh's sudden death, after a few hours' illness. Inside, and unopened, was returned Bluebell's private enclosure revealing her married name.

A year ago this child had been innocent of the existence of nerves, but, from the trying scenes she had lately gone through, they were now so shattered that she was unable to rally. The doctor kept her in bed at first, recommended absolute quiet, and exhausted his formula with as beneficial a result as could be expected considering it attacked the secondary cause only, and was impotent to heal the suffering mind reacting upon the body. Bluebell continued in a torpid condition, scarcely giving any signs of life. One day, Mrs. Markham, who nursed her with unremitting zeal, quickened, perhaps, by the interest of her discovery, observed the patient's hand steal to her neck, and then she glanced uneasily about, as if seeking for something.

They were alone, so Mrs. Markham whispered in a low, cautious tone, "I have it quite safe, locked up in my desk. No one knows of it but myself." An apprehensive look dilated the large, sad eyes, succeeded by an expression of contented resignation. She did not perceptibly improve, her mind was incessantly trying to realize what had happened, and was haunted by a morbid conviction that the anxiety induced by her own strange marriage might have precipitated the sad event, for Miss Opie's letter did not soften the fact that Mrs. Leigh had fretted greatly about it. Still she expressly said that she had succumbed to an epidemic that had already gleaned many victims.

It was, after all, many days before Mrs. Markham remembered the seeds she had been so anxious to obtain, but one favourable afternoon, she set diligently to work to lay the foundation for summer flowers. Though the "even tenour" of her life did not afford much scope for its indulgence, this lady was not devoid of a certain spice of romance. She was also of an independent character, and in the habit of judging for herself on most matters, and had decided not to betray Bluebell's secret to her spouse.

"Men are prejudiced and unpracticable on some points," she soliloquized, "and though I am quite satisfied that the poor girl is married, he may choose to doubt it, or think we had better get out of her. Her illness was entirely occasioned by the shock, so there really is no necessity to explain my little accidental discovery."

But the plot was thickening, for that morning there arrived a letter from Mrs. Leighton written in great perturbation, to the effect that she had heard some very uncomfortable reports about Miss Leigh. Her information was derived from the captain's wife at Liverpool, to whom she had written on Bluebell's obtaining a situation, supposing that, as they had shown her so much kindness, they would feel interested in the fact. But she had received in return a most extraordinary letter from Mrs. Davidson, stating that Miss Leigh had eloped from their house, leaving only a letter containing an improbable story about going to be married, without even mentioning to whom. Her husband, to be sure, had his suspicions as to the lover, but the name had escaped her memory, and Captain Davidson was at sea.

Now Mrs. Markham began to feel her innocent complicity becoming a little embarrassing. It was rather awkward keeping a suspected person about the children. Her husband would be in fits if he knew it, but, however imprudent of Bluebell to elope, she still saw no reason to doubt the marriage. Had she not the wedding-ring in proof of it?

So as she worked and planted, unavoidably decimating a worm here and turning up an ants nest there, she conned it all over.

"The child must really tell me her secrets, or I can do nothing. I will get her out for a drive; sitting alone in one room, as that demented old Chivers prescribes, is the worst thing for a nervous complaint."

So the next fine morning she ordered the car, and, going to the governess's room, asked her, in a matter-of-course manner, to put on her hat and come out.

Bluebell had just received a visit from the local practitioner, who had reiterated his assurances that "we wanted tone, and had better adhere to the iron mixture; that we must not exert ourselves, and must be sure to lie down a great deal," etc.; but she assented to Mrs. Markham's proposal with the same indifference with which she had listened to Esculapius.

They drove on for some distance through a straggling village, with its ivied church guarded by sentinel cypresses, children were playing about with hands full of cowslips, and lilac bushes blossomed within cottage palings. A little beyond they turned into Sir Thomas Farquhar's park, where young rooks were cawing, unwitting of their predestined pastried tomb. On entering a long, shady avenue, Mrs. Markham pulled the horse up to a walk, and said quietly, — "When were you married, Miss Leigh?"

Perhaps this question had not been unexpected since the little episode of the ring, for, with equal calmness, Bluebell replied,—"The last week in November, at Liverpool."

Mrs. Markham felt a triumphant thrill. She would now hear the solution of the mystery that had been exercising her imaginative powers for some weeks. She poured forth question after question. Yet, at the end of half-an-hour, not only had she failed to extort Dutton's name, but had even entangled herself in a promise of inviolable silence as to the only admitted fact.

She had insisted, threatened, got angry; Bluebell sorrowfully offered to go, but remained firm.

"Well, keep your secret, then," cried Mrs. Markham, at last, abandoning the contest; "but I shall find it out if I can. And I must take care that Walter doesn't," thought she, with a mischievous chuckle, for that gentleman, many years older than his wife, was a servile worshipper of Mrs. Grundy, and his hair would have stood on end had he known that he was harbouring a young lady with such suspicious antecedents. Besides her personal liking for Bluebell, Mrs. Markham recollected that if dismissed at this juncture she could scarcely recommend her to any other situation, and then what would become of the poor thing? But what puzzled her most was the total disappearance of the husband to whom she had been so very lately married.

A clue to this, however, she believed herself to have obtained on observing that Bluebell never failed to study the daily papers with an avidity unusual at her age.

"He must be in the army and gone to the Crimea," thought she. "Poor thing! how dreadful! Some day she will see him in the list of killed and wounded."

Some little time after, Bluebell, who had in a great measure recovered her strength, came to her room, and said, with frank, open eyes,—"May I go to Barton and post a letter to my husband?"

A very warm assent drew forth the heartfelt exclamation,—"How I wish I could tell you all, my dear Mrs. Markham."

Without that information, it was not so easy to answer Mrs. Leighton's letter, which she did eventually in very guarded terms, stating that she had proof of the marriage having taken place, but could say no more, except that, "being much pleased with Miss Leigh, she intended to keep her, especially as the children were very much under her own eye, and seldom alone with their governess."

Mr. Markham was generally the first down, and was rather addicted to a curious inspection of the post-mark on the family correspondence, neatly placed by each recipient's plate.

His wife one morning found him standing over a large ship letter directed to the governess, with somewhat the expression of distrustful pugnacity with which a dog walks round a hedgehog.

"Is that for Miss Leigh?" said she, carelessly.

"Yes," with much solemnity. "Apparently she has a correspondent in the Navy. It is not a sort of thing I like, and I must say I have often thought Miss Leigh too young and flighty for me."

"Oh, I believe she is engaged, poor girl!" said Mrs. Markham, slipping out a white one. "And she gets the children on beautifully. You thought Emma already so improved in playing."

"Well if you know all about it, that's another thing. I trust she doesn't put nonsense in the children's heads. Emma is getting very forward and inquisitive."

His wife felt secretly excited, for she was sure this letter must be from the errant husband, especially as the governess would not read it in public, but pocketed it with a slight nervousness of manner.

Time passed on, and Mrs. Markham had discovered nothing.

Bluebell, in her diligent revision of the papers, found much of personal interest. Colonel Rolleston's regiment had been ordered home to proceed to the Crimea, and she well knew the anxiety his family must be enduring.

It seemed cold and ungrateful to be unable to write one word of sympathy to Mrs. Rolleston, but any renewal of intercourse must lead to explanations, and it was her cruel fate to be able to give none. One other name, too, she saw in the public print that ought no longer to have had the power to thrill her as it did. Well, it was not so long ago, after all: but, however mentally disquieted we leave our heroine, as she has now drifted, outwardly, into a peaceful haven, we must return to others in the narrative who have more to do.

CHAPTER XXXVI
IN DEATH THEY WERE NOT DIVIDED

My love he stood at my right hand,
His eyes were grave and sweet;
Methought he said, "In this far land,
Oh, is it thus we meet!
Ah, maid most dear, I am not here,
I have no place—no part
No dwelling more by sea or shore,
But only in thine heart!"

Jean Ingelow.

Bertie Du Meresq, after lingering a while in London, without any tidings of Cecil, began to weary of inaction, and turn his thoughts again to Australia. But just then warlike rumours were becoming rife, and forced his mind into another channel. Good heavens! with such a prospect, possibility even, how could he let his papers be sent in? There was just time to recall them. He rushed to the Horse Guards, despatched a letter to his Colonel, and his retirement, not having yet been gazetted, was cancelled.

But how appease the injured Green, who had advanced the over regulation money for the troop? That must be returned, however expensive it might be to raise the necessary sum. One possible resource remained. He possessed a maiden aunt—of means, whose patience and purse he had completely exhausted some years ago; added to which she had become "serious," and a gentleman of the Stiggens order now diverted her spare cash into the coffers of little Bethlehem.

Du Meresq was aware that he had been predestined to doom by the Rev. Mr. Jackson, and that his aunt had been assured she could not touch pitch without being defiled. "Nevertheless," he thought, "I must try and carry her by a *coup de main*, if I have to pitch her clerical friend out of the window first."

Lady Susan had abandoned the more fashionable precincts of London to be nearer her chapel and districts, and the Hansom cabman who drove

Bertie to Hammersmith had quartered nearly every yard of it before their combined intelligence hit off a square stone house on a bit of a common.

Lady Susan was within, and Du Meresq followed the depressed-looking footman upstairs with as much ease as if he had not been particularly forbidden the house five years ago. He embraced his aunt affectionately before she had collected herself sufficiently to prevent him, and bowed with the utmost grace to a rather vulgar-looking, self-sufficient lady to whom he was presented. This person, however, he contrived to sit out in spite of her curiosity.

"And now, Bertie," said Lady Susan, austerely, "what is it you want? I know from past experience it is not I alone you come to see. I warn you though your hopes are vain. I have, happily, now a more edifying way of spending my poor income than in aiding you in your godless courses."

"I have come to you, my dear aunt, as the kindest-hearted person I know. I am in an awful hole. But let me explain." And then he told how he had sold his troop to pay his debts, but had now, war being eminent, recalled his papers, and so owed all the over regulation money obtained in advance.

For once Du Meresq had a good case. Against her principles almost, Lady Susan listened, and, though pre-determined not to believe a thing he said, his words were making an impression.

"Of course I can get the money; but, going on active service, I should have to pay enormously for it. And, anyhow," he continued, "I thought I should like to say good-bye to you, whether you can let me have it or not."

Bertie's Irish blarney always peeped out in his dealings with women, and Lady Susan of late had been so unaccustomed to anything of the sort, that her heart began to warm to her scape-grace nephew. He was so distinguished-looking, too, with the beauty which comes of air and expression, and a certain winning manner, none of which were conspicuous attributes of the disciples of little Bethlehem. She made him stay to dinner, and Du Meresq, who thought things were looking up, gladly dismissed his Hansom, which had been imparting an unwonted appearance of dissipation to the locality for the last hour. He could make himself quite as agreeable to an old lady as a young one, and this one was a soldier's daughter, and Irish into the bargain. What wonder that her heart beat responsively and her blood fired at the idea of another of her race lending his life to his country! Bertie, to be sure, would have preferred not having to make capital of that, and objected strongly to being treated as a hero in advance. However, it was no use quarrelling with the means that had brought his aunt into so promising a frame of mind; and, before he left that evening, he had actually received the promise of a cheque to the amount of Mr. Green's claims in a few days.

Soon after this, he heard the welcome news that his regiment was ordered home immediately, evidently in consequence of the disturbances in the East. This caused Du Meresq great delight. His corps was, then, certain to be in it, and he would go into action with Lascelles and all his old friends, instead of exchanging into a strange regiment, as he had determined to do if his own were not for service.

With all this other thoughts were associated. Somehow he had never looked upon his rupture with Cecil Rolleston as final, having pretty well fathomed the *motif* of her renunciation of him, which he considered would bear explanation when occasion offered; but now, rather sadly reviewing the past, he said to himself that, after all, it was well for her they had not married.

I do not know that Cecil would have been of the same opinion. She had a brave spirit, that could bear up against known evils, but fretted and suffered in suspense. She was much altered since her illness. Once the most attentive and docile of daughters, she became irritable and uncertain in temper-*difficile*, as the French call it, or, according to a Scotch expression, "There was no doing with her" some days; and Mrs. Rolleston, unhappy about both Cecil and Bertie, looked upon her husband's prejudice against the latter as the cause of all this unsatisfactory state of things.

As to Colonel Rolleston, he was in the condition of a man whose "foes are those of his own household." No one appreciated more the "pillow of a woman's mind"; but really now the pillow might have been stuffed with stones, so many corners and angularities had developed themselves in his feminalities.

The regiment had been ordered to Quebec almost immediately after Bluebell had gone to England; and, as Mrs. Rolleston there heard of Evelyn Leighton's death, the fate of their *protegée* became naturally a subject of anxious speculation. Yet not a line had been received from her; and, after a time, the subject was avoided, for all felt that Bluebell had been ungrateful.

Then Mrs. Leighton wrote out the strange story of her elopement, and having since entered a family as governess in her maiden name. Mrs. Rolleston was painfully shocked; for, coupling it with the girl's silence, she could not but imagine the worst, especially when, as they gazed at each other in mute dismay, she read in Cecil's face a suspicion that Bertie had had some hand in her disappearance, he had not written either; but, unless he were in correspondence with Bluebell, could not have been aware that she was in England. Of course, therefore, it was only the wildest conjecture. Yet how could Cecil believe that a girl who had once cared for Bertie should so utterly have forgotten him as to sacrifice herself to any one else within a few weeks? But a letter from Du Meresq himself did much to banish these gathering doubts and suspicions. It appeared quite open and above-board, and was written to Mrs. Rolleston on the eve of embarking with his regiment for the Crimea. He mentioned one or two houses he had been staying in, related the successful visit to his aunt and wound up in a postcript with the words,—"Give my dearest love to Cecil, if she cares to have it."

Mrs. Rolleston silently put the letter into her hand, and left the room. But the privacy of four walls was insufficient for Cecil while permitting herself the dear fascination of perusing Bertie's handwriting. She was missing for the next two hours, which Lela was able to account for, having observed her going downstairs dressed for walking.

She did not remember to return Du Meresq's letter, nor did Mrs. Rolleston ask for it. Very soon afterwards they also went to England, though the Colonel's regiment was not sent to the Crimea for some months later. It was quartered near London, and he took a house for his family in Kensington. And now a strange fancy possessed Cecil. It happened one day, when they were out driving, that a little boy drifting across the street with the suicidal *insouciance* of his kind, got knocked down by their horses, and, of course, had to be driven straight to the hospital to have his injuries investigated. It was necessary to detain the child, and Cecil walked down most days to bring him toys and inquire into his progress. There she became acquainted with some members of a sisterhood, who were employed in nursing in the accident ward, and, after the boy had been dismissed, convalescent, and ready to be run over again, she still continued her visits.

What the attraction was, neither of her parents could conceive, for, although the sisterhood was of the High Church order, they observed no particular religious enthusiasm or ritualistic tendencies in their daughter. "Cecil's mystery" it was called in the family, for she never spoke of what she had been doing all day, though it was apparently satisfactory, as her spirits were far more even than they had been of late. It was generally supposed that a charitable fervour had seized her, and that she was visiting among the poor; indeed Mrs. Rolleston had little curiosity to spare at present. She was living in dread and daily expectation of Colonel Rolleston being sent to the East; and he was engaged, as a calm, brave man might, in arranging his affairs to provide for his family in any event.

The order came at last; it was almost a relief from the continual suspense, and there were a few days for preparation. On one of these last evenings some of the officers were dining at the Colonel's, and among them—which was unusual now—Fane, who, though believing that Cecil's love affair with Du Meresq must have been broken off, still honourably abstained from her society till she should, by some sign, absolve him from his promise. On this occasion though, to her dread, he appeared sentimentally inclined, and Cecil, to whom a Sir Lancelot even would have been intolerable had he attempted to take the place of the lover she had outwardly discarded and inwardly enshrined, took refuge with Jack Vavasour, who regarded the approaching campaign in about the same light as a steeple-chase—a delightful piece of excitement, with a spice of danger in it.

His cheerful chatter amused and relieved the tension of her mind.

"I shall be sure to come across Du Meresq," he observed, with simple directness. "I shall tell him I saw you the last thing. How glad he will be to hear of any one at home! Have you any message, Miss Rolleston?" looking straight in her face, which was glowing as he spoke.

"Tell him," said Cecil, who liked Jack, and trusted him more than any one, "to be sure and write very often to his sister, who is dreadfully anxious, as, indeed, we *all* are."

"Oh, yes, of course," cried Vavasour; "but is that all? Let me give him that glove," which Cecil had been absently pulling off and on.

"Certainly-not!" flaming up in a moment. "Give it to me back directly, Mr. Vavasour!"

Jack thought she was offended. "I didn't mean to be impertinent, Miss Rolleston. You know this is not like an ordinary occasion; and I am sure I didn't think there would be much in it."

"I know, I know. But don't invent anything from me to Bertie Du Meresq." Then, with a softer manner, and most cordial squeeze of the hand as she saw the other men rising to go,—"Good-bye, and come back safe, you dear, true-hearted boy!"

Next day the mystery came out. She had been qualifying as a hospital nurse, with the view of joining Miss Nightingale's staff at Scutari.

Cecil had quite anticipated the antagonism and ridicule with which this announcement would assuredly be met. A craze to go out to the East possessed many romantic young ladies of the period, too adventurous to be satisfied with merely knitting socks and comforters for their frost-bitten heroes. Colonel Rolleston had frequently expressed a profound contempt for this mania, refusing to perceive any more exalted motive for it than a desire to follow their partners. So his horror may be imagined when his own daughter, whom he had always credited with a certain amount of sense, thus enrolled herself in the ranks of these fair enthusiasts.

Cecil allowed the first torrent of words to expend itself, but, in reply to the contemptuous query of "What earthly use could she be?" reiterated the fact of her having received a certificate of competency from the hospital, and adding, that as five of the sisterhood were shortly to be taken out to Scutari, it would be easy for her to accompany them as a volunteer. Then, evading further discussion by leaving the room, she calmly left the idea to work.

It was not certainly innate love of the occupation that had made Cecil so diligent an attendant of the accident ward. At first she shuddered and faltered at the simplest operation in which her assistance was called for, but it was essential to test her own nerve before dressing gun-shot wounds, besides which, a certificate from the hospital would much facilitate her chance of being taken out to Scutari. And, moreover, she was desperately unhappy, and rushed into anything to escape from herself.

I don't know how it was that Cecil prevailed in the end. A year ago, if she had proposed such a thing, Colonel Rolleston would have a considered her a fit subject for a *maison de sante*, but he had been thinking for some time that his daughter was "odd." She was evidently turning out one of those unmanageable beings, an eccentric woman. Of age, and with an independent income, if baulked in this, she might only do something else equally perverse, and, though a most extraordinary fancy for a girl so brought up, he would not oppose it further.

And then Cecil, when she had got her wish, with a strange inconsistency seemed almost inclined to give it up again. But the Colonel, being in ignorance of her vacillating purpose, took her passage in the same ship as the other nurses.

Work enough was there for every one when that vessel reached its destination. The battle of the Alma had just been fought, and the wounded were being brought in daily to Scutari.

In the mean time, Colonel Rolleston had sailed with his regiment, and Mrs. Rolleston fell into such a state of nervous depression, that Cecil saw it would be cruel to abandon her—another opportunity for going out would soon occur, and defering her journey till then, she remained at home to fulfil the more obvious duty of supporting the sinking spirits of her step-mother.

And so passed many weary weeks. The battle of the Alma had been won, and none of their belongings had appeared in the long list of killed and wounded. Mrs. Rolleston, becoming more accustomed to suspense, bore up with greater fortitude. Letters from the seat of war were, of course, waited for with fearful anxiety, and on the few and far between occasions when these arrived, they were all comparatively happy.

One evening Cecil was sitting alone in her own room, and, being very tired after a long day at the hospital, dropped asleep in her chair. She awoke with a feeling of deadly chilliness. The moon was shining into the room, and the figure of Bertie Du Meresq, keen clearly by its rays, was standing quietly gazing at her.

"Bertie!" shrieked Cecil "Oh, when did you come?"—and she tried to rush forward to greet him, but her limbs seemed paralyzed, and he did not move either, though a sad, sweet smile seemed to pass over his face. *Was* it himself, or only a quivering moonbeam? for when she was able to move there was nothing else to be seen.

A ghost itself could not have been whiter than Cecil, as she fled to the drawing room, and almost inarticulately described what she had beheld.

The very horror it inspired made Mrs. Rolleston repel the ghastly idea almost angrily.

"Good heavens, Cecil, why do you frighten me so! You had fallen asleep, and were dreaming. You say yourself," and she shuddered, "*it* was gone when you awoke."

"You know," said the girl, not apparently attending, "I have never seen Bertie in uniform, but this is what he wore," (describing the dress of the — — Hussars), "and his tunic was torn."

"That is too absurd, Cecil. All Hussar uniforms are more or less alike, and you must have seen many. It *is* this dreadful idea of going to Scutari that has filled your mind with horrors, and hospital work here has been too much for you, and told on your nerves."

But Cecil sat unheeding, as if turned to stone, with such a grey look of despair on her face, that Mrs. Rolleston longed to rouse her in any way.

"Forgive me, Cecil," she cried; "you *do* care for poor Bertie, I see."

She looked up with a vague, uncomprehending glance.

"Who was so brilliant—who so brave—with that sympathetic voice, and warm, endearing manner? He was wicked, I dare say!—he was not cold enough for a saint."

Mrs. Rolleston listened painfully.

"How every one adored him!" pursued Cecil. "I don't mean women—of course *they* did: but all his friends would have done anything for him. I have seen his letters; and who could touch him in countenance, manner, grace? And such a poetic, original mind! But he cared for me *most*,—he must, don't you think?" (looking up with dry, tearless eyes), "or he would not have come to me to-night."

"Then *why*, oh, why, Cecil, did you give him up?"

Her brow contracted for an instant. "I could not bear my sun to shine on any one else," she cried, passionately "I grudged every glance of his eye, every tone of his voice given to another."

"Then, Bluebell *was* the cause—" began Mrs. Rolleston.

"'My eyes were blinded;' he cared no more for her than the rest. Had I believed him, we might have been happy five months, for we should have married the day I came of age."

"It will happen yet!" cried Mrs. Rolleston. "Shake off this fearful dream, my dearest child. I know that Bertie cares only for you."

"We have met to-night, we never shall again."

"She will have a brain-fever," thought Mrs. Rolleston, distractedly, "if tears do not come to her relief." They did eventually, convulsively and exhaustingly, till she dropped into a death-like sleep far into the next morning.

The sun had been shining for hours. Mrs. Rolleston did not disturb her, but the superstitious terror she had battled against the night before returned daring that long day, in an agony of impatience for news.

But no submarine telegraph then existing, nothing was heard for a time. Mrs. Rolleston might have shaken off the gruesome impression, but for the immovable conviction of Bertie's death that actuated Cecil. She assumed the deepest mourning, and passed whole hours alone with her grief, perfectly indifferent to the opinion of any one. Indeed, since his spiritual presence had, as she believed, appeared to her, he seemed nearer than before, when they were parted and unreconciled.

One day, late in the afternoon, Mrs. Rolleston was agitated by that weird sound to anxious ears, the shouting voices of men and boys hawking evening papers, and proclaiming startling news. She saw from the balcony her servant dart down the street for the gratification of his curiosity. He bought a paper, and perused it as he slowly returned. He got "quite a turn," as he afterwards described it, when his mistress, pale as a sheet, met him at the door, and, without a word, snatched the evening journal from his astonished hands.

No occasion to seek far. The sensational paragraph was in capital letters, and contained the intelligence of the battle of Balaklava, and famous charge of the six hundred, with its fearful losses. The cavalry regiments engaged were named. Among them was Bertie Du Meresq's, and mentioned as one that had suffered heavily. The returns of killed and wounded did not appear.

Mrs. Rolleston had a friend at the Horse Guards, and instantly despatched the servant there, with a letter requesting further particulars as early as possible. Ill news does not lag. A letter from General—soon arrived, with its warning black seal. Captain Du Meresq was among the casualties. He had been shot through the heart during the charge.

CHAPTER XXXVII
AN UNEXPECTED RENCONTRE

Into a ward of the white-washed walls,
Where the dead and the dying lay,
Wounded by bayonets, shells, and balls,
Somebody's darling was borne one day.

Song.

Mrs. Rolleston completely sank under this dreadful blow. Bertie had been her darling and pride from his infancy, and her own misery was redoubled, in anticipation of the even greater anguish of Cecil.

Strange to say, though, *she* experienced no new shock. That Du Meresq was dead, she had never doubted, or that his spirit, in the moment of departure, had hovered for an instant near the one who loved him best. It seemed to connect her with that other world whither he had gone. It did not appear so far away, now Bertie was there, and her thoughts were ever in communion with her spirit love.

The hour in which he had, as she believed, appeared to her, she regularly passed alone in the same room, and even prayed for another sign of his presence.

But if such prayers were answered, what mourners would remain unvisited by their dead?

This room became her "temple and her shrine," in which Bertie, all his sins forgotten, was canonized. How incessantly she regretted having parted with those letters, so impulsively affectionate and so entirely confidential! To be sure, they were chiefly about himself; but what subject could be so interesting to Cecil? His normal condition of picturesque insolvency was only a proof of generosity of disposition and absence of meanness. Now she had nothing but a letter not her own, and that one last message, "Give my dearest love to Cecil."

Whether or no the vision was really but a dream, we leave to the decision of our readers. It was not unnatural that the dominant idea should impress that unreasoning moment between sleeping and waking; but Cecil's fervent faith knew no doubts, and thus it was that Du Meresq dead influenced her as much as when living.

They soon heard from Colonel Rolleston. Part of his regiment had been sent to seek and bring in the wounded; his brother-in-law's body had been found and brought back by Vavasour, and he sent his wife Bertie's watch. The newspapers were full of the disastrous but glorious charge of the cavalry, and of their immense loss.

In Du Meresq's regiment all the senior had been cut off. Had he lived, he would have been Colonel of it, a position which Lascelles survived to fill.

There appeared no respite from anxiety for those who had relatives in the East. Within two months the battles of the Alma, Balaklava, and Inkermann had been fought. Colonel Rolleston seemed to bear a charmed life; for, though repeatedly under fire, he had come out unscathed. Many of his officers were killed, Fane slightly wounded, and Jack Vavasour had lost an arm.

In the ensuing spring Cecil roused herself. Though all her hopes were dead, the native energy of her character asserted itself, and rebelled against utter stagnation. Some letters she had received from the nurses in the Crimea rekindled her former enthusiasm, and she determined to execute her original project, and go out to the aid of her suffering countrymen.

Mrs. Rolleston was now more hopeful, and, far from opposing Cecil's wishes, cheerfully forwarded them. She looked upon hers as so cruelly exceptional a lot, that any absorbing occupation capable of distracting her mind was only too welcome. And so when

Spring

Came forth, her work of gladness to contrive,
With all her reckless birds upon the wing,

Cecil, turning "from all she brought," was far on her way to the East, and wishing, as she assumed the black serge hospital dress, that she could as easily transform her internal consciousness as her outward identity.

Hers was not a nature to do anything by halves, and every faculty of mind and body became absorbed in these new duties. The patient who fell into Cecil's hands had little to complain of. She struggled for his life when even the shadow of death had fallen on him, and sometimes, by arduous exertions and devoted nursing, saved one in whom the vital flame had wasted almost to the socket. And then a nearly divine content came to her as she imagined she might have spared some distant heart the pangs that had almost broken her own.

But to follow her through the daily routine of duties, often painful, often touching, would be too long for the present history, so we pass abruptly to one event, a necessary link in it.

Cecil was attending a fever case, and looking anxiously for the doctor, as she fancied her patient was sinking. He was a young man, and had been more or less unconscious ever since he was brought in.

The surgeon came, and shook his head as he felt the feeble pulse.

"Is there no hope?" asked Cecil, sorrowfully.

"Scarcely any. Give him this stimulant whenever you can get him to swallow it; but there seems no reserve of strength." And he passed on to others.

She lost no time in attending to his directions, and a large pair of melancholy brown eyes opened on her. They watched her about persistently, and seeing their gaze, though languid, was rational, she asked "if there was anything she could do for him."

His voice was so inaudible she could but just catch the sentence, "So he gives me over!"

"I don't think he would if he could see you now. Indeed, you seem better."

"I don't think I shall die; but, in case of accidents, will you write something for me?"

Cecil nodded, while holding rapid communion with herself. Ought she to let him exhaust his little strength in dictating probably an agitating letter?

"Will you wait till you are a little stronger?" she said doubtfully.

"If I ever am, it will not be necessary to write; if otherwise I cannot do it too soon."

Cecil, judging by her own feelings that opposition to any strong wish would be more injurious than even imprudent indulgence, glided from the room, and soon returned with writing materials.

She sat down by the bed, and casually felt the attenuated wrist as she did so. The sick man gazed gratefully at her, but waited some minutes for breath to commence. His first words made her almost bound from her chair, and, as he continued in low feeble tones, with long pauses between, Cecil was wrought into an agony of suspense and interest.

The communication was to be addressed to an uncle, and began abruptly:—

> "I was married to Theodora Leigh at a register office at Liverpool in November, 1853, and I make it a dying request to you to acknowledge my widow, who will otherwise be destitute both of money and friends. Forgive, if you can, my deception, and the poor return made for all the benefits lavished on your, notwithstanding, grateful nephew,
>
> "HARRY DUTTON.
>
> "P.S.—My wife is a governess in the family of Mr. Markham, Heatherbrae, Wimbledon."

It was sealed, directed, and the patient had sunk into a heavy stupor; but Cecil felt her heart stirred as she had never expected to do again.

Here, if she had required it, was complete exoneration of any subsequent intercourse having taken place between Du Meresq and Bluebell. The latter evidently had been far otherwise engaged, and, for the first time, she felt her long-cherished resentment melting away.

She gazed with some curiosity at the man who could so soon supplant Bertie, and smiled with irrepressible bitterness at the singular coincidence that she should be striving to preserve a husband to Bluebell, who had deprived her of her own early love.

But where could she have met this man, whom she had married almost immediately on landing in England? Cecil looked again at the address—"Right Honourable Lord Bromley." She had heard that name somewhere, but could not recall any connecting associations.

Harry lingered some time, his life frequently despaired of; and he would probably have succumbed had it not been for the untiring energy and care of the hospital nurse. Her anxiety could not have been exceeded by Bluebell herself, for Cecil's disposition was generous, and she never more truly forgave her *ci-devant* enemy than when thus labouring to return good for evil.

At last the turning-point was reached and Dutton lifted from the very gates of the grave. A wound in his leg was now the chief retarding circumstance; and as it seemed incapable of healing at Scutari, he was ordered on sick leave to England.

In the mean time, a lively friendship had arisen between him and Cecil. Directly she admitted her name and former intimacy with Bluebell, Harry took her entirely into his confidence, and, encouraged by the evident interest with which she listened, related how he had first met and fallen in love with Bluebell on the steamer, and subsequently persuaded her to elope with him.

He did not deny the interested motives which had afterwards induced him to conceal the marriage; but Cecil's upright mind recoiled at the unworthy deception, and the strong view she took of it made short work of the extenuating circumstances advanced by Harry.

The dying appeal to Lord Bromley had, of course, been burnt since its writer's recovery; but Dutton, now thoroughly ashamed of his shabby policy, vowed to Cecil that he would abandon all thoughts of inheritance, and boldly acknowledge his marriage to Lord Bromley as soon as he should set foot in England.

This was their last interview; for, as he had now approached convalescence, she had no further excuse for ministering to Harry.

It was some time since he had received tidings from his wife, having purposely kept her in ignorance when he volunteered into Peel's brigade. Then he was wounded and laid up at Scutari, so whatever letters she might have written would be on board the "Druid."

Now he must apprise her of his approaching return and explain his long silence. As it happened, a homeward-bound steamer sailed within a few days of the one which carried this letter, and Dutton, obtaining a passage in the former, which happened to the faster of the two, arrived in England almost simultaneously.

Without further notice, he rushed down to Wimbledon, and, had she been there, would speedily have solved the mystery that had so exercised Mrs. Markham. But, lo! on reaching Heatherbrae, he beheld with a sinking heart a conspicuous board on the garden-gate, with the words, "To be let, furnished," legibly inscribed thereon.

Weak from his illness and the disappointment, Harry leant against the railings to consider and recover. He had been so secure of finding Bluebell there, and during the whole hurried journey was picturing the meeting. How would she look? He knew so well the fluttering colour that changed in any emotion, pleasurable or otherwise: but would he see a true loving welcome in those transparent eyes? He had considered every probability or improbability of this sort, but not how he should act in such a dead lock as the present.

Repeated rings at the bell at last brought out the woman in charge, her arms covered with soap-suds, and gown drawn through a placket-hole.

"The family had gone abroad," she said. "No, she did not know where. The agent might, perhaps. She was only there to show visitors the house."

Harry turned away in listless perplexity; it was quite evident this person could tell him nothing. Doubtless their change of plans had been communicated to him by post, but he had not waited to send for letters. There was nothing for it but to obtain from the woman the address of the house-agent, get Mr. Markham's from him, and send another letter to Bluebell.

CHAPTER XXXVIII
OLD HEAD ON YOUNG SHOULDERS

How could I tell I should love thee to-day,
Whom that day I held not dear?
How could I know I should love thee away,
When I did not love thee a near?

Jean Ingelow.

We must now see whither the vicissitudes of fortune have conducted Mrs. Dutton. Her pleasant home at the Markhams' was gone. They had lost heavily in the failure of a bank, and were living abroad to retrench, while Mr. Markham pursued his profession in London.

Bluebell was the first luxury to be cut off, though, as a home during Harry's absence was what she chiefly required, she would willingly have remained for nothing. It was unspeakable grief to part with Mrs. Markham, who alone understood how oppressively her secret weighed on her, and her incessant anxiety for news from the seat of war.

One day,—it was after the battle of Balaklava,—when shuddering over, in the *Times*, the ghastly "butcher's bill," Bluebell came upon Du Meresq's name among the killed, and the shock to nerves that had scarcely yet recovered their equilibrium nearly brought on a relapse of her former illness.

Yet, as her mind cleared from its first horror, she was amazed to find it was not Cecil she was most feeling for, and that the cry, "Thank Heaven, it is not Harry!" had arisen spontaneously to her heart. I suppose Bertie's neglect had effected its own cure; but certainly some secret influence was turning the tide of her affections into its legitimate channel.

Yet their correspondence was not only desultory, but constrained. Dutton, never convinced of possessing her heart, and angry with himself at the part he had acted, had no pleasure in writing; and Bluebell was as shy of her new-found feelings as though he were still an unacknowledged lover.

But whenever a ship came in without bringing a letter, she was filled with foreboding and dread. Still, there was always the consolation that he was public property, and as long as she did not see his death reported, might conclude him to be safe.

And he never did write anything to excite alarm. No more perils or hair-breadth escapes could be inferred from his letters than if he were merely residing abroad from choice.

Mrs. Markham obtained her another situation. She had never succeeded in discovering to whom Bluebell was married; but having persuaded herself it was unnecessary to let that stand in the way, simply recommended her in her maiden name.

"I look upon your governessing as a farce, you know, Bluebell, though any one would gladly snap you up for your music alone. But when this war is over, the mysterious husband will return, and you will pay me a visit in your true colours."

And so they parted, with many promises of correspondence.

Bluebell's next venture was at Brighton, and she drove to Brunswick Square one chilly afternoon in March, rather dejected at the prospect of being again thrown among strangers.

"Not at home," said the servant. "Mrs. Barrington is hout-driving."

"Oh, it's all right," said a pert maid, tripping downstairs. "This way, miss. I was to show you your room, and the children's tea will be ready directly."

So saying, she preceded Bluebell upstairs to a chilly, fireless apartment. Houses in Brighton are not generally very substantially built, and the room was furnished on the most approved governess pattern,—just what was barely necessary, no more. Bluebell was impressionable, perhaps fanciful, for hitherto her "lines had fallen in pleasant places," and she shivered a little at the forbidding exterior, but was somewhat cheered by a suggestion of welcome conveyed by a bunch of violets on the dressing-table. "There's some kind person in this house," thought she, yet lingering awhile in a purposeless manner, unwilling to walk alone into the school-room and face the strange children. While thus hesitating, a demure little person came to fetch her, with tight plaited hair, irreproachable pinafore, and stockings well drawn up. Two younger duplicates were in the school-room. The table was laid for the evening meal,—thick wedges of bread-and-butter, calculated to appease but not to allure the appetite, and a large Britannia-metal teapot, with not injuriously strong tea.

There were a couple of globes, an old piano, and book-cases well stocked with grammars and histories, and the fire was guarded by a high fender, effectually dissipating any frivolous notion of sitting with the feet on it. There was neither dog nor cat, nor even a stray doll, to distract attention from the serious business of education.

Such was the impression conveyed to Bluebell, who was instantly filled with well-grounded misgivings as to whether her qualifications might be quite up to the standard expected. Good gracious! those children looked capable of obtaining female scholarships, as they sat, with their keen impassive faces, calmly adding her up, so to speak.

Mrs. Barrington and her eldest daughter had just come in. "Oh, so Miss Leigh has arrived!" cried the former, observing Bluebell's box in the hall. "Dear me, what a bore new people are! I really must rest, as we dine out. Couldn't you go up, Kate, and say I hope she is comfortable, and will ring for the school-room maid whenever she wants anything, and all that?"

"That would console her immensely, I should think," said Miss Barrington, laughing. "Well, I will go and look her over, mamma, and report the result."

As Kate entered, her little set speech, that "mamma was lying down, but hoped," etc., was almost suspended on her lips, as she gazed with unfeigned curiosity at the new governess. Seated pensively behind the urn was a fair girl, dressed in black, with an Elizabethan ruff round a long white throat. Shining chestnut hair contrasted with a complexion of the purest pink and white, while a pair of dewy violet eyes looked shyly up at her. "Good heavens!" thought Kate, "she is the loveliest creature in Brighton at this moment."

"I have also come to ask for a cup of tea. No, thank you, Adela, none of that! What buttered bricks! Goodness, children! don't you ever have cake, or jam, or anything?"

"Miss Steele used to say it would give us muddy complexions, and spoil our digestion."

"Poor little victims! Never mind, you'll come out some day. I must make haste and get married, Mabel, if you grow like that. But Miss Leigh must be starved. Do you like eggs and bacon?" with her hand on the bell.

"Very much," said Bluebell, smiling back, more in gratitude for the good intentions than anything else.

"Poor thing!" cried Kate, impulsively, quite vanquished by the smile; "you will be so dull when the children go to bed. I wish we were not going out to-night. I'll collect the newspapers, and send you up a capital novel I got yesterday from the library."

Bluebell was cheered in a moment. "I am sure it was you whom I have to thank too, for those violets," said she, touching a few transferred to her waist-belt, and beaming up at her new acquaintance.

Kate nodded pleasantly. "Do you like flowers? I bought them in the King's Road this morning." A few minutes later she burst into her mother's room.

"Where does this *rara avis* hail from? I never clapped eyes on such a beauty—Miss Seraphin is not a patch on her!"

"Don't be so noisy, dear—Miss Leigh? Yes I heard she was nice-looking."

"Nice-looking!" echoed Kate, contemptuously. "Just wait till you see her. She will be focused by every eye-glass in Brighton when she takes the children out for their constitutional."

"Dear me! I hope she is a proper kind of person."

"She looks rather in the Lady Audley style—and such a complexion! I could have sworn it was painted if it had not varied so. Now I think of it," said Kate, with *malice prepense*, "she is not at all unlike the photographs, of—,"—naming some one of whose existence she had no business to have been aware.

"It really is too bad of Mrs. Markham not having mentioned this," cried Mrs. Barrington, as if Bluebell had been convicted of a crime. "It is most unpleasant having so *voyante* a person about the children!"

"Oh, what does it matter," said Kate, heedlessly; "you have no grown up sons. And she seems awfully nice. She has a face with a history in it, though. I shall try and make her out to-morrow. No one is ever so innocent as she looks."

Kate's admiration was still further excited next day as she listened to Bluebell's singing.

"You never heard anything like it, mamma—she could fill Covent Garden; and she composes too. I wonder if she has ever been on the stage?"

Less appreciative was the judgment of the erudite Mabel, who reported Miss Leigh unable to continue her arithmetic beyond the decimal fractions she had attained to with Miss Steele. "In fact," said the child, with deep contempt, "I don't believe she has ever-gone beyond the rule of three herself."

Indeed, the exact sciences were not Bluebell's *spécialite*, who now employed many a perplexed hour trying with Sievier's Arithmetic to work herself up a little ahead of this precocious pupil. Fortunately she was tolerably strong in history, having gone through a regular course with the little Markhams; but it was evident, notwithstanding, that Mabel and Adela pretty accurately gauged her acquirements, and held them proportionably cheap.

Kate, too, had become somewhat of a tease. I don't know what led her to suspect that the governess had something to conceal, but she was perpetually putting questions most difficult for her to answer; the incitement being the pleasure of watching, from an artistic point of view, the beauty of Bluebell's ever-ready blushes while essaying to parry her tormentor's inquisitorial efforts.

This cat-and-mouse game would go on till the victim, turning to bay, was on the point of desperately asking, "What she wished to find out?" Then Kate would veil her eyes, and look all innocent indifference. Observing the avidity with which she pounced on newspapers, Miss Barrington one day secreted them, much entertained by watching the governess circling round the room, glancing on every table or couch they were likely to have been thrown on.

"Try behind the sofa cushion, Miss Leigh."

Bluebell started, vexed at being observed, and also at this proof of *espionnage* on her actions, but a little later she fell into more serious self betrayal. They were trying over songs in a locked manuscript book.

"Dear me, what is this air? I know it so well," she cried, incautiously humming it.

"A sea song of my cousin, Harry Dutton's. I had no idea any one else possessed a copy."

There was no answer. She looked up, the blood had rushed over Bluebell's cheek and brow, her lips were apart, and eyes wide open and bright with wonder. Before she could drop a mask over the too eloquent face, Kate's keen eyes were reading her off.

"You know him, I see," with emphasis.

Bluebell, recovering presence of mind, with a desperate effort, replied calmly,—"There was a Mr. Dutton, who came home in the same steamer. Probably I may have heard him whistling the air."—then sat down, and plunged into an instrumental piece, feeling quite unequal to endure further questioning.

But the notes all the time seemed incessantly repeating, "So this is the Cousin Kate he was always talking about."'

Miss Barrington's mind was equally busy.

"I bet Harry flirted with her all the way across, and he never told me a word of it—never so much as mentioned that there was a pretty girl in the ship, and yet she admitted knowing his favourite air 'so well.'"

Then Kate remembered the many unaccounted for weeks between his landing in England and arrival at "The Towers," and her former suspicion that some love affair had intervened.

At first she had only been provoked to curiosity by Bluebell's reserve, but now there really was food for imagination to work on, and perhaps the clue to much that was perplexing in Harry. How curiously it had come out!

The artless Kate smiled re-assuringly at her victim. She was on the track now, and the rabbit might have as much chance of ultimately evading the weasel hunting him by scent.

"What perverse fate has brought me here?" sighed Bluebell, laying her tormented head on the pillow that night. "Miss Barrington will be sure to find out everything. She was so friendly at first; but Harry always said he never trusted her. Then those children! I am sure they are more capable of teaching me. Whenever shall I be extricated from this false position?"

A night's rest did not allay Bluebell's perplexities; on the contrary, more and more complications suggested themselves. Harry must know where she was by this time, and would be frantic at her having dropped into such an ants'-nest. They would recognise his handwriting, too, if a letter came. To be sure that would also strike him. Nevertheless she got into the habit of calling for her letters at the post-office,—a proceeding which the children did not fail to mention, with the rider, "That they wondered at Miss Leigh taking the trouble when she never got any."

Kate was rather inclined to patronize Bluebell. She persuaded her mother to give a musical party for the exhibition of her wonderful voice, and was, on that occasion, quite as solicitous about the young artiste's toilette as her own; and, being not averse to having a girl of her own age to chatter to, bestowed a good deal of her society on Bluebell out of school-hours, which might have been more appreciated were it not for the excessive caution it entailed on the latter.

One day she heard that Mrs. and Miss Barrington were going to Bromley Towers for some theatricals and other gaieties. After her discovery of whose house she was in, that was only a matter of course, and she had only to conceal all interest in it.

Kate was to take a part in one of the plays, and passed the intervening time in getting it by heart, and rehearsing with Bluebell, while the necessary costume was animatedly discussed between them. The latter fancied she had attained sufficient self-command to listen unconcernedly to any conversation about Lord Bromley or "The Towers," but she could not quench the beaming delight in her eyes when Kate one day observed, carelessly,—

"I believe you will see the play, after all, Miss Leigh, as mamma has decided to take Mabel and Adela, which means you also; for Uncle Bromley has rather a horror of children, and would no more have any of the juveniles of the family without a keeper, than he would admit a pack of hounds into the house. Why, Miss Leigh, you look delightful! Do you really care to go?" Then her suspicions awakening, she set a trap like lightning.

"I wonder" (carelessly) "if poor Harry Dutton will get back in time. He is invalided home from Scutari."

Self-command—everything—vanished.

"How did you hear that?" with crimson cheeks and suspiciously dimmed eyes.

"How?" with marked emphasis. "Would it not be stranger if one had not heard it? Uncle Bromley named it in his letter. He was wounded," bringing out the words slowly, "and almost died in the hospital. I hope he will survive the voyage home."

"That girl's a fiend," thought Bluebell, rushing off to her own room in a paroxysm of terror. Then, as she tried to think it out, it became quite evident Harry could not be aware of her change of residence, perhaps had received no letters at the hospital, and would not even know where to find her when he returned. Still, she would be in the right direction, for no doubt he would go to Bromley Towers. But what a place to meet in! And, being ignorant of his address, she could not even send a line of warning.

Romantic notions of fascinating Lord Bromley, and thus facilitating confession when Harry returned, stole through her brain. Kate's play paled in dramatic interest to the possible "situations" that seemed impending. One drawback to taming the lion was the probability of scarcely being on speaking terms with him. Her mission, indeed, seemed to be to keep the children *out* of his way. But there were the theatricals; children, servants, governesses even, would be privileged to look on that one night. The coquette nature, dormant from want of practice, awoke again. Lord Bromley was only a man! Why couldn't she make him like her?

Kate observed renewed smiles and animation, and set it down to the hope of seeing Dutton at "The Towers," especially as she also detected her doing what maids call "a little work for myself," and effecting wonders with a few yards of muslin and ruffling.

CHAPTER XXXIX
THE LOAN OF A LOVER

Parks with oak and chestnut shady,
Parks and ordered gardens great,
Ancient homes of lord and lady,
Built for pleasure and for state.

Tennyson.

This was Bluebell's first acquaintance with a really grand English park, and, during the long drive through it, she gazed in wondering delight at the stately trees, heavy with summer foliage, the herds of deer, the calm lake, with kingly swans gliding over it. Perhaps her greatest surprise was that all this fair domain belonged to one individual. Why, the richest "boss" in Canada possessed no more than a few acres of lawn and pleasure ground, with ornamental trees and shrubs,—all looking new,—the production of a self made man, grown rich within a few years. These stately oaks and beeches must have seen generations live and die, lords of the manor, and she began better to understand Harry's reluctance to risk such an inheritance.

"Oh, they are exercising 'Hobbie,'" cried the children "Then we shall have some rides."

Lord Bromley seldom presented himself to his guests till dinner-time. Polite grooms of the chamber offered tea, etc., the housekeeper showed visitors to their rooms. But on this occasion Mrs. Barrington was virtually lady of the house, and, being too late to receive, was in voluble conversation with a few persons already arrived.

Bluebell was not introduced to any one, and, her first sensations of excited curiosity having subsided, began to feel as if she must stiffen to her chair if no one would speak to her and break the spell. It was a welcome relief when Adela exclaimed,—

"Mamma, may we go up to the nursery?"

"With all my heart, and take Miss Leigh."

The children darted off across a slippery oak hall, up a flight of stone stairs with a velvety carpet, then along a passage leading to a private staircase with a red baize door shutting it off. It opened into a long low room, still keeping the name of nursery, and at each end were bed-rooms, one for the two girls, the smaller for Bluebell.

"This is such a jolly place," cried Adela, who seemed to have left all her primness at Brighton. "You have never seen the spring woods, nor the amphitheatre, nor the waterfall!"

"Nor the terraces and gardens, nor the menagerie, nor dry pond," added Mabel. "Oh, we could not show you everything in a fortnight. Shall we come out now or after tea? It isn't laid yet. Let us have it out of doors."

Bluebell was almost as eager as the children; and they spent the hot June evening under the trees, listening to bird choruses and the rich solo of a lingering nightingale.

Next morning she was conducted by her pupils round the spring woods, the same walk that Dutton and his cousin had perambulated eighteen months ago. It took just twenty-five minutes to make the circuit, returning to the starting point, marked by a summer-house.

When they had got about half way round, they were met by an old, spare gentlemen, slightly bent. He nodded to the children, spoke a casual word, and mechanically raised his hat to Bluebell. The intensity of her interest gave animation to her countenance.

"That's a pretty girl," thought his Lordship, continuing on his way.

He was in the habit of taking this constitutional every morning before breakfast, sometimes twice round, sometimes once. This day it was twice, and, walking at about an equal pace, the school-room party were passing him nearly on the same spot.

Lord Bromley paused again, said something to the children, and took a second glance at Bluebell.

"You are a young mistress of the ceremonies, Mabel; but why don't you present me to this young lady?"

Mabel looked up in astonishment, then said promptly, "Miss Leigh, Lord Bromley."

A slight tremor passed over his face, and he leant a little more on his stick, giving Bluebell an impression of extreme feebleness. After a mechanical observation or two, rather to her disappointment he walked away, without further improving the introduction.

Mrs. Barrington wished lessons to be proceeded with in the forenoon, so they did not leave the nursery. In the evening the children were desired to dress and come down with Bluebell till bed-time. It seems rather a *triste* pleasure for a governess to have the trouble and expense of an evening toilette, with no expectation of entertainment beyond a cup of coffee if the servants remember to offer it, and the enforced conversation of some good-hearted guest, who, in the absence of any subject in common, can think of no more suggestive topic than inquiries into her daily walks, with threadbare remarks on the scenery. If she is lively, and strikes out into fresh fields and pastures new, "she is forward, and a flirt." If otherwise, she mounts the stereotyped smile, and gushes about the singing in church and picturesqueness of the neighbourhood, which, probably, by this time she loathes every feature of. Then come long pauses; the philanthropic guest mingles in general conversation, and edges away, leaving her to retreat upon a photograph book.

Little of all this did Bluebell dread,—she only longed to get downstairs on any terms. Immured in the nursery, how could her little plot proceed? Her simple toilette was carefully considered while brushing out and arranging the shining coils of chestnut hair. Yet it was only a black muslin dress, cut *en coeur*, and relieved with her favourite ruffles. The children had brought handfuls of roses from the rosary—yellow, crimson, white, blush, pink. A York and Lancaster in her hair, a tea-rose in her bosom, and she was ready.

Only the ladies were in the large saloon, which again dazzled the unsophisticated Bluebell with its magnificence. She found herself, as before, little noticed; but, the pictures, which she might study uninterruptedly from a secluded corner, entertained her for some time. There were full-length portraits of Court ladies, by Lely, with wonderful lace on brocaded gowns. One had a little dog half hidden in the folds. The arch face of Nell Gwynne smiled over a door, a life-sized Gainsborough of a lady with a straw hat, reclining on a bank of flowers, was conspicuous over one fire-place. There were cavaliers with long, curled hair, gentlemen of a later date in pig-tails; but the most modern of all was a portrait of a boy playing with a large dog. On this one her eye lingered longest. Whom could it be? It was not in the least like Harry, and yet she fancied something about it familiar to her.

There was a look of Lord Bromley, certainly—perhaps it was a portrait of him in childhood.

Mabel and Adela, meantime, were performing an elaborate duet. It was one of her most irksome duties instructing these children in music, who would never attain to more than mechanical excellence. When they had arrived at the final crash, with not more than half a bar between them, Bluebell was summoned to sing. The gentlemen came in from the dining-room at the last verse, and, after a slight pause, she began another unasked. Mrs. Barrington thought this rather forward, but there was a suppressed murmur of applause when she had finished.

One of the ladies addressed a few words to her, and then Kate carelessly brought up a gentleman who had been tormenting her for an introduction.

Bluebell had hoped that Lord Bromley would have spoken to her, after their encounter in the morning. But he did not, though sometimes she felt sure he was looking at her.

The undercurrent of excitement gave a feverish vivacity to her manner, which Sir Robert Lowther imputed to gratified vanity at his attentions and he continued complacently by her side, till Mrs. Barrington said,—"I think, Miss Leigh, the children should go to bed," and Bluebell understood she was expected to accompany them.

It was very mortifying. Apparently she had been too much at her ease, and perhaps the *empressement* with which Sir Robert had rushed to open the door might exclude her from coming down for the future. Then she reflected, with a little pardonable spite, that, if things turned out according to her hopes, Mrs. Barrington might, perhaps, repent having marched her off with the children like a nursery-maid.

The following morning, at the same hour, Bluebell circulated the spring woods with her pupils, and, had he been a young lover approaching, her heart could not have beat higher than on again perceiving the bent form of Lord Bromley.

Would he pass them with a courteous lifting of the hat to her? Of course; what else would he do? Her fervent aspiration had apparently a magnetic effect; or was it her face that was so tell-tale a mirror? Lord Bromley stopped, spoke a few words, and actually turned back with them!

Bluebell was in the seventh heaven. She had not yet learnt how little even personal liking weighs against ambition when the object of it is unsupported by the merit of being well placed in the world. If well-tochered

Lady Geraldine, pale and plain, had married the heir, every door in Bromley Towers would have been hospitably thrown open to her while the loveliest Peri, whose face was her fortune, might have stood knocking at the portal-gate unnoticed.

"Yet everything will go right if he only likes me!" To be liked, to be loved, that comprises all else with a girl. This one was not quite a fool, only had not outlived her youthful illusions.

An ardent desire to attain anything goes far towards success. Fearful of being thought forward, yet longing to please, she seemed to awaken an interest in Lord Bromley; though he talked playfully to all three, his indulgent smile was for Bluebell. Another expression appeared sometimes on his face, the same that had perplexed her the previous evening—an investigating, speculating glance: and once, when becoming more at ease, her features resumed their play, his were suddenly contorted, as if a sharp pang had seized him.

The walk seemed all too short, for Lord Bromley did not take the second, but retraced his steps to the house. Bluebell fell into a reverie, till something in the children's chatter attracted her attention.

"Wasn't he nice this morning? Never saw him in such a good humour! Why, he hardly ever speaks to us!—hates children, mamma says. Do you know, Miss Leigh, Uncle Bromley never walked with us so far before."

"Perhaps he thinks you are getting to a more companionable age," said Bluebell, blushing; but her heart bounded triumphantly.

It was an intensely hot afternoon. The ladies and some of the gentlemen were grouped under the lime-trees near the house. Kate, standing by a gipsy table, was pouring out tea, and keeping up a running fire of merry nonsense, her usual staff of danglers hovering near. The elder ladies seemed equally content, knitting shawls and weaving scandal. The bees were humming in the limes, "the rich music of a summer bird" overhead. The very air seemed green in the shadow of the trees.

"There," cried Kate, petulantly, "as sure as ever one is innocently happy in this wicked world, some species of amateur police obliges one to 'move on.'" And she glanced over her shoulder at a gentleman approaching.

He walked straight up to the group with a business-like, uncompromising manner, very different to the *dolce far niente* attitudes; yet four of the number rose at once to join him.

"Do have a cup of tea," cried Kate, enticingly, with the view to a reprieve.

"No, thank you; never touch it. There is not *too* much time, Miss Barrington."

"I know, I know," with a resigned air, and a shrug to the four who had risen. And without another word they all mysteriously followed their summoner to the house.

"What can they be going to do with Mr. Barton?" asked one of the ladies.

"Oh, it's a great secret," said Mrs. Barrington, laughing affectedly, "if they can only keep it."

In fact, it was a rehearsal. Mr. Barton was stage-manager, and ruled them with a rod of iron. He made the timid "speak up," the giddy, practise over and over again which side of the stage they were to enter and leave by; threw more spirit in here, checked ranting there, and ventured to object to the key in which Kate, as heroine, sang her song. He permitted "gagging" as a proof of presence of mind, provided the cue was forthcoming; but now his great soul was perturbed by the absence of a prompter.

"We really cannot do without one any longer," cried he, in urgent appeal to Kate, who rang the bell with an air of conviction.

"I will send for Miss Leigh, with whom I have been rehearsing. She almost knows the play by heart, and set my song to music."

Bluebell was starting out with the children, but came very willingly. Acting always had a charm for her, and, the play being pretty well in her head, she could prompt and watch at the same time.

Kate was too clever not to act well; but the *rôle* of the simple, ingenuous heroine was scarcely suited to her. She did not *look* it. The other girl, Miss Heneage, said her part like a lesson, but could not act it. The men were imperfect—incapable of getting through a sentence without the prompter. Sir Robert was the most inattentive of all, being more interested in trying to set up a flirtation with Bluebell, who demurely repressed him.

Such were the elements Mr. Barton was preparing to appear before an indulgent public in two days' time. All the neighbourhood was invited to the theatricals, and the evening was to close with a dance.

This night Bluebell received no invitation to join the party below. The children went down without her, and came up about nine, apparently in a great state of amusement.

"You'll get down to-morrow, I think, Miss Leigh. Uncle Bromley said to mamma, 'Where is your pretty governess, Lydia? Surely she is coming down to sing to us?' And Sir Robert muttered something about 'a beautiful syren,' and wanted to go up and fetch you."

Bluebell was more gratified by the first part of this speech; that silly Sir Robert would spoil everything.

Next day, according to Mabel's prognostications, the ban was removed, and Bluebell made free of the saloon in the evening, continuing, however, rigorously to retire when her pupils did. Somewhat to her discomposure, she found they had been chattering to Kate about Lord Bromley joining their morning walks. Miss Barrington had turned this little circumstance over in her mind rather curiously. Bluebell was apparently so wonderfully discreet with young men, it was strange she should go out early to flirt with an old one.

"Next time say you would rather walk in the Park, Mabel," said she.

And when the children rather confusedly acted on this advice, Bluebell, detecting Kate's hand in it, immediately assented, determined that no reluctance should be reported.

The day of the theatricals arrived, and with it a great reverse of fortune to Miss Barrington. She had driven early into the market-town in a small pony carriage for some essential no one but herself could choose. Now, though a good rider, Kate was a remarkably careless whip; and rattling through the town, the ponies shied at something, or nothing, swerved into a cart, and upset the tittuppy little trap in a moment. The immediate result to the fair driver was a sprained ankle, contused face, and fast blackening eye. Any amount of pain she would have cheerfully endured sooner than give up her evening's excitement; but the unfortunate eye swelled, and got blacker and blacker, and nothing could be done. Her despair was communicated to the whole corps, till Mr. Barton suggested a substitute in Bluebell. It was carried *nem. con.*, with the chilling consent of Mrs. Barrington, who, though she would not hear of Kate appearing thus disfigured, had tried in vain to persuade Lord Bromley to put off the play. But he maintained it was now "too late for postponement; Barton had said the girl could act; and Kate deserved the disappointment, for she had no business to have upset herself," etc. In the meantime Mr. Barton had carried off Bluebell for a severe rehearsal. The play was "The Loan of a Lover," and as Peter Spyk he was interested in his Gertrude. Sir Robert also, as Captain Amesfort, threw considerably more animus into his scene since the change of heroines.

Bluebell had tea with her pupils as usual, and joined in the *dramatis persona* in the green room at nine. The company was arriving. The front benches were soon filled with ladies, while the men stood about in the doorway, or looked over their heads.

Among the latter was Harry Dutton. He had come without notice, too late to join the party at dinner, and, thinking the whole thing rather a bore, scarcely glanced at the stage.

"Mynheer Swizel! Mynheer Swizel!" Dutton started as if he had been shot. In a peasant's dress, and running on to the stage greeted by a round of applause, he recognises Bluebell! Here, at Bromley Towers!

Transfixed to the spot, his moonstruck gaze rivetted on the actors, people spoke to him, and he never heard. Conjecture, wonder, doubts of his own sanity, were whirling his brain. How did she get *here*, of all places in the world? With whom?—and under what name? Heavens, if she should suddenly perceive him, and stop short or scream! He moved behind a pillar, where he could observe unseen. Peter Spyk was singing:—

"To-morrow will be market-day,
The streets all thronged with lasses gay;
And from a crowd so great, no doubt,
Sweethearts enough I may pick out.
In verity, verity, verity aye," etc

And then Gertrude, in a mocking voice, coquettishly sang,—

"Be not too bold, for hearts fresh caught,
Are ne'er, I am told, to market brought
The best, they say, are *given* away,
And are not *sold*, on market-day.
In verity, verity, verity aye," etc

A round of applause and an encore followed. It was long since Harry had heard Bluebell's voice, but he alone did not applaud. The play proceeded, and then Sir Robert came in as Amesfort. It hung a little here. He floundered, gagged, forgot the cue, and the voice of the prompter became distinctly audible. Happily, conceit bore him along. Harry winced as he drawled to Gertrude, "Why, you are very pretty!" But when he proceeded to catch her round the waist and offered to kiss her, he mattered an oath, and half-started forward. Warned by a look of curiosity in a bystander, Dutton fiercely controlled himself, but a burning desire to quarrel with Sir Robert took possession of him.

In the last scene, when she comes on as a bride, Harry remembered, with a curious laugh, she had never been so attired for him. Bluebell was warming to her part. She and Peter Spyk were pulling the whole coach, and when the play was ended they were both loudly called for before the curtains.

Happy and delighted at her success, it was hard to fall from triumph to insignificance; but, in the first flush of the former, Bluebell was left in solitude. Her fellow actors had flown away to exchange their theatrical costume for ball dress, and she had received no *carte blanche* to mingle with the dancers.

Lingering listlessly alone in the greenroom, wishing to join the rest, and hoping some one might think of sending for her, she had thrown herself into an easy-chair, back to the door, which was half-open. There was a slight sound of a rapid, stealthy footstep, and, before she had time to look round, a twisted note was tossed into her lap.

Bluebell started to her feet. Her heart gave one great jump, and her cheeks were blanched.

She rushed to the door. Too late, — the passage was empty. After reading the note, she walked backwards and forwards, in an incoherent state of excitement, pondering its contents, and was returning to the deserted school-room, when she was met and stopped by Lord Bromley.

"Not dressed yet!" he exclaimed. "Or is Gertrude going to dance in this pretty bridal array?"

"This dress is Miss Barrington's. Good-night, Lord Bromley," said Bluebell, trying to pass.

"What! you poor child, are you sent to bed? Come along with me. I'll make it right with Mrs. Barrington."

"I cannot, indeed. I am ill—I am tired," said Bluebell, desperately.

Lord Bromley's eyes were fixed inquiringly upon her; but people were coming along the passage, and, escaping from him, she darted off.

No one was in the nursery. Bluebell hastily changed her dress, wrapped herself in a dark cloak, and drew the hood over her head; then, descending the staircase, listened a moment at the foot. No one seemed about. She flew down a dark passage into the billiard-room, threw open the French window, and stepped out. It was as dark as a summer's night ever is, and a soft shower was falling; but Bluebell took no heed. Avoiding the front of the house, she threaded her way by the back settlements. A dog barked, and a poaching cat was marauding about. The grass felt damp and clinging as she struck into what was called "The West Drive." It was not kept exactly in lawn order there. A hundred yards further on was a summer-house, thatched inside and out with moss, from which, long ere she reached it, Harry Dutton emerged, and, folding her in his arms, drew her within its shelter.

In the meantime, the ball was in full swing; every now and then inquiries were made for the missing heir. "Did not Mr. Dutton come to-night? I wonder what has become of him!" Lord Bromley wondered too; but, before he had time to be really offended at his absence. Mr. Dutton was observed valsing with Lady Geraldine. The young sailor was no whit less interesting for his Crimean campaign, to which his wound lent an additional *prestige*; and it was astonishing what severe remarks were made on the unloveliness of the partner with whom he most frequently danced that night.

And yet such criticism was more undeserved than usual, for a look of gentle happiness softened and inspired her naturally plain features, and lent an unwonted tender grace to a somewhat inexpressive figure.

Lord Bromley did not observe their frequent contiguity with the same satisfaction as of yore. On the contrary, his eye rested on Harry with a somewhat sarcastic expression, and he remained thoughtful and *distrait*.

CHAPTER XL
THE MINIATURE

True, I have married her.
The very head and front of my offending
Hath this extent, no more.

Shakespeare.

Lord Bromley did not suffer the nocturnal festivities to interfere with his morning walk, during which he came upon the governess and her pupils looking as fresh as the dawn.

"I need not ask if you have recovered from last night, Miss Leigh," observed he, dryly, as he bowed demurely, with a somewhat conscious air.

"Did you dance?" asked Mabel; "for I heard you come up just after the stable clock struck one, and the music had been going on for ever so long."

Now, it might have been half-past eleven when Miss Leigh had professed herself to Lord Bromley as too ill and tired to dream of dancing. Looking the consternation she felt at this contradictory piece of evidence, she remained silent, not daring to raise her eyes.

"Who would have taken you for such an actress!" said the peer, in rather ambiguous accents.

Bluebell looked up desperately; her expression was ingenuous, but half imploring.

"Such nerve and command of countenance!" rhapsodized his Lordship, with the same odd fixed look and sarcastic inflection of voice. "The idea of the plot so perfectly conceived and played out! Had you much practice—in Canada."

"I have played in charades and small pieces," wondering how he knew she had been in Canada.

"But you never *really* acted till you came to England? How long was that ago?"

"Some time now," confusedly.

"Nearly two years, perhaps?"

"About that—no, not quite so much," more and more perplexed by his manner.

"I hope you'll come down, and sing to us to-night. Miss Leigh. I am not sure I don't prefer that accomplishment for young ladies—it is *safer*." He turned away, leaving Bluebell in bewilderment.

Kate, recovered by a night's rest, would consent to no more seclusion; the blow was not much of a disfigurement now, and she was making an immense fuss over Harry, which suited him well enough to encourage, as he rather repented the imprudently frequent dances with Geraldine, and felt embarrassed in her society this morning.

The cousins were sitting on an ottoman, in half-teazing, half-affectionate discourse, when Bluebell, feeling like a conspirator of the deepest dye, entered demurely with her pupils. Kate watched Harry narrowly, who did not appear to have observed their entrance.

"You seem to have forgotten Miss Leigh," she remarked. "Did you not travel together from Quebec?"

Dutton, somewhat staggered by her correct information, shot a swift inquiring glance at his cousin.

"To be sure—so it is Miss Leigh. I thought last night I knew the face—"

"Why don't you go and speak to her?"

"I am shy—perhaps she won't remember me."

"Miss Leigh, Mr. Dutton thinks you have forgotten him."

Bluebell bowed stiffly, very much on her guard; for she saw that Lord Bromley was an attentive observer, and his strange behaviour in the morning had given rise to an uncomfortable suspicion that he might (though how, she could not imagine) be cognizant of the tryst in the West Wood. Harry moved to a seat near, and began an indifferent conversation with her, that the whole room might have heard.

"Can it be all—kid," thought Kate, "or was there really nothing between them?"

At that instant Sir Robert lounged up, and threw himself in a familiar manner on the other side of Bluebell.

Dutton's face darkened. He had taken an antipathy to this man, who commenced a sort of condescending flirtation with his wife. He called her

"Gertrude," too, and poured out compliments on her acting, describing his despair at being unable to find her among the dancers afterwards.

Harry was boiling, Kate exultant. "I knew I was right," she thought.

Bluebell was summoned to the piano. Sir Robert followed. It was a semi-grand, and he leant on the other end, opposite to her.

"Where is the music? Oh! you play without. So much the better. One sees the eyes flashing."

It was not the only pair, for Dutton's were fixed upon Sir Robert with a ferocious expression, apparent even to his obtuseness, and somewhat surprised, he returned it with a slight stare and elevation of the eyebrows. That night, in the smoking-room, the antagonism between the two was more pronounced than ever. Sir Robert explained it by a conjecture that "Dutton was sweet on the little governess, and d—d jealous." He was not particularly popular among the other men: but all agreed that Dutton "had been very rough on Lowther, and was not half such a cheery, pleasant fellow as he used to be."

What would not Kate have given for an incident that befell Lady Geraldine one day! She had been much puzzled by Harry's manner since his return: for, though his appreciation of her was more heartily manifested than before, she was conscious of a difference,—or rather, perhaps, analyzed it more truly now. Her adorers had not been so numerous as to disturb the impression of the first man who had ever appeared to care about her; but she could scarcely deceive herself longer—there was evidently now nothing warmer than liking left.

Poor girl! she was easily discouraged, and felt no resentment; she did not even think it necessary to conjure up a rival to account for the discontinuation of his attentions, till a slight incident revealed one to her. She was sitting alone in the morning-room, and, being somewhat of a china fancier, turned a cup on a bracket upside down, to examine the mark at the bottom. In doing so, a bit of paper fluttered out, and as she picked it up, the words, "West Wood, four o'clock," met her startled gaze. She was convinced that the writing was Harry's, but whom could the assignation be intended for? Soon after Bluebell came into the room as it seemed to her with no very apparent purpose Lady Geraldine, not without design, seated herself at a small writing-table, with her back to the bracket, and almost immediately heard a slight clatter. Miss Leigh had vanished, and so had the paper from the teacup.

"I wish I dare go to the West Wood," thought Geraldine, for she was not all perfect, and the indignation in her heart inspired a deep desire to expose the underhand behaviour of the designing governess. That evening Harry had been talking to her longer than usual. Bluebell was singing at the piano, and finally began the Persian song of "The May Rose to the Nightingale." Geraldine listened, attracted by the sentiment. One verse was unfortunately suggestive—

> Moonlight, moonlight, think'st thou he'd leave me
> For one so pale—for one so pale
> But moonlight, moonlight, if he deceive me,
> Tell not the tale—tell not the tale

Then Geraldine's pallid complexion was flushed with resentment, for she imagined the words levelled at herself. Next day—unable to resist again examining the cup—she found another fold of paper, but this time in a female handwriting. Harry, of course, would come for it and she determined to remain till he did so. The room was then tolerably full. Some time after Dutton dropped in with another man, and, all unconscious of *surveillance*, lingered till only he and Lady Geraldine remained in the room.

"Mr. Dutton," she said, in her somewhat reedy voice, "I understand a little about china, but cannot make out the date of that little yellow cup, the mark at the bottom is so defaced."

It was said meaningly, and Harry understood that he was discovered. To throw himself upon her generosity seemed an obvious necessity. With a conscious yet penetrating glance, closing the half open door, he exclaimed, impulsively, "Dear Lady Geraldine, may I tell you something about myself?"

Geraldine flushed hotly. This was somewhat more than she had bargained for. With the slightest *soupçon* of stateliness, dreading what was to follow, she managed to say, that "Whatever he liked to tell her should go no further."

"It will all be known soon enough," cried he. "But I fancy Lady Geraldine, you have some suspicion I know I can trust you, and you have been always so kind and sympathetic to me, it is a much greater comfort telling you than Kate."

Geraldine bowed her head. She was determined not to betray herself, and even felt some little curiosity, though how abundantly that faculty was to be gratified ere she left the room, she certainly had not foreseen. One result was, it had an immediately bracing effect, for, with all her humility,

Geraldine had the pride of self respect, and the confession completely disabused her of the idea that Harry had ever aspired to being suitor of hers. It was a pang, no doubt. Even his confidence might have a double meaning. Had she any of the fury of a woman scorned, what an amount of mischief would be in her power. But Harry's instinct was right, and he never regretted his reliance on Geraldine's honour and pride.

Dutton and his wife continued to meet daily in secret. They had agreed to confess to Lord Bromley directly the visitors should have left, but I think were still young enough to enjoy the stratagems necessary for those stolen interviews. How many narrow escapes they were to laugh at afterwards and, in society, when they appeared on such conventional terms as respectful youth and prudent governess, how many *doubles entendres* Harry hazarded, to see Bluebell struggling with alarmed risibility.

But the rash pair were outwitted at last, and run to earth by Kate in the moss arbour. How much of their conversation had been overheard, or how long she had stood there before springing out, of course could be only conjecture. A violent start had been irrepressible, and, as they both were speechless from the shock, Kate remained mistress of the situation, and evidently not disposed to be merciful. A few sarcastic expressions to her cousin, some cutting remarks on Bluebell's deceitful and designing conduct, and she was gone—apparently for the purpose of exposing the intrigue she imagined herself to have discovered. Dutton sprang after her, and Bluebell, in much vexation and alarm, returned to the house.

Not much breathing time was to be obtained in the nursery, whither she had hurried. The door was half open, and, entering unperceived, she beheld a sight that gave her almost as genuine a start as Kate's inopportune appearance. Yet it was only Lord Bromley sitting by the table, looking pale and shaken, and gazing intently on—could she believe her eyes?—the miniature of Theodore Leigh. The case was broken. Bluebell had been gumming it, and had left it on the table to dry. But why should he be studying it with such absorbing interest?

Lord Bromley raised his eyes, and fixed them sternly on the beautiful girl. "Come here *Theodora*."—and she started. "Whose portrait is this?"

"My father's."

"Exactly. And, such being the case, your presence in this house requires some little explanation."

Unable to see the connexion between the miniature and this attack; Bluebell remained silent and confounded; but, as he continued to gaze severely at her, she roused herself to reply.

"I came here because Mrs. Barrington brought me, and I went to her by the purest accident. Did you *know* my father, my Lord?"

"Simplicity may be rather overdone! Do you think, child, I have not seen through your evident desire to ingratiate yourself?—and scheming yourself into this house will, I assure you, not further your designs!"

Bluebell could not deny the former charge, though guiltless of the latter insinuation. But who could have betrayed their marriage, and why did he only blame her?

"I do not know who may have prompted you, but if he thought duplicity and cunning a recommendation in a grand-child—"

"Grandchild!" echoed Bluebell. "What can you mean, Lord Bromley! Sir Timothy Leigh was *my* grandfather!"

"Which, as you probably very well know, I have not been called for fifteen years!"

Still the intense perplexity of her face was staggering his impression that this adventurous daughter of his disinherited son was trying by a *coup de main* to cancel the edict of banishment, and to obtain favour and fortune at his hands.

"*You* my grandfather!" she reiterated, mechanically, her eyes, wonder wide, staring at the old man with child-like directness, that produced a more convincing effect on his mind than any words. After all, it was quite possible she might not have heard of his succession to a remote peerage, and this amazement was certainly not assumed. Moreover, the expression of her face was conjuring from a dim past a host of memories. He became strangely moved, and could scarcely bear the gaze which recalled so forcibly Theodore in his youth.

Which made the first movement neither knew. "My dearest little girl!" he murmured, and folded her in his arms.

Bluebell was weak and silent from surprise mingled with extreme happiness, and Lord Bromley had gone back in thought to former years, and dare not trust himself to speak; so they were both too absorbed to notice the entrance of Harry Dutton, who remained rooted to the spot (like a stuck pig, as he afterwards elegantly described it), and a smothered exclamation burst from his lips.

Lord Bromley hurriedly withdrew himself from Bluebell, not particularly gratified at being surprized in so romantic a *pose* at his time of life.

"What the d——l are you doing here, sir?" he angrily demanded.

Harry, considering he had quite as good a right to ask that question, turned inquiringly and gloomily to Bluebell, who, feeling if she attempted to open her lips she must either go off into a hysterical fit of laughter or burst into tears, said nothing; and the uncle and nephew continued to glare at each other.

She signed to Dutton to speak; but he was too mystified and sulky; so Bluebell, in desperation, plunged *in medias res.*

"Harry!" she cried, "this is my grandfather as well as your uncle! Why, we must be cousins!" Then, after an instant's pause, with downcast eyes and crimson cheeks, she penitently kissed the old man's hand, and whispered,— "He is my husband too; we meant to have told you to-morrow!"

So the dread secret was out at last! Silence, that could be felt, ensued, and seemed endless to the two culprits, who, with drooping eyes, waited anxiously for him to speak.

Now, this announcement was hardly so unexpected as they supposed, and far more welcome than their wildest dreams could have anticipated. Lord Bromley's agent, who paid the annuity to Mrs. Leigh, was also in the habit of giving him periodical information of the well-being of his grand-daughter. When, however, she eloped from Captain Davidson's house, he had lost sight of her for a time, but afterwards picked up the clue at Mrs. Markham's. When they also disappeared so suddenly, the agent was again at fault, Bluebell having changed her situation in the interval.

Advancing years had softened Lord Bromley. The tidings of her elopement without any positive proof of a *bona fide* marriage preceding it, had shocked him into bitter remorse for having left her, an unprotected waif and stray, to the tender mercies of the world, and now she had passed out of his ken, and he could not but fear the worst.

In this frame of mind he came accidentally upon Bluebell in the spring woods, and the likeness to her father, which was singularly obvious, seemed the reflection of the thoughts that haunted him. Then, when Mabel mentioned her by name, it flashed upon him that what he had taken for a trick of imagination might be, indeed, a sober reality. Lord Bromley sought Mrs. Barrington, and elicited, in reply to his careless inquiries, the fact that the fair governess was a Canadian, and had come into her family from the Markhams'. This was conclusive, and he took every opportunity of observing Bluebell with an almost hungry interest. The elopement rankled unpleasantly in his mind. He watched her conduct narrowly, and was pleased to see that she seemed prudent and careful; but his suspicions received a new direction by the mutual disappearance of Dutton and herself on the night of his return. It was a coincidence, at any rate, for had not Mabel asserted she had not come upstairs till one, before which hour Harry had not entered the ball-room? He also detected two or three looks of intelligence passing between them, then, when Kate remarked that they had returned in the same steamer from Quebec, the mystery began to take a definite shape. He remembered his nephew's confession of an attachment, and his absence for many weeks after landing. At this stage a terrible possibility obtruded itself, and Bluebell's inviting manner, which before had pleased him, seemed all an artful attempt to get into favour.

The accidental sight of Theodore's miniature, which stirred poignantly the stern heart of the father, precipitated the *denouement*, and the artless bewilderment of Bluebell under his reproaches lulled the suspicions which her subsequent avowal of a marriage with Harry nearly set at rest. There only remained those unaccounted for weeks, so that the first sentence he spoke to the peccant pair, whom we left in agitated suspense, surprised them by its calmness.

"When did this happen?" And they could not guess how anxiously he waited for a reply.

Now Dutton had come there expressly to bring Bluebell into Lord Bromley's presence, having resolved to be beforehand with Kate, and make immediate confession. Therefore he was provided with their marriage certificate, which he now produced, and silently presented to his uncle.

The date was satisfactory, and Lord Bromley was relieved from the most harrowing anxiety. Yet his brow did not relax as he turned gravely to his nephew. "What was your motive, Harry, in concealing this marriage?"

Dutton was silent.

"You may well be unwilling to express it. It was because you feared to lose the inheritance I have foolishly brought you up to expect."

Harry looked up frankly, though writhing under his words.

"I cannot wholly deny it, uncle, and if you now change your intentions towards me, it is only what I expect. Bluebell and I were married hastily at Liverpool, she is my best excuse for that. Afterwards, when I came to 'The Towers,' I meant to have told you, but—don't you recollect?—you positively refused to hear what I had to say. Of course I ought to have persisted."

"And did Theodora also see the expediency of concealing her marriage till my death?"

"No, indeed," cried Harry, warmly. "She would have risked everything to have it acknowledged. It puts my conduct in an awfully cold-blooded light, but I hope you don't think me utterly ungrateful."

"As to that, the less said the better," returned Lord Bromley, coolly.

Dutton turned away abashed and deeply wounded, for he really was attached to the relative who had been his best friend and benefactor from infancy to manhood. Lord Bromley slowly left the room, and, sending for his niece, endeavoured to explain to her the astounding facts that Bluebell was the daughter of his disinherited son, and had been married to Dutton for nearly two years.

There was scarcely room in Mrs. Barrington's mind to grasp this new aspect of affairs, it being already taken up with Kate's shocking discovery of the heir, flirting in a secluded summer-house with the treacherous governess. Very earnestly, therefore, she tried to convince her uncle that he must be deceived, and that Bluebell was an impostor and an adventuress.

"There's not a shade of doubt about her identity," contested Lord Bromley "I have known for some time whom she was. Indeed, Lydia, you were my first informant when you told me where you had taken her from. Parker had reported that Theodore's daughter was with some people of the name of Markham, and immediately found out accidentally that she was no longer there and here is further proof"—and he placed before her the portrait that he had carried away. It was difficult to [unreadable]. Convinced against her will, and deprived of the power of giving Bluebell immediate warning, Mrs. Barrington [unreadable] fall back upon her own room, pull down the blinds and take refuge in *petite sante*, till prepared to face her emminent dependent in so new and unwelcome a position.

Certainly this day of elucidation was not a pleasant one. Everybody appeared in a changed point of view, and was feeling its awkwardness. Harry and Bluebell, hardly knowing if they had a right to remain there, wandering disconsolately about, like a modern Adam and Eve awaiting expulsion from Paradise.

Kate felt baffled and dangerous,—angry at her cousin having slipped so smoothly through her fingers, and jealous of his wife.

Lord Bromley, though deeply incensed with Harry, was longing to keep Bluebell, whose every glance and gesture recalled his secretly lamented son. Lady Calvert was on the point of departure with her daughter; and the facts having percolated through the household, all the maids got sick headaches from sympathetic excitement.

Dutton had had a very stormy interview with his cousin when he rushed after her from the arbour. Kate was determined to betray them, and he vainly tried to induce her to be silent. On one condition only would she promise secrecy—that Bluebell should give immediate warning, and that he should never speak to her again. But Harry only laughed, while Kate urged everything she could think of—ruin to his prospects, his uncle's anger, etc.

"It is no business of yours," reiterated Dutton. "If you say anything about it, you'll soon see you have made a fool of yourself, and the little you do know is by prying and listening."

But Kate broke from him and darted into the house, past Lady Geraldine, who was just coming out, and who noticed with surprise the disturbed appearance of the two cousins. To Dutton she seemed a good angel sent to invalidate the spells of an evil one. As the reader knows, she alone had been entrusted with the secret of his marriage, and he now briefly explained that Kate was bent upon betraying his meetings with Bluebell, and entreated her, if possible, by any stratagem, to detain her for awhile.

Geraldine, fully alive to the importance of the request, exclaimed with a gesture of impatience—

"*How* provoking! when you were to have told your own story to-morrow! Be quick, Mr. Dutton, don't lose a moment, and I will undertake to keep Kate and Mrs. Barrington quiet till they can do no further mischief."

A very grateful glance from Harry as he sprang away; and how he fared in the dreaded interview is already known to the reader.

CHAPTER XLI
A LOCK OF HAIR

For which they be that hold apart
The promise of the golden hours;
First love, first friendship, equal powers,
That many with the virgin heart.

In Memoriam.

Another year had gone by since the *denouement* at Bromley Towers. The war was over, peace proclaimed, and what remained of our armies had returned from the East.

General Rolleston then retired from the service, and bought a very nice property near Leamington. He still saw a good deal of his old officers; Fane especially, who now commanded the regiment, spent much of his leave at Pyott's Hill. He retained all his old admiration for Cecil, receiving as little encouragement as ever. Possibly that may have been the secret of his constancy, for certainly, as a Crimean hero, with seven thousand a year to gild the romance of it, he did not find young ladies in general very hard-hearted.

But Fane was ever ungrateful, and, after being petted and feted, sang at, ridden at, and generally made much of, only returned with fresh zest to Cecil's unaffected and pleasant companionship. Yet, after each visit, in spite of manifold opportunities, being alone with her for hours, her constant companion in rides and rambles, and given to her by every one in the neighbourhood, he always found he had never really advanced an inch, and that nothing Cecil expected less than a proposal from him.

So he always went away in despair, to return again at the faintest hint of an invitation from her father.

General Rolleston was by no means displeased to observe this eagerness to avail himself of his hospitality, being quite as alive as heretofore to the advantages of the match—he only wondered why Fane and his daughter were so tardy in coming to an understanding.

Cecil was very much liked in the neighbourhood. Everybody said she was the most unaffected girl in the world. But with all her admirers, she had no flirtations—bright and cold was the verdict pronounced. Some said she was strong-minded, for she was known to read a great deal, and had even had a picture admitted into the Female Artists' Exhibition. She was further convicted of preferring long, solitary rides to joining the numerous equestrian parties got up in the summer; but as public opinion had unanimously agreed that she must be engaged to Fane, the unsocial trait was excused on that hypothesis.

About this period, he having just discovered her whereabouts, Cecil received a long letter from Harry Dutton, relating what he knew would interest her—the strange events and transformations at "The Towers." A similar one came to Mrs. Rolleston from Bluebell, who, now that she was at liberty to speak, wrote something like a volume of narrative and explanation to her friend. The latter, agitated and excited, flew to Cecil with the wonderful news, unaware that she had heard it already from Dutton, or, indeed, of her acquaintance with him: for, considering that all he had told her was in the strictest confidence. Cecil, as the simplest way of keeping it secret, had never mentioned anything at all about him. She must now, however, confess, for her step-mother was in an effusive mood, and bent upon instantly inviting the Duttons to pay them a visit.

Mrs. Rolleston received the information with some coldness and little curiosity, being naturally hurt at her step-daughter's concealment of a fact of so much interest to her; and though she probably told the General, he never afterwards alluded to the episode. Indeed, Cecil's labours at Scutari were rather a tabooed subject, as Harry speedily discovered when one day he attempted to blunder out his gratitude to her father.

The Duttons were invited for a week; also Colonel Fane and Captain Vavasour. Cecil became restless and excited as the day approached. The sight of Bluebell would cruelly re-open old wounds, and she had never met Vavasour (who had brought back the slain body of her lover) since the Crimea. And he would talk to her about it, she was sure, for Jack had long ago fathomed their ill fated attachment. Altogether, it was a relief that other guests were coming to dinner, for they were all too intimate in one way and too far apart in another—a connecting thread seeming to run through all their lives. Jack, an old love of Bluebell's, Dutton, whom she had nursed through deadly peril, and Fane, only prevented being a declared suitor by systematic absence of reciprocity on her side. Well it was a mercy they all came in owl-light, scarcely dusk enough for candles, but pleasantly veiling countenances not too much under command.

Bluebell and Cecil had determined beforehand that they must embrace, and mutually dreaded it. It was not, however, such *a blanc-mange* affair as osculation among ladies often is, for they were both agitated by too vivid memories. Bluebell's feelings were pleasantly diverted by recognising Jack—blushing with delight like the boy he still was. Somehow, he was the only one of the party she felt entirely at ease with, and found herself, as of old, chattering and laughing at as much as with him, just as if three sorrow-laden years had never intervened.

Dutton contrived to get by Cecil at dinner, though he had not taken her down, and their conversation was sufficiently interesting to make them forget their appointed partners.

"And you *are* quite restored to favour?" Cecil was saying, "and the uncle not half so implacable as you expected?"

"I don't know about that," cried Harry. "He has altered to *me*, I think. Bluebell is all the rage now, she actually is admitted into his sanctum every morning, to read him the papers. I shouldn't wonder if she turned out Queen Regnante and I were only Prince Consort!"

Cecil, I think, liked Dutton much better than his wife, with whom it was hard to resume old relations. Besides, she seemed now quite the favourite of Fortune, with every difficulty and hardship smoothed away, and to those who have suffered, it is harder to rejoice with those who do rejoice than to weep with those who weep.

So Bluebell was happier alone with Mrs. Rolleston when the men were hunting or out of the way. Dutton once ventured to question Cecil about Fane, whose hopeless passion was evident to every one in the house. She looked vexed, disconsolate, and gave her usual answer, that there was nothing in it, and never would be.

Dutton gently tried to combat this assertion. He had heard all about Bertie, but of course thought it was useless grieving over spilt milk; that time enough had passed since then; and that she had far better marry and forget.

Cecil smiled with a sort of sad amusement at all this and his slight assumption of marital experience. Harry and Bluebell seemed years younger than herself,—a giddy, happy young couple, the very sunshine of whose lives dazzled them too much to see into the depths of hers.

One afternoon she had started for a lonely walk. The rest of the party were pretty well disposed of—Bluebell driving with Mrs. Rolleston, and the others, she thought were with the General; but it did not much matter. It was a blustering February afternoon—Cecil long remembered it; the north wind had strewn the ground with dead branches, and cawing rooks, on the eve of wedlock, were drifting about incoherently on the breeze. She was following the course of a brook where the grounds widened into a wild, brambly park, and looking over her shoulder she perceived Jack Vavasour some distance off, coming along with rapid strides as if bent on overtaking her.

Cecil sauntered slowly on, not ill pleased at the opportunity of an unreserved conversation with Jack. She noticed, with furtive amusement, that he slackened his pace considerably as he neared her, probably to give an accidental aspect to the encounter. She turned round with a contented smile of expectation, and they wandered on together, Cecil instinctively choosing the most unfrequented and far-off boundary of the park. It was impossible to keep up long a commonplace conversation, and they became more and more *distrait* and nervous, each wishing to approach one subject, and neither liking to begin. In such a case, it is always the woman who breaks the ice. An allusion to the war was sufficient in this instance, and Jack responded so eagerly, she was confirmed in her impression that he had something to tell her. Without waiting for further questioning, he plunged into Crimean reminiscences of Bertie Du Meresq, whom he had seen nearly every day till his death, to all of which poor Cecil listened with breathless interest, and yet she *knew* there was something more to come.

"You know," continued Vavasour, "his watch and things were sent back to England; but when we cut open his tunic, to see if he was breathing, something dropped out that he had worn through the action. I kept *that*, for I thought I would restore it only to the rightful owner."

What intuitive feeling was it that made her wish he would say no more! Jack was opening his pocket-book, and drew out a piece of folded paper.

"I knew it in a moment," he cried, as a long coil of soft, dark hair appeared, so closely resembling Cecil's own as fully to justify his conviction that it was so.

He had expected to see her greatly moved; but the sudden pallor of her face puzzled him, which sensation was still more intensified when her large eyes flashed a moment upon him with an expression he never forgot, and, turning abruptly away, she walked towards the house.

Of all the trouble Cecil had gone through of late, I think for concentrated bitterness this moment was the worst. Though the colour was identical, by feel and texture she knew the tress was not her own, added to which, no such token had ever passed between herself and Bertie.

Well, there was no temptation to linger over the dead past now, which had received its *coup de grace* that wintry afternoon; almost every one felt that some subtle change had passed over Cecil. Perhaps the one who least felt its uncannyness was, Fane, who hovered near her with a brighter air. No doubt some of the party were surprised when, just before it broke up, the engagement of Cecil and Fane was announced; but no one guessed the truth except Jack Vavasour, who, anxious and remorseful, only cursed himself for a blundering idiot.

They were married on her twenty-fourth birthday, much to the relief of her bridesmaid-sisters, who had begun to fear Cecil would be an old maid. Fane sold out, and took his wife abroad, while the old Elizabethan manor-house, which, since his succession to, he had never lived in, was painted and luxuriously refurnished for the reception of the bride.

'Twas a pity Cecil married a rich man. Her best chance would have been having to think, work, deny herself for another, who might thus have become dear from the very sacrifices entailed by him. It was hard on Fane, who had been constant so long, and found he had grasped nothing but fairy gold. The old manor house was generally full, for somehow both dreaded a *tête-à-tête*, and equally, in early days especially, a betrayal of the feeling.

Cecil left her guests pretty much to their own devices in the morning, and read and painted in her own peculiar den, fitted up half as a library, half as a studio. The winter she devoted to hunting, and scarcely any meet was too distant or country too intricate for her. Bertie's riding lessons, at any rate, had not been forgotten, and carelessness of life is certainly conducive to steadiness of nerve. Jack Vavasour, who was out one day, was under the impression she wished to break her neck. Mrs. Fane became noted in her county for going with the most unflinching straightness, but so little did she care for the reputation, that sometimes she would stick unambitiously to the roads and never take a fence.

She had a separate stud of hunters, and rode independently of her husband, who followed the amusement in a less erratic style than his wife, and in more moderation.

Cecil often thought of her dream, when Du Meresq was transformed into Fane, and how singularly it had been realized. Certainly adventitious circumstances were averse to that first love of hers, for, however much appearances were against him, the lock of hair which had decided her destiny was no love token of Du Meresq's. It had been consigned to him by a dying friend, who besought him to write the news to his betrothed, and restore to her the lock of hair she had given him.

When Du Meresq had sent this letter off, he found he had omitted enclosing the tress, but they were then just going into action, and he had placed it inside his tunic.

After long years Cecil met this girl, who had been faithful to the memory of her Crimean hero. Once she spoke of him to Mrs. Fane, mentioning the circumstance of the omission of the lock when Du Meresq's letter had conveyed to her the fatal news. Little did she think how her companion had guarded and hated this *souvenir*. Cecil glanced sharply at the other's hair, harsher and more wiry now, and intersected with silvery threads, still it was like enough to satisfy her of the identity without the confirmatory cry of surprise with which the poor woman received it from her hands. Had she known this earlier, I think Cecil would have clung to her ideal, and never married, but by this time Fane and herself were—well as happy together as other people. Time's "effacing finger" had prepared the way, and since the birth of her only son, Cecil's heart was vitalized by a second passion, as strong though different to the first. So we may leave her, and see how our other heroine ultimately fares before dropping the curtain.

Dutton went to sea once again, but, as his ship was only cruising in the Mediterranean, Bluebell was able to meet him at the different ports they stopped at, and did not at all dislike the changeful variety of the life. However, Lord Bromley found he could not do without her, so, after that one cruise, Harry retired from the navy, and they lived chiefly at "The Towers," where a numerous family was born.

At last Lord Bromley died at a great age, and it was found that he had left Bromley Towers to their eldest boy, Theodore. To the Duttons was bequeathed a small estate worth three thousand a year. So after all Harry never inherited "The Towers," nor Bluebell either.